Bedde

SLEE
THE SHEIKH

Three smouldering heroes from three
sensual, intense writers

We're proud to present

MILLS & BOON
SPOTLIGHT™

*A chance to buy collections of bestselling
novels by favourite authors every month –
they're back by popular demand!*

November 2009

Determined to Protect,
Forbidden to Love

Featuring

Ramirez's Woman by Beverly Barton
Her Royal Bodyguard by Joyce Sullivan
Protecting the Princess by Carla Cassidy

Sleeping with the Sheikh

Featuring

The Sheikh's Bidding by Kristi Gold
Delaney's Desert Sheikh by Brenda Jackson
Desert Warrior by Nalini Singh

SLEEPING WITH THE SHEIKH

KRISTI GOLD

BRENDA JACKSON

NALINI SINGH

 MILLS & BOON

SLEEPING WITH THE SHEIKH © Harlequin Books S.A. 2009.

First published in Great Britain 2009
Harlequin Mills & Boon Limited,
Eton House, 18-24 Paradise Road, Richmond, Surrey TW9 1SR

The publisher acknowledges the copyright holders of the individual works, which
have already been published in the UK in single, separate volumes, as follows:

The Sheikh's Bidding © Kristi Goldberg 2003
Delaney's Desert Sheikh © Brenda Streater Jackson 2002
Desert Warrior © Nalini Singh 2003

ISBN: 978 0 263 87167 8

64-1109

Printed and bound in Spain
by Litografía Rosés S.A., Barcelona

THE SHEIKH'S BIDDING

BY
KRISTI GOLD

Kristi Gold has always believed that love has remarkable healing powers and greatly enjoys writing books featuring romance and commitment. As a bestselling author and Romance Writers of America RITA® Award finalist, she's learned that although accolades are wonderful, the most cherished rewards come from the most unexpected places, namely from stories shared by readers. She welcomes all readers to contact her through her website at http://kristigold.com or by mail at PO Box 11292, Robinson, TX 76716, USA.

To Sandy R for her expertise and her heart of gold.
And to those who go beyond tolerance
and embrace acceptance, acknowledging
that true love knows no cultural boundaries.

One

"Now, who's going to bid first on this fine little lady?"

Andrea Hamilton shifted nervously on the platform situated in the middle of Winwood Farm's impressive arena, wearing the only dress she owned and a self-conscious smile. Resentful of being called "a fine little lady," she reminded herself that the benefit auction was for a good cause, the reason why she had agreed to donate two months' worth of horse-training services. In turn, she was throwing herself onto the block at the risk of being passed over for someone with more experience.

"Come on, ladies and gentlemen," the auctioneer pleaded. "Give her a chance. She's good."

"At what?" a stumbling drunk in a disheveled tuxedo called from the corner.

Andi shot him a scathing look that he didn't seem to heed, evident from his sickening leer. Now nearing the end of the event, the remaining patrons continued to mill around, paying little attention when the auctioneer called her name again. What if no one even bothered to offer the minimum?

"Five hundred dollars," the drunk called out.

So much for that theory.

"Fifty thousand dollars."

The murmuring crowd was suddenly silenced at the sound of the booming voice delivering the astronomical bid from the back of the arena. Andi froze with her mouth agape, unable to fathom who would make such an offer.

"Fifty-thousand. Going once, going twice! Sold to the gentleman near the door!"

Andi craned her neck to try to see the mystery bidder, but because of her small stature, she only caught a glimpse of the back of a man in traditional Arab dress leaving the building. Royalty, she assumed. Not at all uncommon in racing circles.

Perhaps he had more money than sense. Or it could be that he had questionable intentions. She certainly hoped he understood that he was buying only her training expertise. If he counted on another kind of assistance, he would be sorely disappointed. She had no intention of letting him near her, even if he'd offered fifty million dollars.

With a muttered thank-you directed at the auctioneer, Andi sprinted down the steps as fast as the silly high heels would let her, passed her drink off to a roving waiter and shoved her way through the crowd to the exit at the side of the building. She escaped into the warm Kentucky night, grateful to leave behind the well-heeled racing society, not to mention the drunk. Now she could be on her way home and worry about the phantom bidder tomorrow.

Once she made it to the walkway leading to the front parking lot, an imposing dark-skinned man wearing an equally dark suit blocked her path.

"Miss Hamilton, the sheikh would like to speak with you."

"Excuse me?"

"He is the one who bought your services and he wishes to have a word with you." The man gestured toward a black limousine that spanned a good deal of the nearby curb.

No way, no how, would Andi get into a limo with a stranger even if he was some prince who'd invested a great deal of money to benefit a children's clinic. She rummaged through her purse and pulled out her card. "Here. Have him call me on Monday. We can discuss the terms then."

"He insists that he see you tonight."

Andi's patience scattered in the breeze. "Look, mister, I *insist* I'm not interested in doing that right now. Please tell your boss that I appreciate the gesture and I look forward to meeting him soon." Very far from the truth.

The man looked totally composed, unmovable. "He said that if you give me trouble, I am to present a question."

How weird was this going to get? "What question?"

He averted his gaze for a moment, the only hint of

discomfort in his staid expression. "He asks do you still hang your dreams on the stars?"

Andi's heart vaulted into her throat and rapidly fluttered in a frightening rhythm. Haunting memories whirled her back to a time seven years before. Memories of lying in a field of grass beneath a predawn sky, alone, immersed in tears until he had come to her. Memories of a sensual awakening that had begun with tragedy and ended with bittersweet bliss. One special moment, one unforgettable man.

One true love.

Why hang your dreams on the stars, Andrea? Why not something more tangible?

His voice came back to her then, mellow and deep and seductively dangerous. That night in her grief she had turned to him, only to be left behind, left alone except for one precious gift that served to remind her every day what she could never have.

Andi trembled and chafed her palms down her arms, suddenly chilled. "And this man's name?" she asked, although she feared she already knew the answer.

"Sheikh Samir Yaman."

Andi had known him only as Sam, known only of his family's wealth, not his title. He'd been her big brother's best friend who'd spent the better part of his college days at their home as an adopted member of the family. She'd been a teenager smitten by an "older" exotic man who had teased her mercilessly, saw her only as Paul's kid sister, until that night a few weeks after she'd turned eighteen when unforeseen tragedy had created new life. Ironically, only hours before, another life had been taken away.

But that was ages ago, water under the proverbial bridge, and she didn't want to unearth the pain or face him again, knowing she ran a great risk by doing so, both to her heart and the secret she had hidden from him for years.

The man walked to the limo's door and opened it wide. "Miss Hamilton?"

"I don't—"

"Get in, Andrea."

The deep timbre of the magnetic voice drew her forward against her will. She suddenly found herself sliding into the limo as if she had no control over her body or mind. How familiar that concept. From the moment she'd met him, he'd held her captive with his charms, his easy manner, his air of mystery, eventually his touch.

The door closed and a small light snapped on, revealing a man reclining against the rear plush, leather seat facing Andi. A man who was anything but a stranger to her—at least he hadn't been at one time in her life. She stared at him for a long moment, her heart creating a furious cadence in her chest as if it wanted to escape as badly as she did. Yet she couldn't move, couldn't speak when her gaze made contact with his intense eyes.

He raked the kaffiyeh from his head as if to prove he was the man she'd known all those years ago. But he wasn't quite the same. The changes were subtle, no doubt brought about by maturity, yet she couldn't deny he was still beautiful, with the same thick, dark hair that curled at his nape, same masculine jaw, same wonderful mouth now framed by a shading of evening whiskers. Although his near-black eyes held the familiar elusiveness, they also looked weary, not bright and youthful as before. She imagined hers mirrored that disillusionment, only now they more than likely revealed her shock.

Andi struggled to stay strong in his presence. "What are you doing here, Sam?"

His high-impact smile appeared, gleaming white against his caramel-colored skin, revealing the single dimple creasing his left cheek. Yet he seemed to be fighting the smile as much as Andi was fighting her reaction to it. "It's been a while since anyone has called me that." He gestured toward the small built-in bar to his left. "Would you like something to drink, Andrea?"

Something to drink? He expected to waltz back into her life after all these years and ply her with pleasantries?

Andi welcomed the force of her sudden anger, the anchor it provided against the sea of emotions. "No, I don't want a drink. I want to know why you're here. I haven't heard a word from you since Paul's funeral. Not one word."

He shifted in his seat and glanced away. "That was necessary, Andrea. I had obligations to fulfill in my country."

And none to her, Andi decided. "Why didn't you tell me you're a sheikh?"

He pinned her in place with his dark gaze. "Would that have made a difference? Would you have understood what that entailed?"

Probably not. It also didn't change the fact that he'd disappeared without any explanation. Regardless of his status, she was hard-pressed to understand a concept as foreign to her as the clothes he now wore. "So why did you come back?"

"Because I couldn't allow another day to pass without seeing you again."

Andi hated the tiny flutter of her pulse, the glimmer of hope in her heart. "Well, that's great. What did you hope to accomplish after all this time?"

He slipped out of his robes, the final garment that distinguished ordinary man from revered royalty, and tossed them aside, leaving him dressed in a white tailored shirt and black slacks. Try as she might, Andi couldn't help but notice the breadth of his chest and the spattering of dark hair revealed at his open collar. In a matter of years he had gone from a boyishly handsome college student to a devastatingly gorgeous man. And she would be smart to ignore those differences, the heat coursing through her traitorous body.

He scrubbed a hand over his jaw. "I need to know if what I have discovered is true."

A stab of fear impaled Andi's chest, making it almost impossible to breathe, to speak. "What would that be?"

He leveled his serious eyes on her. "I know that you've struggled with the farm, barely managing to get by. Several times over the years I've considered offering my help financially but decided you would have too much pride to accept."

Relief replaced the fear. Maybe he didn't know everything. "You are so right about that. I don't need your help, financially or otherwise."

"Are you certain about that, Andrea?"

"Positive. I'm doing fine."

"But you've never married."

"I'm not interested in finding a husband," she said, when in reality no one had ever come close to being Samir Yaman's equal. No one had ever affected her in the same way, with the same magic. She'd told herself time and again those were the fantasies of a young girl and they shouldn't exist now that she was a woman. Yet no matter how hard she'd tried to convince herself to forget him, forget what it had felt like to be in his arms, it hadn't worked. No man had ever measured up. No man probably ever would. Seeing Sam again brought home that painful truth. Knowing who he was, what he was, only cemented the certainty that she could never be a part of his world.

"I have another question for you," he said quietly.

She was afraid of his questions, afraid of the hold he still seemed to have on her. "If this has to do with the past, I don't want to go there. It's over."

"It's not over, Andrea, no matter how much you wish it to be." His voice, his expression, balanced on the edge of anger as he locked on to her eyes. She couldn't look away even though she wanted to. "How is your son?"

The fear advanced once again. "How do you know about him?"

"I have the means to learn anything I wish about anyone."

Damn his arrogance, his sudden appearance that could very well destroy her world once again. "My son is fine, thank you."

"And his father?"

Bile rose in her throat. Terror closed off her lungs. Protectiveness for her beautiful child pushed it all away. "He's *my* son. Only mine."

"He has to have a father, Andrea."

"No, he doesn't. His father isn't in the picture. He never has been."

"Then he is mine, isn't he?"

Oh, heavens, what was she going to do now? Had he returned to claim his child? She wouldn't let him, not without a fight. "Believe what you will. This conversation is finished."

"It is far from finished."

"What do you want from me?"

"I want to know why you never told me about him."

She released a mirthless laugh to veil her anxiety. "How would I have done that? You disappeared with no number to call, no way to get in touch with you."

"Then you admit I am his father?"

"I'm admitting nothing. I'm saying it doesn't matter, *Sheikh* Yaman. None of this matters. The past is over. I don't want to dredge it up again."

"It doesn't matter what either of us wants, Andrea. What matters is our child. I'm determined to settle this. If not now, then later. And soon."

Andi opened the door and tried to slide out, but not before he caught her hand and said, "I will be in touch."

She responded with tingles where his fingers curled around hers, with regret when she saw a sadness in his expression that she'd only seen one other time. But that surprising display of vulnerability soon disappeared, and his eyes once again took on the mystery—deep, dark waters that threatened to suck Andi into their shadowy depths. Without breaking his gaze, he turned her hand over and slid a slow fingertip along her palm, reminding Andi of that long-ago night when his masterful touch had made her beg him to stop, beg him to never stop.

Andi yanked her hand from his grasp and hurried away to her truck, sprinted as fast as her heels would let her. She raced from the panic that he might intend to take her child away from her, ran from the love for him that had never died.

But in her heart she knew that no matter how hard she tried to get away, Andrea Hamilton could never escape Sam Yaman, even after he left her again.

Samir Yaman sat alone in darkness in the hotel suite, surrounded by the luxury he had known most of his life. He needed a drink and would welcome the bitter taste of whiskey on his tongue, but he didn't dare give in to the craving, not when he needed a clear head. Truthfully, he hadn't touched alcohol since that night—the night he had made two grave mistakes.

After all this time Sam had not been able to escape the guilt over his best friend's demise. He had realized all too late that he should have stopped Paul's postgraduation drinking binge, but he'd allowed him his freedom that night, feeling it had been hard-earned due to the responsibility placed upon Paul after his father's death. That freedom had cost Paul his life, and Sam still paid the price for his own poor judgment.

And if only he hadn't gone to Andrea after he'd left the hospital with the knowledge that her brother had not survived. If only he had waited until dawn instead of following her to the pond where she always went to think, that night to mourn. If only he hadn't forgotten that she was no more than a grief-stricken girl who had needed comfort. Giving in to that need had been his second mistake. He'd been powerless to resist her, perhaps because of his own need to forget or perhaps because she had always been his ultimate weakness.

She still was.

He had recognized that tonight the moment he'd glimpsed her standing before the masses, wearing a black dress that revealed a woman's curves. She had looked poised and proud until no one offered a decent bid—the reason he had spontaneously decided to remedy that situation.

Leaning his head back, Sam closed his eyes against images of Andrea that burned in his mind, a flame that would not die, had not died since he'd left her the day they had buried her brother, his friend. No matter how he tried, they refused to disappear, forcing him to acknowledge what he had known all along— time and distance had changed nothing.

Her eyes were still azure, her long hair still the color of a desert sunset, reds mixed with gold. He imagined she still possessed a free spirit, an undeniable passion for life, a strong heart, the attributes that had attracted him to her from the beginning. Qualities he still admired. Yet he had sensed defiance when she'd entered the car, perhaps even hatred. He couldn't blame her. She had much to hate about him. At times he hated himself. He had thrust himself into his duty, losing his honor in the process by not facing his failures.

Since his return to Barak, he'd had his guard and

confidant, Rashid, covertly track Andrea's life as much as possible. But a few months ago, when he had planned the trip to the States, Rashid had finally revealed that Andrea had a six-year-old son. No matter what Andrea had told him tonight, Sam knew the boy was his. The timing was too coincidental for it not to be the case. He intended to prove it and make certain the child's needs were being met, though he could never claim him, or Andrea.

He could promise Andrea nothing beyond providing for her and their child. He could never tell her all the things he felt as a man. He could never speak of the times he had considered giving up his wealth, his legacy, to be with her again. She would never know that not one day had passed when he hadn't thought of her, longed for her.

Sheikh Samir Yaman, first son of the ruler of Barak, heir to his father's legacy, was bound by duty to his family, his country, groomed from birth to lead, and tied to an arrangement of marriage to a woman he had never touched. A woman he would never love, for his heart always had, always would, belong to a woman he could not have—Andrea Hamilton.

''Mama! There's a big black car in the driveway!''

Andi froze with her arms full of the clothes she'd gathered for her son's summer trip to camp. She had hoped this wouldn't happen today. Hoped that Sam would have waited to contact her until tomorrow. If only she'd hurried and gotten Chance out of the house sooner, she might have been able to avoid this scene. Maybe she still could.

''Get away from the window, Chance.''

He looked back over his shoulder, confusion calling out from dark eyes much like his father's. "Why, Mama?"

"Because it's not nice to stare at strangers, that's why."

Ignoring her, Chance continued to look out the window. "He's got a towel on his head and a big man with him."

"Chance Samuel Paul Hamilton, come over here right now and help me get your things together, otherwise you'll miss the bus."

With a sigh he turned and trudged toward her. "I just want to look at the man."

That's the last thing Andi wanted, at least now. She would prefer to put Sam off until she could get her child on his way to camp. Then she would deal with the questions that were sure to come—or demands as the case might be.

Andi stuffed the clothing into the nylon tote and told Chance, "Get your toothbrush and put it in the plastic bag in the bathroom with your medicine. Then pick out some books and make sure you pack your paper so you can write home."

Chance's lip pooched out in a pout. "Then can I meet him?"

"Not today. I'm not sure what he wants." A less-than-truthful version. Andi knew exactly what he wanted, to see his son. "He'll probably be gone before you're finished packing."

"I'll hurry up." With that, Chance sprinted into the hall.

Andi was right behind him, relieved that he'd gone toward the hall bathroom, not down the stairs. Her son was well behaved most of the time, although he could be determined. He came by it naturally, she guessed, considering she was much the same way. That had gotten her into trouble on more than one occasion. A particular summer night came to mind.

The doorbell sounded, jarring Andi into action. "I'll get it," came from the first floor.

"I'll get it, Tess," she called to her aunt in hopes of stopping her. "I—"

"Well good gracious! Sam!"

Too late. Andi should have forewarned Tess that they might be having a visitor, and exactly who that visitor would be.

Andi slowly walked down the stairs that ended in the entryway now containing her aunt, a bodyguard and her son's father. Sam immediately looked up and met her gaze. She hugged her arms across her middle as she spanned the remaining stairs. When she came to the last one, she was afraid to go any farther, especially when Sam kept staring at her as if he could see all the secrets she had held in her heart for years.

Tess turned a huge grin on Andi. "Well, looky here what the cat dragged in, Andi. It's our Sam."

Our Sam. How odd that sounded at the moment. That's exactly what they'd called him years ago. But he wasn't Andi's. Beyond that one night he never had been, nor would he ever be.

Andi managed a fake smile and spoke through clenched teeth. "I thought you would call first."

"And give you fair warning?" he said with a cynical grin.

"What's this get-up you're wearing?" Tess asked with a one-handed sweep toward Sam's robes.

He finally took his attention away from Andi, allowing her to release her breath. "My straitjacket, I'm afraid."

"You don't look crazy," Tess said. "You look like a break in the clouds after the rain. Now come here and give me a hug."

Sam complied, lifting Tess off her feet as he had so many times before. After setting her down, he asked, "You don't happen to have any of your famous coffee on to brew, do you?"

Tess favored him with a sunny smile. "You know I always keep a pot on. Come into the kitchen and sit a spell."

The bodyguard remained positioned at the door while Andi followed Tess and Sam into the breakfast room. Once there, Tess poured him a cup of coffee and said, "I'm going to run upstairs and check on the boy. You two have a nice visit." She hurried away, leaving Andi alone to face her past.

Sam took the chair with its back to the bay window, the place he'd always sat during family dinners. Andi refused to sit, resenting the fact that Sam had made himself comfortable as if he planned to stay awhile. Except for his clothing, he even looked comfortable, at home, as if he'd never left. But he had left, and Andi couldn't believe that Tess had acted as if he'd only been gone for a week or so, as if nothing had changed. When in fact everything had changed. But Tess had always loved Sam just the way she loved Andi and Paul. Just the way she loved Chance.

"Mama?"

Andi's gaze shot to the doorway leading to the hall where her son now stood, his large brown eyes focused on the man he considered a fascinating stranger. Tess was nowhere to be seen, leading Andi to believe that her aunt had a hand in this spontaneous introduction of father and son.

Andi didn't know what to do, what to say. But if she didn't act normal, Chance would immediately sense something was wrong, and she didn't want to frighten him.

She held out her hand to him. "Come here, sweetie."

When Chance walked forward and stood in front of her, Andi braced her palms on his frail shoulders. "Honey, this is Mr. Yaman."

Sam rose, and Andi immediately noticed the wonder in his eyes, the undeniable emotion as he looked upon his child. With his thick dark hair, his coffee-colored eyes, Chance was almost the mirror image of his father. There was no longer any use in denying the truth.

"I'm Samir," he finally said, his smile now aimed at his child, not Andi. "You may call me Sam."

Chance's mouth opened in surprise. "That's kind of like my name, the Sam part, anyway. Chance Samuel Paul Hamilton. Aunt Tess sometimes calls me Little Bit." He sounded as if that was totally distasteful.

"You have a good strong name." Sam sent only a cursory glance in Andi's direction before turning his attention back to his son, but not before she saw another glimpse of regret and sadness. He was probably thinking about Paul, maybe even thinking about how much he'd missed in Chance's life. Andi couldn't let that sway her. She had to stay strong for her child's sake.

Tess suddenly reappeared into the kitchen. "Don't be scared, Little Bit. Shake the man's hand. He's an old friend."

Chance looked back at Andi, and she nodded her approval, then he moved forward and took the hand his father offered. Sam's smile revealed his pride. Andi couldn't blame him. She had felt that way about her child from the moment he was born.

After a hearty, exaggerated shake, Chance asked, "What's that on your head?"

"It's a kaffiyeh," Sam said.

"What's it for?"

"It's part of my official dress. I come from a country far away. I am a sheikh."

"Well, I'll be durned," Tess muttered.

Chance still looked confused. "A sheet?"

"A prince," Andi stated, grateful that Sam had enough wherewithal not to announce he was her son's father.

Chance glanced back at her. "Like *The Little Prince?*"

Andi smiled over the reference to one of his favorite books. "More like *Aladdin.*"

"Oh." He stared at Sam a moment longer. "Do you have a flying carpet?"

Sam laughed then, a low rich laugh that brought back more of Andi's cherished memories. "I'm afraid I have no magic carpet."

"Just a big black car," Chance said, sounding awed over that fact.

Andi took Chance's hand, determined to usher him out before he asked more questions. "Honey, it's time to go to camp. If we don't leave, you'll miss your bus.''

Amazingly, Chance looked disappointed over leaving his newfound friend. He'd been bugging her for weeks, counting the days until his first trip to camp, something Andi had been dreading even though she knew it would be good for him. Now he looked as if he couldn't care less. ''Can I stay and talk to the prince a little longer?''

''How long will you be away at this camp?'' Sam asked.

''Two weeks,'' Andi answered for her son. ''I'm sure you'll be gone—''

''I promise I will be here when you return,'' Sam said, his eyes still leveled on his child.

Chance's grin widened, revealing the left-sided dimple that served as another reminder of his parentage. ''Can I ride in your car when I get home?''

''Most certainly.''

Andi gave Chance a nudge toward the door. ''Let's go.''

''Andrea,'' Sam said from behind her. ''One other thing.''

She looked back to find that Tess had taken a chair across from Sam who had seated himself once again, his hands folded before him, looking much too cozy for Andi's comfort.

''What other thing?'' she asked, although she wasn't certain she really wanted to know.

''I will be here when you return.''

Exactly what Andi had longed for through many yesterdays, and what she greatly feared today.

Two

He had viewed the many ruins in Rome, Sacré Coeur at Montmartre in Paris, the Acropolis in Athens. Yet those experiences had paled in comparison to gazing upon his child for the first time.

Now Sam could only sit in silence, holding fast to the wish that he could recapture the years and experience every one of his son's milestones. But that was not possible, and not enough hours existed to make up for lost time.

"Are you okay, Sam?"

He looked up from his untouched coffee and met Tess's compassionate, gray eyes. "As well as can be expected."

"I guess finding out about the boy kind of shocked you."

"I knew about him before I arrived."

Tess's eyes widened. "You knew?"

"Did Andrea not tell you that we spoke last night following the auction?"

"Heck no, she didn't tell me that. She only told me that some guy paid a truckload of money for her to train his horse."

"I was the one. A small price to pay for the opportunity to know my child." And the opportunity to once again be in Andrea's presence, if only for a while. Perhaps he was somehow torturing himself, knowing he could never touch her, never hold her or make love to her again. Some things had not changed with the passage of time.

"How long have you known?" Tess asked.

"I found out a few months ago, when I knew I would be returning. I had someone investigate Andrea's whereabouts. I didn't know for certain that he was mine until I spoke with her last evening."

"She admitted you're his father?"

"No, but I surmised that fact because of his age and some of what she said to me. I had no doubts after I saw him." Sam pushed the cup aside and leaned back. "How long have you known?"

Tess propped her cheek on her palm and sighed. "I knew something was wrong with Andi after Paul's death, something more than losing her brother. I finally nagged her enough until she told me she was pregnant. The girl tried to convince me she'd been with some boy in town, but when Chance was born, that's when I knew for sure he was yours."

The guilt fisted in Sam's belly and held on tightly. "It was the night Paul died, Tess. We turned to each other for comfort. Never before Andrea had I been so careless. I know that doesn't relieve me of the responsibility, but I want you to know that I never intended it to happen.''

"I know you didn't. I also know that Andi had her sights set on you the minute you walked through the front door that first time. Add that to her mourning Paul's death, it's not surprising at all.''

"That does not excuse my behavior, my failure to protect her,'' Sam said adamantly. "I should never have allowed it to happen.''

Tess leaned forward and laid a hand on his arm. "It's too late to worry about the what-I-should-havedones. Question is, what are you going to do now?''

Sam knew what he wanted to do. He also knew what he could not do. He couldn't get involved with Andrea again knowing what he faced on his return home. He also could not abandon his child. "I would like to take the month I have here in the States to get to know my son.''

Tess frowned. "So you're gonna try to cram six years into a few weeks?''

"I suppose I am. I also want to set up a trust fund to make sure that his needs are met.''

Tess glared at him. "Let's get one thing straight, Mr. Sheikh. Andi has worked like the devil to meet that boy's needs. After the life insurance money ran out last year, she broke horses no one else wanted to break, all at the risk of getting herself hurt, or worse, just to pay the bills and put food on the table. I've done my part, too, and you can bet Chance has been happy, except for the diabetes.''

Searing panic rushed through Sam. "Diabetes?''

"Yeah. Guess Andi didn't bother to tell you that,

either. The camp he's going to is a summer program for diabetic kids. It almost killed Andi to let him go, but she decided it would do him a world of good.''

"How long has he had this diabetes?"

"He was diagnosed a little over a year ago. But he's doing okay after having a few setbacks. He's a regular little trooper, I tell you."

Sam experienced an overwhelming pain for his child, the need to take that pain away, if only he could. "If I had known, I would have done more. I would have sent him to the finest doctors, the best hospitals."

"And it wouldn't have changed a thing, Sam. He's stuck with this disease, and we can only hope and pray that someday they'll find a cure. In the meantime, we plan to treat him like a normal kid. Or at least I try to do that. Andi's pretty protective."

That much he'd witnessed earlier. "With my money, she can have more financial freedom."

"She won't take your money."

"She won't refuse as long as she knows I have our son's best interest at heart."

"Maybe, but you hurt her pretty badly by just running off and not staying in touch. I'm not sure how you're going to deal with that."

Neither did Sam, but he had to try. "After we've had the opportunity to talk further, I hope we can come to an understanding."

She stared at the cup a few more moments before looking up once again. "Okay, so you want to spend some time with Chance, and I think that's a good idea, which means you need to be close by. So the way I see it, you'll need to move in here with us."

Sam secretly admitted he had thought about that, living once again in the place he had considered his true home in America, but he could only imagine Andrea's reaction. "I doubt your niece will agree to that plan."

"Let me handle her. I suggest that you get in that limo and hightail it out of here to go and get your things. She won't be back for another hour or so, since she's got to stop by the feed store. That should give you enough time to settle in. You can have my room. I'll stay in the bunkhouse."

"With Mr. Parker?"

Tess patted her short, gray hair and glanced away. "No. Riley's working for someone else because Andi couldn't afford to keep him on. He still stops by now and then."

Sam grinned when color rose to Tess's careworn face. "He has yet to propose marriage?"

"He has, every day, but I'm too old to consider getting married."

"But not too old to…?" Sam let his words trail off on a question, unable to resist teasing her a bit.

"Too old for a good old-fashioned tumble? No one's too old for that, Sam. Not when it comes to someone you care about."

Images filtered into Sam's consciousness, visions of making love to Andrea, seeing satisfaction in her eyes, not sadness or hatred. But he could not consider something so foolish again, no matter how much he ached to do that very thing.

"Perhaps I should wait until Chance returns from camp," he said, thinking that might be favorable to being alone in the house with Andrea.

Tess shrugged. "You could, but I figure while you're here, you could earn your keep. The place is falling down around our ears, especially the barn. Might be nice if you could help fix the place up a bit. You could take the time to do that before Chance gets back."

At least that would occupy his hands during the day. But during the night… "I would be happy to do that. I must admit, I've missed engaging in manual labor since I've been away."

She sent him another questioning look. "You know, I'm surprised some girl hasn't snatched you up."

Sam mentally winced. "I am to be married by the end of summer."

"Does Andi know about this?" Tess did well to keep the shock from her expression, but it resounded in her tone.

"No. I prefer not to speak about it."

Tess stood and went to the counter to refill her coffee. "I guess you know what you're doing."

He knew exactly what he was doing—entering into a union with a woman for whom he felt nothing, an alliance that would benefit both their families. A life that held little promise of satisfaction all in the name of producing an heir with royal blood. "I have no choice in the matter."

Tess carried her cup back to the table and reclaimed her seat, staring at him intensely. "You're wrong, Sam. Life is about choices. Can you live with this one?"

Before he had returned to Andrea, he had come to

accept his fate. Now that he had seen her again, he wasn't as certain as before.

He could not consider that now. First and foremost, he had to consider his child's well-being, to make memories that would last a lifetime. And in order to have that opportunity, he must convince Andrea to trust him again.

Andi didn't trust Sam or his motives. Worse, she didn't trust herself around him. Today she had cried more than a few tears seeing her son off for the first time. She wasn't sure she had enough strength to deal with his father. But she had to deal with him. Chance's welfare was of the utmost importance, and she intended to find out what Sam had planned in that regard.

Pulling up behind the limo, she put the truck in Park and slid out, bolstering her courage. The bodyguard was seated on the front porch glider, looking serious, his arms folded across his chest. When Andi approached, he stood.

She stuck out her hand for a formal introduction. "I didn't catch your name."

He glanced at her hand then reluctantly took it for a brief shake. "Mr. Rashid."

"Nice to meet you, Mr. Rashid. You're welcome in the house, you know."

"It is best I remain here to allow you and the sheikh some privacy."

Andi shrugged. "Suit yourself, but I'm sure this won't take long."

Rashid executed a slight bow. "As you say, Miss Hamilton."

Andi yanked open the door, prepared to face whatever might come, yet she couldn't have prepared for Sam sitting on the living room sofa, dressed in casual slacks and knit shirt, his dark head bent as he thumbed through a photo album containing pictures of Chance from birth to the present day. So engrossed was he in the task, he didn't bother to look up. His preoccupation gave Andi a chance to study him while he journeyed through the pictorial history of their child.

Leaning back, he propped the album on one crossed leg and smiled. His smile faded and his expression turned melancholy, wistful. Andi closed her eyes and willed away the threatening emotions, the regrets.

Once she felt more composed, she approached the sofa. "He was such a beautiful baby."

Startled, Sam looked up and erased the tenderness from his features, but it didn't quite leave his eyes. "Yes, he was."

Andi joined him on the sofa, leaving as much distance between them as she could and still be able to view the pictures with Sam. How many times had she dreamed of this? How many times had she hoped that one day he would return? More times than she could count. And now that the moment had arrived, she wasn't sure how to handle it.

"What made you decide to call him Chance?" Sam asked.

"Other than I like the name, I guess you could say he was my chance to have someone who loved me without conditions." Her chance to have part of Sam that she could have with her always, but she wouldn't admit that to him.

She pointed to the photo of Chance on his first birthday, a mound of icing on top of his dark head. "He really tore into that cake. He wore more than he ate."

He turned the page to a picture of Chance on a pony. "I see that he has inherited his mother's love of horses."

"Yes. That's Scamp. She's still with us although I'm not sure for how long. She's about twenty years old now. I don't know what he'll do when we lose her."

"I'll buy him another."

"Some things can't be easily replaced."

He kept his attention focused on the photograph. "I have learned that to be a strong truth."

Now seemed like a good time to tell him her greatest concern. "I can't let you take him from me, Sam."

He closed the album, slipped it onto the coffee table and leaned forward, hands clasped between his parted knees, but he failed to look directly at her. "Is that what you think I've come to do, take him away from you?"

"Is it?"

"No, Andrea. He belongs here with you."

Although he sounded certain, doubts still hounded Andi. "So now that you've seen him, you're going to turn your back and walk away?"

He pinned her with his fiery dark eyes, his expression hard, angry. "I have no intention of turning my back on him. I will set up a bank account in your name to pay for his expenses. As I understand it, his medical bills have been a burden on you, according to Tess.''

Damn Tess. ''He's doing okay, and I'm managing to pay the bills a little at a time. So it's really not necessary for you to give us any money.''

His features softened. ''I insist that you let me do this for him. For you.''

''I'll think about it.'' And she would, but not for herself. After all, Sam did have an obligation to their son, and she could use the extra money for his expenses. Not to mention, the sheikh probably had several fortunes to spare. Because of Chance, she would put away her pride and allow him to help.

Sam walked to the shelf across the room and ran a fingertip along the edge of the frame that held the most recent picture of Chance, as if trying to connect to the child he'd only known for a few hours. ''Do they know why he has this diabetes?''

''No. It just happened. It's not anyone's fault.''

He glanced back. ''And he's doing well?''

''Most of the time, now that we have his insulin and diet regulated. He's so brave. He doesn't even complain when he has to have his shots.''

''I hate that he has suffered.'' Turning his attention back to the photo, he released a long sigh. ''Has he asked about me?''

Andi rose and stood behind him. ''Yes, several times in the past few years.''

''And what did you tell him?''

''I told him that you couldn't stay, that you lived far away in another land. I told him that you loved him and you'd be with us if you could.''

Slowly Sam faced her. "Then you did not lie to him."

"I don't know. Did I?"

He lowered his head. "It's true. I couldn't stay in America, Andrea. And now that I have seen him, I know that I would die before I let any harm come to him."

Andi swallowed hard around the lump in her throat. "I'm glad you feel that way, but I'm also worried about what we should tell him."

Sam raised his dark eyes to her. "I will leave that up to you, but I would like for him to know that I'm his father."

In a perfect world Andi would consider that to be a good idea. But this wasn't a perfect situation by any means. "Then what? 'Hey, Chance, I'm your dad and I'm sorry about this, but I have to go back and do my princely duties'?"

"I can return to visit during the summers when he's not in school."

"Is that enough, Sam? Will that ever be enough for him?"

He streaked a hand over his nape and sighed. "Would you have given up the opportunity to have spent time with Paul and your father even knowing they would be taken from you?"

Andi cursed his logic. "No, I wouldn't take anything for that time with them. But that's different. You'd be absent by choice, not death."

"Sometimes choices are made for us."

"You mean your duty? I'm not sure he'd understand why your position takes precedence over him. In time he might come to resent you."

"As his mother does?" Sam asked in a low, steady voice.

Andi had to admit that she'd resented his sudden departure. Resented that he had made love to her, created a child then left her alone to raise their son, left her alone to deal with her grief over her brother's death. But she couldn't fault him, at least when it came to Chance, since he hadn't known about him until now. He also hadn't made that possible because of his loyalty to a way of life that Andi couldn't even begin to understand. Worse, he hadn't even tried to explain or to stay in touch.

Still, she had to do what was best for everyone, even if that included calling a truce.

"I'm past my resentment, Sam."

"But you'll never forgive me, will you?"

"I have forgiven you." To a point, but she would never be able to forget.

His eyes took on the cast of satisfaction. "I'm pleased by that, Andrea. I only hope that I can earn your trust."

That would be a bit harder, in Andrea's opinion. She still feared that Sam might change his mind and try to take her son back to his country, especially after he got to know him. Yet she was willing to give him the benefit of the doubt, at least for the time being. "So where are you staying?"

"Here."

"I beg your pardon?"

"Tess told me it would be best if I remain nearby, and I agree. She wishes to reside in the bunkhouse during my stay, though I argued against it. But she insisted. I've brought a few of my things and I'll send

Rashid back to the hotel in Lexington to wait for me until I'm ready to leave."

Andi fought the bite of apprehension. If Sam stayed under the same roof, she couldn't avoid seeing him on a daily basis. And with their son away at camp for two weeks, she worried that she might not be able to resist him. "I think you should wait until Chance returns before you move in."

"I have promised Tess I will help do some repairs while I'm here, before Chance comes back."

Tess. Always thinking of everything, darn it. "I guess I could use the help," Andi admitted. She could also use some courage. Right now it was all she could do not to reach out and touch him, send her fingertips over the fine lines framing his mouth, his incredible lips that now formed a grim line as he studied her. Be brave, she told herself.

As if he intended to test her nerve, Sam took her hand into his, creating pleasant warmth that flowed through her whole body. One simple touch, and already she was battling for control. But she had to remain in control, prove to herself, and to him, that she was much stronger than before. Prove that her memories were colored by the fantasies of a young girl, dreams that no longer existed in a woman's reality. She intended to conduct her own test.

Putting her best smile forward, she pulled her hand from his grasp and opened her arms. "Welcome home, Sam."

His gaze roved over her from head to toe in a long, lingering look of appreciation, then finally he accepted her embrace. He felt good against her, strong and solid and warm. She remembered how wonderful it had been to hold him close, remembered his exotic scent, his overwhelming heat. Remembered how she had missed having him in her life, left only with her hopes of his return and memories of one night when he had been completely hers.

Trembling with the force of her reaction, she pulled out of his arms and stepped back. Her greatest fear was now realized.

Nothing had really changed, even after all these years.

Sam brushed a tender kiss across her cheek and studied her with those damnable mysterious eyes, dark and intense and capable of bringing her to her knees.

"Thank you, Andrea. It's good to be home."

If only it was home, Sam thought as he stood in the middle of the aged barn. He had chosen to come to the stable first, his favorite place. A place where he had spent many an hour with Paul and Andrea, assisting with the daily chores, shoveling manure, unloading feed, watering the remaining two horses that had belonged to Paul and Andrea's father before his death, and any others that had happened upon the premises, thanks to a young woman who couldn't say no.

Even then, Andrea would bring home someone's colt or filly to break, most of the time solely for the thrill of it, not for the pay. Today, out of the dozen or so stalls, only four were occupied, one by Chance's pony.

This would never do, Sam decided. He needed to help Andrea acquire some horses to train immediately. Most of those he owned belonged to a syndicate, but that did not mean he couldn't purchase one that belonged solely to him. He had a gift for choosing good prospects, the reason why he had come to Kentucky to attend the sales. In fact, he had been approached at the auction regarding a promising two-year-old filly. One phone call and the mare would be his, though she was priced at half a million U.S. dollars. That didn't matter. After all, he had paid for Andrea's training expertise; he might as well put that investment to good use. But first he must repair a few stalls.

After rummaging through the tack room for a hammer and nails, Sam set out to make the barn more serviceable. Unfortunately, he pounded his thumb on more than one occasion, yet he welcomed the pain. For seven years he had done nothing more than paperwork, since manual labor was considered demeaning for royalty. But Sam was in America now, in a barn, not Barak, therefore he could labor to his heart's delight.

"What on earth are you doing?"

He turned toward the entry to find Andrea staring at him as if he had grown fangs. He had no fangs, only two nails in his mouth. He spoke around them. "I'm repairing these stalls before an injury occurs." Considering his deplorable skills, an injury could very well occur. To him.

She took a few steps forward and braced her hands on her hips. "In case you haven't noticed, there isn't a horse in that stall, and I doubt there's going to be one anytime soon."

Turning away from her, he removed the nails from

his mouth and hammered one into the wooden slat. "You're wrong, Andrea."

"What are you talking about?"

He faced her again and swiped the sweat from his brow with a forearm. "I've recently purchased a filly." Or he would by day's end. "If you recall, I bid an obscene amount of money for your services, and I expect to collect."

At the moment he would like to collect on several things, none having to do with her training skills. He couldn't seem to pull his gaze away from the ragged white T-shirt she now wore or the faded jeans that adhered to the bow of her hips like a second skin. His body stirred, calling attention to a need that had been denied far too long. Reminding him that Andrea could still affect him without attempting to do so.

She strolled to his side and leaned a shoulder against the stall, facing him. "You mean to tell me that you actually intend for me to train your horse."

"That's precisely what I'm telling you." He should be telling her that, if she knew what was best for her, for them both, from this point forward she would wear a bra.

She frowned. "And when is this horse supposed to be here?"

"I will arrange for her to arrive in two days. That should give me time to repair the stall."

Andrea smiled, amusement dancing in her blue eyes. "You intend to do this in your good clothes?"

Sam looked down at his slacks and shirt, then back up again. "I'm afraid this is all I have at the present. I'll go into town and buy something suitable tomorrow."

"Can't you have Mr. Rashid do it for you?"

"I've sent him back to the hotel to field calls. I prefer that no one knows where I am." Then perhaps he could avoid his father's questions.

"You don't need his protection?"

Only from his desire for Andrea, and he doubted Rashid could aid him in that regard. "I am relatively safe at the moment." Yet still in danger of losing his control in her presence.

"You really don't have to buy anything, at least not today," she said. "I'm sure I can find you something to wear."

He let his eyes travel down the length of her—very much at his own peril when he noticed her nipples had hardened beneath the thin shirt. "I doubt that I will fit into your jeans."

She crossed her arms over her chest, much to his disappointment and relief. "Not mine. Yours. You left some jeans here. They're in the cedar chest in the attic."

"And they are still intact?"

"I'm sure they are. Of course, there could be one major problem. You were much skinnier then."

"Skinnier?"

She sent a long glance down his body, much the same as he had hers. "Yep. You've filled out quite a bit."

He was definitely filling out in some very obvious places. To avoid embarrassment, he turned back to the stall and surveyed his handiwork. "Give me a moment and we can go to the attic."

"Why can't we go now?" she asked, sounding confused.

Obviously she was still somewhat naive. He took in a deep draw of air but refused to turn around. "As soon as I'm finished with this board, I will join you. At the moment I prefer not to stop what I'm doing."

He, as well, preferred to stop his craving for her, but he doubted that would happen soon—if ever.

Three

____

Sitting cross-legged on the attic floor, Andi pulled the jeans from the cedar chest where she'd kept them along with other special mementos—Chance's baby clothes, his first shoes, a few of Paul's things, treasures that she couldn't bear to part with. She fought back more tears, already missing her son and he'd only been gone a few hours. Admittedly, already missing Sam even though he wouldn't leave again for several weeks.

She set the jeans aside and rummaged through the pile in the chest, coming upon Paul's high school football jersey sporting the number seven. Lucky seven, Paul had said. If only his luck had held out, before he'd been ripped from her life, never having children of his own, never knowing Chance.

How Paul would have loved his nephew, loved

playing uncle. If he hadn't died, maybe things would have been different. She probably wouldn't have made love with Sam. And she wouldn't have Chance.

She couldn't imagine not having her son in her life. She also couldn't turn back time and she couldn't keep wondering about what might have been. Even if Paul had survived, Sam would have returned to his country, his duty. Hadn't he all but admitted that to her?

Dropping the jersey back into the chest, she grabbed up Sam's jeans and held them against her heart. Clung to his old clothes as if they were a replacement for the man.

"You're so stupid, Andrea Hamilton," she muttered. "Still pining away over a man you can't have, so stop thinking about him. *Stop it!*"

"Did you find what you're looking for?"

Still clutching the jeans in her arms, Andrea stiffened. With her back to the door, she could only hope Sam hadn't witnessed her foolishness, hadn't heard her declaration.

Glancing over her shoulder, she thankfully found his eyes focused on the open cedar chest, not her. He strolled over with hands in his pockets, then hovered above her like some dark, imposing monument to sheer male beauty.

He nodded toward the jersey laid out on top of the other items. "I remember Paul wearing that often."

Andi tossed the jeans aside and shifted to where she could get a better look at Sam, his reaction. He hid his emotions behind that steel facade, those impenetrable eyes. Tearing her gaze away, she leaned forward again and produced another keepsake. "Do you remember this?"

Sam crouched beside her and took the baseball from her grasp, turning it over and over with his strong fingers. His expression mellowed with remembrance. "I recall this very well. My first major league game. Cleveland Indians. In April, the year Paul and I met."

"And Paul caught the ball after a two-run homer."

Sam grinned. "The ball rolled from two rows above us and landed at his feet. It was a foul, not a home run. Paul thought the other story sounded more favorable."

Andi laughed. "That was just like him, making up something that sounded more exciting."

"Yes. Exactly like him." Sam's tone turned weary and so did his eyes.

When he tried to hand the ball back to her, she said, "Keep it."

"I could not—"

"He'd want you to have it, Sam. Besides, you two didn't bother to take me along, so why would I want it?"

His smile reappeared. "We did not take you because Paul worried that you would distract me from the game."

"He did not!"

"Perhaps he was not worried, but I was, the reason I didn't encourage your attendance."

Andi's face flushed hot as a summer sidewalk. "Always the charmer," she murmured.

"It's the truth, Andrea. You were very distracting. You still are."

Determined to move away from that topic, Andi patted the wooden floor next to her. "Have a seat. There's something else I need to give you."

Sam joined her on the floor, his long legs crossed the same as hers, and set the ball beside him. Andi reached into the corner of the chest and found the present in the same place she'd left it years before. The newspaper was yellowed, the blue bow tied around it somewhat flat. Tucked underneath the ribbon was an envelope that read "Sam, The Man."

She offered it to him. "It's Paul's graduation gift to you. I found it in his room when we were converting it to Chance's nursery."

Sam took it from her and placed the present in his lap. Andi noticed a slight tremor in his fingers when he slit open the envelope and withdrew the card. While he read to himself, his expression took on a pain so intense it stole Andi's breath.

"What does it say?" she asked.

He handed her the card and she, too, read in silence.

Hey, Sam. Just a little something for you to take back home. I'd send Andi with you, but she'd just give you grief. So I'm keeping her here for the time being, unless you decide to come back and take her off my hands. Seriously, if anything should happen to me, take care of her. She deserves to be happy.
Remember me.
Your bud, Paul

Tears burned Andi's eyes. Her throat ached and her

chest contracted with the sorrow that she'd kept at bay for more days than she could count.

"He knew," she said, her voice shaking with the effort to hold back the threatening tide of emotions.

"Knew what?"

She raised her eyes from the card to Sam. "When we were cleaning out his things, we also found two Christmas presents, one for me and one for Tess. Paul never shopped until Christmas Eve. I think he knew what was going to happen."

Sam sighed. "Andrea, I refuse to believe that Paul would drink himself to death, take his own life."

"That's not what I'm saying. Tess calls it 'angels' intuition.' The ability to know your fate."

"And you believe this?"

"I think anything's possible." Or she had at one time.

Andi glanced at the unopened package still resting in his lap. "Are you going to see what's inside?"

He carefully tore away the paper, revealing a framed photo that Tess had taken of Andi standing between Sam and Paul, arms wrapped around each other's waists, all three sporting bright grins on their dirt-spattered faces, the result of a mud-slinging contest after the boys had dumped Andi in the trough.

They all looked so happy, carefree. If only they'd known what the future held. If only they'd played a little longer, clung to each other a little tighter, told each other what they were feeling inside....

Andi could no longer hold back the tears. They fell at will, rolled down her cheeks and onto her T-shirt. Sam wrapped his strong arms around her, absorbing her sobs against his solid chest. He rocked her back and forth as she had rocked his son so many nights. She didn't want to need his consolation, his strength, but she did. She needed *him,* more than she should.

Tipping her face up, Andi brushed a kiss across his jaw, knowing that he could very well refuse this kind of comfort. But the possible benefit outweighed the probable rejection. Yet he didn't push her away. Instead, he cupped her face in his palms and kissed her. All the sadness melted away and desire took its place, as it had before.

Oh, how she remembered this, his gentle persuasion, the soft glide of his tongue, the velvet feel of his lips, his extraordinary skill. Those memories had served her well. No one had kissed her this way before or since. No one.

Sam abruptly broke the kiss, pushed away from her and stood. "I apologize," he said, sounding like the prince, not the man.

Andi felt angry, ashamed, weak. She lowered her eyes to the discarded photo and card, reminders that the kiss had come about from Sam's need to provide comfort and perhaps receive some comfort in return, not his need for her. From grief, not from desire. Although they were in a dusty attic, not stretched out by a pond, history seemed intent on repeating itself.

"This cannot happen again, Andrea," he stated, then quickly left the room without the jeans, Paul's gift or the baseball. Left Andi alone to mull over what to do about Samir Yaman.

She agreed it shouldn't happen again if she wanted to protect her heart, even if she still wanted him, and she did. Regardless, she had to accept that he was here, at least for the time being, and she needed to deal with it.

Andi gathered the jeans and laid the picture and card on top, then on second thought, grabbed the baseball in her free hand. She stood and sprinted down the stairs to find Sam standing in the second-floor hallway beside the attic entry, his forehead tipped against the wall.

"Here," she said, offering him the jeans. "Try these on. Maybe they still fit."

He pushed off the wall with both palms and faced her. "I doubt they will, at least at the moment."

When her confusion cleared, Andi lowered her eyes to the evidence below his belt stating loud and clear that he wasn't at all unaffected by the kiss.

She raised her gaze to his espresso eyes that expressed self-consciousness and, amazingly, the same desire she had seen the night he'd made love to her.

Maybe this was the answer. By making love with him again, maybe she could somehow, some way get him out of her system, find out for certain if the precious memories were nothing more than the imaginings of a girl who had turned to a man during her sorrow. Not love, only a need for solace.

She doubted Sam would be so quick to accommodate her, but that certainly didn't mean she couldn't try to persuade him, beginning now.

She shoved the jeans and photo against his chest, forcing him to take them from her. Then, with a courage she didn't know she possessed, she rolled the baseball slowly down his groin and slipped it into his pocket. Before she retreated, she ran a fingertip over the obvious bulge below his belt. "If you need any help with this, let me know."

With that she hurried to the first floor, not daring to look back to see his reaction. Before she made it out the door, she heard what sounded like a baseball hitting plaster, and she figured she'd probably driven home her point. Now she would attempt to drive him crazy with need, drive him back into her arms, and in doing so, drive him from her heart for good.

She'd have to take it slowly, plan carefully and, most important, remember she intended to tell him goodbye, once and for all.

Sam sat at the breakfast table, exhausted from physical labor and lack of sleep. After the way Andrea had touched him two days before, the kiss, the promise in her words, he had stayed awake both nights in Tess's room, tensing at every sound, worried that Andrea might come to him and he might not be able to turn her away. But in fact she had barely spoken to him as she carried on with her normal activities, not once mentioning the kiss or her proposition.

Sam had avoided her, but he couldn't avoid her now, especially when she occasionally glanced at him while moving the scrambled eggs around on her plate. He found himself staring at her mouth several times, watched while she nibbled at her food. Everything about her enthralled him, from the slight spattering of freckles across her nose, to the fragile column of her throat and that same fire in her eyes that caused his heart to pound in a fearsome rhythm.

He had tried to listen for the sound of the transport scheduled to bring the filly, but he hadn't been able to concentrate. Before, the family dog, an Australian shepherd named Troubles, would have alerted everyone. Odd, he hadn't noticed until today that the dog was no longer around.

Pushing his plate back, he asked, "Where is Troubles?"

Tess shook her head and spoke around a bite of toast. "He ended up on the wrong side of a tire when Chance was four."

"And you haven't found another?"

"I haven't had time," Andrea said as she stood.

Or the money, Sam thought. "I could provide one."

Andrea picked up their plates and slipped them in the sink. "That's not a good idea. With the traffic on the highway, I'm afraid we might lose another dog, and I don't want to put Chance through that again."

Sam hated the thought that his son had suffered through such a loss, but he was coming to realize that loss was a part of life that could not be avoided. "Then he remembers?"

Tess swiped at her mouth with a napkin. "Yeah, he remembers, but he's okay with it. Andi told him that Troubles was with Uncle Paul, jumping from star to star."

Obviously, Andrea still maintained a fascination with stars. The night Paul died she'd insisted that the brightest held his soul, and that she would hang her dreams on him for safekeeping. In that moment Sam had recognized that his love for her was as infinite as those stars. Making love with her had been a natural expression, a means to show her, since he had never told her.

The sound of a truck brought him out of his recollections and back into the present.

Andrea wiped her hands on a towel and faced him. "Do you think that's them?" Her excitement came through in her tone and the widening of her blue eyes. The first time Sam had witnessed her joy since Chance had left.

"Perhaps we should go see."

Before he could move, Andrea had already raced down the hall toward the front door.

"I swear," Tess said, then chuckled. "Nothing gets that girl more excited than a good horse."

Sam knew all too well what else excited her, but he would be wise to keep that out of his mind. "True. I hope this one doesn't disappoint her."

Tess propped her legs on the opposing chair and sent him a wicked grin. "I doubt she'll be disappointed. I'm sure you'll see to that while you're here, if you haven't already."

Without response Sam left the room, determined to ignore Tess's veiled suggestion. Nothing would please him more than to please Andrea in every way possible. But he would have to settle for providing a prize filly, otherwise he would be repeating past mistakes, knowing that he would have to leave her once again.

He joined Andrea at the rear of the massive trailer and waited for the filly to be unloaded. Sam was more than a bit apprehensive since he had never purchased a horse sight unseen. But when the man backed the filly down the ramp, Sam acknowledged that she was a treasure, as was Andrea who stood staring at the two-year-old. The woman had wonder in her eyes as she watched the filly prance about, restless with the need to run after her journey.

"Sam, she's unbelievable," Andrea said, almost in a whisper.

"I have to agree."

The man held the lead rope up. "She's all yours."

When Andrea failed to move, Sam said, "What are you waiting for?"

Andrea stepped forward and took the rope, then allowed the filly to sniff her free hand before scratching her behind the ears. As if the horse somehow knew she had found a friend, she settled down, accepting the display of affection without protest.

"What's her name?" Andrea asked.

"At the stables we called her Sunny," the man said. "Her registered name is Renner's Sun Goddess."

"Sunny it is." Andrea turned the horse and led her toward the stable. "I'm going to put her on a longe line and see how she moves," she tossed over one shoulder.

"Good," Sam said. "I'll join you in a moment."

By the time Sam had signed the appropriate paperwork and paid the handler before sending him on his way, Andrea had the filly in the outdoor arena, working her at a trot.

Sam propped one heel on the arena's bottom rung and watched both horse and trainer in action. The mare's flaxen mane and tail flowed with her fluid movements. Andrea's red-gold hair fluttered in the June breeze, the color very close to the horse's near-copper coat. Together they were a matched set, a tribute to beauty and grace with a wildness that lingered immediately below the surface.

Sam kept his attention on the filly only a brief moment, now that he had the opportunity to look his fill at Andrea without her knowledge. She had matured into a woman in every way, and that concept unearthed a searing heat low in Sam's belly that had nothing to do with the Kentucky sun.

She wore a light-blue shirt that barely reached the top of her jeans, jeans that fit every curve to perfection. When she raised her arm to keep the filly moving, Sam caught a glimpse of flesh at her waist. He imagined how it would feel to have his hands there, lower still, molding them to her bottom, pulling her against him, letting her know how strongly she could affect him, how being in her presence aroused him beyond all bounds. He was definitely aroused now and had been for two miserable days with no possible end to that misery, unless...

No, he could not act on those desires. It would be unfair to both of them, even though Andrea had made the offer of her assistance in that matter.

Andrea drew the filly into the center of the arena, turned to face him and called, "She's a winner, Sam."

Her vibrant smile had him smiling, too. Pleasing her did please him, and again he thought of many ways he could bring her more satisfaction, ways that would leave them clinging to each other, breathless, sated....

The crunch of gravel turned Sam's attention to the drive. A massive red truck pulled up next to the pen and a man dressed in typical cowboy garb got out.

Without invitation he opened the gate to the round pen and joined Andrea.

Because of his proximity, Sam couldn't hear the conversation though he assumed they were discussing the filly. Then their shared laughter floated over the breeze, and the man moved closer to Andrea. Too close.

Sam despised the sudden intimacy between them, hated even more that the cowboy touched Andrea's face then patted her bottom as if he had the right to do so. It took all of Sam's strength not to scale the fence and go after the idiot with fists raised. Luckily the man turned and left before Sam acted on that impulse. He had no cause to intervene. Andrea could do as she pleased with any man she pleased.

Still, Sam couldn't seem to get a grasp on his anger. It stayed with him all the way to the barn as he followed Andrea and the filly. The sway of her hips only fueled his fury when he thought about the man touching her with such intimacy, any man aside from him.

Once inside, Andrea turned the filly loose in the stall and came out holding a water bucket.

Sam leaned back against the opposite stall, hands fisted at his sides, no longer able to maintain his silence. "Who was that man?"

Andrea kept her back to him while she gathered the hose and began to fill the bucket. "Caleb? He's a friend."

"Only a friend?"

She regarded him over one shoulder. "The bay gelding at the end of the aisle is his. He stopped by to check on his progress. He's letting me have him for thirty more days for the basics, before he takes him to a cutting horse guy.''

''Then you're saying that his only interest in you has to do with your training skills?''

She shut off the water and turned, the hose still clutched in her fragile hand. ''Of course.''

''Are you still so naive, Andrea?''

Her face melded into a frown. ''About what?''

''That man has designs on you as a woman.''

She rolled her eyes. ''Get off it, Sam. Caleb wants me to train his horse and that's all.''

''He wants *you*, Andrea.''

''Good grief. What on earth makes you think that?''

''The way he touched you.''

''Touched me?''

''Are you saying you didn't notice when he put his hand on your…on your…butt?''

When Andrea laughed, Sam's temper flared again. ''You find this funny?''

After recovering somewhat, she said, ''I'm laughing because your assumptions about Caleb are ridiculous.''

''My observations cannot be denied.''

She tossed the hose to the ground. ''You sound like a jealous lover.''

Sam acknowledged that fact, but he couldn't stop his reaction. ''Is *he* your lover, Andrea?''

Her eyes narrowed with anger. ''That's really none of your business.''

Regardless, Sam had to know. ''Is he, Andrea?''

She leaned back against the stall. ''Let me ask you

something. Have you been celibate all these years, Sam?''

"That's not the point.''

"Oh, I think it is. If we're going to get into my business, then that gives me the right to get into yours.''

"I'm concerned about our son,'' Sam said, grasping for anything so he would not have to admit there had been other women, but not so many as she might think, and none that could compare to what he had found with her. "I'm wary of those who would enter your life but have no intention of treating Chance appropriately.''

"If you must know, I've dated a couple of men, but it didn't work out because Chance didn't like either of them. For me that's the test. Chance's approval. Now are you satisfied?''

Only one thing would satisfy him, kissing the defiance from her expression, making her lips soften beneath his. "Obviously, this Caleb would like to be the next in line.''

"Your imagination is running wild, Sheikh Yaman.''

She was driving him wild, her eyes now as blue as flames. Sam wanted to touch her, to make her forget the fool who'd had his hands on her earlier. To forget every man she had ever let touch her. Yet he didn't dare give her more than advice.

"Your clothing leaves little to the imagination, Andrea. I suggest that you consider how you dress from now on.''

"I'm wearing what I wear every day of the week. Plain jeans and T-shirt.''

"Tight jeans and a very thin T-shirt."

She took a visual journey from his chest to the boots he had bought on a trip into town yesterday. "I'm thinking you've got the tight jeans market cornered. But I have to admit they look pretty darned good. I'm still surprised they fit."

They did, but barely, and the fit at the moment was less than comfortable. "My attire is not the issue at present." His gaze slid to her breasts. "You have on no bra. How can you expect a man to ignore this?"

She grabbed the hem of her shirt and pulled it out. "This provides plenty of cover."

"It shows far too much. Hides too little." Made Sam ache.

"I don't have that much to see, Sam. But thanks, anyway."

"You are wrong, Andrea. Wrong and foolish to think otherwise."

Her sudden smile caught him off guard. "Does this plain old T-shirt get your blood pumping, Sheikh Yaman?"

He couldn't deny that. "It is practically transparent."

She reached down and picked up the bucket. Sam believed she meant to carry it into the filly's stall. Instead she tipped it toward her, spilling the contents down the front of her, then tossed the bucket aside. She pointed at her breasts. "Now, this is transparent."

Sam could only stare at the dark shading of her nipples that showed through the saturated material. His hands opened and closed with the urge to touch her.

"Like what you see, Sam?" she asked, her tone full of challenge that he dared not answer.

But he couldn't keep from answering. He spanned the space between them before his brain registered that he had moved. Yet his body was very aware that he now had Andrea against the stall. He took her mouth without consideration of the consequences, thrusting his tongue between her parted lips with the force of his need while his hands searched beneath the wet fabric to cup both of her breasts. She whimpered when he thumbed each peak. Her hips ground against him in a torturous rhythm that made him hard and aching, balanced on the point of losing all restraint. He wanted to take her right there, right then, without regard to location or lack of privacy.

When she raised her arms, Sam pulled the drenched shirt over her head and dropped it to the ground behind her back while he trailed a path of wet kisses down the valley of her breasts. She arched her back, and her chest rose and fell rapidly in sync with his pounding heart, then her breath completely stopped when he drew one nipple into his mouth.

So lost in the taste of her dampened flesh, in the feel of her softness against his tongue, it took him a moment to notice the downward track of his zipper. Realization caught hold and he clasped her wrist.

"No, Andrea." He stepped back, away from her, then realized, with her standing there bare from the waist up, he was in danger of forgetting himself once again.

Yanking his own shirt over his head, he held it against her, shielding her from his eyes. "Put this on."

"But—"

"Put it on."

When she finally took the shirt, Sam walked to the opposite stall, braced his hands above his head and leaned into them. His chest burned from the effort it took to recover his breath and to calm his body.

When he turned again, thankfully she had honored his request. The knit shirt hit her at the knees, but the sharp sting of awareness was still present within him, even though she was now completely covered.

"I promised myself this would not happen between us," he said, his voice thick with the desire that he couldn't disregard.

She folded her arms across her breasts. "Wouldn't be the first time you've broken a promise, Sam."

"What promise have I broken?"

She strolled down the aisle a few steps then turned. "That night at the pond, you promised you wouldn't leave me."

"I meant that moment, Andrea. That night. Not forever."

"That's not at all how it seemed."

Sam recognized that he probably had led her to believe that he had meant always, bringing about more guilt. "I said many things to you that night, but we were both in pain." Lost in each other, lost in love both timeless and forbidden.

"Then you didn't mean any of it?"

He had meant most of it, but he hadn't stopped to consider that he couldn't keep those promises. "With you in my arms, I had forgotten who I was, what was expected of me. I regret that I was such a fool."

Andrea shrugged. "Guess that goes for both of us. Except there's one thing I don't regret."

"What is that?"

"Our son. Having him made Paul's death more bearable, easier to accept that you had left for good. I thank you for that gift. For him."

Sam doubted that he could feel any worse, any lower. "I regret that I have not been here for him, or for you."

"And you're going to have to leave us again. Do you regret that?"

More than she would ever know. "I do not have the luxury to dwell on regrets, Andrea. I've very little time left to know my son before I have to return home."

"Then why don't we make the best of that time together?" She sent him another lazy smile. "Do what comes naturally."

Sam clenched his jaw tight. "If you are saying that we should make love, then that would be unwise."

She moved closer to him, almost close enough for him to touch her again. It took all his fortitude not to reach out to her once more, finish what they had begun.

"In case you haven't noticed, Sheikh Yaman, I'm a grown woman now, not a girl. I'm not going to fall apart when you leave." Her gaze faltered, belying her confident tone. "So just in case you decide to change your mind…"

She brushed past him and headed toward the tack room. After a moment she came out and called, "Catch."

Sam grabbed the baseball midair, confused. "And the point to this is?"

She smiled a devious smile. "Just wanted to let you know that the offer still stands, in case you decide to play ball. Unless, of course, you can't handle it."

He could not handle hurting her again, and he would, once he told her the reasons why he could not stay.

She pivoted on her booted heels and swayed toward the barn's opening. Without turning around, she said, "Water the horse, will ya? I seem to be a little clumsy this morning."

For the second time in as many days, Sam slammed the ball against the wall, thinking it might be best if he did the same to his head. Perhaps he could pound Andrea out of his brain.

But a thousand blows and a million years would not begin to force Andrea Hamilton from his heart.

Four

When Andi stepped through the back door, she was suddenly assaulted by a cold draft of air and a strong case of chills. But it wasn't the air-conditioned kitchen that had her shivering, or her still-damp skin. Sam was the cause of her present condition.

She could still feel his soft abrading tongue on her breasts, his hands molding her bottom, his body pressed intimately against hers. Just thinking about him made her feel feverish, the low throbbing ache having yet to subside.

Andi hugged her arms across her chest, a sorry replacement for Sam, but she needed to hide the effects of their recent interlude. She realized all too late that she couldn't escape her aunt's scrutiny.

Standing at the sink, Tess grabbed a towel from the counter and surveyed Andi from chin to toes. "Correct me if I'm wrong, but wasn't Sam wearing that shirt this morning?''

Heat skimmed up Andi's throat and settled on her face. At the moment she felt like a schoolgirl caught necking in the pasture. Okay, so it wasn't the pasture, but it was pretty darned close. ''I had a mishap with the water bucket. He lent me his shirt since mine was soaked.''

Tess's knowing grin appeared. ''You two already having to cool yourselves off after just three days?''

She released a sigh. ''Don't let your imagination run away with you, Tess.'' Andi's, on the other hand, was long out of the starting gate and still running full-steam ahead, thanks to Sam.

Tess's forehead wrinkled from a frown as her gaze settled on Andi's mouth. ''I'm not imagining the whisker burn on your face, little girl. I might be old, but I'm not stupid.''

Andi walked to the cabinet and retrieved a glass. Her hands shook as she tried to fill it with water. ''I didn't say you're stupid, Tess. I'm just saying don't make too much out of this.''

''I won't if you won't. In fact, I think it's best if you stop and consider what you're doing before you make another mistake.''

Andi glanced up from the cup to Tess, who now looked considerably more serious. ''I don't consider Chance a mistake, Tess, if that's what you're suggesting.''

Tess leaned against the counter looking primed for a parental lecture. ''Of course he's not a mistake. He's been a godsend. But getting involved with Sam would be a mistake. He won't stay this time, either, Andi. You'd do well to remember that.''

If only Tess realized that's all Andi had thought about the past few days. She didn't need to be reminded that Sam would leave once again in the name of duty to his country. Knowing didn't make it any easier to deal with, yet she was determined to keep everything in perspective. She also didn't expect Tess to understand what she intended to do—make love with Sam in order to get him out of her system.

"By the way," Tess said as she swiped at the kitchen counter, "the camp called."

Andi's chest tightened with panic, and she nearly dropped the glass. "What's wrong?"

"Nothing's wrong. They called to remind you about parents' day on Saturday. You have to be there by 8:30 a.m."

Relief flowed through Andi knowing that her baby was okay. After taking a long drink, she dumped the water into the sink and set the glass aside. "I remembered it was this weekend, but I didn't know I'd have to be there quite that early. I guess I can ask Sam to feed and water the horses."

Tess tossed the towel aside and faced Andi, her expression no less stern. "I'll feed the horses. Sam should go with you."

The panic returned to Andi once more. "I can't do that, Tess. Chance might start asking questions. He doesn't need to deal with any stress while he's away."

"And when do you intend to tell him, Andi? Never?"

She hadn't gotten that far in her thinking. She only

knew she didn't want to deliver any confessions during her son's first opportunity to establish his independence. "I don't know when I'll tell him. Soon, I guess. Before Sam leaves."

Tess sighed. "That's up to you, but I still think Sam should go with you."

"Where are you proposing I go?"

Andi tensed at the sound of Sam's deep voice coming from behind her. Trapped like a caged rabbit. She had no choice but to tell him about the event.

After facing Sam, Andi's well-rehearsed smile disappeared when she immediately contacted his bare chest, now at eye level. Her gaze skimmed over the territory marked by sinewy muscle and scattered with dark hair. Her fingers opened and closed with the urge to explore as if they'd been offered a masculine playground designed with a needy woman in mind.

In the barn she hadn't taken the time to study the details. In fact, she'd intentionally *avoided* the details after Sam thwarted her seduction. But she couldn't ignore them now, though she thought it best to stop looking with Tess playing audience.

She put on a casual smile and pulled her gaze back to his face. "Actually, it's no big deal really. The camp is holding a parents' day on Saturday."

His brows drew down into a frown. "Parents' day?"

She shrugged. "You know, games, a barbecue, that sort of thing. Pretty boring stuff." Especially for a man like Sam who probably spent his days in some elaborate palace surrounded by jewel-encrusted bowls of fruit and scantily clad women provided for his entertainment. She almost laughed over the absurdity of that stereotypical image, and silently cursed to think it might be an accurate assumption.

Forcing the thoughts away, she turned her attention back to Sam and noted her drenched shirt gripped tightly in his grasp. "I would like very much to go," he said.

"You would?"

"Yes. It would provide the opportunity to spend more time with my son."

"Exactly what I was thinking," Tess said.

Andi quelled the urge to tell her aunt that no one had asked her opinion on the matter. "I'm still not sure it's a good idea. Chance might wonder why you're there."

Sam's features turned tightrope tense. "You may tell him I'm there as a friend. I will not force you to say anything more, if that's your concern."

The anger and hurt in his tone made Andi flinch internally. She had already denied him many opportunities to know his child, though not intentionally. After all, *he* had been the one to disappear from their lives. He had been the one to discard her as if what had existed between them meant nothing at all.

Still, she had to consider Chance's opportunity to know his father. "I'll think about it." And she would, long and hard.

Tess brushed past Andi on her way toward the hall. "I'll leave you two alone to discuss it while I sit on the porch and snap some peas."

After Tess left the kitchen, Sam offered her the soggy T-shirt. "Perhaps you would like to return my clothes to me."

Andi couldn't suppress a devilish smile. "Do you want to do it now?"

"Do what?"

"Exchange shirts." She took a few steps and stopped immediately before him, close enough to touch the copper surface of his bare skin. "Unless you need something else from me?"

He released a frustrated sound, somewhere between a growl and a groan. "I prefer you stop making offers I cannot accept."

Determined to keep his attention, she ran a fingertip down his sternum along the stream of dark hair, and paused at his navel. "You can't accept them or you won't?"

"We've been through this, Andrea. I am not able to accept."

She sent a quick glance at the proof that he was still willing to play along. "You seem more than able to me."

He held her hand against his belly and kept his gaze fixed on hers as he exhaled slowly, his muscles tightening beneath her palm. Andi held her breath, wondering if this time he might decide to accept her offer. Maybe this time he would give up and give in, knowing this was what they both wanted. Even though he tried to deny that he did want her, she wasn't too dumb to read the signs. His eyes were dark, almost desperate, warring with indecision and desire. A slight sheen of perspiration covered his chest and forehead. His respiration sounded unsteady.

No, she wasn't too dumb to recognize that he wasn't at all unaffected, either here in the kitchen, or earlier in the barn. As affected as he had been seven years ago.

"Is this really all you want from me, Andrea?" he asked in a low, controlled voice as his fingertips stroked her knuckles. "This and nothing more? And afterward, will you then be satisfied?"

"Yes, I will," she said in a voice she didn't recognize.

He pushed her hand away and took a step back. "Perhaps you will, but I will not. If I have you, I promise I would want you more than once, and often, until I again must leave. Ask yourself truthfully if you would want to make love knowing nothing more will ever exist between us."

With that he tossed her wet shirt onto the table and strode out of the room, leaving Andi to ponder his words, the raw truth she heard in them. If she did have him once again—all of him—would it ever be enough?

There would never be enough time now.

Sam tossed his cell phone onto the sofa next to him and sent a string of mild curses directed at his duties. According to his father, the current situation in Barak demanded Sam return home immediately. Sam had bargained for two more weeks instead of four, on the pretense that he still had investments he needed to oversee. Only one week to spend with his son upon his return. Never enough time.

He shoved the newspaper's financial section off his lap, then scolded himself for acting like a child in the throes of a tantrum. Anger wouldn't serve him well at this time. He could only make the best of a situation beyond his control.

"Problems, Sam?"

Sam watched as Andrea strolled into the room and dropped down onto the sofa next to him, wearing a guarded expression and a pair of silk pajamas the color of fine champagne. The scent of orchids filtering into his nostrils served to make him forget his current troubles as did the sight of her dressed in feminine attire. Yet he refused to let her distract him. Now that he'd learned he would have to leave sooner, he had much to discuss with her.

"I'm afraid I must cut my visit short. I have been summoned home."

Her blue eyes widened. "Tonight?"

"No, but I will not be able to stay as long as I'd intended. I must return in two weeks."

Seeming to relax somewhat, she tucked her legs beneath her and sipped a glass of iced tea. "Was that Rashid on the phone calling to deliver the good news?"

"I spoke with my father. It is his wish that I return."

She frowned. "Do you always do what he tells you to do?"

Sam had expected her disapproval, but he hadn't expected her forthright query. "I have obligations, Andrea. Surely you understand, now that you have a child."

"I don't see Chance as an obligation," she said, ire in her tone. "I see him as a joy, not as a chore or a servant."

Sam lowered his eyes to his hands, clasped tightly

in his lap, biting back the sudden surge of anger. "Would you expect me to ignore my responsibilities?"

"I'd expect that being a prince might make you a little happier."

His gaze snapped to hers. "On what do you base this assumption, that I'm not happy with what I am?"

She shrugged. "You don't look happy, not like before. I've rarely seen you smile, much less laugh. In fact, most of the time you look way too serious. That's not the Sam I remember."

Sheikh Samir Yaman had replaced the Sam she remembered. The Sam she had known had yet to be tainted by the responsibility placed on his shoulders as the eldest son of a king. "That carefree college student you knew no longer exists."

"Oh, I think he's still in there just dying to get out."

"Unfortunately, that is not the case."

She set her glass on the coffee table before them and hugged her knees to her chest. "I'd hate to think that's true, Sam. I'd also hate to think that Chance would ever be subjected to the kind of pressure that would make him lose his spirit and his love of life."

If the truth were known, so would Sam. "I doubt that he will ever lose those attributes considering his mother."

Andrea's smile curled the corners of her beautiful mouth. "I suppose that's a compliment."

"Yes, very much so. I greatly appreciated your free spirit, your passion for living."

"And I appreciated your passion, too."

Sam was inclined to believe that she meant the passion they had experienced in each other's arms. He refused to travel that road of regret tonight, not with her so near, looking like temptation incarnate. He wasn't that strong.

He cleared his throat and leaned back against the sofa, hoping to seem relaxed when in fact he was anything but. "I have learned to deal with the demands of my station. It is who I am."

"It's a title, Sam, not who you are. My father never tried to make me something I'm not. Neither did Paul. They just let me be myself."

"If my memory serves me, Paul once said that it would take a front-end hauler, a steel cable and an ancient oak to tie you down."

Andrea tossed back her head and laughed, filling Sam with joy over the sound. "That's a front-end loader, and yes, he did say that, and I've heard you say worse. You guys were always teasing me. You lived to drive me nuts."

"You were an easy target."

She smiled. "A moving target most of the time, you mean. Especially when you both came at me and threatened to tickle me senseless."

Sam grinned at the memories. "I believe you have very sensitive knees."

Andrea hugged her legs tighter against her chest. "Don't you even think about it, mister."

He inched a little closer despite the voice that told him to keep his distance. "It might be amusing to see if that continues to hold true."

"Still the bully, just like before."

"Before it was the only way to make you do my bidding."

Her smile faded and her expression softened, taking on the appearance of a woman more than willing to submit to his demands. "That wasn't the only way."

Sam was suddenly catapulted back to that night at the pond. Never had any woman given him as much with such sweet abandon. And considering she'd been barely more than a child all those years ago, he could only wonder what she would be like now as a woman.

Inching closer until she was flush against his side, she brushed his hair away from his forehead. "Do you ever think about that night, Sam? Not about Paul, but about what happened between us?"

Even after seven years, those memories still haunted his dreams in sleep and his thoughts upon waking. "I remember."

"Do you ever wish that it hadn't happened?"

How could he explain so she would understand? He caught her hand and brushed a kiss across her palm. "I suppose that if I could change anything about that time, it would only be two things."

With fine fingertips she traced a path along his jaw. "What would they be?"

"That I could have saved Paul from his fate. And that I could have stayed."

Her face lit up as if he had offered her the stars that held her dreams. Leaning forward, she whisked a kiss across his cheek. "Thank you."

He did not deserve her gratitude, then or now. "Nothing has changed, Andrea. We cannot go back. I will still leave you again."

She framed his jaw in her slender fingers. "We could make up for lost time. There are a lot of hours in fourteen days."

Not nearly enough, Sam decided. Not nearly enough distance between them, either. Normally he was a man with a firm resolve, but Andrea unearthed his weakness, could mold him as easily as if he were made of clay. As he stared at her lips, he became caught in the grip of longing.

Sam claimed her mouth for a kiss fueled by a power he didn't know he possessed. In the far reaches of his mind, he realized he should be experiencing some guilt, since he was promised to another. But that woman was as unfamiliar to him as the concept of turning his back on his country and his legacy. He could only consider the sweet heat of Andrea's mouth, the gentle foray of her tongue against his, the feel of her lithe body curled against him as he deepened the kiss and tightened his hold on her.

The passion that was so much a part of Andrea came out in the kiss. Her hands roved over his back in steady strokes as if she were memorizing this moment. He caught a handful of her hair as if to moor himself against the onslaught of heat, of desperate desire. When she draped one leg over his thigh, he curved his palm over her waist. They parted for a moment, but only a moment, to draw air before their mouths united again. How easy it would be to touch her, Sam thought. How easy to show her pleasure. He slipped his hand between her thighs and Andrea wriggled her encouragement.

Reality soon caught hold and Sam became aware that if he continued, he would not be able to stop. He would toss away all his reasons for avoiding this very thing and carry her to bed, make love to her all through the night, destroying his determination not to hurt her more than he already had.

Breaking the kiss, he tipped his forehead against hers as he tried to regain his respiration. "You are still too hard to resist."

"Then why even bother?"

He pulled back and searched her blue eyes. "You know the reasons why. Because I—"

"Have to go back to the magic kingdom," she said, then scooted away from him to the other end of the sofa. "You don't have to remind me again."

"I'm glad you are finally beginning to understand."

She picked up a throw pillow and held it against her breasts. "Now that we've established you'll be leaving, for about the hundredth time, I've come to a decision."

"About?"

"Chance. I've decided you can go with me to the camp."

Sincerely pleased, Sam smiled. "Good. We can travel in the limo instead of that wreck you call a truck."

He snared the pillow she tossed at him in one hand before it hit his face. "What's wrong with my truck?"

"Nothing if you're hauling feed and hay and traveling only a short distance. I believe my mode of transportation provides more comfort and reliability. And if you'll recall, our son expressed his desire to ride in it. Rashid can drive us."

Andrea chewed her bottom lip for a moment before raising her eyes to his. "Maybe that is a good idea.

Plenty of room in the limo. Lots of room, in fact.''
She smiled once again. A smile that could only mean
trouble for Sam. ''In fact, I just bet you could stretch
out if you wanted to.''

''Andrea,'' he said in a half-warning tone, a great
effort considering the arrival of visions of Andrea beneath him, naked, in the dimly lit limousine.

She stretched her arms above her head, giving him
a good view of her breasts unencumbered beneath the
satin, then rose and stood above him. ''Relax, Sam. I
promise I won't make you do anything you don't
want to do.''

Exactly what he feared, for if given the opportunity, Sam knew precisely what he would want to do—
make love to her as if tomorrow would not arrive.

In many ways, at least in regard to his time with
the mother of his child, that was very close to the
truth.

''Got a minute to gab, Andi?'' Tess asked the following day.

Andi looked up from gathering a few things for the
trip to camp and gave her attention to Tess. ''Sure.
What's up?''

Pacing the length of the bedroom, Tess paused to
toy with various keepsakes on the bureau. ''I have
something I need to tell you.''

Andi tossed the picnic blanket aside and took a
roost on the edge of the bed, gearing up for a ''Sam''
lecture. ''I've agreed to let him go with me, if that's
what's bugging you.''

Tess finally faced her. ''I know. Sam told me. But
this doesn't have a thing to do with him.''

Realizing Tess meant serious business, Andi patted the mattress beside her. "Have a seat and tell me what's got you in such a mood."

Tess joined her and wrapped an arm around Andi's shoulder. "Honey, Riley has asked me to marry him."

"So what else is new?"

"This time I said yes."

Andi's heart took a nosedive over the prospect of losing the one person she had come to count on through thick and thin, a proverbial port in the storm, her touchstone.

Hiding her selfishness with a smile, Andi proclaimed with a goodnatured pat on Tess's thigh, "Well it's about damned time."

Tess gave Andi's shoulder a motherly squeeze. "Then you're okay with this?"

"Are you asking my approval?"

"I'm asking how you feel about it."

Rising from the bed, Andrea took her place at the bureau where Tess had been a few moments before, her back turned to her aunt so she wouldn't give herself away. "Of course I'm okay with it. I'm thrilled." She didn't sound at all thrilled.

Biting back the tears, Andi drew in several cleansing breaths. Tess's careworn hands coming to rest on her shoulders almost proved to be her undoing.

"I know the timing seems pretty bad with Sam here again," Tess said, "but Riley bought himself one of those new-fangled homes on wheels and he wants to travel."

That brought Andi around to face Tess. "You mean you'll be gone all the time?"

"A lot of the time. We'd like to see the country in our golden years, before we're too old to enjoy it."

Andi attempted another smile, but her lips felt as stiff as a metal pipe. "That sounds great, Tess."

Tess tried to smile, as well, but it, too, seemed forced. "During the summers you and Chance can come along with us, when he's out of school."

"Oh, yeah, Tess. I'm sure Riley would love having us along while you're still on your honeymoon."

"Next year, silly girl. We're not going to tie the noose until after Sam leaves."

Andi shrugged. "Why not now? Sam can be Riley's best man. Heck, how many people can say they have a prince standing up for them during the nuptials?" Her attempt at humor rang false, and she realized her aunt saw right through her.

Tess brushed Andi's hair away from her shoulders, a gesture so endearing and familiar it made Andi's heart ache, and the stubborn tears threatened to appear once again. "Your time will come, Andi girl. You only have to open yourself up. You can do that once Sam's gone again."

Did everyone have to keep reminding her about Sam's impending departure? Was everyone so bent on believing that her world revolved around him?

Andi swallowed past the boulder in her throat, determined not to cry over something she couldn't control. "Whether Sam's here or not makes no difference to me, except where Chance is concerned. There's nothing more between us." If only Andi had sounded more convincing. If only she really believed that.

"There will always be something between you two, Andi. A child, and two different worlds. He can't give you what you need, but someday you'll find a man who can.''

Andrea wanted to stomp her foot and cuss like a ranch hand. She wanted to scream that this supposed ''special'' man didn't exist in any world, especially hers. Instead, she said, ''I'm satisfied with my life, Tess. My work and Chance are all I need. And I'm thrilled for you and Riley. You've been the only mother I've ever known, and if you hadn't been there when Daddy and Paul died, I don't know what I would've done. You deserve some happiness, too.''

Tess tugged her into a solid embrace. ''I'll always be here for you, honey, God willing.'' She pulled back and studied Andi's face through the eyes of a mother concerned for her child. ''Just like I was for all the hurts and heartaches, and for Chance's entry into this crazy world, I'll be there when your prince leaves again.''

Your prince. Andi had never been one to put much stock in fairy tales, or to believe that some knight would come along and rescue her. Sheikh Samir Yaman had shattered those dreams long ago, and he would shred her life again if she let him.

But she wouldn't let him destroy her. As always, she would survive. She and Chance together. Andi didn't need a prince, even one she would probably love forever.

Five

Sam regarded Andrea over the magazine he'd pretended to read for the better part of the trip to the camp. Thankfully she had retired early the night before without further mention of lovemaking. In fact, she had said very little at all, then and now. At the moment she sat across from him wringing her hands and staring with an unfocused gaze out the tinted window.

Curious over her uncharacteristic silence, Sam tossed the magazine aside and studied her. "Are you afraid that our son has forgotten his mother?"

She turned startled eyes on him. "Of course not. Why would you think that?"

"You seem very nervous."

She tightened the rubber band around her hair. "Can you blame me? I mean, I'm about to take you to camp. Even if Chance doesn't question your resemblance to him, other people are going to automatically assume you're his father.''

''That is not necessarily so.''

''Oh, come on, Sam. He looks just like you, right down to the blasted dimple.''

Sam couldn't contain his pride or his smile. ''He has your nose.''

Andi placed her fingertips on the tip of her nose as if to verify that fact. ''He does at the moment, but he's still just a baby. I'm sure he'll have your aristocratic honker by the time he's a teenager.''

''Honker?''

''That's what Chance calls noses.''

''You do not care for my nose?''

''Your nose is fine. Very sophisticated.''

''I am relieved it meets with your approval.''

Her grin came out of hiding. ''Everything about you meets with my approval. All those parts seen and unseen, or as best I can remember, because it's been a while since I've seen all your parts.''

Sam shifted in his seat and resisted the urge to offer an inspection. At least they had survived the duration of this trip without utilizing the privacy of the limo. But on the ride home…

''Looks like we're here.'' The limo had barely come to a stop before Andrea slid out the door. Sam hurried out behind her, afraid she would abandon him and leave him to his own devices. He knew nothing about how he should act at this camp. He had no idea how to answer any questions that might arise about his relationship with Andrea and Chance. He would simply have to allow Andrea to handle the situation in the way she saw fit. He suspected he would not care for her explanations.

Sam caught up with Andrea immediately outside a large cedar cabin surrounded by several adults. A young woman approached them and held out her hand. "Hi, I'm Trish, Ms. Hamilton."

"Nice to meet you, Trish," Andrea replied politely.

"You don't remember me? We met when you came to check out the camp."

Andrea continued her hand kneading. "I'm sorry. It's been a long drive."

Trish seemed unfazed by Andrea's lack of memory and continued on at a vibrant pace. "We're glad you could come today. Chance is so excited. He's a fantastic little boy. Quite the happy camper."

Andrea's gaze roamed the immediate area. "Where is he?"

"In the dining hall finishing up breakfast. He'll be right out." Trish turned her smile on Sam. "And you must be Mr. Hamilton."

"His name is Mr. Yaman," Andrea added quickly. "A family friend."

The woman looked flustered. "Well, I'm sorry. It's just that Chance looks so much like you."

Andrea produced a nervous smile. "I know. Isn't that weird?"

Sam hated the denial, hated that Andrea didn't see a need for the truth. "Chance's father and I are from the same country," Sam offered along with his hand.

"Cool," Trish said after a brief handshake.

A spattering of laughter and shouts broke the awkward moment as myriad children came rushing out the doors of the largest cabin to the left.

"Mama! You came!"

Chance rushed Andrea and engaged her in a voracious hug. She picked him up and held him tightly against her breasts. "I've missed you, sweetie. Are you having fun?"

He squirmed in her grasp. "Yeah. Lots of fun. Put me down, Mom, before the other guys see."

Looking heartsick, Andrea complied but kept her hand on his shoulder. "Guess that wouldn't be cool," she said in a voice that sounded much like the camp counselor.

Chance stared up at Sam with surprise as if he'd only now realized his presence. "How come you didn't tell me you were bringing the prince?"

Andrea sent a quick glance at Sam, then said, "We only decided a few days ago."

Sam held out his hand. "I hope that is all right with you, Chance."

Chance displayed his approval with a jerk of his head and a hearty handshake. "Sure. Did you bring the car?"

Sam hooked a thumb over his shoulder. "In the parking lot."

His son's eyes grew large with wonder, reminding Sam of Andrea. "Can I take the guys for a ride?"

"Not now, sweetie," Andrea said. "Maybe before we head back. Right now we have to play some games."

Andrea took Chance by the hand and headed off toward the group of parents gathered at the flagpole. Sam stood in place watching mother and child walk away, hand in hand, without concern that they had left him behind. He despised feeling the outsider, welcome only because of his car—a symbol of his wealth—not as a part of this family.

Perhaps it would be best if Chance never knew the

truth. Perhaps he should walk away and never look back, knowing it would be favorable for everyone concerned, especially his son. Yet it would prove to be a most difficult choice.

Then suddenly Chance tugged his hand from Andrea's grasp and came running back to Sam. He toed the dirt beneath his feet then stared at Sam with eyes much like his own. ''Can I ask you somethin'?''

Sam ruffled the boy's dark head. ''Certainly.''

''It's kind of a favor.''

Kneeling on Chance's level, Sam's expression softened as did something deep inside him. ''Do not be afraid to ask anything of me.''

''Can you pretend to be my dad today?''

Andi hadn't minded that Chance requested Sam be his ''pretend'' father, even though it wasn't at all pretend. She hadn't minded that Sam seemed to garner all the attention during the day-long activities. After all, he was a prince. She hadn't minded that he had been chosen to anchor the tug-of-war rope for Chance's team since he was well built for the challenge. Nor had she really cared that Chance took great pains in introducing Sam to everyone while she seemed almost inconsequential. Besides, when Chance scraped his knee during the softball game, he had sought out his mother to kiss away the hurt.

Yet she couldn't help but feel a little jealous when Chance told Sam that he'd had the best time ever, even more fun than when Andi had entered him and his pony in the local Fourth of July parade. How could she compete with that?

She couldn't, and she shouldn't want to. In fact, she should be thrilled that father and son had hit it off. But she couldn't be totally happy, knowing that in a matter of days Sam would be gone from their lives, maybe even for good, before Chance really got to know him as his father.

While Rashid took one last circle around the parking lot in the limo accompanied by Sam, Chance and a half dozen other boys, Andi stood alone and waited patiently. She would give them these special moments together without complaint, knowing they might be some of the last.

The car came to a stop nearby and a group of chatty boys piled out, then headed off at a run toward the dining hall for the evening meal. Chance hung back to talk with Sam while Andi leaned into the limo to load her bag and blanket into the car. After she was done, she found Sam crouched on Chance's level near the trunk, explaining the finer points of Thoroughbred racing. Funny, Chance had never seemed to care all that much about Andi's explanations of the sport.

She approached quietly and rested her hand on Chance's hair still damp from their afternoon swim. "It's time for you to go on back, honey. Dinner's ready and we need to get home to check on the horses."

Chance looked up, disappointment in his eyes. "Okay. But can Sam pick me up in the limo next weekend?"

"I don't know, sweetie. You'll have to ask—"

"I will make it a point to be here," Sam interjected.

Andi pulled Chance into an embrace, thankful that he allowed it. "You be good."

"I will, Mom."

"Eat right and check your levels."

"Yeah, Mom."

"Be sure to get plenty of rest and—"

"Can I go now, Mother? I'm hungry."

Mother? Since when had she stopped being Mama?

After popping a kiss on his cheek, Andi released Chance knowing that she would eventually have to learn to let him go, something that was all too familiar where the men in her life were concerned.

Chance turned to Sam and gave him a high-five. "Later, Mr. Sheikh."

Sam grinned. "Later."

With a last wave, Chance set off toward the cabin, taking a tiny piece of Andi's heart with him.

Sam gestured toward the open door. "Shall we?"

Andi took another glance toward the cabin only to discover that her son had disappeared. "I guess so," she said, then slid inside the limo.

For the first few minutes they rode in silence, yet Sam couldn't seem to stop smiling. Andi reluctantly admitted she appreciated his joy and understood it. Spending time with your child was the greatest experience on earth.

"So did you have fun, Sheikh Yaman?" she asked in a teasing tone.

His grin deepened. "Yes, I did most certainly."

"I'm glad." Andi paused for a moment, frustrated that he was going to make her drag a conversation out of him. "I noticed you really seemed to enjoy the swim."

"Very much."

"The women sure seemed to enjoy watching you swim."

He frowned. "I do not understand."

"Are you saying you didn't notice they were all

staring at you when you rose from the water like some Arabian god?''

Sam laughed. ''Andrea, your imagination is second only to your love of good horseflesh.''

''I'm not imagining things. I thought I might have to do CPR on them when you executed that perfect dive. Of course, those swim trunks did tend to enhance your finer features.''

''They are plain, Andrea. Simple black. Adequate cover.''

''Nancy sure seemed to like them, and everything in them.''

He raised one dark brow. ''Nancy?''

''Yeah. Little Bubba's mother. The divorced one who wore four-inch heels with her metallic gold thong and kept gushing over you all day.''

''I do not remember her.''

''Oh, I'm so sure.''

His gaze slid over Andi, and she suddenly found herself covered in gooseflesh. ''I would not have noticed this Nancy with you present. The suit you wore drew attention, as well, and not from me alone. The blue brought out the color of your eyes and the fit enhanced your figure. Very nice indeed.''

Andi wanted to laugh. Her suit was a relatively modest two-piece, and for most of the day she'd worn her oversize cover-up. ''I just bet you say that to all the girls in your harem.''

''I have no harem.''

Andi tossed up her hands in mock exasperation. ''Well, darn. There went my desert fantasy.''

Sam rubbed a large hand down his thigh, bare because of the shorts he now wore, capturing Andi's attention. ''I am sorry to disappoint you.''

In reality he hadn't disappointed her. Yet. But the night was young, and she had only one major goal in mind—to convince Sam that spending the next two hours in the limo could be as boring, or as exciting, as they chose to make it.

On that thought, she fanned her face. "It's rather warm in here, don't you think?"

His expression went as taut as the black leather covering the seats. "I am comfortable."

"Well, I'm not." She unbuttoned her blouse and let it fall open to reveal the top of her less-than-comfortable bra. "That's a little better."

"I will ask Rashid to adjust the air." Depressing the intercom button to his right, he made the request then settled back against the seat with the magazine he'd been reading earlier.

This would not do, Andi thought. She refused to let him ignore her. Feeling brave, she reached for the button on her denim shorts then reconsidered. "Speaking of Rashid, can he see back here?"

Sam sent her a suspicious look. "Not as long as the privacy window is intact. Why do you ask?"

"Just wondering."

Muttering something in Arabic that Andi couldn't understand, Sam went back to the magazine and Andi went back to tugging off her shorts. On afterthought, she unfastened her bra and slipped it off through the armholes then tossed it onto the floor to join her shorts. Now she wore only a white sleeveless cotton shirt and a pair of skimpy black panties. If that didn't get his attention, Andi doubted anything would, short of leaning out the window naked and hollering at the top of her lungs.

When Sam failed to look at her, she decided to take

matters into her own hands, or whatever else she needed to take into her hands to earn his notice. All day long she'd endured the sidelong glances aimed at Sam. And all the while she'd had to pretend they were old friends.

She was tired of the whole charade because he was more than a friend. He was the father of her child, and at one time her lover. Just once more before he disappeared again, she wanted to experience all that he had to offer, if she could just convince him to cooperate.

On that thought, Andi slipped to her knees and crawled to the opposite seat to move between Sam's parted legs. When he looked up, she noted a hint of surprise in his expression.

She grabbed the magazine and tossed it behind her, then slipped her fingertips immediately underneath the hem of his khaki shorts. "Is that magazine so darned interesting that you can't give me a little of your time?"

He nailed her with his dark eyes. "Is my time all you want, Andrea? If so, you do not have to resort to such measures as crawling on your knees."

"You don't like me on my knees?" she asked, topped off with a suggestive grin.

His glance fell to her open blouse that now revealed a good deal of her breasts. "I would like you to return to your seat and put your clothes back on before I..."

His words trailed off, leading Andi to believe that he was entertaining some of the same naughty ideas.

"Before you what?"

"Before Rashid sees you."

She frowned. "I thought you said he couldn't see back here with the window up."

"I do not believe he can, but I've never ridden in the front to test the window's merits. It would be unwise to take that risk."

Andi's wicked side surfaced, and she climbed onto the seat on her knees, straddling Sam's thighs. "Why don't we just hope for the best? Besides, you can always say you had something in your eye and I was trying to remove it."

He braced his hands on her waist but didn't attempt to move her out of the way. "I doubt that Rashid would buy such a weak excuse."

"Considering this car's owner, I'd just bet Rashid has probably seen it all."

"What are you saying?"

"You and other women engaging in some hanky-panky."

"I use this car for business purposes and nothing more."

She rimmed her tongue along the shell of his ear and whispered, "Then maybe we should get down to business."

"Andrea, why are you so intent on pursuing this?"

Pulling back, she locked into his dark gaze, determined to have her say—and her way. "Because I have to know if I only imagined how wonderful you made me feel, or if it's just the fact I had no one to compare you to." She ran the tip of her tongue across the seam of his lips. "I want to know if you're really all that great."

Sam tightened his grip on her waist, and his eyes went almost black. "Are you saying that you wish to know how I compare to other men? Have there been so many, Andrea?''

There had been only one other man, a brief affair that had been more than disappointing, but revealing that fact wouldn't help her cause. ''I'm saying it was a long time ago and that maybe my recollections are incorrect.''

''Yet you have told me repeatedly you do not wish to resurrect the past.''

''I'm telling you now that I *need* you to refresh my memory.'' She moved against him, immediately noting the slight swell beneath her bottom. ''Is that a camel in your pocket, or are you just glad to see me?''

Sam's grin surfaced. ''You can be a very devious woman, Andrea.''

''You don't know the half of it, but I'd be glad to show you.''

Indecision warred in his expression. Andi knew the moment he lost the battle when he released a strained breath. ''Perhaps I should show you a few things.''

Sliding his hands to her hips, he pressed down until she could feel every glorious part of him. He nudged her forward then back ever so slightly against his erection, creating an amazingly erotic friction and a rush of damp heat where Andi's body contacted his.

''I remember much about that night,'' he said in a voice only a degree above a whisper, deep and grainy and sensual. ''I remember the way you looked, trusting and innocent. I remember how your skin felt beneath my hands.''

He slipped his hands beneath her panties and stroked her bare bottom. ''Do you remember me touching you this way, Andrea?'' He asked the question while continuing to glide her hips back and forth against him in a steady rhythm.

She combed her hands through his dark hair then closed her eyes. "Maybe."

Like some love-starved woman, she savored the feel of his mouth as he feathered a kiss across the rise of her breast, grazing his tongue over her nipple just enough to tease and entice. "I remember the soft sounds of pleasure you made when I kissed you this way, how you begged me to continue."

Right now she was primed for some more begging if he dared to stop. "It's beginning to come back to me, but I could use a little more detail." In reality, she hadn't forgotten one incredible detail.

He began to move his hips in sync with hers, increasing the contact of their bodies that fitted so perfectly together. "I remember how brave you were, how you ignored the pain."

The pain had been nothing compared to the pleasure. And the pleasure was upon her now as Sam continued his erotic motion, rubbing cotton against silk, creating delicious sensation against the place that needed his attention the most. He undid two more buttons on her blouse and a cool draft of air streamed over her bare breasts.

Andi kept her eyes closed, lulled by the sound of his sensual voice. "I remember how you trembled beneath me. How warm and wet and soft your body was surrounding mine. I remember being totally lost to you at that moment."

She remembered being lost, too. She was quickly losing her way once more, especially when he took her breast completely into his mouth and laved his tongue back and forth over her needy flesh. But it only lasted for a short time until he commanded, "Look at me, Andrea."

She opened her eyes slowly to find him staring at her intently as he began to speak again. "Do you remember how it felt to be so close?"

He tilted his pelvis upward, causing her to gasp. "Yes, I remember," she said with all the adamancy she could muster at such a moment.

"Do you remember what I told you?"

She could hardly breathe, much less think. "Tell me again, just in case I don't."

"I told you that I had never been so lacking in control. That I had never had such feelings or that I had never wanted a woman so badly."

Coherent words escaped her, but Sam's enticements came through loud and clear and compelling, his movements more insistent, bringing Andi to the brink, though he had yet to use his hands on her. And, oh, did she want him to do that very thing. But he continued his assault on her senses, touching her only with his words and heady movements. "I also recall that as I brought you to a release, you called my name."

And that's exactly what Andi did again as a searing climax overtook her. She literally saw stars this time, too, only they weren't those found in the night sky above them.

Andi collapsed against Sam's broad chest and shuddered uncontrollably while he held her close to his heart, which pounded a steady rhythm against her cheek. When the world finally came back into focus, she felt a little foolish. She also realized he had his palm over her mouth.

"No doubt Rashid heard that," he said, followed by a chuckle. "Do you feel inclined to shout again?"

She managed to shake her head no, still mute even after he dropped his hand from her mouth.

"Have I adequately jarred your memories?" he asked.

He'd done much more than that. "Every last one."

"Good." As if the interlude was an everyday occurrence, he set her aside and claimed the opposing seat.

Andi could only stare at him with mouth and shirt gaping until the shock subsided. "That's it?"

He had the nerve to look surprised. "That was not enough?"

She refused to let him off the hook until she had exactly what she'd been seeking since that first day he'd reentered her life. "I want you to finish this, dammit."

"It is finished, Andrea."

"You mean to tell me that you're willing to leave it at that? Even when you didn't—"

"That should not matter to you."

She sent a pointed glance at the obvious ridge beneath his shorts, proof positive that he still had issues he needed to settle. "It does matter to me. I want it all, and I'd bet all the hay in the barn that you want more, too."

"You want more than I can give you."

"I want sex, Sam. Hard, lusty limo sex. That's not too much to ask."

His eyes took on a solemn cast. "I want to leave knowing that I have done nothing to hurt you."

This time Andi wanted to scream with frustration instead of passion. "If you're worried about getting me pregnant, I've prepared for that.'' She yanked her bag from the floor and opened the zippered pocket to show him the condoms she had purchased the day before.

He still seemed totally immovable as he eyed the foil packets. ''That is a wise choice, Andrea, but have you considered how you will protect your heart?''

Anger impaled Andi soul deep, baring the wound that had festered like an inflamed blister for seven years. He still viewed her as that same girl who had hung on his every word, his every touch, too naive to know her own mind. That girl was long gone.

She gripped her open blouse with one hand and tossed the condoms back in the bag with the other. ''You just don't get it, Sam. I don't want anything except a quick roll. That's it. No promises of tomorrow. No *I love you*s. Heck, you don't even have to sleep in the same bed with me.''

The lie sat like a rock in her belly, but she was too proud to admit that she did want more. She wanted everything, not just sex. She wanted to be with him the next day and the next. She wanted him to be a part of Chance's life. But most of all she wanted his love, something she knew she would never have.

Six

He had sworn never to hurt Andrea again, yet that's exactly what he had done by acting as though touching her had meant nothing. In reality it had meant everything.

On the return home the silence in the car had been stifling, and as soon as they pulled up in the drive, Andrea had gathered her belongings and exited the car without speaking. Only, she had not returned to the house. But Sam knew precisely where she had gone.

He could not let so much go unsaid between them. He would need to attempt once more to explain why he could promise her nothing. Perhaps he should tell her about his impending marriage to Maila so she would understand his resistance. Though the young woman meant nothing to him, he felt honor bound to his commitment. He doubted Andrea would understand, yet she needed to hear the truth.

As he set out on the path that led through the fields, the air was heavy with mist, almost stifling, and so were his thoughts as he silently rehearsed what he would say to Andrea. But when he came upon her seated on the blanket facing the pond, her elbows resting on bent knees and her beautiful face cast in the light of a half-moon, everything he had thought to say vanished.

Quietly he came up behind her and dropped to his knees, then circled his arms around her. "I knew I would find you here."

When she shuddered, he wondered if he should let her go. Instead he held her tighter. "Are you cold?" he asked.

"No. I'm just having a strong sense of déjà vu."

Sam moved around to face her and took her hands into his. He was uncertain where to begin but decided seven years ago would be an appropriate place to start. "I am sorry for leaving you without an explanation after Paul's funeral. I feared that if you'd asked me to stay, I wouldn't have been strong enough to deny you, and I knew that I must."

She turned her face to the stars. "Let's not go there tonight, Sam. You did what you thought you had to do."

He drew in a sharp breath. "I do also wish to apologize for my behavior in the car. It was unfair to you."

Inclining her head, she surveyed him a moment with soulful blue eyes. "You've told me all along that you don't want me, so you have nothing to be sorry for.''

He released a frustrated sigh. "I do want you. I have never stopped wanting you."

Her expression brightened somewhat, yet she still looked wounded. "You have a strange way of showing it."

He attempted a smile. "I thought it was quite evident."

Finally Andrea's smile returned, a smile that had stayed with him over many days. Would stay with him always. "Okay, so maybe it was a little obvious." Her features went solemn once again. "But that's just a physical reaction, Sam. It doesn't really mean anything."

Framing her face in his palms, he said, "You have no idea how much you mean to me. How much you have always meant to me. But I cannot promise you anything."

"I told you I don't expect any promises." She pulled his hand away and held it against her breast. "Life is so very short. No one can predict what will happen tomorrow. We both know that. I'm only asking for here and now. I just want to be with you. And when it's over, then we'll both move on with our lives knowing that we've found some joy in each other one more time."

Sam considered what she was saying and then considered his marriage contract. Arrangement, he corrected. Only verbal to this point. His father had called because of that impending contract. Maila's father was growing impatient with his absence, a greedy man willing to sell his daughter into a union for the sake of finances.

Maila was several years younger and a virtual stranger to Sam. The two times they had met, she had barely spoken to him and only then to give her vow that she would try to produce a son although he sensed that prospect wasn't all that appealing to her. But Sam already had a son—a cherished child mothered by a woman for whom he cared deeply. A woman who now offered herself to him without condition. At the moment all he could consider was forgetting his obligations and turning his attention to that woman one last time.

"Are you certain you want this, Andrea?"

"Are you saying you're willing to consider it?"

"As I told you before, I fear hurting you."

"You'll only hurt me if you keep acting as if there's nothing going on between us, if you deny me this opportunity to be with you again in every way."

"Are you not worried that I will disappoint you?"

Rising from the blanket, she began once more to undo her blouse and slipped it completely away. She then removed her shorts and panties, leaving her cloaked only by the night. "Do I look worried to you?"

"No. You look exquisite." And she did, more captivating than he remembered. Priceless perfection. All his, if he so chose.

Heat surged through him and settled in his groin. A deep, abiding heat that made him hard and desperate to be inside her once more. That frantic need forced all consideration of the consequences from his brain. He only knew that he could no longer resist her.

Coming to his feet, he stood before her and tugged his shirt over his head. When he reached for the snap on his fly, Andrea stopped him with a gentle hand. "Let me do it. You didn't give me the opportunity last time. In fact, I recall we didn't completely remove our clothes."

"True, but we were in a hurry."

She slid his zipper down slowly. "Not tonight."

When she had him completely undressed, they continued to stare at each other in the muted light until Sam could stand it no longer. He reached for her and she moved easily into his embrace. He held her a long while, relishing the soft feel of her bare skin against his raging body. Then he kissed her with all the yearning he felt in his soul, with all the need he had harbored since that final moment they were together seven years ago.

The kiss born of emotion soon turned to a kiss of sheer desire. Andrea pressed harder against him, meeting his tongue thrust for blessed thrust. Determined to show her more pleasure, he broke the kiss and settled his lips on her delicate throat then worked his way downward.

She sighed as he plied her breasts with tender kisses. She whimpered as he bent and traced a damp path down her belly with his tongue. She moaned as he fell to his knees and took her with his mouth.

With her hands gripped tightly in his hair, she swayed slightly as he explored the soft folds with his tongue, holding fast to her hips to steady her. But with every sound that escaped her lips, every tremor that ran through her body, he, too, began to feel unsteady. When she tensed and her breathing halted, Sam slipped a finger inside her to prolong her climax, to experience with his own hands the pleasure she now enjoyed.

As her knees began to buckle, he pulled her down onto the blanket and rocked her gently until she seemed to calm.

"That was—" she drew in a broken breath "—remarkable."

He stroked her hair and pressed a kiss against her forehead. "I very much wanted to do that the first time we were together."

"Why didn't you?" she asked, her words muffled against his shoulder.

"I did not want to overwhelm you."

She laughed softly. "I would have definitely been overwhelmed." Pulling away from him, she nudged his chest. "Lie back."

He complied, no longer able to withstand even her slightest command. She set a course down his body with her warm lips, driving him insane with desire when he realized what she intended.

As she reached the plane of his belly below his navel, he laid a hand on her silky hair. "This is not necessary, Andrea."

She raised her head and showed him a determined look. "For me it is. But just so you know, I've never done this before, so you'll have to be patient."

That pleased Sam, knowing she had not had such intimacy with another man. It also forced every thought from his mind when she took him into the silken heat of her mouth and tested its limits. Perhaps she had no experience, but Sam would be hard-pressed to believe that at the moment. She was handling the challenge quite well. He only wished he could say the same for himself.

Nearing the edge, he pulled her head up and kissed her once more. Then he rolled her over and poised himself to enter her. But before he could sink into her, she said, "No."

Sam sighed. "Have you suddenly changed your mind?"

"I've almost lost my mind. We're forgetting something. Again. As much as I love Chance, I don't think it's a good idea to give him a brother or sister."

Sam rolled onto his back, laid an arm over his eyes and cursed his stupidity. How could he be so careless a second time? How could he almost disregard something so very important? Because his only thoughts were of Andrea and making love to her.

"I'll take care of it," she said in a whisper, and before he realized she had moved, he felt her sheath him. "It's okay now," she said quietly.

Sam removed his arm and found her staring at him expectantly, waiting for him to take the next step. He vowed he would not disappoint her.

When Sam pulled Andi back into his arms, she experienced a rush of anticipation. Everything in her life seemed to have come down to this one moment, this reunion of bodies and souls with this one man.

He rolled her to her back and nudged her legs apart with his leg, then entered her with an easy thrust. She had a strong sense of being where she belonged, so close to this man who had lived within her heart for almost a decade.

He moved once more and seated himself deep inside her. A steady moan climbed up her throat and slipped out between her parted lips.

Sam stilled against her. "Have I hurt you?"

"Not in the least." Not yet. But he would when he left again.

"Good. You feel better than I remember," he said with a soft kiss on her brow, his voice strained with his effort to speak.

"So do you," she said, then tilted her hips up to take him completely inside her body. As he set a steady rhythm, she tried to memorize the moments, every incredible sensation, Sam's face as it showed the tension of a man trying to maintain control. How she could relate to that. Right now the bliss of this union was almost more than she could bear without giving in to tears of elation.

"Come with me," Sam murmured, then pulled her over so they faced each other, her leg draped over his hip, their eyes connected as well as their bodies.

"I'm with you," she whispered, and she was. At least for now.

Never in all her imaginings did she ever believe this would happen again. Never did she think that Sam would be making love to her once more, touching her inside and out, drawing another incredible climax from her as he quickened the pace.

She clung to his solid shoulders, held on as if to never let him go. He whispered to her softly in both English and Arabic, heightening the erotic quality of the night and this act. And with one final thrust, he said her name over and over as she relished his climax as well as her own.

The night sounds surrounding them seemed to stop, or maybe it was only Andi's imagination. But she hadn't imagined Sam, the power of his body, the gentleness of his touch, the way he had loved her as if she did mean something to him.

She turned onto her back, breaking the intimate connection between them. She needed to regroup, assess what had happened to her resolve to avoid any emotional entanglement.

How could she have been such an idiot? How could she have believed that by letting him back inside her body, she'd push him out of her heart when she had only drawn him further in?

Sam came up on one bent elbow and braced his cheek on his palm as she stared at the night sky. "Have I disappointed you, Andrea?"

She glanced at him and smiled, though she felt like crying. "No. Not at all." If only he had disappointed her, then she wouldn't be facing such a predicament.

"Perhaps you are wishing on stars again?"

She sighed. "I don't do that anymore, Sam." She had learned long ago that nothing could be gained by such a frivolous activity. She was in charge of her destiny now, at least where Sam was concerned. No matter how wonderful the experience had been, she needed to stay grounded and remember this was only a temporary thing between her and the prince. She couldn't do that with her head off somewhere in the galaxy.

He drew lazy circles around her breasts, and darned if she wasn't reacting as if he had yet to touch her. "Do you not have dreams any longer?"

Oh, she had them. She just refused to buy in to any

of them that dealt with what could never be. "I want to be the best horse trainer the racing world has ever known."

"Much like your father?"

"Daddy was good at what he did, but he never aspired to be the best," Andi replied, more than willing to discuss anything except what had just happened.

"People will know that you are the best," he said adamantly.

She released a humorless laugh. "If you say so."

"They will if I have a say in the matter."

Her gaze zipped to his, fueled by a burst of pride and a spear of anger. "I can do it on my own, Sam. I have to make a name for myself, by myself. It's the only way I'll earn it."

"And you will not accept my help?"

"You've already done enough by letting me train your filly."

"She is yours when I leave, Andrea."

Great. A consolation prize. "You don't have to do that."

"I already have, and I will arrange—at my expense—for her to race when you feel she is ready."

"If you insist that she stay here, I'd like her to belong to Chance."

"As you wish."

Sitting up, she reached for her discarded clothes and began to dress again, before she told him that she loved the horse but she loved him more. Before she did something really crazy like beg him to stay.

"Where are you going?" he asked.

"I imagine Tess is wondering where we are."

"I imagine she has already retired to bed, considering the late hour."

Andi slipped on her panties and shorts then stood. Seeing Sam stretched out on his back still gloriously naked, his dark skin contrasting with the pale-blue blanket, made Andi almost reconsider her departure. But she had to regain her emotional bearings.

Bending down, she retrieved his shorts and tossed them at him. "Put these on, Your Highness. Tess doesn't take too kindly to naked men in her kitchen."

His grin lit up the night. "How do we know that she has not had a naked man in her kitchen?"

Andi groaned. "I don't even want to go there." She thought about what Tess had told her the day before. "I guess you probably know that she and Riley are finally getting married."

"Actually, no."

That surprised Andi. Tess had been an open book since Sam's reappearance. "Well, they are in a few weeks." She sighed. "I can't even imagine Tess being away from the farm."

"They will not live here?" Sam asked.

"They plan on traveling the country."

"You will miss her terribly," he said, a simple statement of fact.

"Of course I will. So will Chance. But we'll manage," she said, although she wasn't sure how. Yet somehow she had always managed the losses in her life, only this time she would feel truly abandoned, especially after Sam left.

"Perhaps you would like me to turn your thoughts to more pleasant things," he said, as if he had somehow tuned in to her mind. Before she could prepare, he tugged her back down against him, amazed to find he was already aroused. And she was more than willing to forget all the sadness, all the tough times to come, in his welcoming arms.

"You're not going to tickle me, are you?" she asked with mock exasperation.

"Not in the way you might imagine, but I'm certain I will find some means to make you feel better."

When he nuzzled her neck, she said, "A good prince is hard to find," feeling lightheaded and light-hearted in his arms. "Or maybe it is the other way around."

"Perhaps we should find out."

Once again Andi's clothes ended up on the nearby grass. And in very little time, Sam had her clinging and gasping and praising his skill.

Too much, she thought as he guided her back to a paradise of his own making. Too little.

Never enough.

Sam stood over Andrea and watched her while she continued to sleep completely unaware he was keeping vigil. He'd been up for hours, had already tended to the horses since he had decided to allow her the luxury of spending extra time in bed. After last night she deserved the added rest.

Silently he admonished himself for his weakness. Scolded himself for not feeling as guilty as he should after making love to her well into the early hours of the morning. Yet he had no regrets except one—their time together was limited.

Seating himself on the edge of the bed, he continued to observe Andrea lying on her belly, still beautifully naked and his to behold a few moments longer. He recalled each and every detail of the night before, unearthed all the feelings for her that should be buried with the past. Yet they were not, nor would they ever be even if miles once again separated him from her.

He glanced at his watch and noted the time. Now nearing 10:00 a.m., he thought it best to wake her or, no doubt, suffer her wrath. Moving closer, he traced his finger down the curve of her spine and onto her buttock. She stirred a little and a sleepy sigh escaped her lips. But he couldn't discern if her eyes had opened, since her hair covered her face in a tangled disarray to match the twisted sheets.

She finally lifted her head, pushed her hair back and regarded him over one shoulder. "What time is it?"

"Time for you to be up and about, I'm afraid."

She rolled onto her back without concern for her nudity. Sam, on the other hand, was very concerned, considering what she was doing to him at that moment. What she had been doing to him since the day of his return.

After glancing at the clock, she sat up with a start. "My gosh, I've wasted most of the day."

"You needed your sleep."

Blessedly she smiled. "I guess so, considering I was up most of the night, thanks to you."

He leaned and kissed her softly on the lips. "No. Many thanks to you."

She stretched and draped her arms around his neck. "I think I used parts of my body that I haven't used in years."

"Then you are in pain?"

"Nice pain. Very nice."

Unable to help himself, he kissed her throat and couldn't resist kissing her breasts. "Perhaps I should do something to alleviate that pain."

"Sorry. We don't have time for that now," she said, then bolted out of the bed, leaving Sam alone to deal with his own discomfort and the emotional wall she had seemed to raise.

After slipping on her robe, she faced him. "I have to put Sunny through some more ground work if I'm going to have her saddled by the end of the month."

Just as well, he decided. If he had his way, they would stay in bed all day without regard for their responsibilities. How easy that would be, now that he had rediscovered the pleasure of making love with Andrea. But he could not disregard what he had to do, not only today but also in a matter of weeks, as much as he would like to forget what awaited him at home. "Riley is in the barn. He's agreed to assist me in making it more serviceable."

She grabbed a brush from the dresser and ran it through her hair with a vengeance. "I can't afford to pay Riley."

"I will see to that."

Tossing the brush aside, she simply said, "Fine, I'm heading to the shower," then left through the door.

Sam was shocked she had not protested his financial offer. Perhaps she was finally beginning to see that his money could only aid in her future and that of their son's.

When he again returned to the stable a few moments later, he discovered that Riley had almost finished removing the old bedding from the first stall in preparation to replace the rubber matting beneath.

Riley looked up and leaned against his shovel, then stroked his too-long mustache. "Andi still sawin' logs?"

Sam frowned. "She is awake at the moment."

He chuckled and scooped another shovelful of bedding into the wheelbarrow. "I forget you don't always understand the language. Guess it's because I remember the way it used to be when Paul was still around. You were more loose back then. Relaxed. Even the way you talked."

That was before he had carried the weight of a kingdom on his shoulders. "I have been away for a long time."

An uncomfortable silence hung between them until Riley spoke again. "Did Andi tell you about me and Tess deciding to get hitched?"

"Yes. Last night. Congratulations to you both."

"Tess told me you're about to do the same come end of the summer."

"It has been arranged."

"That's a strange way of putting it."

Sam saw it exactly as it was, an arrangement. No emotional ties. No vows of love. "I prefer you not speak of this to Andrea until I have a chance to inform her."

Riley lifted one shoulder in a shrug. "That's your business, I guess, but I'm thinkin' she deserves to know." He appeared to go back to work, but before Sam could leave to gather more wood to brace the stalls, Riley stopped his departure. "You know, Andi's dad was a good friend of mine."

Sam paused and faced the open stall once more. "I remember." He wondered where the conversation might be leading, yet he suspected it would come in the form of a lecture.

"I think he would've liked you a lot."

Sam had not bargained for that presumption. "It is my understanding he was a very good man."

"The best. And he thought the sun rose and set in Andi. Now, I'm not saying he didn't love the boy because he did. But Paulie was more like his mother than Bob—into book learning and that sort of thing." Riley smiled. "Andi was just like her dad, and the apple of his eye. According to him, she could do no wrong."

Sam greatly related to that. "She is a good woman."

"Yep, which is why I have to say something to you."

Exactly as Sam suspected. "I am listening."

Riley raked off his cap and forked a hand through his silver hair, then shoved it back on his head. "Chance is a good kid. He deserves the best. He deserves a dad like Andi's. I've tried to be there for him, to teach him what I know and that ain't too much. But I'm too old to keep up, which is why I'm telling you that if you can't fill those shoes, then maybe you should consider stepping aside to let Andi find someone who can be there for him all the time."

Sam silently cursed Riley's interference, but he understood that it came out of protectiveness for Andrea and Chance. He also realized there was much logic in his assertions. "I will consider your advice."

"That's good. But I also know how hard it is to

ignore a woman like Andi. Tess is much the same. Strong-willed, hard-headed, wild but in some real nice ways. It's not easy to let that kind of woman go.''

Yet that's exactly what Sam had to do—let her go. He'd known that all along. He had known getting involved with her again would be a grave mistake. But he *had* become involved, and now he would have to deal with severing their emotional ties when the time came.

''I promise that whatever I decide to do about my son, it will be best for all concerned.''

''I'm counting on that, Sam.'' Riley set the shovel aside and wiped his hands on his jeans. ''I've got to go do a few things back at the Hammonds' place, but I'll be back at sundown.''

''I will try to finish this stall before you return.''

''You do that.''

Sam stepped aside and allowed him to exit, but before he reached the open door, Riley turned once again. ''And one more thing, Sam. Since I was Andi's dad's best friend, I want you to know that I'm standing in for him.'' He pointed a crooked finger. ''And if you hurt her, you'll have to answer to me.''

With that he was gone, leaving Sam to ponder his words. He had no intention of hurting Andrea, if he could avoid it. But the closer they became, the more the risk increased that he again would shatter her heart. And most likely do a great deal of damage to his own.

Seven

After lunch Sam headed to the stable to resume the repairs. Andrea had only made a brief appearance in the house, grabbed a sandwich then returned to work the horses in the round pen, barely acknowledging him or her aunt.

As Sam neared the barn, he noted the red truck belonging to the man named Caleb parked in the drive. He approached the entrance slowly as he heard the sound of Andrea's laughter, pausing outside to listen. He acknowledged that he had no right to intrude, yet he couldn't stop his eavesdropping.

"Dinner would be great," Andrea said. "But it will have to be in a couple of weeks. Chance will be home and my guest should be leaving."

Her guest? Sam experienced a pang of anger that she considered him only a guest, then admonished himself for such foolishness. He was a guest, not a member of the family. Only a friend, a stranger to his son. Her lover for the time they had remaining, if he had any say in the matter.

That thought sent him forward, but he hesitated once more when the man began to speak. "I'll give you a call next week, unless you decide you want to get together sooner."

Sam could only imagine what this Caleb had in mind for Andrea, and he couldn't contain the spear of jealousy hurling through him. That jealousy thrust him into the barn to find Andrea and Caleb facing each other at the stall containing the filly.

Andrea turned and met Sam's gaze, then smiled. "Speak of the devil, here he is now." She gestured toward him. "Caleb, this is Sam, a family friend."

Sam reluctantly accepted the handshake offered by the cowboy but did not return his smile.

"Nice to meet you, Sam," Caleb said. "Andi tells me you're some kind of a prince."

"A sheikh," he said as politely as his current mood allowed.

"That's great." He gave his grin to Andrea. "Keep up the good work, Andi. I'm pretty pleased with you so far."

Sam wondered what other pleasure he had in mind for Andrea. Forcing the thoughts away, he moved aside and gladly let the man take his leave.

When they were alone once again, Sam lost the tenuous grasp he'd placed on his control. "You will be dining with him after I leave?"

Andrea picked up a plastic box containing supplies and walked into the tack room. "Looks that way."

Propelled by his insane envy, Sam followed her inside. "Will Chance be in attendance?"

"Yes," she answered curtly.

"Does our son like this man?"

"He's not been around him all that much."

"Then you have no way of knowing if this Caleb will be an acceptable suitor."

Andi dropped the box at her feet and turned, leaning against the saddle set atop the stand. "I personally don't think Caleb is an appropriate suitor, because he's married and has two kids."

"He has a wife?"

"Yes, he has a wife, and she'll be coming with us. Are you satisfied now?"

Sam was still reluctant to trust the man. "I'm admittedly concerned about his motives regardless of his marital status."

Andrea rolled her eyes to the ceiling, then turned her back and began oiling the saddle. "Look, Sam, Caleb is a nice guy. He's really done me a favor by letting me train his horse, and that's the only thing he's asked of me."

"To this point."

She faced him, twisting the rag in her fist. "I don't know why you keep thinking he has other things in mind. You don't even know him."

He knew his type, and he knew how tempting Andrea could be. She was tempting him greatly now with the fire in her eyes and the clothes she wore, a sleeveless rag of a shirt cut short at her midriff, giving him a glimpse of her navel, where her jeans rode low at her shapely hips. The cowboy might be wed but he was still a man. And Sam had no right to judge anyone, considering what he had done with Andrea last night, knowing he was bound to another. Considering that he had not yet had his fill of her, as if he ever would.

"I will not mention it again," he conceded, though he knew he would think about it often in the days to come, as well as when he returned to Barak. He would think about her often, wondering if she would find her way to another man's arms, another man's bed.

But until that time she was his, and although it would be inadvisable to pursue a physical relationship with her, he was not strong enough to resist. He had no intention of resisting. If all he could have was a few stolen moments, then so be it.

Sam could only stare at Andrea as she cleaned the saddle, bending down now and then to retrieve supplies for the task. His body raged with need when the denim pulled tight over her hips, revealing the shape of her buttocks. Her hair was secured and bound high on her head in a band, leaving the back of her slender neck fair game. Sam imagined kissing her there. Kissing her everywhere.

"Do you need my assistance?" he asked.

She sent him a coy look over her shoulder. "I've cleaned so many saddles I could probably do it blindfolded."

"I assume you could do many things blindfolded."

Andi froze with her hand midswipe when she felt the heat of Sam's body at her back. A pleasant tremor crept up her spine as he tugged the bandanna from her back pocket then snaked it across her shoulder and over one breast before drawing it up slowly.

"Should we see if it is true that you are skilled without the benefit of sight?" His voice was a warm, midnight breeze at her ear.

Before she could respond, he placed the cloth over her eyes and tied it, throwing her into darkness, throwing her body into a carnal tailspin.

"You're really going to make me clean the saddle blindfolded?" she asked, her voice little more than a croak, knowing that's not what he'd meant at all.

Taking her by the shoulders, he turned her around and nudged her back against the saddle. "I propose that we ignore the saddle for more pleasant endeavors." He softly kissed her with an added sweep of his tongue across her lower lip. "I want you to concentrate on what I am doing to you."

A wave of heat ignited low in her belly then alighted between her thighs. "I've been working, Sam. I'm hot and sweaty." A feeble protest that she hoped he would ignore.

"So am I," he said. "But my hands are clean."

His hands were wonderful as he skimmed them down her sides, grazing her breasts. "What about Tess?" She worried they might get caught, yet that prospect heightened her desire.

"Tess has gone to the market," he whispered as he laved his tongue over her earlobe. "Riley will not return until sundown."

When she clutched his arms to secure herself, he pulled her hands away and held them at her sides. "Do not touch me yet," he said.

Andi gripped the metal stand to remain upright when her knees threatened to give way. She stood and waited for the longest moment until Sam caught her hands once more and placed a kiss on each palm before resting them against his face.

"Touch me now, Andrea. Remember me."

How could she ever forget him? Heavens, she had tried, but without success. She was tired of trying.

On that thought, she explored his wonderful face with her hands, a face that had invaded her dreams in great detail so many nights before—details deeply engrained in her memory and her heart. She traced a finger over the strong plane of his nose, the bow of his beautiful, full mouth, the solid jaw covered by a spattering of whiskers. It didn't matter that she couldn't see him now—he would always be with her, branded into her brain.

Gliding her hands down the column of his throat, she continued on to his chest, pausing when she realized he had removed his shirt, much to her delight. His skin was damp and hot beneath her palms as she set a course across the crisp hair and on to his nipples that peaked into tiny pebbles beneath her fingertips. She traveled down his abdomen, and his muscles clenched when she circled a finger in his navel. Intending to continue her erotic exploration, she slipped her fingertips beneath the band of his jeans, only to have him stop her as he gripped her wrist.

"Raise your arms," he said.

As if a master puppeteer was controlling her, she complied, leaning back against the saddle for support while he tugged her shirt over her head, leaving her completely naked from the waist up. He ran a fingertip across her chest from shoulder to shoulder, much the same as she had done to him. He traced her breasts with sensuous strokes of his fingertips, with agonizing slowness as he decreased the circles when he reached her nipples.

"You are very beautiful in the daylight," he said in a deep, slow-burn voice that complemented his avid touch.

"This isn't fair," she said on a broken breath. "You can see me but I can't see you."

"You only need to feel at the moment."

No problem, Andi thought as the heat of his mouth engulfed her nipple. She bucked at the pleasurable sensations, giving everything over to feeling. He paid equal attention to both breasts as she molded her hands to his scalp and followed his movements. Then suddenly he raised his head and commanded, "Turn around."

She did as she was told, bracing her hands on the saddle to regain her ground. Sam tracked his way down her spine, first with his thumbs then with his lips, leaving a trail of wonderful chills in his wake. Tuned in solely to Sam's sensual torture, it took Andi a moment to realize he had slipped one hand between her and the saddle. She felt the downward track of her zipper and went weak with anticipation, and weaker still when he lowered the denim to her thighs, taking her panties with it. A wisp of warm air whisked over her now-exposed bottom, but it was nothing compared to the heat Sam generated as he pressed more kisses to her lower back, then kissed her bottom.

Andi lowered her chin to her chest, savoring the feel of his mouth, gasping at the tiny nip of his teeth that he soothed with his tongue.

"A very nice dessert," he added with a low chuckle that sounded from deep within his chest.

She couldn't argue that point. This was much better than a hot-fudge sundae with whipped cream and nuts. Better than anything she had imagined to this point.

After working his way back up, he cupped his palm between her thighs while feathering kisses across the back of her neck, yet he only toyed with the cover of curls. Overcome with the need for him to pacify the insistent throbbing, she pressed against his hand in encouragement.

Andi couldn't stifle the moan of frustration when he took his touch away. "Patience," he scolded. "I will see to your needs but first I must see to something else."

When she heard the sound of his zipper followed by the rattle of paper, Andi realized that Sam had planned this all along. Planned to make her mindless with wanting despite his initial opposition. And more important, he was ruining her for other men. Convincing her with every kiss, every touch, that no one would ever measure up to him. But she really didn't care. She only cared about right now, the absolute need, the undeniable ache that could only be relieved by this particular prince.

He was soon flush against her back, returning his hand to the place that wept for his attention. This time he delved into the damp folds until he found her center to caress and cajole with firm yet tender fingertips. She was soon caught up in a whirlwind of sensory details surrounding her—freshly cut hay, mingled with the scent of leather and Sam. She heard his shallow breathing and the sounds of horses chomping their hay. But all sounds, all smells disappeared as he fondled her straight into oblivion.

The climax began to build and build, and she only knew that she wanted him inside her *now.* Reaching back to grasp his hips, she pulled him forward, and he entered in one sharp, enthralling thrust, bringing about an earth-moving climax.

She turned her face toward him and accepted his deep, penetrating kiss. His tongue captured the rhythm of his body as he explored her eager mouth while he moved inside her, stifling her gasps as he filled her completely.

He continued to stroke her even after her release had subsided. "Again, Andrea."

"I'm not sure—"

"I am," he insisted. "You will."

Amazingly, she did, moments before Sam found his own release. He gripped her hips, and a steady groan escaped his mouth as she absorbed the weight of his body against hers. Burying his face between her shoulder blades, he held her tightly. She couldn't tell who was shaking more, him or her. They were so close it was hard to tell where one began and the other ended. So close that Andi wanted to stay this way forever.

"You take me to limits I have never known before," he whispered. "I have never known anything such as this."

Neither had Andi. And she would probably never know anything like it again.

Reality took hold when she suddenly realized that someone had pulled up into the drive. And, considering the familiar sound of the noisy tailpipe, she knew exactly who that someone might be.

"Tess!"

Shoving Sam away with a push of her hips, she yanked the bandanna from her eyes and pulled her pants back up. She fumbled for her shirt, now covered in sawdust and straw, and pulled it over her head.

Awareness finally hit Sam but he seemed in no hurry. "Get dressed," Andi hissed. "She might come in here."

"I assume she would put away the groceries first," he said, taking his sweet time redoing his jeans.

She shoved his shirt at him. "Your assumptions could be wrong, and we'd have the devil to pay."

He had the gall to grin.

Sam Yaman was much too confident, Andi decided. Too practiced in his efficiency, she thought, when he calmly tossed the condom and package into the trash bin then covered it with a feed sack.

He turned his deadly grin back on her. "All evidence has been disposed of, and no one will know what deeds have been done in this room."

Andi glanced down at her disheveled clothes and could only imagine how she would look to her aunt. "Guess I could tell Tess that we had an unexpected tornado come through the barn."

He kicked the door closed, taking Andi by surprise. "We could lock out the world and stay in here the remainder of the afternoon." He stalked toward her and pulled her into his arms. "After all, we still have much to learn about each other."

"I'd be willing to spend a lifetime having you teach me."

His expression went serious. "If only that were possible."

Suddenly chilled, she backed out of his embrace. "Don't look so worried, Sam. I told you I don't expect anything. I was just spouting off."

"You have no idea how much I wish that we could be together." Her heart soared, then fell once again when he declared, "But that is not possible."

She propped a hand on her hip and glared at him. "I've always believed that anything's possible."

"Not in this instance, Andrea."

She forced back the unexpected tears burning hot behind her eyes. "Why? Because of your duty? Don't you realize you could be happy here with us? I've seen your happiness, Sam. You smile more now. You're enjoying yourself, especially with Chance. You might as well be wearing a blindfold if you don't see it, too."

He kicked the barrel containing the feed, causing a loud thump that would surely give them away if anyone were nearby. "Of course I am happy here. I have always been happy here. But that does not change my circumstance. I have to see to my obligations."

How many more times would she have to hear this? "Obligations to whom? Your father?"

"To my…" He looked away. "Yes, to my father. To my people."

Andi swiped away one rogue tear. "Well, great. I guess that doesn't include your son." *Or me.*

"I have told you I will provide—"

"Money. I know. But that won't buy you his love, Sam. Your money and your station won't buy you happiness, either."

Without a word he yanked open the door and left Andi alone with her sorrow once more. If only he knew how much she loved him. If only he would consider the possibilities. But something was keeping him from doing that, and she wondered if there was more to his resistance than his duty. Something he was failing to tell her.

She intended to find out the sheikh's secrets, even if it was the last thing she did before he left.

Sam spent the coming days working on the stable with Riley, but he spent the nights in Andrea's arms. She had proved to be an uninhibited lover, wild in the ways that she pleased him. Each time they were together, he discovered something new about her, acknowledged that she was forever imbedded in his soul.

He engaged in a constant battle between guilt and desire, love and responsibility. His desire and love for Andrea had won out, at least for now. When he took Maila as his wife—if he took her as his wife—he was sentencing himself to a loveless union. And when he took her to his bed, he would forever imagine Andrea.

That would be doing a grave disservice to Maila. She was a good woman who deserved a man who could give more of himself. An educated woman who, like him, agreed to the union out of a sense of obligation to their families. Yet if Sam ended the arrangement, in doing so he would encounter his father's scorn.

He would have to decide what would be best for everyone involved, a decision that would not come easily. And in a scarce few days, he would be leaving his son, and Andrea.

After his shower, he walked downstairs to find Andrea on the phone. She worried her bottom lip as she spoke quietly. "Okay, sweetie. You sleep tight now, and I'll see you tomorrow."

Sam seated himself on the sofa and gestured for Andrea to join him after she replaced the phone in its cradle. The concern in her expression could not be denied, even when she smiled at him.

"That was Chance," she said. "He wanted to make sure we're going to pick him up in the limo."

Sam returned her smile to mask his own worry. "And you assured him that we would?"

"Yes."

Sam patted the seat beside him. "Come tell me what is troubling you."

Instead of taking her place next to him, she curled into his lap. He held her tightly, savoring the scent of her shower-damp hair and the softness of her fragile body encased in satin.

"I'm worried about Chance," she said.

"Is he not well?"

She glanced up at him, then tucked her head beneath his chin. "He says he's fine, but he sounds tired."

"I would assume he is tired."

"I hope that's all it is."

He brushed a kiss over her forehead and stroked her hair. "What would lead you to believe otherwise?"

"Mother's intuition. Or maybe I'm just being paranoid like always."

"You are only concerned for his well-being, Andrea."

She sighed. "I know. But when he was almost three, he climbed up on a fence rung and fell backward. He seemed to be okay, but then the next morning he complained about his shoulder. I took him to the doctor and found out he'd broken his collarbone. I should've taken him that night."

Sam tipped her chin up, forcing her to look at him. "It was a simple mistake, Andrea. It does not mean that you don't care for him."

"I realize that, but I felt horrible, like a bad mother."

"You are a wonderful mother," Sam said adamantly. "I could not have picked a better mother for my child."

She touched her lips to his cheek, stirring his body and his soul. "Thanks." After studying him a long moment, she said, "Now tell me what's bugging you."

Sam should be surprised that she so easily saw through him, but he wasn't. It seemed that over the past week they had become totally tuned in to each other's moods, each other's needs. Perhaps it had always been that way. Perhaps it always would.

"I'm afraid I have some less-than-satisfactory news."

Andrea's frame stiffened in his arms. "What is it?"

"I spoke with my father earlier today. I must return to Barak on Thursday."

"You weren't supposed to leave until Sunday." She stared at him with fire and frustration in her eyes.

"So he snaps his fingers and you come running. Wish I knew his secret."

"It is complicated, Andrea. I do not have the luxury of coming and going as I please."

She slid off his lap and claimed the place at the end of the sofa. "I'm sorry for you, Sam. It must be awful to have that kind of burden, to not have free will."

Anger gripped Sam and he struggled to temper his fury. "I have free will. I also have responsibilities."

She rolled her eyes to the ceiling. "I know, I know. But what about your responsibility to your child? You've barely spent any time with him. Is this what he'll have to count on in the future, a father who may or may not come to see him?"

Sam sat forward and lowered his head. "I have been considering that. I can only promise that I will try to be here as much as possible."

Andrea sighed. "We don't have much time to decide when to tell him, do we?"

They had little time to be together, as well. "No, we do not."

Andrea rose from the sofa. "Guess we'll cross that bridge when we come to it."

Sam stood. "What time will we leave tomorrow morning to pick up Chance?"

She folded her arms across her breasts and faced him. "Not we, Sam. You."

He frowned. "I do not understand."

"I've decided *you* should pick him up by yourself. That way you can have time alone with him to get to know him."

"But you—"

"I'll see him when you get back. Besides, I'll have him with me for the rest of my life. You, on the other hand, have very little time."

Sam realized the difficulty of her decision and the heartache he was causing her. "Are you certain this is what you want?"

"Yes, I'm sure."

"Do you wish me to tell him—"

"No, I don't want you to say anything about you being his father. I think I should be there."

"I will honor your request."

She started toward the stairs. "Good night, Sam."

"I will join you in a few moments."

She turned to him once again. "I'd like to sleep alone tonight. I'm exhausted."

In her own way she was already preparing to let him go, that much Sam knew. "I will do what you ask, Andrea, but I would like to spend this last night with you, before Chance returns."

"It's okay, Sam," she said in a weary tone. "We've both known all along this wasn't forever. Might as well end it now."

He wanted to shout that he wanted no part of this ending, that he wanted to forever be by her side, in her bed, in her life. Instead he turned his back and said, "I wish you pleasant dreams, Andrea."

Her sharp, mirthless laugh stopped him cold. "I don't believe in dreams, Sam. Not anymore."

Eight

"**W**here on earth are they?" Andi paced the length of the kitchen as she stared at the clock that read 3:00 p.m. Long past time for Sam and Chance's arrival home from the camp.

"Maybe they stopped off for some lunch," Tess offered as she poured her and Riley another glass of tea at the table.

"I packed them a lunch," Andi responded, unable to keep the panic from her voice. "I wanted to make sure Chance has the right things to eat."

"I'm sure they just stopped off for a picnic, then," Riley said. "Sam seems like a fairly responsible guy."

Andi spun around to face the pair. "Yeah, that's how he seems, but how well do we really know him?"

Tess frowned. "Andi, you're talking nonsense. This is Sam, the boy who practically lived here for four years. The same one who worked on the barn for the past two weeks like some hired hand."

"He's changed, Tess. He's not the same. What if he's decided to go to the airport and just keep going from there? What if he takes Chance back to his country?"

Tess rose from the kitchen table and took Andi by both arms. "Just listen to yourself, Andi. You're not making any sense. Sam promised he wouldn't try something like that."

"He promised a lot of things, Tess, and he didn't keep those promises, either. How can I trust that he won't do the same thing again?"

Tess narrowed her eyes and studied Andi dead-on. "Trust your heart, Andi."

Andi didn't dare. She'd done that before only to be crushed in the process.

The shrill of the phone caused Andi to jump. Pushing away from Tess, she grabbed it on the second ring. "Hello?"

"Could I please speak to Ms. Andrea Hamilton," a soft feminine voice asked.

Frustrated that it wasn't Sam, Andrea sighed. She didn't need home repairs or a magazine subscription. "That depends on who you are."

"I'm Mrs. Murphy with the hospital in Lexington, and I'm calling concerning your son."

Sheer panic pierced through Andi's momentary shock. "Has there been an accident?"

Tess quickly came to Andi's side as the woman

continued to speak. "No, no accident. A Mr. Yaman brought Chance in. The boy's blood sugar is low."

"Is he okay?"

"He's in the E.R. being examined now. Mr. Yaman asked if I would notify you."

"I'm on my way." Andi hung up without saying goodbye and grabbed her keys from the hook by the back door. "Chance is at the hospital," she called to Tess on her way out.

"Let me drive you, Andi," Tess said at the door while Andi crossed the yard to the pickup.

"I'll call you."

"Andi, are you sure?"

She dismissed Tess with a wave. "I'm fine."

But was Chance?

Andi managed the thirty-mile drive in record time. She rushed into the emergency room barking inquiries to anyone who would listen. Finally one nurse directed her to a curtained cubicle down a narrow corridor.

Stepping inside, Andi stopped short at the scene playing out before her. Among the all-too-familiar sterile scents and scenery, Sam was stretched out in the small hospital bed, Chance curled against his side with his face turned in profile as his head rested against his father's solid chest.

Andi covered her mouth to stifle a sob when she caught sight of the IV tubing trailing from Chance's slender arm. But she couldn't hold back the emotions when she noted how natural they looked—one beautiful man with his large hand enfolding the equally beautiful child's smaller one, an overt display of protection. The identical dark hair, the dark lashes fanned against their cheeks as they slept, presented a picture of peace that starkly contrasted with the colorless surroundings.

As Andi took another step forward, Sam's eyes snapped opened and he attempted a smile. Quietly he slipped his arm from beneath Chance and slid out of the bed without disturbing their son. He gestured for Andi to step outside. Reluctantly she complied, torn between wanting to hold her precious child and needing to hear what Sam had to say.

"What happened?" she said, her voice hoarse with fear, clouded with emotions that she tried to keep at bay.

Sam rubbed a hand over his jaw. "On the ride home he became very pale. I offered him some juice, as you'd instructed, but he refused. Then he began to perspire and became agitated. We were nearing Lexington so I instructed Rashid to come here. I knew not what else to do."

"You did the right thing, Sam."

He glanced away but not before Andi glimpsed the worry in his near-black eyes. "I have never feared much in my lifetime, Andrea. But this terrified me." He finally turned his gaze back to her. "I only now realize how much you have been through with this disease."

"What Chance has been through," Andi corrected. "It's something you learn to deal with as a parent of an ill child. My love for him has seen me through."

"I suppose I am only beginning to understand that concept."

Andi bit the inside of her cheek to stop another

onslaught of tears over Sam's obvious pain. She had to stay composed. "Has the doctor seen him?"

"Yes, a few minutes ago. He said that his levels seem to be stable, but he would like him to stay for a few hours to be certain."

Andi drew in a slow breath of relief and released it on a shaky sigh. "That's routine."

"Then he has suffered this before?"

"Yes. Several times at first, but not in a while."

"The doctor believes that Chance's exhaustion perhaps brought on this attack."

Andi silently cursed her stupidity. "I should never have let him go to camp."

Sam took her by the arm and guided her against the wall opposite the cubicle. "Do not blame yourself, Andrea. Chance told me how much he enjoyed his time at the camp. You had no reason to believe this would happen."

She shot a glance at the parted curtain to see that Chance still slept. "I should've known."

Sam brushed a lock of hair away from her face, damp with the tears she had shed on the ride to Lexington. "The doctor also said you should consider putting Chance on a medicine pump to replace the shots."

"I've wanted to do that," Andi said. "But it's very expensive. I've been trying to save enough money to cover what the insurance won't pay."

"I will take care of it," Sam insisted. "You need not worry about funds."

She was worried about many things at the moment. "Did you tell anyone you're Chance's father?"

"I told the physician, but Chance did not hear me, if that is your concern."

Andi felt incredibly selfish to question him at such a time. "I wasn't worried exactly. I'd just hate to think that Chance learned something so important while he's sick."

"I've told him nothing, even when he asked many questions on the ride back."

Andi's concern came calling again. "What questions?"

"He wanted to know if I knew his father. I told him that I did, but not very well. And that is the truth, Andrea." He streaked a hand over his face. "I realize I don't know myself at all."

Andi laid a hand on his arm. "I know you, Sam. You're a good man. A good father."

He studied her with weary eyes. "Am I, Andrea? I am a father who must leave his son. There is nothing good in that."

"You can enjoy the time you have with him now so he can get to know you as his father."

"Perhaps it would be best if he never knows."

Best for whom? Andi wanted to shout. Best for him, no doubt. No ties except for providing money. No commitment to their son, or to her. "Let's not talk about this here. I need to be with Chance."

"I only wanted you to know that I am considering our son's well-being. If that entails giving him up, I will not hesitate to consider it."

Andi's heart plummeted, causing a painful ache in her chest brought about by an overwhelming sadness. "If that's what you want."

''I promise you, Andrea, it is not what I wish at all. But it could be the best decision for Chance.''

Too tired to fight, too heartsick to talk, Andrea walked away to see her son, the only constant in her life.

Sam spent the better part of the week getting to know his son. While looking on with the eye of a concerned parent, he'd taught Chance how to hammer a nail. Yet he felt it necessary to treat the boy as if he had no deficit. On the surface Chance appeared to behave as any normal boy would, active and enthusiastic, embracing life to its fullest. But now that Sam had witnessed the effects of his disease, he worried all the more.

At least Andrea seemed to be very optimistic, now that Chance had begun using a pump that kept the medication flowing into his body. She had told Sam that his levels were much better, and that Chance was much more energetic than before. A very good thing, Sam decided. And he certainly could confirm his son's zeal for activity.

Presently Chance was helping him sweep the aisle between the stalls. With his small hand—a miniature version of Sam's own—poised on the push broom that was almost as tall as the child, he asked, ''Do I look like my dad?''

Sam carefully weighed the question. ''Yes, to some degree.''

''Like how?''

''The color of your skin and your hair. I believe your eyes are lighter in color.''

Leaning the broom against one stall, Chance studied his arms then wrinkled his nose. "I've got Mama's freckles."

Sam laughed as he had many times in previous days over his child's antics. "Yes, you do."

Chance toed a pile of hay with one booted foot. "My friend Bobby says that where you live it's nothing but sand."

As Chance had done, Sam propped his broom against the opposite stall. "That is true to a point, we do have quite a bit of sand. But we also have trees and mountains. And a very good university we've built in the last few years as well as an excellent hospital."

Chance frowned. "I hate hospitals."

Sam's first fatherly faux pas. "I'm certain you do, and with good reason. But they are necessary."

"I still hate 'em." Chance turned his eyes to Sam, eyes so very much like his own. "Do all the people look alike in your country?"

"Most have dark skin and features, but they are all very different."

"Are they nice?"

"As it is in America, there are some very good people and some not so good people. There are mothers and fathers, sisters and brothers who play together and argue with each other. Teachers, doctors and builders. Overall, it is a very peaceful place to live."

"Do you live in a palace?"

"Yes. It has been in my family for many generations."

"Can I come visit you sometime?"

Sam's chest tightened with remorse, wishing that were possible. "Perhaps when you are older."

He released a long sigh. "I sure wish you could stay here. Don't you like America?"

"I like it very much. In fact, I was born here, in the state of Ohio."

"Then if you're American, how come you don't live here?"

At times Sam had desired that very thing, now more than ever, but he still had a strong allegiance to his country. Although they had made many strides, there was still much to be done. "I cannot live here because my father is the king of my country and I am to take his place one day."

"Maybe you could call him and tell him to hire someone else to do it." His eyes widened with innocence. "One of the girls at camp said her dad doesn't have a job. Maybe he'd do it."

Sam knelt at Chance's level with a tenderness radiating from his heart over the child's simple logic. "It is very complicated, Chance. I was born to lead my country, to help my people." He brushed a tendril of hair from his forehead. "Do you understand now why I must leave?"

He shrugged. "I guess, but I still wish you would stay." Chance wrapped his frail arms around Sam's neck in an embrace, taking Sam by surprise and his heart by storm. "I still wish you were my dad."

Andi stood outside the barn, frozen in place while awaiting Sam's response to Chance's wish. Yet he only said, "Let us finish our work so we're not late for supper."

She leaned back against the outside wall of the barn, closed her eyes against the setting sun and released a slow uneven breath. He'd had the perfect opportunity to tell Chance. Maybe he was still honoring her request that she be there when the moment arrived. Or maybe Sam was serious about not telling Chance the truth.

That made her incredibly troubled that she would continue to live a lie. If Sam insisted that Chance not know, should she tell him anyway? Maybe when he was much older, then she would make the revelation—and more than likely face his wrath because of her deceit. Would Chance blame her or would he blame Sam? Would he ever understand that his father thought it best? Would he realize that Sam was being unselfish in his decision, and that it had caused him great pain?

"You're looking a little pale, Andi girl. Did you work too hard today?"

Andi opened her eyes to find Tess staring at her inquisitively. She pushed off the wall and folded her arms across her chest. "Sam leaves tomorrow," she said.

Tess patted Andi's shoulder. "I know, honey. And I wanted to talk to you about that very thing."

"I'm going to be okay."

"You will if you do what I tell you to do."

Andi rolled her eyes skyward. "Do I really have to hear this?"

"Yes, you do." Tess forked a hand through her short gray hair. "Tonight I want Chance to come to the bunkhouse and stay with me. That will give you the opportunity to say your goodbyes to Sam, and I want you to do it properly."

"I don't think that's necessary."

Tess sent her a stern look. "Yes, it is. You take tonight and you spend it with him. You make those memories because they'll be all you'll ever have. You keep them in your heart and you bring them out when times are tough."

It sounded simple enough, but past experience had taught Andi it was anything but simple. "I don't need more memories, Tess."

"Yes, you do. I could never have made it without mine all these years."

Andi sported a frown of her own, confused over Tess's veiled revelation. "Does this have to do with you and some man other than Riley?"

Glancing away, Tess muttered, "Yes," then after a pause continued. "It was a long time ago. He was a soldier, a real good-looking fellow, not that I couldn't hold my own back then," she added with a grin. "He asked me to marry him before he left for the war, and I turned him down."

Andi shifted her weight from one hip to the other. "And he didn't ask again when he came home?"

"He never came home."

"Oh, Tess," Andi said, hugging her aunt against her. "I'm so sorry."

"Don't be," Tess said when they parted. "I confess I regret that I didn't say yes, but I regret more that the should-have-beens have kept me from living my life all these years. I don't want that to happen to you."

Andi sighed and pushed back the tears. "It's going to be so hard, letting him go." Harder than the first time. Harder than anything Andi had ever done before.

Tess braced Andi's shoulders and gave her a little shake. "But you have to let him go. You have to for your sake and for your son's. You take tonight and you show him that you love him. Tell him that you love him, because I know you do. If he walks away after that, then it was never meant to be in the first place."

The "give them wings" theory that Andi was coming to despise. But she saw the logic in her aunt's advice, and she made the decision to have one last night with Sam, her lover, the love of her life.

Chance came bounding out of the barn door shouting, "I'm hungry!" interrupting the emotional moment.

Tess caught him on the fly and whirled him around. "You eat as much as a moose these days."

"I am a moose," Chance proclaimed, followed by a high-pitched giggle.

Tess set him on his feet and grinned. "Tell you what, Mr. Moose. Why don't you come spend the night in the bunkhouse with me? Riley's coming over and we can play some checkers."

Chance's expression brightened. "Can Riley teach me how to play poker?"

Both Andi and Tess laughed then. "I guess we can do that, Little Bit," Tess said. "As long as your mama doesn't mind."

Andi pretended to think long and hard before saying, "As long as you don't bet away the house and the horses."

"We'll stick to pennies," Tess said. She turned her attention back to Chance. "Then it's settled. Right after dinner, we'll play some poker."

"Can Sam play, too?" Chance asked.

Tess sent Andi a meaningful glance. "I think Sam has a few things to tend to tonight with your mama."

Sam had longed to tell Chance the truth, yet he hadn't. He had longed to declare that he was the father Chance had wished for, yet he couldn't. If he had made that admission knowing he would leave the next day, never to return, it would have been selfish on his part and totally unfair to his son. And he couldn't return, not after knowing what it would be like to remain a part of this blessed family. Knowing each time it would be more difficult to leave. He could only hope that one day Andrea would find a suitable father for Chance. That consideration made him wince with a pain so deep that it threatened to consume him.

"It is for the best," he kept repeating to himself as he had during dinner, quite possibly the last meal he would ever share with his son or Andrea.

The finality sat heavily on his heart as he began to pack the rest of his belongings. He'd saved the most significant for last—the baseball, Paul's graduation gift to him, even the pair of tattered jeans he had left behind before. All mementos from the past that he would cherish throughout his future. Yet when he opened his suitcase once more, he found lying atop his clothing a souvenir that captured the present.

The photograph was much the same as the one of him, Andi and Paul except Chance had replaced his uncle. Tess had taken it earlier in the week, but he had no idea when she'd had it developed or how it had ended up among his things. Perhaps she had placed it there when he had returned to the stable for one last look after the evening meal. Perhaps it wasn't Tess's doing at all. If his instincts served him correctly, Andrea had left the keepsake, another precious gift she had given him.

Andrea.

He wanted desperately to go to her, to take her in his arms one final time, to spend a few more moments in her presence, to make love to her as he had desired to do the past week. He would deny himself that pleasure for he did not deserve her attention. And more than likely she would refuse if he dared make the offer tonight.

He picked up the photo and studied it a moment longer, admiring the faces of the woman he had always loved, of the child he had grown to love. Tomorrow he would say goodbye to them both and wish them well, then return to his homeland and pretend that nothing had changed. Yet everything had changed, especially Sheikh Samir Yaman.

"It's a nice picture, isn't it?"

His hands froze on the framed photo at the soothing sound of Andrea's voice coming from behind him. After carefully tucking the photo beneath a few garments to protect it, he closed the suitcase and closed the chapter on what could never be.

Slowly he turned to face the woman who had so easily secured his heart years ago. "I will cherish it always," he said. "Thank you."

She took a tentative step forward and stopped at the end of the four-poster bed. "It's the least I could do."

"It is very much appreciated."

As a heavy silence hung between them, she pushed her red-gold hair away from her face but failed to look directly at him. Finally she walked forward and stood face-to-face with him, so close that he could see that her heartache had settled in her beautiful blue eyes. He opened his arms to her, and she moved into his embrace.

Andi settled her cheek against Sam's chest, not certain whose heart was beating more rapidly, his or hers. But her heart was in the process of totally splintering.

On that thought she kissed his whisker-rough jaw and gathered all her courage to tell him the one thing she had avoided until now. "I love you, Sam."

He touched her face with tenderness and gently kissed her brow. "As I love you."

She experienced an overwhelming joy that raced to her soul and settled on her wounded heart. "Then stay with me. Be a part of our lives."

"You know that I cannot do that."

She stared at him in frustration. "Then you don't really love me."

His rough sigh echoed in the silent room. "Yes, I do, more than you will ever know. But that does not change my situation."

"It could if you wanted it to."

"If only that were true." He guided her to the edge of the bed and seated her next to his side, then took her hands into his. "I also love our son, which is why I have decided that he need never know I am his father."

Exactly what she'd feared. "But what about when you come back?"

He glanced away but not before revealing an abiding sadness in his stoic expression. "I will not be coming back."

Andi's heart started another descent. "But you have to come back. Chance needs you. *I* need you."

"You need to resume your life without me. You need to find someone who will care for you and our son. Someone who is deserving of your love."

"I don't want anyone but you," she said, warm tears now raining down her cheeks in a stream of sorrow.

"You say that now, but you will change your mind once I am gone."

He pulled her tightly into his strong arms. If only Andi could absorb some of that strength. If only she could have foreseen where this would lead. In reality she'd known all along what would happen, that he *would* leave her again, but she had chosen to believe that somehow, some way, it would be different this time. That he might actually change his mind, that she would change his mind. How foolish she'd been.

She had no choice but to claim the sadness, to accept defeat. But she didn't know how to accept his leaving. "I don't know how to let you go."

"You must."

She raised her head and looked at him straight-on, determined to try one more time to make him see things her way. "Even if you give up your wealth, your status, just look at what you'd be getting in return."

"How well I know this."

"Then why does it have to be this way? Why do

you have to go? Why? And what is it you're not telling me?''

He remained silent for a moment before drawing in a deep, cleansing breath. ''I am to marry another.''

Nine

Sam had been prepared for Andrea's shock over his sudden announcement. He had not been prepared for the seething anger boiling beneath the surface of her calm facade, apparent from the narrowing of her blue eyes.

"And you've known this all along?" Her tone was surprisingly controlled.

Sam wished she would shout at him. He deserved her hostility, her fury. "Yes, I have, but I must explain what this involves."

She bolted from the bed, away from him. "You are damned right you must explain."

He knew not where to begin, since there seemed to be no excuse for his behavior. "This marriage is an arrangement and nothing more. The details are to be finalized when I return. But rest assured, I do not love her, Andrea."

She wrapped her arms about her middle. "Well, great. That makes me feel a whole lot better."

"I have also decided that I will discuss this marriage with my father on my return. I am considering not going through with it."

She glared at him. "Bully for you."

How could he get through to her? How could he convince her that his heart was solely in her possession? He rose and clasped her slender arms. "I've decided I cannot live that lie, Andrea, not with what I've found with you. Maila is a good woman, and like you she deserves a man who can give all of himself to her."

"When did you figure this out, Sheikh Yaman? Before or after you had sex with me?"

Anger roiled within Sam. "I made love to you, Andrea, and if you recall, at your insistence. I have always been weak in your presence. Always. I have never been able to resist you from the moment that Paul brought me here."

"So it's my fault that you cheated on your fiancée, is it?"

"It is my fault for not being a stronger man."

"So answer this," she said sternly. "If you're getting out of this marriage, then why can't you be with us?"

"Must I remind you again about my status?"

She took a few more steps away from him. "Heavens, no. If I hear that one more time, I'll scream. But it seems to me that you just don't get it. All the finest things in the world will never replace love, Sam. Your son's love. My love. But if your riches and your title mean so much to you, then you're right, it's better that you leave for good.''

With that, she started for the door. Sam quickly came to his feet. ''I beg you Andrea, please stay. Let us take this time to talk things through, to be with each other. This last night will be all that we ever have.''

Slowly she turned to face him. ''No, Sam, I won't. I'm letting you go, starting now.''

Andrea realized there had been a lot of truth in Sam's words the night before. She had been the one to entice him. She had insisted they make love. Yet he had refused to tell her about his impending marriage, and that not only stung but it angered her, as well.

All that wounded pride and horrible hurt had prevented her from spending more time with him, making more memories. In some ways she'd regretted that decision, but no matter how hard it had been to walk away, she had known that she would only have more trouble seeing him off this morning.

Obviously she had been wrong to trust him. Maybe he didn't really love her. Maybe in reality he viewed her only as a convenience. But he had made love to her so sweetly, and he had told her that he loved her. Regardless of her anger, her pride, the horrible hurt stinging her heart, the betrayal, she would never forget the time she'd spent with him. And she still didn't love him any less, as foolish as that seemed.

She would also never forget the scene playing out before her at the moment. Chance was standing near the hood of the limo, and Sam was crouched down at his level, preparing to say goodbye. They spoke softly and Andrea strained to hear Sam's parting words. When she couldn't quite make them out, she moved a little closer.

"You must promise me that you will take care of your mother."

"Okay," Chance said reluctantly.

"And you must promise me to take care of Sunny now that she is yours. She's a fine filly, and I trust that you will watch out for her."

Chance frowned. "Will you tell Mama to let me ride her sometime?"

"I'm sure she will allow it once the time is right."

They both remained silent for a moment before Sam laid his palm on Chance's thin shoulder. "Be proud of who you are."

"I am. I'm gonna tell my friends about your country, that it's not just all sand, and that the people are nice and look sort of like me."

Sam attempted a weak smile before his expression turned somber once more. "And most important, you must remember that no matter where he is, or what he is doing, your father will always love you."

Andi looked away before her son could glimpse her tears.

"How do you know that?" Chance asked.

"Because I know you. He would be very proud to have such a strong, wise boy."

Andi forced herself to look at father and son once more, to remember.

After a moment's hesitation, Chance drew Sam into an awkward hug and said, "I love you, Sam, like you're my dad."

Andi's heart completely shattered in that moment, and she wanted desperately to reveal that Sam was, in fact, her son's father. But if Sam had no intention of returning, then it would serve no purpose but to confuse Chance even more. Yet deep down she wondered if on some level Chance did know the truth. Regardless, it would be up to her to provide a happy home, to take care of his needs, and to answer his questions when they happened to come. She also hoped that someday she could love again, find a good father for Chance, although that seemed impossible at the moment. .

"Time for breakfast, Little Bit," Tess called from the back door.

Chance headed off at a sprint but stopped and pointed at the limo. "One day I'm gonna get me one of those."

Sam laughed then, a rich deep laugh that Andi would take to memory to add to the rest.

Once Chance was safely inside, Andi approached Sam with tentative steps. "Guess it's time for you to go, huh?"

He surveyed her face a long moment then bracketed her cheeks in his palms. "Take care, Andrea."

"I'm going to be fine, Sam. We're all going to be fine." She said the words with false bravado, determined to act as though she would survive his departure. And she would, even if it took years to get over him.

"I will have my banker send you the information on Chance's trust. I will see that all yours and Chance's financial needs are met."

But not the one need she desired the most, to have him in her life permanently. "I appreciate that."

He softly kissed her lips. "I will forever be sorry for what I have put you through, but I will never regret what we have shared."

"Neither will I," she said sincerely. "And I'll never forget you." Despite the heartache.

He stared at her long and hard. "You must forget, Andrea. You must go forward."

"I could never forget, Sam, and I'm afraid the same holds true for your son."

"The memories eventually will fade for him, and for you."

"If you say so," she said, knowing that years of trying would never erase him from her memory. They never had before. At least Chance was young, resilient, and he had a lifetime ahead of him, even if he wouldn't have the pleasure of knowing his father.

Andi jumped when Rashid started the engine, yet Sam didn't let her go. He lowered his lips to her ear and whispered, "No matter where I am or what I am doing, I will always be thinking of you. I will always hold you close in my heart and love you with all that I am."

Andi swiped furiously at her eyes, now clouded with unwanted tears. "Don't do this to me, Sam. Please go."

He met her gaze. "Before I do go, will you allow me one more kiss?"

Though she knew she shouldn't, she nodded her agreement. His lips were soft and warm and gentle as they claimed hers in a heartfelt kiss, a kiss that expressed the emotions Andi felt so deep inside her soul. Yet it only lasted a brief time before he pulled away.

"Live well, Andrea." With one more soft kiss, he stepped into the limo and closed the door, closed out all that they had known in each other's arms.

After Rashid drove away, Andi stood and watched until she could no longer see the car's taillights. In that moment she made a vow. She would take all the memories and store them away for safekeeping, as Tess had told her she should. Life would go on without Sam, though she might always live with some regrets. But she would have her beloved son, the greatest gift to be had. Sheikh Samir Yaman had given her that much, even if he couldn't give all of himself. For that she would always be grateful.

Sam sat alone in the airport terminal while awaiting the pilot's summons. He watched with new interest the people passing by, yet the families traveling together held his interest most of all. He could see the affection in their faces, the protectiveness of a father tightly gripping his daughter's hand. He viewed the pride in a mother's face when her son said, "Excuse me," as he passed in front of Sam to claim a seat nearby.

A soul-wrenching emptiness flowed through Sam as he acknowledged how much he would lose by not experiencing the same relationship with his son. One day he might have other children, and he would love them equally, but he would always wonder about what might have been had he taken a different path. Had he not been born to royalty.

"The plane is ready, Prince Yaman."

Sam looked up to see Rashid standing over him with his usual detachment. "I am ready." Yet he did not feel ready for this trip. For what awaited him at home. He could only concentrate on what he was leaving behind.

As they traveled down a corridor and onto a tarmac where the private jet awaited them, Rashid began a litany of duties Sam would be facing upon his return. The list continued even after Sam had settled in to his seat for the journey.

"Your father says that you are to report immediately to the palace to sign the agreement."

Not surprising, Sam thought. "I assume my father will be there?"

"Yes, and so will your bride and her father."

Something Sam was already dreading. Since he had decided to call off the arrangement, he preferred to meet with his father alone. "What else?" he asked, although that was quite enough.

"You are to meet with the parliament tomorrow morning to discuss the upcoming election."

"I am aware of that."

"And your father also requests that you speak with your brother."

Sam waved off the male attendant offering a drink. "Which one?"

"Jamal. It seems the young prince is secretly seeing a woman, although her identity has not been revealed."

Good for Jamal. It would please Sam if his brother made his own decision about his life partner. "I refuse to interfere."

Rashid frowned. "This will not sit well with your father."

Neither would refusing to marry Maila. "I understand that, and I will handle it."

Rashid fell silent for a moment then once again took up where he'd left off. "You also have…"

A child that needs you, Sam thought. *A woman who loves you. A place by her side if you so choose. Another home. Another family.*

Sam no longer heard Rashid's voice. He could only hear his son saying how he had longed for Sam to be his father. Andrea saying that she loved him, that she needed him. That she wanted him to stay.

The roar of the plane's engines snapped him back into the present situation. Tightly he gripped the arms of the seat as the plane began to taxi toward the runway.

You must return, echoed in his mind. *You are Samir Yaman, firstborn son of the ruler of Barak.*

Yet another voice overshadowed the other.

You are Chance Samuel Paul Hamilton's father….

He was no longer able to fight the urge to run back to Andrea, back to his son, away from his responsibility, toward a new life. He would only be half a man if he left Andrea behind. An inadequate human being if he disregarded his child.

"Tell the pilot to halt and return to the terminal," he shouted at Rashid as he yanked the seat belt away and stood.

Rashid regarded him with a confused look. "Is there a problem?"

Yes, he had been totally blinded by his royal duties until now.

Duty be damned.

When Sam didn't respond, Rashid gave the order to the pilot. After a moment the plane turned around. When they once again reached the position near the terminal, Sam said, "Open the door." The attendant came to his feet but seemed unable to move. "I said open this door," Sam repeated, more demanding this time.

The man reluctantly complied, and Rashid joined Sam at the opening. "Sheikh Yaman, have you forgotten something?"

Sam looked at him earnestly. "Yes, Rashid, I've forgotten who I am, what I desire as a man, not as a prince. I've forgotten what is important in life."

"Are you saying you will be remaining here?"

"Yes, that is exactly what I am saying. I will remain here with my son and the woman I intend to make my wife."

"But your father—"

"Will more than likely disown me. My mother will cry, yet she has the capacity to understand. I will lose my position as future king but in doing so I will gain some peace. Tell me, Rashid, can you blame me?"

Rashid slowly shook his head. "I suppose I cannot, yet I worry over the fate of our country without your leadership."

Sam braced a hand on Rashid's shoulder. "Do not concern yourself with that. Omar is next in line and he is more adept at leading. He will serve our people well."

Sam started down the steps but halted when Rashid asked, "Will you not be returning?"

Looking back over his shoulder at his faithful companion of seven years, Sam smiled. "That is entirely up to my father's mandate. And my mother's powers of persuasion."

For the first time in many years, Rashid smiled. "I would wager my life on your mother's powers."

Sam hurried down the stairs and headed back toward the terminal at a fast clip, resisting the urge to run. He had not felt such freedom in years, such joy over the prospect of spending his life with Andrea and his child.

If Andrea agreed to welcome him back. If not at first, Sam would make sure she would eventually. In the meantime he had much to do.

"That was the third call in three days." Andi turned from the phone to address her aunt seated at the kitchen table.

"More business, I take it."

"Yes, and that was Adam Cantrell. He has a prospect he wants me to train."

Tess slapped her hands on her thighs and stood. "About time people figured out what a good hand you are."

Andi chewed her bottom lip for a moment. "But how would anyone know?"

"Word of mouth I suppose."

"Or word of Sam."

Tess frowned. "Now why would you think Sam had something to do with this?"

"Because he told me that he wanted to help me establish my career, so this has his mark all over it."

"And what's the big deal if he made a few calls?"

"I want to do this on my own, Tess. I want to build my reputation by myself."

"Speaking of building," Tess said. "You're going to have to add onto the barn if things keep going the way they have been."

Andi had considered that for the past week since Sam left, when she hadn't been thinking about him. "I know, but I need to make some money first."

"It's none of my business, but what about the money Sam put in the bank for you and Chance?"

"I want to save that for Chance's education and any medical expenses."

"If you don't mind me asking, how much money is it, anyway?"

Actually, Andi did mind Tess asking even though she shouldn't. After all, Tess had helped make ends meet by taking in sewing and working part-time at the local grocers. They'd never hidden anything from each other since Chance's birth, so she might as well come clean—at least partially. "Let's just say I've never had that many zeroes in my bank account."

Tess raised a thin brow. "That much, huh?"

"That much."

The roar of a truck pulling up behind the house grabbed their attention. Andi walked to the back door and peered out the window. "I wonder who that is?"

Tess came up behind her. "I dunno, but they sure as heck have a fancy enough truck."

Andi tightened her ponytail and swiped away the straw from her shirt. "I'm a mess. Go see what they want."

Tess shrugged. "If you insist, but if he's cute and

single I'm invitin' him in for something cool to drink.''

''Don't you dare!'' Andi's glare was lost on Tess since she'd already headed out the door.

Keeping her post by the back door, Andi watched curiously as a young man left the truck and handed Tess a small white envelope. The guy looked familiar, but she couldn't place him.

When Tess returned to the kitchen, Andi asked, ''What was that all about?''

Tess offered her the envelope. ''It's for you. That was the Masters kid. Seems he's taken a job nearby.''

Unable to contain her curiosity, Andi tore open the envelope to find a card inside. She read silently until Tess cleared her throat. ''Care to let me in on that?''

''It's an invitation to some kind of reception down the road at the old Leveland Place. It's called Galaxy Farms now.''

''I thought that place was vacant.''

So had Andi. ''It was, but apparently not anymore. Someone must have bought it, although there isn't any name indicating the new owner.''

''Someone rich, no doubt,'' Tess allowed. ''That place is prime horse farm all the way around.''

''No joke.''

Leaning back against the counter, Tess eyed Andi for a moment. ''So?''

''So what?''

''So are you going?''

Andi tossed the card onto the table. ''No.''

''Why not?''

Because she didn't feel like socializing at the moment. Because she'd rather be with her son. ''First of all, it's tonight, and that's very short notice. Second, I don't have anything proper to wear.''

''Sure you do. The little black number you wore to the auction. And you need to go because it will be good for business. I'm sure there'll be quite a few bigwigs there for a little practical schmoozing.''

She sent Tess a semidirty look. ''If you're so gung-ho, then why don't you go schmooze?''

Tess let loose a grating laugh. ''Oh, yeah. I'm sure I'd make quite an impression.'' She pulled a stray piece of hay from Andi's hair. ''If you get cleaned up, you'll fit right in. Of course, I'll need to cut up some cucumbers for your eyes so you can get rid of those duffel bags underneath.''

Andi's fingertips automatically went to the bags in question. ''They're not that bad.''

''No, not too bad, but it's obvious to me you haven't been sleeping.''

No, she hadn't been, not much. She'd stayed awake at night for hours, but she hadn't been alone. Sam still stalked her mind and even her dreams when she finally did nod off. Several times she'd awakened and reached for him as if she couldn't quite register he was really gone. But he was gone, and she needed to move on with her life as she'd been told time and again by everyone she loved. Although she had no desire to meet a man at the moment, she probably should attend the reception for the business's sake.

''Okay, I'll go.'' Andi released a long, weary sigh. ''But I'm not going to stay long. I want to be here to put Chance to bed.''

''I'll put him to bed,'' Tess stated firmly. ''You go and have a good time.''

Mingling with money didn't sound like a good time at all. "I'll be home by ten."

"Okay, but I won't wait up just in case the new owner is some high-falutin' unmarried hunk."

"He's probably some overindulged, married drunk."

Tess chuckled as she left the kitchen, and Andi already regretted the decision.

Oh, well. She'd just get lost in the crowd.

There was absolutely no one around.

Maybe everyone had parked behind the massive barn, Andi thought as she pulled up behind the truck stationed in the driveway—the same shiny, extended-cab-with-all-the-options truck Donny Masters had been driving that morning.

Confused and concerned, Andi opened the glove compartment and retrieved the invitation. The date was correct and so was the time, only Andi had decided to arrive a half hour later to shorten the duration. Surely the party hadn't been so dull that everyone had taken their leave early. Or maybe no one had bothered to show. Not likely.

But if that were the case, she'd simply march up to the door, introduce herself to the new owners, maybe have a drink, then be on her merry way.

Andi opened the door and slid from the truck, cursing the tight black dress until her feet hit the ground. How she hated this kind of thing. Hated having to get all fixed up for the sake of some strangers.

When she entered the walkway leading to the front door of the sprawling stone house, a series of tiny lights lining the hedge snapped on. Very impressive, Andi thought as she stepped up onto the front porch.

After taking a deep breath, she pushed the bell, worried when she didn't hear any noise coming from inside. No muffled conversations. Not even any music. More than likely she had been correct in her assumptions that either the guests were gone, or they had never come in the first place. Or it could be the party was in the arena. If so, surely some kind soul would direct her to the festivities.

Soft footfalls signaled someone was about to answer her summons. The door opened to a petite woman—obviously a maid—wearing a neat, black uniform and functional shoes. Andi coveted those shoes at the moment, considering she now wore the hated high heels.

"Welcome," the woman said in a voice as soft as her gray eyes. "We're glad you could join us, Miss Hamilton."

She knew her name? Obviously the owners had done their homework, whoever they were. Andi decided to let the introductions unfold naturally. "Thank you. I very much appreciate the invitation." And she very much wanted to get this over with and get out of there.

Once inside, Andi studied the lengthy corridor with awe as she followed behind the maid. The polished Italian tile beneath her feet and the ornate chandeliers above her head shouted big bucks. And so did the massive room that she entered, a room filled with fine furniture and tasteful treasures set about the room. A room that was completely deserted otherwise.

"Is the party in the stable?" Andi asked when she saw no sign of food or drink.

The woman only smiled. "He will be with you shortly to answer any questions you might have."

"He who?" Andi asked, totally baffled.

"The master of the house, of course." With that she disappeared.

The maid obviously had vagueness down to a fine art, and this was just a little too weird, in Andi's opinion. Her first instinct told her to get out. Her second involved blatant curiosity.

Although she really didn't sense she was in imminent danger, Andi shot a glance over her shoulder, making sure the path to the door was clear should she have to make a hasty escape. In the meantime she opted to do a little exploring around the area in search of some clue that might indicate who the mysterious "he" might be. Her gaze immediately traveled to the paned window to her right, or more accurately the glittering mobile that hung between the heavy parted curtains.

When she moved closer, she noted the individual crystals were replicas of planets flanked by tiny shimmering stars. Of course, she thought. Galaxy Farms. Very clever.

Unable to resist, Andi reached out and touched the tiny diamond-like stars, setting the mobile in motion. The gentle sway shot beams of color around the immediate area. Absolutely breathtaking, Andi thought. At least the mysterious owner had good taste, whoever he was.

"Are you still so fascinated with the stars, Andrea?"

Ten

Her hand froze midair at the sound of the familiar voice. The deep, endearing voice forever engrained in her memory, in her heart.

Andi shuddered, and a soft keening ring filtered into her ears. No way could this be happening again. Her mind was playing nasty tricks on her, playing havoc with her pulse. She was totally losing it. Sam had left. Gone for good. Forever.

But the reference to the stars…

Unable to turn around, she visually searched the room for some sign that she wasn't totally nuts. Something that would indicate she hadn't completely lost her grip on reality.

Then she saw it.

On a nearby oak table sat a photograph of a beautiful little boy, his adoring mother and dark, handsome father, holding on fast to each other. To any casual observer, they would appear to be any happy family. The family Andi had always wished for, and still did.

She closed her eyes and inhaled deeply, immediately drawing in the familiar, welcome scent of the man whom she'd said goodbye to six days ago. Six long, torture-filled days.

"You did not answer my question, Andrea."

How could she answer his question when she couldn't begin to speak? How could she just stand there and not turn around to verify this was real?

His fingertips skimmed down her arm, and she shivered as if she were totally exposed. In some ways she was, laid emotionally bare once again because of his unexpected return.

"I think I must be dreaming at the moment." Her voice sounded broken, unsure. Hopeful.

His warm breath fanned across her neck and cheek. "This is no dream, Andrea."

Finally she turned around and met his dark, dark eyes. "What are you doing here, Sam?"

He showed a hint of a smile. "I am the new owner."

Too surreal, she thought. Too, too surreal. "You're telling me you've bought this place?" Suddenly it was all too apparent that this was Sam's money and means at work. Sam's way of trying to provide for her without asking. More than likely, he wasn't back to stay. "If you think Chance and I are going to live here, then you—"

He held a fingertip against her lips to silence her. "I do hope you and Chance will decide to live here."

"We already have a place to live, so we'll do no such thing—"

"With me."

"With—" she swallowed hard "—you?"

He slid his knuckles along her jaw in a slow, heavenly rhythm. Andi wanted to close her eyes but feared if she did, he would evaporate into thin air. "Of course we will keep your father's place for Tess and Mr. Parker, and then our son if he so chooses to live there."

Andi blinked once, twice. "I don't understand."

"It is very simple, Andrea. I've realized that my place is here with you and our son."

How long had she waited to hear that? "But what about your duty?"

"My duty lies in my responsibility to you and to Chance. Admittedly it took me some time to realize this, but now that I have, I am hoping you will trust that I intend to stay. Always."

Oh, how Andi wanted to believe him, but it was simply too good to be true. "You'll have divided loyalties, Sam. You'll miss your family."

He circled his arms around her waist and pulled her to him. "You are my family now, Andrea. The rest will work itself out in due time."

"Are you sure, Sam? Are you really sure this is what you want to do? Be with us, day in and day out? No one waiting on you hand and foot, just your average, everyday work?" Another thought crossed her mind. "What would you do here?"

"Other than work very hard to make you happy, I would establish this place as a premiere training facility. With your expertise and my eye for fine stock, we could be very successful.''

Regardless of her caution, Andi couldn't contain her excitement. ''Do you think maybe we could consider breeding?''

Sam grinned. ''I would propose we put that at the top of the list.''

She pinched his side. ''I meant horses.''

''I suppose we could breed those, as well.'' He brushed a chaste kiss across her lips. ''Then you are considering my suggestions?''

How easy it would be to say yes. How very, very easy. After all, wasn't this what she had dreamed about for so long? Sam returning, for good. If it was, in fact, for good.

She moved back, putting some distance between them in order to reclaim her emotional bearings. ''The past few days I've ached to have you back, but I was getting by, the same as I did when you left the first time. But if you ever decided to leave again, I'm not sure if I would survive it the next time.''

''There will be no next time.''

He sounded so sincere, but one very important question still hounded her. ''What about the woman you're supposed to marry?''

''I have spoken with her, and she is very much relieved. It seems she has fallen in love with another man. I am pleased by that fact.''

So was Andi, but she still had more questions. ''And your parents? What do they think about you staying in America?''

He sighed. ''My father has not taken the news well. My mother is somewhat saddened by my decision, yet she told me she knew that when I was born in America, a significant part of my being would always remain in this country.''

Andi realized there were still many things she didn't know about him. ''Are you saying you have dual citizenship?''

''Technically, yes. My parents were traveling in the states on a diplomatic mission, visiting with various governors. My mother insisted on accompanying my father despite the fact she was only a few weeks away from delivery. I chose to arrive early on American soil. That is the reason I attended university here, to experience this place, this life.''

''But you've always preferred your father's country.''

''I've always considered it my country, regardless of where I was born. If my father sees fit, I will visit there often, with you and Chance. But I consider my true home to be with you and my son.''

He seemed so convincing, every plan so well thought out. Then why was she still so scared?

As if sensing her reticence, Sam reverently touched her face and searched her eyes. ''Trust me, Andrea. I give you my word that I will never leave you again. Never.''

''Do you promise?''

''With all that I am.''

This time Andrea's heart told her that he meant what he'd said. This time she decided to listen.

She opened her arms and smiled through joyful tears. ''Welcome home, Sam.''

In a sudden explosion of passion, he kissed her with a fervor that momentarily deprived her of the ability to breathe, to think. She didn't want to think. She didn't want to do anything but be with him, to prove that this was real, the offer of a home and his love. That he was real.

"Come with me," he whispered softly and took her hand. She followed as if she had no will of her own, and that somehow seemed appropriate. Having strength of will seemed unnecessary. Following Sam to wherever he might lead her took priority over protest at the moment.

They walked through another long hallway and to an atrium filled with myriad plants at the rear of the house. One wall of windows provided a view of a large yard with a fountain illuminated in blue. Sam guided her to a plush chaise longue wide enough for two people. Once they'd settled on the edge, Andi turned her face to the glass ceiling that revealed a blanket of stars.

"This is so beautiful, Sam."

"Our very own place under the heavens," he said in a deep, sensual voice. "A place where we can make love regardless of the weather."

She regarded him with a smile. "What? And give up the pond? We can't do that. I'd miss getting eaten alive by bugs."

He laughed. "That I will not miss at all, but I see no reason not to visit there for the sake of remembrance." Suddenly serious, he caught her hands and held them against his pounding heart. "You honor me by your presence alone, yet I would be more honored if you would agree to be my wife."

Wife. That one word staggered her soul, set her mind to reeling. She had always said she had no use for being anyone's wife, and all along she had been lying to herself. She'd only wanted to be Sam's wife, his life partner. Although she wanted to cry out *yes!* she didn't. Not yet.

Leaning closer, she tickled his ear with the tip of her tongue. "Where's the maid?"

"She took her leave soon after she greeted you, as instructed."

"Good, because I'd really like you to convince me that agreeing to your proposal would be worth my while."

He smiled a beautiful, endearing smile. "I see that you are determined to be obstinate."

She slipped the first button on his nice white shirt that now sported a nice pink lip print on the collar. She'd always wanted to do that, and she planned to do much more. "I'm determined all right, but it has nothing to do with being obstinate, as you will soon find out."

"So be it." He attempted to turn off the nearby floor lamp and she stopped him.

"No," she said adamantly. "No darkness this time, Sam. I want to see you in the light. Every detail."

He reached behind her and slid the zipper down on her dress, his ragged respiration echoing in the room. "Anything you wish, Andrea. Anything at all. You only have to tell me and I will do whatever you ask. Tonight I am yours for the taking. Every night from this point forward, if you so desire."

She desired to sleep with him every night, to wake with him every day, to work with him not only to build a successful business but also to make a secure, loving home for their son. For the remainder of her life.

But tonight she wanted once again to concentrate on showing Sam how much she loved him.

After undressing in a rush, they stretched out on the chaise facing each other. The mutual exploration began with tender touches and ended with fevered caresses. They took turns pleasing each other, committing to memory every detail with hungry hands. Then touches gave way to intimate kisses, leaving no parts of their bodies unexplored.

Feeling bold and brave, Andi nudged Sam onto his back and straddled his thighs, intending to take control over the situation. But awareness of what they needed to do suddenly hit her.

"Do you have any protection, Sam?" she asked.

He clasped her hips in his large hands and inched her forward, very close to dangerous territory. "Will you think I am insane if I ask that we do not consider that tonight?"

"You mean—"

"That I want nothing between us, but only if you are in agreement."

"But I could—"

"Become pregnant again. I know." He cupped the back of her head and brought her forward, then kissed her thoroughly before saying, "Nothing would please me more than to have another child with you. One that I would know from the beginning."

The ultimate proof of his commitment, Andi decided. He would never leave her alone to raise another child, this much she knew. He would never abandon her this time.

Instead of responding with words, she lifted her hips and slowly lowered herself onto him. They kept their gazes locked as well as their bodies as they moved in sync.

It seemed as if they had never made love before, at least to Andi. Every sensation as Sam moved smoothly inside her seemed new, untried. Every passionate word he spoke to her seemed as if she were hearing it for the first time.

Watching his face and knowing her own reflected the same pleasure he enjoyed at this moment only heightened her desire, solidified her love for him.

When neither could hold out any longer, they came apart in each other's arms. Came together in one act of love that would always be beyond compare.

After Andi collapsed against Sam's chest, he told her, "You have yet to give me an answer."

Andi rolled to her side to face him. "I'm thinking we have someone else to ask first."

He raised a dark brow. "Our son?"

"Yes, although I can't imagine he'd put up a fuss once we tell him you're his father."

"I am very much looking forward to that moment."

Andi tucked her head beneath his chin and held him tightly. "In the morning."

"I'd prefer to tell him tonight."

She raised her head and stared in surprise. "Tonight?"

He cupped her breast in his hand. "In a while. I fear that I still have more convincing to do."

Andi wriggled against him, eliciting a groan from Sam. "I believe you do, at that."

* * *

By the time they reached the farm, it was nearing 11:00 p.m. Sam realized that his son could very well be in bed, but he hadn't been able to keep his hands off Andrea, nor had she put up much protest.

Fortunately, the lights still burned bright from the kitchen window as they made their way to the entrance. Once they arrived on the top step, Andrea stopped him from opening the door. "Wait just a sec, okay? I want to have some fun."

He cupped her bottom and pulled her to him, amazed that he was again aroused after such a brief time. Yet he probably shouldn't be amazed at all. Andrea was capable of keeping him in such a state both day and night. "Are you not afraid that Tess might see us?"

She batted at his hand. "Not that kind of fun. I want to play this up with Tess. Boy, will she ever be surprised."

No, she would not, but Sam decided against revealing that fact.

Andrea opened the door, and he glimpsed Tess and Riley Parker seated at the table.

"Hey, you two," Andrea said. "I'd like you to meet the new owner of Galaxy Farms."

Grabbing Sam's hand, she pulled him forward. Tess and Riley did not bother to appear the least bit shocked, as he'd expected.

"Howdy, Sam," Riley said. "Nice night out, ain't it?"

"Real nice," Tess said with a vibrant grin.

Andrea glanced at Sam, then at the couple, before

affording him a stern, suspicious stare. "These two knew about it all along, didn't they?"

"Now don't get your tail in a wringer, Andi," Tess said. "If Sam hadn't told me about his little plan, I wouldn't have tried so hard to convince you to go tonight."

Andrea's mouth opened, no doubt to deliver a protest. "That was not even nice."

"But necessary," Tess stated.

In hopes of calming her down, Sam wrapped his arms around Andrea from behind and pulled her against him. "I will make it up to you in some manner."

"You can bet on that, buster," she muttered, a smile in her voice.

Feeling greatly relieved, he addressed Tess once more. "Has our son already retired?"

Tess nodded toward the hall. "I just tucked him in. I would've told him he might be getting a surprise tonight but I wasn't sure what our girl here was going to do."

Sam was still uncertain since she had yet to give him a solid answer to his marriage proposal. "Do you think he is still awake?"

"Probably so," Riley said. "I imagine he's countin' his fortune. The kid took all my pennies during poker. He's a regular little card shark."

"Even if he's not awake," Tess said, "you need to get him up. He wouldn't want to miss this."

Andrea glanced back at Sam. "She's right, as bad as I hate to admit it."

Sam gestured toward the stairs. "Lead the way."

On the upper floor Andi pushed open the door to

Chance's room. The light from the hall spilled across his son's small body turned toward the wall. Andrea perched on the mattress, snapped on the bedside lamp and gently shook his shoulder. "Chance, sweetie, are you awake?"

"I am now," came a sleepy and somewhat irritable voice. He turned over and rubbed his eyes. "What's up, Mama?"

"You have a visitor."

"Can't be Santa 'cause it's not Christmas." He raised his head and when his gaze met Sam's, a bright smile illuminated his face. He sat up in a rush. "Sam! You came back."

Sam sat on the other side of his son. "Yes, I have returned."

Chance's grin reflected his joy. "I knew you would. Every night I said my prayers and asked for you to come back. I also asked Uncle Paul in case he and God are good friends."

Andrea touched his cheek. "I'm sure they are, honey. Your uncle Paul was always a good friend."

"The best," Sam said in earnest. He felt assured that Paul would very much approve of his love for Andrea and would gladly bless their union, if Andrea acquiesced. He would know in a matter of minutes.

Andrea sent a nervous glance at Sam, then turned her attention to Chance. "We have something very important to tell you, sweetie. Something I hope you will understand."

"What is it?" he asked.

"Well, Sam isn't just a friend. He's your—"

"Father." His knowing smile expanded. "I know,

Mama. I bet Billy Reyna that Sam was my real dad back when we were at camp.''

Sam took a moment to recover his voice. Obviously, they had been wrong to underestimate their son's intuitiveness. ''You have known all along, then?''

He nodded his head with a jerk. ''Sure did. But how come you two waited so long to tell me?''

''It's kind of complicated, Chance,'' Andrea said.

Sam took Chance's hand into his. ''We waited until the moment was right, until I knew for certain that I would be able to stay with you forever.''

Chance's eyes widened. ''Then you are going to stay?''

''Yes, I am. If that is favorable to you and your mother.''

He looked at Andrea. ''It's okay, isn't it, Mama?''

''More than okay. And one more thing.'' She looked lovingly at Sam. ''Your father would like me to marry him so that we can be a family.''

Chance hopped feetfirst onto the bed and released an ear-piercing ''Whoopie!''

Andrea tugged him back to her side. ''I guess that's a yes.''

''Yep, it is.'' Chance frowned. ''As long as you don't kiss and do a lot of that mushy stuff.''

''We'll try to restrain ourselves,'' Andrea said, then laughed. ''At least when you're around.''

Overcome with joy, with love, Sam pulled Chance to his side. ''I am grateful that you understand, my son.''

Awareness dawned in his child's joyous expression. ''Can I call you Daddy now?''

"It would be my fondest wish for you to do so."

Chance pulled him into a voracious hug. "I'm really glad you're back, Daddy."

Sam's heart took flight over that one simple word. "As I am glad to be back."

"Can I go to sleep now?" Chance said through a yawn. "I wanna get up early and call Billy."

Andrea ruffled his hair and kissed his forehead. "Of course. Sweet dreams and see you in the morning."

"Will you be here in the morning, Daddy?"

"Yes, and every morning from this point forward."

Epilogue

From this day forward. How very sweet to have had those words included in their vows, Andi thought as she and Sam arrived hand in hand at the reception in their new home.

She had been so nervous during the wedding, not because of the ceremony itself, just a simple gathering at a nearby wedding chapel. It seemed she'd been waiting a lifetime for the moment when she and Sam were truly together. Her apprehension resulted from the prospect of meeting Sam's family, but only his mother and Sam's brother Omar and his two children came. Now expecting another child, Omar's wife had stayed behind. And Sam's father had refused to join them.

Andi had been shocked to learn that anyone in the family had agreed to come. If only they'd had the opportunity to spend some time together beforehand, then Andi might not be so shaky. But as it had turned out, the royal family hadn't arrived in time for the wedding.

Even though she'd asked Sam a lot of questions about his culture, Andi wasn't sure how she was supposed to act, what she was supposed to say. After all, she was entering a different world. Sam's world. Never before had she shied away from a challenge, but she wanted so badly to please them for Sam's sake.

Sam gave Andi's hand a reassuring squeeze as they paused in the hallway. "You need only be yourself," he said as if he'd read her thoughts.

"I hope that's good enough," Andi said through a forced smile.

He brushed a kiss across her cheek. "Always know that you are the best in my eyes."

Andi took comfort in his words and her anxiety lessened somewhat—until they entered the tent set up outside the atrium. The moment of judgment had arrived, and she sure hoped Sam's family didn't find her lacking. No matter, she decided. She would always have her own little family.

The makeshift ballroom glistened with twinkling white lights crisscrossed on the ceiling, providing the only illumination aside from candles set out on the round tables. Along the perimeter of the tent's walls, banquet tables brimmed with every food imaginable. Main courses on one side, canapés and desserts on the other. At the front of the tent a huge cake draped with lilac flowers flanked a fountain flowing with champagne. And near the chocolate groom's cake sporting a baseball in the center, sat a photo of a smiling young man, the very man who had been responsible for this union.

"Thank you, Paulie," Andi whispered, followed by a smile. Although he wasn't physically present, Andi had no doubt that her brother was looking on from his position among the stars and probably saying, "Poor Sam. Now he has to put up with you."

"It's about time you two got here. I thought you'd stopped somewhere to start the honeymoon." Several people looked up from the feasting over Tess's rather loud greeting.

Blazing heat crept up Andi's face as Sam nudged her forward into the middle of the crowd composed of community leaders, clients and family. Yet Andi couldn't see anyone that she thought to be Sam's mother among the masses, but she had glimpsed her son running about with two beautiful olive-skinned children that she assumed could be Sam's niece and nephew. Chance continued to be totally oblivious to their arrival, and that was okay with Andi. She would visit with him later. Right now she wanted him to get to know his new cousins.

After numerous greetings and good wishes, hugs and happy tidings, Andi followed Sam to the head table and accepted the champagne he offered her. From the corner of her eye, Andi noted a tall, elegant woman wearing a long navy gown, her hair pulled back into a neat chignon. She had no doubt this was Sam's mother. The resemblance was truly remarkable. Nearby stood a man in traditional Arab dress, and Andi assumed this to be Sam's brother.

Sam nudged her forward. "Come. I will introduce you."

After gulping a long drink, Andi allowed Sam to take her elbow and guide her toward the pair. Her heart drummed in her chest with every footstep.

Once they arrived at the place where the strangers now stood, Sam said, "It is my honor to present my wife, Andrea. Andrea, my mother, Amina, and my brother Omar."

Omar gave her a courteous nod, looking somewhat aloof and very much like Sam, aside from a neatly trimmed goatee. On the other hand, Sam's mother smiled, catching Andi off guard. "My son has done very well, I see," she said. "We are very happy to welcome you into the family, Andrea." Her voice was kind, sophisticated and laced with a lyrical accent.

Andi held out her hand that Amina took without hesitation. "I am very happy to be in the family."

Omar's serious expression suddenly melted into a dimpled grin. "I welcome you as well, Andrea. You are to be commended for taming my rogue brother."

Sam looked totally incensed. "You are one to talk, Omar. Had it not been for Sadiiqa's kindness in accepting you as her husband, I have no doubt you would still be jet-setting throughout Europe, bedding every woman—"

"Enough," Amina stated firmly with the hint of another smile. "Do you both wish to have Andrea believe I have raised two hellions?" She laid a dramatic hand on her heart. "Forgive them, Andrea. No matter how many years pass, they are still inclined to behave like young boys."

Andi laughed. "I understand completely." And she did. Years before, Sam and Paul had acted much the same. How wonderful to see it happening again.

Omar gestured across the room. "I believe I must tend to my children since I see that Jassim is unhappy. No doubt a minor crisis has arisen between him and his sister."

"No doubt your daughter has only defended herself," Amina said. "She is as strong as any boy, I am proud to say."

"Obviously you have taught her well, Mother," Sam said in a mock-serious tone. "Omar, would you tell Chance that his mother has summoned him?"

Omar nodded again. "Most certainly."

After Omar took his leave, Amina turned to Andi once more. "I have enjoyed visiting with your aunt. She has shared with me the finer points of Southern cooking, although I am still not certain about the collard greens."

Leave it to Tess to bridge the cultural gap with country cuisine. "If I were you, I wouldn't worry about it. They're not exactly my favorite."

Taking Andi by both hands, Amina stepped back and looked her up and down. "Your dress is simply exquisite."

Andi sneaked a quick glance over her sleeveless satin bridal gown. "It's simple, like me."

Amina released Andi's hands and gently patted her cheek. "There is much beauty in simplicity. One only has to look at the heavens to realize this. The stars are beautiful in their simplicity.''

In that moment Andi felt a true affinity with Sam's mother. Maybe she might fit in after all. ''I couldn't agree more.'' Sam only smiled.

Amina's features turned solemn as she regarded her son. ''Samir, I will not attempt to apologize for your father's absence. I will ask you to be patient.'' She addressed Andi once more. ''He is a somewhat stubborn man, yet he truly loves his family. He sees this as a loss of his child.''

''It does not have to be that way, Mother,'' Sam said adamantly.

She laid a slender hand on Sam's arm. ''I realize this, my beloved son, and he will realize the same eventually. I do hope you can make amends at your brother's wedding in three months' time. You will consider attending?''

Sam frowned. ''What wedding?''

''Jamal's wedding.''

Rubbing his jaw, Sam smiled. ''Ah, so I assume the mystery woman has been revealed.''

Amina glanced away and wrung her hands. ''Yes, she has, and I hope it will please you.''

''Who is this woman?''

''Maila.''

Andi stifled a gasp and Sam looked no less shocked and somewhat angry. ''So Father has replaced me with Jamal. How convenient.''

''You are very wrong, Samir,'' Amina scolded. ''Jamal and Maila are together at their own insistence, without the benefit of an arrangement. It is a love match in every sense of the word.''

''I am glad,'' Sam said sincerely.

And so was Andi. She could greatly appreciate two people falling in love. Sometimes destiny just couldn't be denied.

''Have you told Father about Chance?'' Sam asked.

Andi had wondered if Amina knew that Sam was Chance's father but hadn't asked. She decided that Sam would be the best judge of how to handle that news. Obviously he had handled it.

''I believe it best that he meet his grandson in person,'' Amina said. ''I, too, am waiting for an official introduction. And it seems that moment has arrived.''

In that instant Chance rushed to Andi and grabbed her around the waist. ''That man said you want me, Mama, but I'm playing with these kids from Daddy's country and we're having fun. Can I go back now?''

''Not yet,'' Andi said as she turned Chance around to face Amina. ''First, there's someone we'd like you to meet.''

Amina knelt on Chance's level. ''Chance, I am your *jadda.*''

He wrinkled his nose, a sure sign of his confusion. ''My what?''

''Your grandmother,'' Sam stated. ''My mother.''

Looking as if they'd handed him the world in a basket, Chance grinned. ''For real? I don't have one of those.''

Amina drew him into a quick, heartfelt hug. ''You most certainly have one now, little one.''

Andi half expected Chance to protest another relative referring to him as "little," but he only continued to smile.

"Do you live in my daddy's country?" he asked.

"Yes, I do, and I hope you will come visit one day." She touched his face with maternal reverence. "The children with whom you are playing are your cousins, and their father is your uncle Omar."

Chance glanced back at Andi. "Like Uncle Paul?"

"Yes," she said. "Like Uncle Paul."

"Cool." He looked back at the place where Omar stood with his son and daughter. "Can I go play with my cousins now? I want to take them to the barn to see Sunny."

"Okay, but make sure you go with an adult," Andi said.

"I will go," Amina offered. "But first, who is this Sunny?"

"My horse," Chance said, taking Amina by the hand. "You're going to love her, Grandma. Can I call you Grandma?"

"Oh, most certainly. Did you know you look very much like your father did when…"

As she watched Amina drape her arm around Chance's shoulder, as she observed the children jumping up and down with excitement as they headed away, Andi realized there wasn't so much difference after all. Family was family, regardless of cultural diversity. That diversity made the moments all the more special. After all, love knew no real boundaries.

"Would you care to escape with me for a moment?" Sam whispered.

"I suppose I could for a while," she said. "But

eventually we're going to have to cut that mammoth cake.''

"The cake can wait a few more moments. At present I would like to be alone with my bride.''

Andi followed Sam from the tent and back into the atrium. Once there he turned her into his arms and kissed her, but good—very, very good.

Just when Andi considered saying, To heck with the cake, let's go upstairs, Sam broke the kiss.

"I am losing my control,'' he said, winded.

"Do you hear me objecting?''

"No, but I do believe I heard you moan.''

She playfully slapped at his hand that had somehow landed on her bottom. "I'm sure it won't be the last time tonight.''

"I do wish you had allowed me to take you somewhere for a honeymoon,'' he said.

"You know we can't do that right now. We have to be here for Riley and Tess's wedding next week. I need to get Sunny well underway, not to mention the other ten horses in the barn. Besides, we have a nice big bed upstairs with a huge whirlpool tub in the bathroom. Who could ask for more?''

"I suppose you are right,'' he said, looking too, too somber. "And as it now stands, we should probably be prudent with our funds. I have spent a great deal on this place, and until we begin to see a profit, we will have to rely on what I have left of my own investments since my father has withdrawn his support.''

Andi touched his face. "We have so much now, Sam. We're going to do fine. And I know how badly you hurt over your father's attitude, but I'm inclined to believe your mother. He'll come around.''

"I do most admire your optimism, but I also know my father very well."

"And I never believed we would be together, either.''

Sam caught her hands and kissed each palm. ''Nor did I.''

Andi shrugged. ''Besides, once we see him face-to-face, once he sees how much we love each other, he'll have to believe it was meant to be. And I'm sure he'll be very taken with his charming grandson.''

"On the topic of children, will there be another child in our near future?''

"I hope so,'' Andi said with a smile. ''But not this time.''

"Then you are not—''

"Pregnant. No. At first I was disappointed, then I decided that it will happen when the time is right.'' She pulled him close and couldn't resist executing a little wriggle against one of Sam's finer qualities. ''I'm sure you'll eventually get the job done, and quite sufficiently.''

He tugged at the collar of his tuxedo. ''I believe we shall have a lengthy practice tonight.''

"I'm willing to give for the cause.''

Sam sighed. ''I wish that I could give you everything your heart desires.''

Andi rested her cheek against his chest, against his strong heart. ''You *have* given me everything, Sam. A wonderful home. A family. A beautiful child. But you know what?''

Andi looked into the eyes of her husband and no longer saw any real mystery there. She only saw his love, bold and beautiful beneath the stars that shone above them.

''The best gift you have given me, the greatest gift anyone could ever receive, is your love. Without that, all the gold in the world would mean nothing.''

Softly he kissed her lips. ''How very true, Andrea. How very, very true.''

*   *   *   *   *

DELANEY'S DESERT SHEIKH

BY
BRENDA JACKSON

Brenda Jackson is a die-'heart' romantic who married her childhood sweetheart and still proudly wears the 'going steady' ring he gave her when she was fifteen. Because she's always believed in the power of love, Brenda's stories always have happy endings. In her real-life love story, Brenda and her husband of thirty years live in Jacksonville, Florida, and have two sons at university.

An award-winning author of ten romance titles, Brenda divides her time between family, writing and working in management at a major insurance company. You may write to Brenda at PO Box 28267, Jacksonville, Florida 32226, USA, or visit her website at www.brendajackson. net.

Brenda Jackson has a new Mills & Boon® Desire™ novel, *Quade's Babies*, available in January 2010.

To my husband, Gerald Jackson, Sr – you are my hero.
To my editor, Mavis Allen – you are super!
To my agent, Pattie Steele-Perkins –
once again you have outdone yourself!
To the "Hotties" of the Color of Love Forum.
You ladies know who you are, and this is one author
who truly appreciates your love for steamy romance.
To Martha Shina Bowes – this one is definitely for you!

Two can accomplish more than twice as much as one,
for the results can be much better.
—Ecclesiastes 4:9

One

This was the first time he had been between a pair of legs and not gotten the satisfaction he wanted.

Jamal Ari Yasir drew in a deep, calming breath as he slid his body from underneath the table. Standing, he wiped the sweat from his brow. After an entire hour he still hadn't been able to stop the table from wobbling.

"I'm a sheikh and not a repairman, after all," he said with a degree of frustration, tossing the handyman tools back in the box where they belonged. He had come to the cabin to get some rest, but the only thing he was getting was bored.

And it was only the second day. He had twenty-eight to go.

He wasn't used to doing nothing. In his country a man's worth was measured by what he accomplished each day. Most of his people worked from sunup to sundown, not because they had to, but because they were accustomed to

doing so for the good of Tahran. And although he was the
son of one of the most influential sheikhs in the world, he
had been required from birth to work just as hard as the
people he served.

Over the past three months he had represented his country
as a negotiator in a crucial business deal that also involved
other nations surrounding Tahran. When the proceedings
ended with all parties satisfied, he had felt the need to escape and find solitude to rest his world-weary mind and
body.

The sound of a slamming car door caught Jamal's attention, and he immediately wondered who it could be. He
knew it wasn't Philip, his former college roommate from
Harvard, who had graciously offered him the use of the
cabin. Philip had recently married and was somewhere in
the Caribbean enjoying a two-week honeymoon.

Jamal headed toward the living room, his curiosity
piqued. No one would make the turnoff from the major
highway unless they knew a cabin was there—five miles
back, deep in the woods. Walking over to the window, he
looked out, drawing in a deep breath. Mesmerized. Hyp-
notized. Suddenly consumed with lust of the worst kind.

An African-American woman had gotten out of a late-
model car and was bending over taking something out of
the trunk. All he could see was her backside but that was
enough. He doubted he could handle anything else right
now.

The pair of shorts she wore stretched tightly across the
sexiest bottom he had ever seen—and during his thirty-four
years he had seen plenty. But never like this and never this
generous. And definitely never this well-defined and pro-
portioned. What he was looking at was a great piece of art
with all the right curves and angles.

Without very much effort, he could imagine her backside

pressed against his front as they slept in a spoon position. A smile curved his lips. But who would be able to sleep cuddled next to a body like hers? His gaze moved to her thighs. They were shapely, firm and perfectly contoured.

For an unconscious moment he stood rooted in place, gazing at her through the window. Reason jolted his lust-filled mind when she pulled out one large piece of luggage and a smaller piece. He frowned, then decided he would worry about the implications of the luggage later. He wanted to see the rest of her for now.

No sooner had that thought crossed his mind than she closed the trunk and turned around. It took only a split second for heat to course through his body, and he registered that she was simply gorgeous. Strikingly beautiful.

As she continued to toy with her luggage, his gaze began toying with her, starting at the top. She had curly, dark brown hair that tumbled around her honey-brown face and shoulders, giving her a brazenly sexy look. She had a nicely rounded chin and a beautifully shaped mouth.

He reluctantly moved his gaze away from her mouth and forged a path downward past the smooth column of her throat to her high round breasts, then lower, settling on her great-looking legs.

The woman was one alluring package.

Jamal shook his head, feeling a deep surge of regret that she had obviously come to the wrong cabin. Deciding he had seen enough for one day—not sure his hormones could handle seeing much more—he moved away from the window.

Opening the door he stepped outside onto the porch. He was tempted to ask if he could have his way with her—once, maybe twice—before she left. Instead he leaned in the doorway and inquired in a friendly yet hot-and-bothered voice, "May I help you?"

* * *

Delaney Westmoreland jerked up her head, startled. Her heart began racing as she stared at the man standing on the porch, casually leaning in the doorway. And what a man he was. If any man could be described as beautiful, it would be him. The late-afternoon sun brought out the rich-caramel coloring of his skin, giving true meaning to the description of tall, dark and handsome. Her experience was limited when it came to men, but it didn't take a rocket scientist to know this man was sexy as sin. This man would cause a girl to drool even with a dry mouth.

Amazing.

He was tall, probably six foot three, and was wearing a pair of European-tailored trousers and an expensive-looking white shirt. To her way of thinking he was dressed completely out of sync with his surroundings.

Not that she was complaining, mind you.

His hair, straight black and thick, barely touched the collar of his shirt, and dark piercing eyes that appeared alert and intelligent were trained on her, just as her gaze was trained on him. She blinked once, twice, to make sure he was real. When she was certain that he was, she forced her sanity to return and asked in a level yet slightly strained voice, "Who are you?"

A moment of silence passed between them before he responded. "I should be asking you that question." He moved away from the doorway and stepped off the porch.

Feeling breathless but trying like hell not to show it, Delaney kept her eyes steady as he approached. After all, he was a stranger, and there was a good chance the two of them were all alone in the middle of nowhere. She ignored the foolish part of her mind that said, There's nothing worse than not taking advantage of a good-looking opportunity.

Instead, she gave in to the more cautious side of her mind

and said, "I'm Delaney Westmoreland and you're trespassing on private property."

The sexy-as-sin, make-you-drool man came to a stop in front of her, and when she tipped her head back to look up at him, a warm feeling coiled deep in her stomach. Up close he was even more beautiful.

"And I'm Jamal Ari Yasir. This place is owned by a good friend of mine, and I believe *you're* the one who's trespassing."

Delaney's eyes narrowed. She wondered if he really was a friend of Reggie as he claimed. Had her cousin forgotten he'd loaned this man the cabin when he'd offered it to her? "What's your friend's name?"

"Philip Dunbar."

"Philip Dunbar?" she asked, her voice dropping to a low, sexy timbre.

"Yes, you know him?"

She nodded. "Yes. Philip and my cousin, Reggie, were business partners at one time. Reggie is the one who offered me the use of the cabin. I'd forgotten he and Philip had joint ownership to this place."

"You've been here before?"

"Yes, once before. What about you?"

Jamal shook his head and smiled. "This is my first visit."

His smile made Delaney's breath catch in her throat. And his eyes were trained on her again, watching her closely. She didn't like being under the scope of his penetrating stare. "Do you have to stare at me like that," she snapped.

His right eyebrow went up. "I wasn't aware I was staring."

"Well, you are." Her eyes narrowed at him. "And where are you from, anyway? You don't look American."

His lips lifted into a grin. "I'm not. I'm from the Middle East. A small country called Tahran. Ever heard of it?"

"No, but then geography wasn't my best subject. You speak our language quite well for a foreigner."

He shrugged. "English was one of the subjects I was taught at an early age, and then I came to this country at eighteen to attend Harvard."

"You're a graduate of Harvard?" she asked.

"Yes."

"And what do you do for a living?" she asked, wondering if perhaps he worked in some capacity for the federal government.

Jamal crossed his arms over his chest thinking that western women enjoyed asking a lot of questions. "I help my father take care of my people."

"*Your* people?"

"Yes, *my* people. I'm a sheikh, and the prince of Tahran. My father is the amir."

Delaney knew amir was just another way of referring to a king. "If you're the son of a king then what are you doing here? Although this is a nice place, I'd think as a prince you could do better."

Jamal frowned. "I could if I chose to do so, but Philip offered me the use of this cabin in friendship. It would have been rude of me not to accept, especially since he knew I wanted to be in seclusion for a while. Whenever it's known that I'm in your country, the press usually hounds me. He thought a month here is just what I needed."

"A month?"

"Yes. And how long had you planned to stay?"

"A month, too."

His eyebrow arched. "Well, we both know that being here together is impossible, so I'll be glad to put your luggage back in your car."

Delaney placed her hands on her hips. "And why should I be the one who has to leave?"

"Because I was here first."

He had a point, though it was one she decided not to give him. "But you can afford to go some place else. I can't. Reggie gave me a month of rest and relaxation here as a graduation present."

"A graduation present?"

"Yes. I graduated from medical school last Friday. After eight years of nonstop studying, he thought a month here would do me good."

"Yes, I'm sure that it would have."

Delaney breathed a not-so-quiet sigh when she saw he was going to be difficult. "There's a democratic way to settle this."

"Is there?"

"Yes. Which do you prefer, flipping a coin or pulling straws?"

Her options made his lips twitch into an involuntary smile. "Neither. I suggest that you let me help you put your luggage back in the car."

Delaney drew in a deep, infuriated breath. How dare he think he could tell her what to do. She'd been the only girl with five older brothers and had discovered fairly early in life not to let anyone from the opposite sex push her around. She would handle him the same way she handled them. With complete stubbornness.

Placing her hands on her hips she met his gaze with the Westmoreland glare. "I am not leaving."

He didn't seem at all affected when he said, "Yes, you are."

"No, I'm not."

His jaw suddenly had the look of being chiseled from stone. "In my country women do what they are told."

Delaney flashed him a look of sheer irritation. "Well, welcome to America, *Your Highness*. In this country women have the right to speak their minds. We can even tell a man where to go.''

Jamal's eyebrows shot up in confusion. ''Where to go?''

''Yes, like go fly a kite, go take a leap or go to hell.''

Jamal couldn't help but chuckle. It was apparent Delaney Westmoreland was potently sassy. He had learned that American women didn't hesitate to let you know when they were upset about something. In his country women learned very early in life not to show their emotions. He decided to try another approach, one that would possibly appeal to her intelligence. ''Be reasonable.''

She glared at him, letting him know that approach wasn't going to work. ''I *am* being reasonable, and right now a cabin on a lake for a month, rent free, is more than reasonable. It's a steal, a dream come true, a must have. Besides, you aren't the only one who needs to be in seclusion for a while.''

Delaney immediately thought of her rather large family. Now that she had completed medical school, they assumed she was qualified to diagnose every ache and pain they had. She would never get any rest if they knew where to find her. Her parents knew how to reach her in case of an emergency and that was good enough. She loved her relations dearly but she was due for a break.

''Why are you in seclusion?''

She frowned. ''It's personal.''

Jamal couldn't help wondering if perhaps she was hiding from a jealous lover or even a husband. She wasn't wearing a wedding band, but then he knew from firsthand experience that some American women took off their rings when it suited them. ''Are you married?''

''No, are you?'' she responded crisply.

''Not yet,'' he murmured softly. ''I'm expected to marry before my next birthday.''

"Good for you, now please be a nice prince and take my luggage into the house. If I'm not mistaken, there are three bedrooms and all with connecting bathrooms, so it's plenty big enough and private enough for the both of us. I plan to do a lot of sleeping, so there will be days when you probably won't see me at all."

He stared at her. "And on those days when I do see you?"

Delaney shrugged. "Just pretend that you don't. However, if you find that difficult to do and feel things are getting a little bit too crowded around here to suit you, I'd completely understand if you left." She glanced around the yard. "By the way, where's your car?"

Jamal sighed, wondering how he could get her to leave. "My secretary has it," he responded dryly. "He checked into a motel a few miles away from here, preferring to be close by just in case I needed anything."

Delaney lifted a cool eyebrow. "Must be nice getting the royal treatment."

He ignored her chill and responded. "It has its advantages. Asalum has been with me since the day I was born."

Delaney couldn't help but hear the deep affection in his voice. "Like I said, it must be nice."

"Are you sure you want to stay here?" His tone was slightly challenging as his black eyes held her dark brown ones.

The question, spoken in a deep, sexy voice, gave Delaney pause. No, she wasn't sure, but she knew for certain that she wasn't ready to leave; especially not after driving seven hours straight to get there. Maybe she would feel different after taking a shower and a very long nap.

She met Jamal's dark gaze and almost shuddered under its intensity. A shiver of desire rippled through her. She felt it now, just as she had when she'd first seen him standing on the porch. At twenty-five, she was mature enough to recognize there was such a thing as overactive hormones. But then, she was also mature enough to know how to control them and not yield to temptation. Getting involved with a male chauvinist prince was the last thing she wanted, and she hoped getting involved with her was the last thing he wanted, as well.

She met his gaze and lifted her chin in a defiant stance and said, "I'm staying."

The woman was as stubborn as they came, Jamal thought as he leaned against the doorjamb in the kitchen. He watched Delaney as she unpacked the groceries she had brought with her. When she finished she turned around. "Thanks for bringing in my luggage and those boxes."

He nodded as his gaze held hers. Once again he felt that sudden surge of lust that made his body tighten and knew she had noticed his reaction. Nervously she licked her lips as she dragged her eyes away from his. It was obvious that she was also aware of the strong sexual chemistry arcing between them.

"If you're having second thoughts about staying…"

Her eyes filled with the fire he was getting used to. "Forget it."

"Remember it was your decision," he said evenly.

"I'll remember." She walked over to him and glared up at him. "And I would suggest that you don't get any ideas about trying to do anything underhanded to run me off. I'll leave when I get ready to leave and not before."

Jamal thought that the angrier she got the more beautiful she became. "I'm too much of a gentleman to behave in such a manner."

"Good. I'll take your word on that." She turned to leave the room.

He watched the sway of Delaney's hips until she was no longer in sight. His nostrils flared in response to the enticing feminine scent she had left behind, and the primitive sultan male in him released a low growl.

One thing was for certain, he would not be getting bored again anytime soon.

With a soul-weary sigh, Delaney ran her fingers through her hair and leaned against the closed bedroom door. A jolt of heat ripped from the tip of her painted toes all the way to the crown of her head. Jamal's gaze had been hot and hungry.

What had she gotten herself into?

The thought that she was actually willing to share a cabin with a man she didn't know was plain ludicrous. The only thing to her credit was the fact that while he had been outside getting the boxes out of the car, she had used her cell phone to call Reggie.

Born the same year, she and Reggie had forged a closeness from the time they had been babies, and over the years he had become more than just a cousin. He was sort of like her best buddy.

He had always kept her secrets, and she had always kept his. Since his interest had been in working with numbers, no one was surprised when he had established an accounting firm a few years ago after earning a graduate degree in Business Administration from Morehouse College.

After apologizing for the mix-up, Reggie had assured her that Jamal was legit. He had met him through Philip a few years ago. Reggie further verified Jamal's claim that he was a prince and had gone on to warn her that according to Philip, Jamal had very little tolerance for Western women.

She had ended the conversation with Reggie, thinking that she couldn't care less about the man's tolerance level, and had no intention of letting him dictate whether or not she would stay. She deserved thirty days to rest and do nothing, and by golly, come hell or high water, she planned to enjoy her vacation.

Crossing the room, she plopped down onto a reclining chair. She glanced at the luggage on her bed, too tired to unpack just yet. Putting up the groceries had taken everything out of her. Jamal had stood there the entire time watching her.

Although he hadn't said anything, she had felt his gaze as if it had been a personal caress. And a few times she had actually looked across the room and caught him staring. No, *glaring* was more like it.

She knew his intent had been to try to unnerve her. But as far as she was concerned, he had a long way to go to ruffle her feathers. The Westmoreland brothers—Dare, Thorn, Stone, Chase, and Storm—made dealing with someone like Jamal a piece of cake.

Her cheeks grew warm when she imagined that he was probably just as tasty as a piece of cake. Utterly delicious. A mouthwatering delight. Even now her body felt the heat. He had evoked within her the most intense physical reaction and attraction to a man she had ever experienced.

She shook her head, deciding she definitely needed to take a cool shower and not get tempted.

No matter how crazy her body was acting, she didn't need a man. What she needed was sleep.

Two

Delaney stood in the kitchen doorway and stared for a long moment at the masculine legs sticking out from underneath the kitchen table. Nice, she thought, studying the firmness of male thighs clad in a pair of immaculately pressed jeans.

Since arriving four days ago, this was only her third time seeing Jamal. Just as she'd told him that first day, she intended to get the sleep she deserved. Other than waking up occasionally to grab something to eat, she had remained in her bedroom sleeping like a baby.

Except for that one time he had awakened her, making a racket outside her bedroom window while practicing some type of martial art. She had forced her body from the bed and gone to the window to see what the heck was going on.

Through the clear pane she'd watched him. He'd been wearing a sweat top and a pair of satin boxing trunks that were expertly tailored for a snug fit.

She'd watched, mesmerized, as he put his body through a series of strenuous standing-jump kicks and punches. She admired such tremendous vitality, discipline and power. She had also admired his body, which showed an abundance of masculine strength. For the longest time she had stood at the window rooted in place, undetected, while she ogled him. A woman could only take a man like Jamal in slow degrees.

Deciding that if she didn't move away from the window she would surely die a slow and painful death from lust overload, she had made her way back to the bed and nearly collapsed.

"Dammit!"

Jamal's outburst got her attention and brought her thoughts back to the present. She couldn't help but smile. No matter how well he mastered the English language, a curse word coming from him didn't sound quite the same as it did coming from an American. Her brothers had a tendency to use that particular word with a lot more flair.

She walked over to the table and glanced down. "Need help?"

At first he froze in place, evidently surprised by her presence. "No, I can manage," was his tart reply.

"You're sure?"

"Positive," he all but snapped.

"Suit yourself," she snapped back. She turned and walked over to the kitchen cabinet to get a bowl for the cereal she had brought with her, ignoring the fact that he had slid from underneath the table and was standing up.

"So, what got you up this morning?" he asked, tossing the tools he'd been using in a box.

"Hunger." She put cereal into her bowl, then poured on the milk. Seeing the kitchen table was not available for her to use, she grabbed the cereal box and a spoon and went outside onto the porch.

Already the morning was hot and she knew it would get hotter, typical for a North Carolina summer. She was glad the inside of the cabin had air-conditioning. This was sweaty, sticky heat, the kind that made you want to walk around naked.

Her brothers would be scandalized if they knew she'd done that on occasion when it got hot enough at her home, which was one of the advantages of living alone. She released a deep sigh as she sat down on the steps thinking that with Jamal sharing the cabin walking around naked wasn't an option.

She had taken a mouthful of her cereal when she heard the screen door opening behind her. The knowledge that Jamal was out on the porch and standing just a few feet behind her sent every instinct and conscious thought she had into overdrive. Out of the corner of her eye she saw him lean against the porch rail with a cup of coffee in his hand.

"You've given up moonlighting as a repairman already, *Your Highness?*" she asked in a snippy voice, dripping with sarcasm.

He evidently decided to take her taunt in stride and replied, "For now, yes, but I intend to find out what's wrong with that table and fix it before I leave here. I would hate to leave behind anything broken."

Delaney glanced over at him then wished she hadn't. It seemed his entire face, dark and stunning, shone in the morning sunlight. If she thought he'd been classically beautiful and had dressed out of sync four days ago, then today he had done a complete turnaround. Shirtless, unshaven and wearing jeans, he looked untamed and rugged and no longer like a wolf in sheep's clothing. He looked every bit a wolf, wild and rapacious and on the prowl. If given the chance he would probably eat her alive and lick his chops afterward.

There was nothing in the way he looked to denote he was connected to royalty, a prince, a sheikh. Instead what she saw was an extremely handsome man with solid muscles and a body that exuded sheer masculinity.

He lowered his head to take a sip of his coffee, and she used that time to continue to study him undetected. Now that he was standing, she could see the full frontal view. His jeans were a tight fit and seemed to have been made just for his body. Probably had since he could afford a private tailor. And even if she hadn't seen him doing kickboxing, it would be quite obvious that he kept in shape with his wide, muscular shoulders, trim waistline and narrow hips.

She imagined having the opportunity to peel those jeans off him just long enough to wrap her legs tight around his waist. And then there was his naked chest. A chest her hand was just itching to touch. She was dying to feel whether his muscles were as hard as they looked.

Delaney's heart began pounding. She couldn't believe she was thinking such things. She was really beginning to lose it. Incredible. Nothing like this had ever happened to her before. She couldn't think of one single man in all her twenty-five years who had made her feel so wanton, so greedy, so…needy.

The only need she had experienced with the guys she had taken the time to date in college and medical school had been the need to bring the date to a quick end. And her only greed had been for food, especially her mother's mouthwatering strawberry pie.

No longer wanting to dwell on her sex life—or lack of— she racked her brain, trying to remember the question she had intended to ask Jamal a few minutes earlier. The same brain that had helped her to graduate at the top of her class just last week had turned to mush. She collected her scattered thoughts and remembered the question. ''What's wrong with the table?''

He raised his head and looked at her as if she was dense. ''It's broken.''

She glared at him. ''That much is obvious. How is it broken?''

He shrugged. ''I have no idea. It wobbles.''

Delaney raised her eyes heavenward. ''Is that all?''

''A table is not supposed to wobble, Delaney.''

And I shouldn't be getting turned on from the way you just said my name, she thought, turning her attention away from him and back to her food. That was the first time he had called her by name, and her body was experiencing an intense reaction to it. His tone of voice had been low and husky.

Her eyes stayed glued to her cereal box as she ate, thinking that her fixation with Tony the Tiger was a lot safer than her fascination with Jamal the Wolf. The last thing she needed was a complication in her life, and she had a feeling that getting involved with Jamal would definitely rank high on the Don't Do list. She had no doubt he was a master at seduction. He looked the part and she was smart enough to know he was way out of her league.

Satisfied that she was still in control of her tumultuous emotions, at least for the time being, Delaney smiled to herself as she continued to eat her cereal.

Releasing a deep sigh, Jamal commanded his body to take control of the desire racing through it. Ever since he had begun business negotiations with the country surrounding Tahran for a vital piece of land lying between them, he had been celibate, denying his body and freeing his mind to totally concentrate on doing what was in the best interest of his country. But now that the negotiations were over, his body was reminding him it had a need that was long overdue.

He scolded himself for his weakness and tried to ignore the sexual urges gripping him. If he had returned home after Philip's wedding instead of taking his friend up on his offer to spend an entire month at this cabin, he would not be going through this torment.

In Tahran there were women readily available for him— women who thought it a privilege as well as an honor to take care of their prince's needs. They would come to his apartment, which was located in his own private section of the palace, and pleasure him any way he wanted. It had always been that way since his eighteenth birthday.

There was also Najeen, the woman who had been his mistress for the past three years. She was trained in the art of pleasing only him and did an excellent job of it. He had provided her with her own lavish cottage on the grounds not far from the palace, as well as personal servants to see to her every need. At no time had he ever craved a woman. *Until now.*

"Tell me about your homeland, Jamal."

Jamal arched a brow, surprised at Delaney's request. He shifted his gaze from his cup of coffee and back to her. Her honey-brown face glowed in the sunlight, making her appear radiant, golden. She wasn't wearing any makeup, so her beauty was natural, awe-inspiring. He swallowed hard and tried once again to ignore the urgent need pounding inside him, signals of desire racing through his body.

"What do you want to know?" he asked with a huskiness he almost didn't recognize.

Delaney placed her empty bowl aside and leaned back

on both hands as she looked at him. "Anything you want to tell me. It must be an interesting place to live."

He chuckled at the curiosity in her voice, then stared down at her for several moments before he began speaking. "Yes, interesting," he said slowly, "and quite beautiful." She couldn't know that he had just referred to his country…as well as to her.

Fighting for total control, he continued. "Tahran is located not far from Saudi Arabia, close to the Persian Gulf. It's a relatively small country compared to others close to it like Kuwait and Oman. Our summers are intensely hot and our winters are cool and short. And unlike most places in the Middle East, we get our share of rain. Our natural resources in addition to oil are fish, shrimp and natural gas. For the past few years my people have lived in peace and harmony with our neighbors. Once in a while disagreements flare up, but when that happens a special regional coalition resolves any disputed issues. I am one of the youngest members of that coalition."

"Are both your parents still living?"

Jamal took another sip of his coffee before answering. "My mother died when I was born and for many years my father and I lived alone with just the servants. Then Fatimah entered our lives."

"Fatimah?"

"Yes, my stepmother. She married my father when I was twelve." Jamal decided not to mention that his parents' marriage had been prearranged by their families to bring peace to two warring nations. His mother had been an African princess of Berber descent, and his father, an Arab prince. There had been no love between them, just duty, and he had been the only child born from that union. Then one day his father brought Fatimah home and their lives hadn't been the same.

His father's marriage to Fatimah was supposed to have been like his first marriage, one of duty and not love. But it had been evident with everyone from the start that the twenty-two-year-old Egyptian beauty had other plans for her forty-six-year-old husband. And it also became apparent to everyone in the palace that Fatimah was doing more for King Yasir than satisfying his loneliness and his physical needs in the bedroom. Their king was smiling. He was happy and he didn't travel outside his sheikhdom as often.

King Yasir no longer sent for other women to pleasure him, bestowing that task solely upon his wife. Then, within a year of their marriage, they had a child, a daughter they named Arielle. Three years later another daughter was born. They named her Johari.

Arielle, at nineteen, was now married to Prince Shudoya, a man she had been promised to since birth. Johari, at sixteen, was a handful after having been spoiled and pampered by their father. Jamal smiled, inwardly admitting that he'd had a hand in spoiling and pampering her as well.

He simply adored his stepmother. More than once during his teen years, she had gone to his father on his behalf about issues that had been important to him.

"Do the two of you get along? You and your stepmother?"

Delaney's question invaded his thoughts. "Yes, Fatimah and I are very close."

Delaney stared at him. For some reason she found it hard to imagine him having a "very close" relationship with anyone. "Any siblings?" she decided to ask.

He nodded. "Yes, I have two sisters, Arielle and Johari. Arielle is nineteen and is married to a sheikh in a neighboring sheikhdom, and Johari is sixteen and has just completed her schooling in my country. She wants to come to America to further her studies."

"Will she?"

He looked at her like she had gone stone mad. "Of course not!"

Delaney stared at him dumbfounded, wondering what he had against his sister being educated in the United States. "Why? You did."

Jamal clenched his jaw. "Yes, but my situation was different."

Delaney lifted her brow. "Different in what way?"

"I'm a man."

"So? What's that supposed to mean?"

"Evidently it means nothing in this country. I have observed more times than I care to count how the men let the women have control."

Delaney narrowed her eyes. "You consider having equal rights as having control?"

"Yes, in a way. Men are supposed to take care of the women. In your country more and more women are being educated to take care of themselves."

"And you see that as a bad thing?"

He gazed at her and remembered her sassiness from the first day and decided the last thing he wanted was to get embroiled in a bitter confrontation with her. He had his beliefs and she had hers. But since she had asked his opinion he would give it to her. "I see it as something that would not be tolerated in my country."

What he didn't add was that the alternative—the one his stepmother used so often and had perfected to an art—was for a woman to wrap herself around her husband's heart so tightly that he would give her the moon if she asked for it.

Taking another sip of coffee, Jamal decided to change the subject and shift the conversation to her. "Tell me about your family," he said, thinking that was a safer topic.

Evidently it's not, he thought when she glared at him.

"My family lives in Atlanta, and I'm the only girl as well as the youngest in the third generation of Westmorelands. And for the longest time my five brothers thought I needed protecting. They gave any guy who came within two feet of me pure hell. By my eighteenth birthday I had yet to have a date, so I finally put a stop to their foolishness."

He smiled. "And how did you do that?"

A wicked grin crossed her face. "Since I never had a social life I ended up with a lot of free time on my hands. So I started doing to them what they were doing to me—interfering in their lives. I suddenly became the nosy, busybody sister. I would deliberately monitor their calls, intentionally call their girlfriends by the wrong name and, more times than I care to count, I would conveniently drop by their places when I knew they had company and were probably right smack in the middle of something immoral."

She chuckled. "In other words, I became the kid sister from hell. It didn't take long for them to stop meddling in my affairs and back off. However, every once in a while they go brain dead and start sticking their noses into my business again. But it doesn't take much for me to remind them to butt out or suffer the consequences if they don't."

Jamal shook his head, having the deepest sympathy for her brothers. "Are any of your brothers married?"

She stared at him, her eyes full of amusement at his question. "Are you kidding? They have too much fun being single. They are players, the card-carrying kind. Alisdare, whom we call Dare, is thirty-five, and the sheriff of College Park, a suburb of Atlanta. Thorn is thirty-four and builds motorcycles as well as races them. Last year he was the only African-American on the circuit. Stone will be celebrating his thirty-second birthday next month. He's an author of action-thriller novels and writes under the pen name of Rock Mason."

She shifted in her seat as she continued. "Chase and Storm are twins but look nothing alike. They are thirty-one. Chase owns a soul-food restaurant and Storm is a fireman."

"With such busy professions, how can they find the time to keep tabs on you?"

She chuckled. "Oh, you would be surprised. They somehow seem to manage."

"Are your parents still living?"

"Yes. They have been together for over thirty-seven years and have a good marriage. However, my mother bought in to my father's philosophy that she was supposed to stay home and take care of him and the kids. But after I left home she found herself with plenty of spare time on her hands and decided to go back to school. Dad wasn't too crazy with the idea but decided to indulge her, anyway, thinking she'd only last a few months. I'm proud to say that she graduated three years ago with a graduate degree in education."

Jamal set his empty coffee cup aside. "For some reason I have a feeling that you influenced your mother's sudden need to educate herself."

Delaney chuckled. "Of course. I've always known she had a brilliant mind—a mind that was being wasted doing nothing but running a house and taking care of her family. You know what they say. A mind is a terrible thing to waste. And why should men have all the advantages while women get stuck at home, barefoot and pregnant?"

Jamal shook his head. He hoped to Allah that Delaney Westmoreland never had the opportunity to visit his country for an extended period of time. She would probably cause a women's rights revolution with her way of thinking.

He stretched his body, tired of the conversation. It was evident that somewhere along the way Delaney had been given too much freedom. What she needed was some man's firm hand of control.

And what he needed was to have his head examined.

Even now his nostrils were absorbing her feminine scent, and it was nearly driving him insane. As she sat on the steps, her drawn-up knees exposed a lot of bare thigh that the shorts she was wearing didn't hide.

"Do you have female doctors in your country?"

He looked at her when her question pulled him back into the conversation. It was the same conversation he had convinced himself a few moments ago that he no longer wanted to indulge in. "Yes, we have women that deliver babies."

"That's all they do?" she asked annoyed.

He thought for a second. "Basically, yes."

She glared at him as she pursed her lips. "Your country is worse off than I thought."

"Only you would think so. The people in my country are happy."

She shook her head. "That's sad."

He lifted a brow. "What's sad?"

She drew his gaze. "That you would think they are happy."

Jamal frowned, feeling inordinately annoyed. Had she given him the opportunity, he would have told her that thanks to Fatimah, a highly educated woman herself, things had begun to change. The women in his country were now encouraged to pursue higher education, and several universities had been established for that purpose. And if they so desired, women could seek careers outside of the home. Fatimah was a strong supporter of women enjoying political and social rights in their country, but she was not radical in her push for reform. She simply used her influence over his father to accomplish the changes she supported.

He moved from the rail. It was time to practice his kickboxing, but first he needed to take a walk to relieve the anger consuming his mind and the intense ache that was gripping the lower part of his body. ''I'm going down to the lake for a while. I'll see you later.''

Delaney scooted aside to let him walk down the steps, tempted to tell him to take his time coming back. She watched as he walked off, appreciating how he filled out his jeans from the back. There was nothing like a man with a nice-looking butt.

She pulled in a deep breath and let it out again. Every time he looked at her, directly in her eyes, sparks of desire would go off inside of her. Now she fully understood what Ellen Draper, her college roommate at Tennessee State, meant when she'd tried explaining to her the complexities of sexual chemistry and physical attraction. At the time she hadn't had a clue because she hadn't yet met a man like Jamal Yasir.

Standing, she stretched. Today she planned to explore the area surrounding the cabin. Then later she intended to get more sleep. For the past three weeks she had studied all hours of the day and night preparing for final exams and had not gotten sufficient rest.

Now that she could, she would take advantage of the opportunity to relax. Besides, the less she was around Jamal, the better.

Jamal kept walking. He had passed the lake a mile back but intended to walk off as much sexual frustration as he could. The anger he'd felt with Delaney's comment about the people in his country not being happy had dissolved. Now he was dealing with the power of lust.

He stopped walking and studied the land surrounding the cabin. From where he stood the view was spectacular. This was the first time since coming to the cabin that he had actually taken the time to walk around and appreciate it.

He remembered the first time Philip had mentioned the cabin in the Carolinas, and how the view of the mountains had been totally breathtaking. Now he saw just what his friend had meant.

His mind then went back to Delaney, and he wondered if she had seen the view from this spot and if she would find it as breathtaking as he did. He doubted she had seen anything, since she rarely left the confines of her bedroom for long periods of time.

Jamal leaned against a tree when he heard his cell phone ring. He unsnapped it from the waist of his jeans and held it to his ear. "Yes, Asalum, what is it?"

"I'm just checking, Your Highness, to make sure all is well and that you don't need anything."

He shook his head. "I'm fine, but I have received an unexpected visitor."

"Who?"

He knew that Asalum was immediately on alert. In addition to serving as his personal secretary, Asalum had been his bodyguard from the time Jamal had been a child to the time he had officially reached manhood at eighteen.

He told him about Delaney's arrival. "If the woman is being a nuisance, Your Highness, perhaps I can persuade her to leave."

Jamal sighed. "That won't be necessary, Asalum. All she does most of the time is sleep, anyway."

There was a pause. Then a question. "Is she pregnant?"

Jamal arched a brow. "Why would you think she is pregnant?"

"Most women have a tendency to sleep a lot when they are pregnant."

Jamal nodded. If anyone knew the behavior of a pregnant

woman it would be Asalum. Rebakkah, Asalum's wife, had borne him twelve children. "No, I don't think she's pregnant. She claims she's just tired."

Asalum snorted. "And what has she been doing to be so tired?"

"Studying for finals. She recently completed a medical degree at the university."

"Is that all? She must be a weak woman if studying can make her tired to the point of exhaustion."

For some reason Jamal felt the need to defend Delaney. "She is not a weak woman. If anything she's too strong. Especially in her opinions."

"She sounds like a true Western woman, Your Highness."

Jamal rubbed his hand across his face. "She is. In every sense of the words. And, Asalum, she is also very beautiful."

For the longest moment Asalum didn't say anything, then he said quietly, "Beware of temptation, my prince."

Jamal thought about all that he had been experiencing since Delaney had arrived. Even now his body throbbed for relief. "Your warning comes too late. It has gone past temptation," Jamal said flatly.

"And what is it now?"

"Obsession."

Three

After being at the cabin a full week, Delaney finally completed the task of unpacking and put away the last of her things. With arms folded across her chest she walked over to the window and looked out. Her bedroom had a beautiful view of the lake, and she enjoyed waking up to it every morning. A number of thoughts and emotions were invading her mind, and at the top of the list was Jamal Yasir. She had to stop thinking about him. Ever since their talk that morning a few days ago, he had been on her mind although she hadn't wanted him there. So she had done the logical thing and avoided him like the plague.

A bit of anger erupted inside of her. In the past she had been able to school her thoughts and concentrate on one thing. And with that single-minded focus she had given medical school her complete attention. Now it seemed that with school behind her, her mind had gotten a life of its own and decided Jamal deserved her full consideration.

She was always consumed with thoughts of him. Intimate thoughts. Wayward thoughts. Thoughts of the most erotic kind. She wasn't surprised, because Jamal was the type of man who would elicit such thoughts from any woman, but Delaney was annoyed that she didn't have a better handle on her mental focus. Even with medical school behind her, she was still facing two years of residency, which would require another two years of concentration. An intimate relationship with any man should be the last thing on her mind.

But it wasn't.

And that's what had her resentful, moody and just plain hot, to the highest degree. Deciding to take a walk to cool off—like she really thought that would help—she grabbed her sunglasses off the dresser. She stepped outside of her room only to collide with the person who had been dominating her thoughts.

Jamal reached out to grab her shoulders to steady her and keep her from falling. She sucked in a quick breath when she noticed he was shirtless. Dark eyes gazed down into hers making her knees go weak, and the intensity of her lust went bone deep.

The rate of her breathing increased when his hand moved from her shoulder to her neck and the tip of his fingers slowly began caressing her throat. She could barely breathe with the magnitude of the sensations consuming her. The chemistry radiating between them was disturbingly basic and intrinsically sexy, and it was playing havoc with all five of her senses.

The sound of thunder roared somewhere in the distance and jolted them. He slowly released his hold, dropping his hands to his side. "Sorry, I didn't mean to bump into you," he said, the sound a throaty whisper that hummed through every nerve in Delaney's body before flowing through her bloodstream. And from the look in his eyes she could tell he wasn't immune. He was as aware as she was of the strong sexual tension that held both of them in its clutches.

"That's okay since I wasn't looking where I was going," she said softly, also offering an apology and inhaling deeply to calm her racing heart. She watched as his gaze slowly raked over her. She was wearing a pair of shorts and a crepe halter top. Suddenly she felt more naked than covered. More tensed than relaxed. And hotter than ever.

"Delaney?"

With the sound of her name spoken so sensually from his lips, her gaze locked with his, and at the same time he began leaning down closer to her. It was too close. Not close enough. And when she felt the warm brush of his breath against her throat, she responded softly, in an agonized whisper, "Yes?"

"It's going to rain," he said huskily.

She saw flickers of desire darken his gaze. "Sounds that way, doesn't it?" she managed to get out with extreme effort. She licked her lips slowly, cautiously. She was no longer aware of her surroundings, and barely heard the sound of the first drops of rain that suddenly began beating against the rooftop. Nor did she feel the tartness of the cold, damp air that suddenly filled the room.

All of her thoughts, her total concentration, was on the imposing figure looming before her. And she didn't consider resisting when he gently pulled her to him.

Go ahead, let him kiss you, a voice inside her head said. *Indulge yourself. Get it out of your system. Then the two of you can stop acting like two animals in heat. All it will take is this one, single kiss.*

A deep, drugging rush of desire filled Delaney. Shivers of wanting and need coursed down her spine. Yes, that's all it would take to get her head back on straight. A sexual attraction between a man and woman was healthy. Normal. Fulfilling. She just never had time to indulge before, but now she was ready. Now, with Jamal, indulging was necessary.

That was her last thought before Jamal's mouth covered hers.

Jamal took Delaney's lips with expertise and desperation. The need to taste her was elemental to him. Relentlessly his tongue explored her mouth, tasting and stroking, slowly moving beyond sampling to devouring. And when that wasn't enough he began sucking, drawing her into him with every breath.

He slipped his hand behind her head to hold her mouth in place while he got his fill, thinking it was impossible to do so, but determined to try anyway. He was at a point where he was willing to die trying.

He had kissed many women in his lifetime but had never felt a need to literally eat one alive. Never had any woman pushed him to such limits. He had been raised in an environment that accepted sex and intimacy for what they were—pleasure of the most tantalizing kind and a normal, healthy part of life.

But something deep within him believed there wasn't anything normal about this. What could be normal about wanting to stick your tongue down a woman's throat to see how far it could go? What was normal about wanting to suck her tongue forever if necessary to get the taste he was beginning to crave?

He pressed his body closer to hers, wanting her to feel him and know how much he desired her. He wanted her to know he wanted more than just a kiss. He wanted everything. He wanted it all.

And he intended to get it.

Jamal's fingers were insistent as they moved down her body to come to rest on her backside, gently pulling her closer. His body hardened at the feel of the tips of her nipples pressing against his bare chest through the material of her top. The contact was stimulating, inflaming, arousing.

And it was driving him insane.

The area between his thighs began to ache and get even harder. Grasping her hips he brought her more firmly against him, wanting her to feel his arousal, every throbbing inch. He knew she had gotten the message when he felt her fingers tangle in his hair, holding him close as he continued to devour her mouth.

Moments later, another loud clap of thunder, one that seemed to shake the entire earth, broke them apart. Delaney gasped so hard she almost choked. She bent over to pull air into her lungs, and seconds later, when she looked up and met Jamal's hot gaze, she felt her body responding all over again.

One kiss had not gotten him out of her system. That thought made her aware that unless she backed away, she would be in too deep. Already she felt herself sinking, drowning, being totally absorbed by him.

She backed up and he moved forward, cornering her against the wall. "I don't think we should have done that," she said softly, unconvincingly. Her voice was shaky, husky.

Jamal was glad they had done it and wanted to do it again. "It's been a week. We would have gotten around to kissing eventually," he said in a low, raspy voice. His body was still radiating an intimate intensity, although they were no longer touching.

"Why?" she asked, her curiosity running deep. When she saw the way his eyes darkened, a part of her wished that she hadn't asked him. He was looking at her in that way that made certain parts of her body get hot. And at the moment she couldn't handle the heat and doubted that she ever would.

"Because we want each other. We want to have sex," he replied, bluntly and directly. Although the words sounded brusque even to his ears, it was the truth and when it came to satisfying his body he believed in complete honesty. In his country such things were understood, expected and accepted.

Delaney's body trembled with Jamal's words. He'd made having sex sound so simple and basic. She thought of all the guys she had dated in her lifetime. She'd never wanted to have sex before. But Jamal was right—she *was* tempted now. But a part of her held back.

"I'm not a woman who makes a habit of getting into a man's bed," she said softly, feeling the need to let him know where she stood, and determined not to let him know that for the first time she was rethinking that policy.

"We don't have to use a bed if you don't want. We can use the table, the sofa or the floor. You pick the place. I'm bursting at the seams ready."

Delaney glanced down and saw his erection pressing against his zipper and knew he was dead serious. She inhaled deeply. He had missed her point entirely.

"What I mean is that I don't sleep with a man just for the fun of it."

He nodded slowly. "Then what about for the pleasure of it? Would you sleep with a man just for the pleasure it would give you?"

Delaney stated at him blankly. Indulging in sex mainly for pleasure? She knew her brothers did it all the time. They were experts in the field. None of them had a mind to marry, yet they bought enough condoms during the year to make it cost efficient to form their own company.

"I've never thought about it before," she answered truthfully. "When I think of someone being horny, I immediately think of men, more so than I do women."

"Horny?"

She shook her head, thinking he was probably not familiar with a lot of American slang. "Yes, horny. It means needing sex in a bad way, almost to the point where your body is craving it."

Jamal leaned down close to her mouth. "In that case, I'm feeling *horny*," he murmured thickly against it. "Real horny. And I want to make you feel horny, too."

"That's not possible," she whispered softly, barely able to breathe.

A half smile lifted one corner of his mouth. "Yes, it is."

Before she could say anything, his hand reached down and touched her thigh at the same time his tongue licked her lips, before slowly easing inside her mouth. Once there he began stroking her tongue with his, as if he had all the time in the world and intended to do it all day at his leisure.

Delaney's entire body shivered when she felt his fingers at the zipper of her shorts, and a part of her wanted to push his hand away. But then another part, that foolish part that thrived on curiosity, the one that was slowly getting inflamed again, wanted to feel his touch and wanted to know how far he would take it.

She held her breath when he lowered the zipper slowly and deliberately, easing her into submission. His breathing was getting just as difficult as hers, and her entire body felt hot all over.

And then he inserted his hand inside her shorts, boldly touching her through the flimsy material of her panties. He touched her in a place no man had ever touched her before, and with that intimate touch, every cell in her body ignited.

He began stroking her, slowly, languidly, making her feel horny. Just as he said he would do.

Never had she experienced anything so mind numbing, so unbelievably sensuous as one of his hands gently pushed her thighs apart even more while his fingertip gave complete erotic attention to that ultrasensitive, highly stimulated spot between her legs, while his tongue continued to suck on hers.

The combination of his fingers and his tongue was too much. She felt faint. She felt scandalized. She was feeling pleasure of the highest magnitude.

Another rumble of thunder with enough force to shake the cabin jolted Delaney out of her sexual haze and back to solid ground. She pushed Jamal away. Taking a deep breath she slumped against the wall, not believing what had just happened between them. What she had let him do. The liberties she had given him.

She had been putty in his arms.

A totally different woman beneath his fingers.

She appreciated the fact that evidently someone up there was looking out for her and had intervened before she could make a total fool of herself. Just as she'd thought, Jamal was a master at seduction. He had known just how to kiss her and just where to touch her to make her weak enough to throw caution to the wind. And she was determined not to let it happen again.

Forcing her gaze to his, she knew she was dealing with a man who was probably used to getting what he wanted whenever he wanted it. All he had to do was snap his fingers, ring a bell or do whatever a prince did when he needed sexual fulfillment.

Did he think she would fit the same bill while he was in America? The thought that he did angered her. She was not part of his harem and had no intentions of being at his beck and call.

Furious with herself for letting him toy with her so easily, she glared at him. "I plan to take a cold shower. I suggest you do the same."

He didn't say anything for a long moment, and then he smiled at her. It was a smile that extended from his eyes all the way to each corner of his lips.

"A cold shower won't help, Delaney."

"Why won't it?" she all but snapped, refusing to admit he was probably right.

"Because now I know your taste and you know mine. When you get hungry enough you will want to be fed, and when that happens I will feed you until your body is full and content. I will provide it with all the sexual nourishment it needs."

Without giving her an opportunity to say anything, he turned and walked away.

After pacing the confines of her bedroom for what seemed like the longest time, Delaney sat on the edge of the bed. She couldn't ever remember being so irritated, so frustrated…so just plain mad.

"I'll feel better once I get my head back on straight," she said, as she stood and began pacing again. How could one man have the ability to set a body on fire the way Jamal had hers still burning.

All she had to do was close her eyes and she could actually still feel the essence of his tongue inside her mouth or the feel of his hands…more specifically, his fingers, on her flesh. And she could still feel the hardness of him pressed against her stomach.

A silky moan escaped her lips, and she knew she had to leave the cabin for a while and take a walk. But the problem was that it was raining, and not just a little sprinkle but a full-fledged thunderstorm.

She touched a finger to her lips, thinking that it was too bad the thundershowers couldn't wash away the memories of her kiss with Jamal.

A part of her wondered what Jamal was doing right now. Was his body being tormented like hers?

She sighed deeply. She had to stay determined. She had to stay strong. And most important, she had to continue to avoid Jamal Ari Yasir at all cost.

Four

"Going someplace?"

Delaney stopped in her trek across the room to the door. She wished she had waited until she'd been absolutely sure Jamal was asleep before leaving to go to the store. After their encounter a few days ago, she had avoided him by staying in her room most of the time.

But she had been too keyed-up to hide out in her room any longer. Heated desire flowed like warm wine through all parts of her body, making her feel things she had never felt before. Restless. On edge. Horny.

The rain for the past two days had kept them both inside the cabin. And whenever she got too hungry to stay in her room, she would go into the kitchen to find him sitting at the wobbly table sketching something out on paper. His black gaze would pierce her, nearly taking her breath away, and although he didn't say anything, she knew he watched her the entire time she was in close range. Like a wolf watching his prey.

She sighed as her gaze moved slowly down the length of him. He was dressed in a pair of white silk pajamas. The first thought that entered her mind was that she had seen her brothers in pajamas many times, but none of them had looked like this. And then there was the white kaffiyeh that he wore on his head. Silhouetted in the moonlight that flowed through the window, he looked the epitome of the tall, dark and handsome prince that he was.

Inhaling deeply, she needed all of the strength she could muster to hold her own with him, especially after the kiss they had shared; a kiss that made her breathless just remembering it. And it didn't help matters that she was noticing things she hadn't noticed before; like his hands and how perfect they looked. The fingers of those hands were long, deft and strong. They were fingers that had once swallowed hers in a warm clasp while he had kissed her; fingers whose tips had touched her cheek, traced the outline of her lips, and fingers that had touched her intimately. Then there were his eyebrows. She had been so taken with his eyes that she had failed to notice his brows. Now she did. They were deep, dark, slanted, and together with his eyes were deadly combinations.

"Delaney, I asked if you were going somewhere," Jamal said.

She swallowed as she gazed across the room at him and nearly came undone when he nailed her with his dark, penetrating eyes and those slanted brows.

"I'm going to the store," she finally responded. "There are some items I need to pick up."

"At this time of night?"

Even in the dim light Delaney could see the frown darkening his face. She met his frown with one of her own. "Yes, this time of night. Do you have a problem with it?"

For a long moment they stood there staring at each other—challenging. Delaney refused to back down, and so did he. To her way of thinking he reminded her of her brothers in their attempts to be overprotective. And that was the last thing she wanted or would tolerate.

"No, I don't have a problem with it. I was just being concerned," he finally said. "It's not safe for a woman to be out at night alone."

The quiet tone of his voice affected her more than she wanted it to. And the way he was looking at her didn't help matters. Intentionally or not, he was igniting feelings she had been experiencing lately; feelings she had tried ridding herself of by staying in her room. But now she felt the slow pounding of blood as it rushed to her head and back down to her toes. She also heard the ragged pant of her breathing and wondered if he heard it.

"I'm used to living alone, Jamal," she finally responded. "And I can take care of myself. Because of my study habits, I'm used to going shopping at night instead of in the daytime."

He nodded. "Do you mind some company? There are some things I need to pick up, as well."

Delaney narrowed dark eyes, wondering if he actually needed something or if he was using that as an excuse to tag along. If it was the latter, she wasn't having any of it. "If I wasn't here, how would you have managed to get those things?"

He shrugged. "I would have called Asalum. And although he would be more than happy to do my shopping for me, I prefer doing things for myself. Besides, it's after midnight and he needs his rest."

Delaney was glad to hear that he was considerate of the

people who worked for him. Slowly nodding, she said, "Then I guess it will be all right if you come along."

Jamal laughed. It was a deep, husky, rich sound that made heat spread through the lower part of her body. She slanted him a look. "Something funny?"

"Yes. You make it seem such a hardship to spend time with me."

Delaney sighed, looking away. He didn't know the half of it. Moments later she returned her attention to him. "Mainly because I had thought I would be here alone for the next few weeks."

He grinned at her suddenly. It was so unexpected that her anger lost some of its muster. "So had I," he said huskily, slowly crossing the room to stand in front of her. "But since we're not alone and it was your decision to stay, don't you think we should stop avoiding each other and make the most of it and get along?"

Delaney fought her body's reaction to his closeness. It wasn't easy. "I suppose we can try."

"What do we have to lose?"

Oh, I can think of a number of things I have to lose. My virginity for one, Delaney thought to herself. Instead of responding to his question, she turned and headed for the door. "I'll wait in the car while you change clothes."

"Did you get everything you need?" Delaney asked Jamal as they got back into her car to return to the cabin. Once they had gone inside the all-night supermarket he seemed to have disappeared.

"Yes, I got everything I need. What about you?"

"Yes. I even picked up a few things I hadn't intended to get," she said, thinking of the romance novel she had talked herself into buying. She couldn't remember the last time she'd been able to read a book for pleasure.

They drove back to the cabin in silence. Delaney kept her eyes on the road but felt Jamal's eyes on her all the while.

"What kind of doctor are you?" he asked after they had ridden a few miles.

His question got him a smile. She enjoyed talking about her profession and was proud of the fact that she was the only doctor in the Westmoreland family. "I will be a pediatrician, but first I have to complete my residency, which will take another two years."

"You like working with children?"

Delaney's response was immediate. "Not only do I enjoy working with kids, I love kids, period."

"So do I."

Delaney was surprised by his comment. "You do?" Most men, especially a single man, wouldn't admit that fact.

"Yes. I'm looking forward to getting married one day and having a family."

She nodded. "Me, too. I want a houseful."

Jamal chuckled and gave her a curious look. "Define a houseful."

The words leaped from Delaney's mouth without thinking about it. "At least six."

He smiled, finding it amazing that she wanted pretty close to the same number of children that he did. "You are asking for a lot, aren't you?"

She grinned. That was what her brothers always told her. They were convinced it would be hard to find a man who'd want that many kids. "Not a whole lot, just a good even number to make me happy and content."

When the car stopped at a traffic light, Jamal glanced over at Delaney. He thought she was too beautiful for words. Even with a face scrubbed clean of makeup and a fashionable scarf around her head to keep her hair in place, she was definitely one nice feminine package, a right sassy one at that.

His thoughts drifted to Najeen. She would remain his mistress even after he took a wife. That was understood and it would also be accepted. He knew that Western women tended to be possessive after marriage. They would never tolerate a husband having a mistress. But then, most American women fancied themselves marrying for love. In his country you married for benefits—usually heirs. His marriage would be no different. Since he didn't believe in love he didn't plan on marrying for it. His would be an arranged marriage. Nothing more. Nothing less.

He could not see Delaney ever settling for that type of arrangement with any man. She would want it all: a man's love, his devotion, and his soul if there was a way she could get it.

Jamal cringed inwardly. The thought of any woman having that much control over a man was oddly disconcerting. The possibility that a woman would demand such a relationship would be unheard of in his country.

"Think you can juggle a career and motherhood?" he asked moments later. He wondered how she would respond. Western women also tended to be less domesticated. They enjoyed working just as hard as a man. He smiled. The woman he married would have only one job—to give him children. She could walk around naked all day if she chose to do so. She would be naked and pregnant the majority of the time.

"Sure," Delaney said smiling. "Just like you'll be able to handle being a prince *and* a father, I'll be able to handle being a doctor and a mom. I'm sure it will be a little hectic at times but you'll be successful at it and so will I."

Jamal frowned. "Don't you think your child would need your absolute attention, especially in the early years?"

Delaney heard the subtle tone of disapproval in his voice. "No more than your child would need *yours* as his father."

"But you are a woman."

She smiled in triumph, pleased with that fact. "Yes, and you are a man. So what's your point? There's nothing written that says a mother's role in a child's life is more important than a father's. I tend to think both parents are needed to give the child love and structure. The man I marry will spend just as much time with our children as I do. We will divide our time equally in the raising of our child."

Jamal thought about the amount of time his father had spent with him while he'd been growing up. Even when his father had been in residence in the palace, Jamal had been cared for by a highly regarded servant—specifically, Asalum's wife, Rebakkah. And although his father had not spent a lot of time with him, he had always understood that he loved him. After all, he was his heir. Now that he was older, he knew their relationship was built on respect. He saw his father as a wise king who loved his people and who would do anything for them. Being his father's successor one day would be a hard job and he hoped he was at least half the man his father was.

Delaney was fully aware that Jamal had become quiet. Evidently she had given him something to think about. The nerve of him thinking that a woman's job was to stay barefoot and pregnant. He and her father, as well as her brother Storm, would get along perfectly.

It was a long-standing joke within the family that her youngest brother wanted a wife who he could keep in the bedroom, 24/7. The only time he would let her out of bed was when she needed to go to the bathroom. He wanted her in the bed when he left for work and in the bed when he came back home. His wife's primary job would be to have his children and to keep him happy in the bedroom, so it wouldn't matter to him if she were a lousy cook in the kitchen. He would hire a housekeeper to take care of any less important stuff.

Delaney shook her head. And all this time she'd thought that Storm was a rare breed. Evidently not. When they had made Storm, the mold hadn't been broken after all.

She glanced quickly at Jamal and wondered how she had gotten herself in this predicament. When she hadn't been able to sleep, going to the store in the middle of the night for some things she needed had seemed like a good idea. But she hadn't counted on Jamal accompanying her.

She sighed as the car traveled farther and farther away from the city and back toward the cabin. She stole another glance at him and saw that he was watching her. She quickly returned her gaze to the road.

When they finally arrived back at the cabin, Delaney felt wired. Too keyed-up to sleep. She decided to start cutting back on the hours of sleep she was putting in during the day. At night, while the cabin was quiet, her mind had started to wander and she didn't like the direction it was taking.

She quickly walked past Jamal when he opened the door, intending to make a path straight for her room. The last thing she could handle was another encounter like the one shared before. The man was definitely an experienced kisser.

What he had predicted was true. She hated admitting it but her body was hungry for him. A slow ache was beginning to form between her legs, and heat was settling there as well.

"Would you like to share a cup of coffee with me, Delaney?"

The sound of his voice, husky and sexy, like always, did

things to her insides. It also made that ache between her legs much more profound. Sharing a cup of coffee with him was the last thing she wanted to do. She would never make it through the first sip before jumping his bones. "No, thanks, I think I'll go on to bed."

"If you ever get tired of sleeping alone, just remember that my room is right across the hall."

Delaney tightened her lips. "Thanks for the offer, but I *won't* keep that in mind."

He reached out and brought his hand to her face and caressed her cheek. The action was so quick she hadn't had time to blink. His touch was soft, tender, gentle, and her breathing began a slow climb. He leaned toward her and whispered. "Won't you?"

Delaney closed her eyes, drinking in the masculine scent of him. Desire for him was about to clog her lungs. Fighting for control, she took a step back as she opened her eyes. "Sorry, *Your Highness,* but no, I won't." She then turned and walked quickly to her room, thinking she had lied to him and that she *would.*

"Oh, my goodness." Delaney shifted her body around in the hammock while keeping her eyes glued to the book, not believing what she was reading.

She hadn't read a romance novel in nearly eight years and then the ones she'd read had been those sweet romances. But nothing was sweet about the book she had purchased last night. The love scenes didn't leave you guessing about anything.

She had awakened that morning, and while Jamal had been outside doing his kickboxing routine, she'd sat at the wobbly table and had eaten a bagel and had drunk a cup of orange juice. Jamal was still outside by the time she had finished. She had passed him when she had left to find a good spot near the lake to read her book.

She took in a deep breath, then returned to the book once more. A few minutes later the rate of her heart increased, and she wondered if two people could actually perform that many positions in bed?

Stretching her body and giving herself a chance to catch her breath, she admitted that reading the book had turned her on. In her imagination, the tall, dark, handsome hero was Jamal and she was the elusive and sexy heroine.

Rolling onto her back she decided she had read enough. There was no use torturing her body anymore. The next thing Delaney knew, she had drifted off to sleep with thoughts of romancing the sheikh on her mind.

She dreamed she was being kissed in the most tantalizing and provocative way; not on her lips but along her shoulder and neck. Then she felt a gentle tug on her tank top as it was lifted up to expose her bare breasts. It had been too hot for a bra so she'd not worn one, and now, with the feel of her imaginary lover's tongue moving over her breasts, tasting her, nibbling on her, she was glad that she hadn't. A rush of heated desire spread through the lower part of her legs as a hot, wet tongue took hold of a nipple and gently began sucking, feasting on the budding tip.

A name, one she had given to her imaginary lover, came out on a gasp of a sound. Her mind began spinning, her breathing became even more erratic and her body hotter. A part of her didn't want the dream to end, but then another part was afraid for it to continue. It seemed so real that she was almost tortured beyond control, just on the edge of insanity.

Then suddenly her lover lowered her top and ceased all

action without warning. Her breathing slowed back to normal as she struggled to gain control of her senses.

Moments later, Delaney lifted her dazed eyes and glanced around her. She was alone, but the dream had seemed so real. The nipples on her breasts were still throbbing and the area between her legs was aching for something it had never had before—relief.

She closed her eyes, wondering if she could dream up her lover again and decided she couldn't handle that much pleasure twice in the same day. Besides, she was still sleepy and tired. As she drifted off to sleep she couldn't help remembering her dream and thought it had been utterly amazing.

Jamal breathed deeply as he leaned back against the tree. What had possessed him to do what he'd just done to Delaney? It didn't take long for him to have his answer. He had been attracted to her from the first, and when he had come upon her sleeping in the hammock wearing a short midriff top and shorts, with a portion of her stomach bare to his gaze, he couldn't resist the thought of tasting her. A taste he had thought about a lot lately.

Her breasts, even while she slept, had been erect with the dark tips of her nipples showing firmly against her blouse. Without very much thought, he had gone to her and had knelt before her to feast upon every inch of her body. But he hadn't gotten as far as he wanted before coming to his senses.

Just thinking about making love to her made him aroused to the point that his erection, pressing against the fly of his jeans, was beginning to ache. And when she had moaned out his name, he'd almost lost it.

A woman had been the last thing on his mind when he

had arrived at the cabin. Now a woman, one woman in particular, was the only thing he could think about.

His body felt hot. It felt inflamed. He wondered if he should pack his things and ask Asalum to come for him. Maybe it was time for him to return to Tahran. Never before had he wanted any woman to the point of seducing her while she slept.

But he knew he couldn't leave. She had moaned out his name. He hadn't imagined it. She may deny wanting him while she was awake, but while she slept it was a different matter.

His libido stirred. He wanted to taste her again. In truth, he wanted more than that. He wanted to make love with her. And every muscle in his body strained toward that goal.

Five

Jamal was sitting at the wobbly table drinking a cup of tea when Delaney came inside for lunch a few hours later. She glanced over at him as she made her way to the refrigerator to take out the items she needed for a sandwich.

"I'm making a sandwich for lunch," she said, opening the refrigerator. "Would you like one, too?"

Jamal shifted in the chair as he looked at her. He didn't want a sandwich. He wanted sex. And as a result, he felt restless and on edge. Earlier in the week he had tasted her mouth, today he had feasted on her nipples. There wasn't much of her left to discover, but what there was sent his hormones into overdrive.

When he didn't answer, she turned away from the refrigerator and looked at him curiously. "Jamal?"

"Yes?"

"I asked if you wanted a sandwich?"

He nodded, deciding to take her up on her offer. He

needed to eat something, since he would need all his strength later for something he would enjoy. At least that was what he was hoping. "Yes, thank you. I would love to have a sandwich." *I would love to have you.*

He continued to watch as she took items out of the refrigerator and assembled them on the counter. The enticing scent of her perfume was filling the kitchen and he found himself getting deeply affected by it. And it didn't help matters that he knew she wasn't wearing a bra under her top and that her breasts were the best kind to lick and suck. The moment his tongue had touched the taut nipple, the tip of it had hardened like a bud, tempting him to draw the whole thing in his mouth and gently suck and tease it with a pulling sensation. And the way she had moaned while squirming around on the hammock had let him know she enjoyed his actions.

He shifted his gaze from her chest to her bottom. Her backside had been what had caught his attention that very first day. It was also the main thing that had him hard now. She liked wearing shorts, the kind that showed just what a nice behind she had. Nice thighs, too. The shorts placed emphasis on the curve of her hips. He wondered what her behind looked like without clothes. He bet her buttocks were as firm and as lush as her breasts.

"Do you want mayonnaise on your bread?"

Her questions made him return his gaze to her face when she tossed him a glance over her shoulder. "No, mustard is fine," he answered, briefly considering pinning her against the counter and taking her from behind. He could just imagine pumping into her while pressed solidly against her backside.

He took another sip of his herbal tea. Usually the sweet brew calmed him. But not today and certainly not now.

"Be prepared to enjoy my sandwich," she was saying.

"My brothers think they're the bomb and would give anything for me to make them one. They have my special touch."

He nodded. He could believe that and suddenly felt envious of a slice of bread and wished he could trade places with it. He would love to have her hands on him, spreading whatever she wanted over his body, preferably kisses. She wouldn't even have to toast him since her touch would burn him to a crisp, anyway.

She glanced over his shoulder and smiled again. "You're quiet today. Are you okay?"

He was tempted to tell her that no, he wasn't okay, and if he were to stand up she would immediately see why he wasn't. But instead he said, "Yes, I'm fine."

Satisfied with his response, she turned back around to continue making their sandwiches. He leaned back in his chair. He watched her pat her foot on the hardwood floor while she worked. She was also humming. He wondered what had her in such a good mood. Unlike him, she must be sleeping at night and not experiencing sexual torment.

"Did you finish your book?" he decided to ask. She had been reading it all morning. The only time he noticed her not reading was when she'd fallen asleep on the hammock.

"Oh, yes, and it was wonderful," she said, reaching up in the cabinets to get two plates. "And of course there was a happy ending."

He lifted his brow. *So she had been reading one of those kind.* "A happy ending?"

She nodded turning around. "Yes. Marcus realized just how much Jamie meant to him and told her that he loved her before it was too late."

Jamal nodded. "He loved this woman?"

Delaney smiled dreamily. "Yes, he loved her."

Jamal frowned. "Then what you read was pure fantasy.

Why waste your time reading such nonsense and foolishness?''

Delaney's smile was replaced with a fierce frown. "Nonsense? Foolishness?''

"Yes, nonsense and foolishness. Men don't love women that way.''

Delaney braced herself against the counter and folded her arms across her chest. Her legs, Jamal noted, were spread apart. Seeing her stand that way almost made him forget what they were discussing. Instead his gaze moved to the junction of those legs and wondered how it would feel fitting his hard body there.

"And just how do men love women?''

Jamal's gaze left her midsection and moved up to her face. She was still frowning. Evidently she was no longer in such a good mood. "Usually they don't. At least not in my country.''

Delaney lifted a brow. "People do get married in your country, don't they?''

"Of course.''

"Then why would a man and a woman marry if not for love?''

Jamal stared at her, suddenly feeling disoriented. She had a way of making him feel like that whenever he locked on her dark brown eyes and lush lips. "They would marry for a number of reasons. Mainly for benefits,'' he responded, not taking his gaze off her eyes and lips. Especially her lips.

"Benefits?''

He nodded. "Yes. If it's a good union, the man brings to the table some kind of wealth and the woman brings strong family ties, allegiances and the ability to give him an heir. Those things are needed if a sheikhdom is to grow and prosper.''

Delaney stared into his eyes, amazed at what he had just

said. "So the marriages in your country are like business arrangements?"

He smiled. "Basically, yes. That's why the most successful ones are arranged at least thirty years in advance."

"Thirty years in advance!" she exclaimed, shaking her head in disbelief.

"Yes, at least that long, sometimes even longer. More often than not, the man and woman's family plans their union even before they are born. Such was the case with my father and mother. She was of Berber descent. The Berbers were and still are a proud North African tribe that inhabits the land in northwestern Libya. As a way to maintain peace between the Berbers and the Arabs, a marriage agreement between my mother, an African princess, and my father, an Arab prince, was made. Therefore, I am of Arab-Berber descent, just as the majority of the people of Tahran are. My parents were married a little more than a year when my mother died giving birth to me."

Delaney leaned back against the counter. At the moment what he was telling her was more interesting than making a sandwich. "What if your father, although pledged to your mother, had found someone else who he preferred to spend the rest of his life?"

"That would have been most unfortunate. And it wouldn't have meant a thing. He would still marry the woman he'd been pledged to marry. However, he could take the other woman he fancied as a mistress for the rest of his days."

"A mistress? And what would his wife have to say about something like that?"

He shrugged. "Nothing. It's common practice for a man to have both a wife and mistress. That sort of an arrangement is accepted."

Delaney shook her head. American men knew better.

"That's such a waste, Jamal. Why would a man need both a wife *and* a mistress? A smart man would seek out and fall in love with a woman who can play both roles. In our country wives are equipped to fulfill every desire her husband may have."

Jamal lifted a brow. He could see her fulfilling every man's desire since he saw her as a very sensual woman. She would probably make a good *American* wife, if you liked the outspoken, sassy and rebellious type. She would keep a man on his toes and no doubt on his knees. But he had a feeling she would also keep him on his back—which would be well worth the trouble she would cause him.

He sighed, deciding he didn't want to talk about wives and mistresses any longer, especially when he knew how possessive American women were. "Are the sandwiches ready?"

Evidently, she wasn't ready to bring the subject to an end and asked, "The first day we met you indicated you were to marry next year."

He nodded. "Yes, that's true. In my country it's customary for a man to marry before his thirty-fifth birthday. And I'll be that age next summer."

"And the woman you're marrying? Was your marriage to her prearranged?"

Seeing she would not give the sandwich to him until her curiosity had been appeased, he said, "Yes, and no. My family had arranged my marriage to the future princess of Bahan before she was born. I was only six at the time. But she and her family were killed a few years ago while traveling in another country. That was less than a year before we were to marry. She was only eighteen at the time."

Delaney gave a sharp intake of air into her lungs. "Oh, that must have been awful for you."

Jamal shrugged. "I guess it would have been had I

known her.'' Like I know you now, he thought, watching her eyes lift in confusion. The thought of anything ever happening to her…

''What do you mean if you had known her? You didn't know the woman you were going to marry?'' Her mouth gaped open in pure astonishment.

''No, I had never met her. There was really no need. We were going to marry. Her showing up at the wedding would have been soon enough.''

''But…but what if she was someone you didn't want?''

Jamal looked at her, smiling as if she had asked a completely stupid question. ''Of course I would have wanted her. She was pledged to be my wife, and I was pledged to be her husband. We would have married regardless.''

Delaney inhaled slowly. ''And you would have kept your mistress.'' She said the words quietly, not bothering to ask if he had one. A man like him would, especially a man who thought nothing of marrying a woman he had never met to fulfill a contract his family had made. He would bed his wife for heirs, fulfilling his duty, then bed his mistress for pleasure.

''Yes, I would keep my mistress.'' He thought of Najeen, then added, ''I would never think of giving her up.''

Delaney stared at him and his nonchalant attitude about being unfaithful. Her brothers, possibly with the exception of Thorn when he was in one of his prickly moods, were players, enjoying being bachelors to the fullest. But there was no doubt in her mind that when…and if they each found their soul mate, that woman would make them give up their players' cards. They would not only give her their complete love but their devotion and faithfulness, as well.

She was suddenly swamped by a mixture of feelings. There was no way she could get serious about a man like Jamal and accept the fact that he would be sleeping with another woman. She appreciated differences in cultures, but there were some things she would not tolerate. Infidelity was one of them. Violation of marriage vows was something she would not put up with.

Crossing the room with both plates in her hands, she set his sandwich down in front of him with a thump, glaring down at him. "Enjoy your sandwich. I hope you don't choke on it. I'm eating in my room, since I prefer not to share your company at the moment."

Jamal was out of his chair in a flash. He reached out and grabbed hold of her wrist and brought her closer to him. "Why?"

Her eyes darkened. "Why what?"

He studied her features. "Why did my words, spoken in total honesty, upset you? It's the way we do things in my country, Delaney. Accept it."

She tried pulling her hand free but he held on tight. "Accept it?" Her laugh was low, bitter and angry. She tilted her head back and glared up at him. "Why should I accept it? How you live your life is your business and means nothing to me."

Their faces were close. If they moved another inch their mouths would be touching. She tried to pull back, but he wouldn't let her. "If you truly mean that, then it would make things a lot easier."

Delaney tried not to notice that his eyes were focused on her mouth. "What do you mean by that?" she snapped, hating the fact that even now desire for him was spreading through all parts of her body. How could she still want him, after he admitted he would not marry for love and proudly boasted of having a mistress? A mistress he would never give up.

"If how I live my life means nothing to you, then it won't be an issue when we sleep together."

"What!"

"You heard what I said, Delaney. Western women tend to be possessive, which is one of the reasons I've never gotten too involved with one. You sleep with them once and they want to claim you forever. I've pretty much spelled out to you how my life will be when I will return to Tahran. I want you to fully understand that, before you share my bed. I make you no promises other than I will pleasure you in ways no man has pleasured you before."

Delaney shook her head, not believing the audacity of Jamal. He was as arrogant as they came. In his mind it was a foregone conclusion the two of them would sleep together. Well, she had news for him. It would be a damn cold day in July before she shared his bed.

She snatched her hand from his. "Let me get one thing straight, Prince." Her breath was coming in sharp; as sharp as her anger. "I have no intention of sleeping with you," she all but screamed, thumping him on his solid chest a few times for good measure. "I don't plan on being number three with any man, no matter the degree of pleasure. Your body could be made of solid gold and sprinkled with diamonds, I still wouldn't touch it unless it was mine exclusively. Do you hear me? I get exclusive rights from a man or nothing at all."

His gaze hardened as he stared at her. "I would never give any woman exclusive rights on me. Never."

"Then fine, we know where we stand, don't we?" She turned around to leave the room.

"Delaney…"

She told herself not to turn around, but found herself turning around, anyway. "What?"

He was frowning furiously. "Then I suggest you leave here. Now. Today."

Delaney inhaled deep. Of all the nerve. "I've told you, Jamal, that I'm not leaving."

He stared at her for a long moment, then said. "Then you had best be on your guard, Delaney Westmoreland. I want you. I want you so badly I practically ache all over. I want you in a way I have never wanted a woman. I like inhaling your scent. I like tasting you and want to do so again…every part of you. I want to get inside your body and ignite us both with pleasure. Ever since you got here all I do is dream about having you, taking you, getting on top of you, inside of you and giving you the best sex you've ever had."

He slowly crossed the room to her. Ignoring the apprehension in her eyes, he lifted his hand to her cheek and continued. "For the two of us it all comes down to one word. *Lust*. So it doesn't matter who or what comes after we leave here. What we're dealing with, Delaney, is lust of the thickest and richest kind. Lust so strong it can bring a man to his knees. There is no love between us and there never will be. There will only be lust."

He stared deeply into her eyes. "Chances are when we leave here we will never see each other again. So what's wrong with enjoying our time together? What's wrong with engaging in something so pleasurable it will give us beautiful memories to feast on for years to come?"

His hand slowly left her cheek and moved to her neck. "I want to have sex with you every day while we're here, Delaney, in every position known to man. I want to fulfill your fantasies as well as my own."

Delaney swallowed. Everything he said sounded tempting, enticing. And a lesser woman would abandon everything, including her pride, and give in to what he was suggesting. But she couldn't.

For too many years she had watched her brothers go from

woman to woman. She would shake her head in utter amazement at how easily the women would agree to a night, a week or whatever time they could get from one of the Westmoreland brothers, with the attitude that something was a lot better than nothing.

Well she refused to settle for just anything. She wasn't that hard up. Besides, you couldn't miss what you never had, and although she would be the first to admit that Jamal had awakened feelings and desires within her that she hadn't known existed, she could control her urge to sample more.

With a resolve and a stubborn streak that could only match her brother Thorn, she took a step back. "No, Jamal, I meant what I said. Exclusive or nothing."

His eyes darkened and she watched his lips tilt in a seductive smile. "You think that now, Delaney, but you will be singing a different tune in the end."

His voice was husky, and the look in his eyes was challenging. She swallowed the lump in her throat. "What do you mean?"

His smile became biting. "I mean that when it comes to something I want, I don't play fair."

Delaney stared pointedly into his eyes, her heart slammed against her ribs, completely understanding what he meant. He would try to wear down her defenses and didn't care how he did it as long as the end result was what he wanted—her in his bed.

Well, she had news for him. Westmorelands, among other things, were hard as nails when they chose to be. They were also stubborn as sin, and some were more stubborn than others were. They didn't back down from a challenge. A light flickered in her eyes. The prince had met his match.

Delaney smiled, and her eyes were lit with a touch of humor. "You may not play fair, but you can ask any one of my brothers and they will tell you that when it comes to competition, I play to win.''

''This is one game you won't win, Delaney.''

''And this is one game I can't afford to lose, *Your Highness*.''

His eyes darkened as he frowned. ''Don't say I didn't warn you.''

She met his frown with one of her own. ''And don't say I didn't warn *you*.'' With nothing else to say, Delaney turned, and with her head held high she strutted out of the kitchen and headed to the porch to eat her sandwich alone.

Six

Jamal looked up when Delaney walked into the living room later that evening. War had been declared and she was using every weapon at her disposal to win. She was determined to flaunt in his face what she thought he would never have. Which he assumed was the reason for the outfit she had changed into. There was only one way to describe it—sinfully sensual.

It was some sort of lounging outfit with a robe. But the robe enticed more than it covered. He couldn't do anything but lean back in his chair and look at her from head to toe. A surge of raw, primitive possessiveness, as well as arousal of the most intense kind, rushed through him. He couldn't pretend indifference even if he wanted to, so there was no sense trying. Instead he tossed the papers he was working on aside and placed his long legs out in front of him and gave her his full attention, since he knew that is what she wanted, anyway.

He knew her game. She wanted to bring him to his knees with no chance of him getting between her legs. But he had news for her. He would let her play out this little scene, then he intended to play out his.

The outfit she wore was peach in color and stood out against the color of her dark skin. The material was like soft silk, beneath a lacy robe that gave the right amount of a feminine allure. The sway of the material against her body as she crossed the room clearly indicated she didn't have on a stitch of undergarments. The woman was foreplay on legs.

His groin throbbed as he watched her sit on the sofa across the room from him, real prim and proper and looking incredibly hot. Of its own accord his breathing deepened, making it difficult to pass oxygen through his lungs, yet he continued to torture himself by looking at her.

"So, what's up?" she asked in a deep, sultry voice.

He blinked when it occurred to him that she had spoken, and the sexy tone and the way she was looking at him made him aware of every male part of his body. "I can tell you of one thing in particular that's up, Delaney," he said smoothly. He may as well state the obvious since it had to be evident to her, even from across the room, that he had an erection the size of Egypt.

She didn't answer him. Instead she smiled saucily, as if she had scored a point. And he had to concede that she had. He wondered if she enjoyed seeing him sweat. He would remember just what she was putting him through when it was his turn to make his move. And when that time came he wouldn't let her retreat. She had started this, and he damn well intended to see her finish it. He intended to teach her a thing or two about tempting a desert sheikh.

The CD he had been listening to stopped playing, and a lingering silence filled the room. She watched him and he watched her. Inside he smoldered, his body was heating to a feverish pitch and from the look on her face she was savoring every moment.

"Do you want me to put on some more music?" he asked, slowly standing, not caring that she could see his obvious masculine display.

After taking it all in, seeing how big he was, she just nodded, unable to respond. The look on her face gave him pause, and he couldn't help but smile. Hell, what had she expected? Granted he'd been told by a number of women that he was very well endowed, but he thought surely she had seen a fully aroused male before.

Crossing the room he walked over to the CD player. "Is there anything in particular you would like to hear?" he asked huskily, in a quiet whisper. When she didn't answer he glanced at her over his shoulder.

She shrugged. He saw the deep movement of her throat as she swallowed before responding. "No. Whatever you decide to play is fine."

He picked up on her nervousness. Evidently, she didn't have this game of hers down as pat as she thought she did. With five brothers she should have known that a woman didn't stand a chance against a man with one thing on his mind. You play with fire you got burned, and he was going to love scorching her in the process. By the time he lit her fire she would be ready to go up in smoke.

He put on Kenny G and it wasn't long before the sound of the saxophone filled the room. He turned around slowly and walked over to the sofa toward her. *Stalked* over to the sofa was probably a better word. He intended to see just how much temptation she could take.

Coming to a stop in front of her he reached out his hand. "Would you like to dance?" He saw the movement of her throat as she swallowed deeply again. Her gaze held his and he knew she was giving his question some thought.

He had an idea what her response would be. She had started this and she intended to finish it. There was no way she would let him get the upper hand, even if it killed her. He smiled. He definitely didn't want her dead. He wanted a live body underneath him tonight when he made her admit defeat.

She slowly slid off the sofa, bringing her body so close to his that his nostrils flared with her scent. "Yes, I'll dance with you," she said softly, taking the hand he offered.

He nodded and pulled her into his arms. They both let out a deep rush of breath when their bodies connected. He closed his eyes, forcing his body to remain calm. She felt good against him, and when she leaned closer he groaned.

Neither of them said a word, but he could hear her in-drawn breath each and every time his erection came into contact with her midsection, which he intentionally made happen a lot.

As Kenny G skillfully played the sax, he masterfully began his seduction to prove to Miss Westmoreland that she couldn't play with the big boys, no matter what her intent. When she rested her head against his chest, he opened his hand wide over her backside, cupping her to him as he slowed their movements even more.

He groaned again as he felt her lush bottom in his hand. He smoothly rubbed his hand over it, loving the way it felt. He decided not to speak. Words would only break the sensuous spell they were in. So he pulled her closer to his swollen erection, wishing they were in bed together instead of dancing, but grateful for what he could get; especially after she had been so adamant about him not getting anything.

When the music stopped playing, he didn't want to release her from his arms. And since she didn't take a step back he got the distinct impression she wasn't ready for the moment to end yet, either.

He knew what he had to do and what he wanted to do. And if tasting her led to other things, then so be it.

He leaned back slightly from her, which forced her head to lift from his chest. She met his gaze and he saw desire, just as potent, just as raw, in her eyes. He had to kiss her.

She must have had the same idea since without any protest her lips parted for him. A ragged moan escaped the moment he captured her mouth in his.

The movement of his tongue in her mouth was methodically slow and she reacted with a groan deep in her throat, which he absorbed in the kiss. He was an expert on kissing and used that expertise on her. He had been schooled in various places but found he had learned more during his stay in the Greek Isles than any other place. It was there he had mastered Ares, an advanced form of French kissing.

Some people preferred not using it because it could get you in such an aroused state, if you weren't careful things would be over for you before you even started. Only men with strong constitutions, those capable of extending the peak of their pleasure could use it. And it wasn't unusual for a woman to climax from the pleasure it gave her. Ares was developed around the belief that certain parts inside of your mouth, when stroked in the right way, gave you immense pleasure. He had never tried it on any other woman other than the person who had taught it to him at the age of twenty-one. It boggled his mind that he had never wanted to try it on Najeen, yet more than anything he wanted to experience it with Delaney. It was something about her taste that made it imperative for his state of mind.

Closing his eyes he took their kiss to another level. He could tell she noted the change but continued kissing him.

Moments later he felt her arms reach up and encircle his neck as she became as much a part of their kiss as he did.

Moments later, startled, she pushed back out of his arms, her breasts rising and falling with every uneven breath she took. He wasn't through with her mouth yet. He'd barely started.

"Give me your tongue back, Delaney," he whispered in a low guttural tone. "Just stick it out and I'll take it from there."

She stared at him for a moment. Then closing her eyes she opened her mouth and darted her tongue out to him. Angling his head so he wouldn't bump her nose he captured it with his and drew it into his mouth. Slowly, gently, he set out to seduce her with the kiss he now controlled.

Delaney heard a soft moan from deep within her throat as she stroked her hands through Jamal's hair. She was in a state of heated bliss. She had no idea what he was doing to her but whatever it was, she didn't want him to stop. There were certain areas in her mouth that his tongue was touching that were driving her insane to the point that the heat between her legs was becoming unbearable.

She felt him rubbing against her and that combined with what he was doing to her mouth was too much. He sucked her tongue deep when she felt the first inkling of desire so strong it shot through her body like a missile and exploded within her.

She groaned, long and deep in her throat. Her body began to tremble. Every nerve ending seemed electrified. Her knees felt weak, her head began spinning and the last conscious thought that flooded her mind was that she was dying.

Delaney slowly opened her eyes and gazed up at Jamal. She was draped across him, sitting in his lap on the sofa.

She blinked, her breathing was heavy, ragged. "What happened?" she asked in a whisper, surprised that she was able to get the words out. She felt so weak.

"You passed out."

She blinked again, not sure she had heard him correctly. "I passed out?"

He nodded slowly. "Yes. While I was kissing you."

Taking a deep breath, she closed her eyes remembering. She may be a novice but she had the sense to recognize a climax when she experienced one. Her first and she was still a virgin. It seemed that every part of her body had become detached, as pleasure the degree of which she had never felt before had flooded through her. It had been just that intense.

She took another deep breath, closing her eyes, trying to gather her thoughts. She was a doctor, right out of medical school, and fully understood the workings of the human body. All through life she had aced all her biology classes. Under normal circumstances people didn't pass out during a kiss.

She frowned. But what she had shared with Jamal had not been a regular kiss. It had been a kiss that had made her climax all the way to her toes. She opened her eyes and looked up at him. He was studying her intently. "What did you do to me?" she asked breathlessly, as the aftereffects sent shivers through her body. Her mouth felt sensitive, raw, and his taste was embedded so deeply in the floor and roof of her mouth that she savored him every time she spoke.

He smiled and it was a smile that made her stomach clench in heat. "I kissed you in a very special way."

She licked her lips before asking. "And what way was that?"

"Ares. It's a very volatile form of French kissing."

Delaney stared up at him, unable to say a word. When she had entered the room earlier that evening she had thought she had everything under control. In the end he had brought out his secret weapon. But he had warned her from the very beginning that he didn't play fair.

"Is that the way you kiss your mistress?" she whispered, suddenly wanting to know, although she knew how she would feel when he gave her the answer.

His eyes darkened and a surprised look came into his face. "No, I've never kissed Najeen that way. Other than the woman who taught me the technique when I was twenty-one, I've never used it on anyone."

Delaney blinked. Now she was the one surprised. Not only had he given her the name of his mistress, but had admitted to sharing something with her he had not shared with any other woman. For some reason she felt pleased.

"You climaxed while I was kissing you."

Delaney's mouth opened in silent astonishment, not believing he had said that. A part of her started to deny such a thing but knew he was experienced enough to know she would be lying through her teeth. She searched her brain for a response. What could a woman say after a man made a statement such as that?

Before she could gather her wits he added, "You're wet."

She swallowed, the soreness of her mouth almost made the task difficult. She knew what he meant and wondered how he knew? Had he checked? She was sitting in his lap, draped over him in a position that was downright scandalous. Had he slipped his hand inside her clothes and fingered her the way he had done the last time? Evidently the question showed on her face. He responded.

"No, I didn't touch you there, although I was tempted to. Your scent gave you away. It was more potent and overpowering, which is usually the case after a woman has a climax.''

Delaney stared at him, not believing the conversation they were having. At least, he was talking. She was merely listening, being educated and suddenly, thanks to him, was becoming aware of the intensity of her femininity.

He smiled again and as before her stomach clenched. He stood with her in his arms. ''I think you've had enough excitement for one night. It's time for you to go to bed.''

He began walking down the hall and she was surprised when he carried her into her bedroom instead of the one he was using. He gently placed her in the middle of the bed, then straightened and looked down at her.

''I want you, Delaney, but I refuse to take advantage of you at a weak moment. I will not have accomplished anything if you wake up in my arms in the morning regretting sleeping with me.''

He sighed deeply before continuing. ''As much as I want to bury myself inside of you, it's important to me that you come to me of your own free will, accepting things the way I have laid them out for you. All I can and will ever offer you is pleasure. What you got tonight was just a fraction of the pleasure I can give you. But it has to be with the understanding that my life is in Tahran, and once I leave here you can't be a part of it. I have obligations that I must fulfill and responsibilities I must take on.''

He leaned down and cupped her cheek, his dark gaze intense. ''All you can and ever will be to me is a beautiful memory that I will keep locked inside forever. Our two cultures make anything else impossible. Do you understand what I'm saying?'' he asked quietly in a husky voice filled with regret.

Slowly Delaney nodded her head as she gazed up at him. ''Yes, I understand.''

Without saying anything else Jamal dropped his hand from her face, turned and walked out of the room, closing the door behind him.

Delaney buried her head in the bedcovers as she fought back the tears that burned her eyes.

Seven

Delaney slowly opened her eyes to the brilliance of the sun that was shining through her bedroom window. Refusing to move just yet, she looked up at the ceiling as thoughts and memories of the night before scrambled through her brain.

She lifted her fingers to her mouth as she remembered the kiss she and Jamal had shared. Her mouth still felt warm and sensitive. It also felt branded. He had left a mark on her that he had not left on another woman. He had given her his special brand of kissing that had been so passionate it had made her lose consciousness.

Closing her eyes, Delaney gave her mind a moment to take stock of everything that had happened last night, as well as come to terms with the emotions she was feeling upon waking this morning.

Yesterday Jamal had pretty much spelled everything out to her. He had told her in no uncertain terms that he wanted her. But then in the same breath he had let her know that the time they spent at the cabin was all they would have together. He had obligations and responsibilities in his country that he would not turn his back on. He had a life beyond America that did not include her and never would. In other words, she would never have a place in his life.

As a woman who had never engaged in an affair, casual or otherwise, she had felt indignant that he would even suggest such a thing to her. But last night after he had left her alone in her bedroom, she had been able to think things through fully before drifting off to sleep.

Jamal's life was predestined. He was a prince, a sheikh, and his people and his country were his main concerns. He admitted he wanted her, not loved her. And he had stated time and time again that what was between them was lust of the strongest kind, and as two mature adults there was nothing wrong in engaging in pleasure with no strings attached.

What he offered was no different from what her brothers consistently offered the women they dated. And she had always abhorred the very thought of any woman being weak enough to accept so little. But now a part of her understood.

Things had become clear after Jamal had brought her into the room and placed her on the bed. And after listening to what he had said then, she had known: she was falling in love with Jamal. And now, in the bright of day, she didn't bother denying the truth.

Although her brothers were dead set against ever falling in love, a part of her had always known that she would be a quick and easy victim. Everyone knew that her parents had met one weekend at a church function and less than two weeks later had married. They claimed they had fallen in love at first sight and always predicted their children would find love the same way.

Delaney smiled, thinking of her brothers' refusal to believe their parents' prediction. But she had, which was one of the reasons she had remained a virgin. She had been waiting for the man she knew would be her one true love, her soul mate, and had refused to sell herself short by giving herself to someone less deserving.

Over the years she assumed the man would be a fellow physician, someone who shared the same love for medicine that she did. But it appeared things didn't turn out that way. Instead she had fallen for a prince, a man whose life she could never share.

She opened her eyes. What Jamal had said last night was true. When they parted ways, chances were they would never see each other again. Somehow she would have to accept that the man she loved would never fully belong to her. He would never be hers exclusively. But if she accepted what he was offering, at least she could have memories to treasure in the years to come.

She inhaled deeply, no longer bothered that there would not be a happy ending to her situation with Jamal. But until it was time for them to leave, she would take each day as it came and appreciate the time she would spend with him, storing up as many memories as she could.

She wanted him, the same way he wanted her, but in her heart she knew that for her, lust had nothing to do with it. Her mind and her actions were ruled by love.

"Are you sure you are all right, my prince?" Asalum asked Jamal as he gave him a scrutinizing gaze.

"Yes, Asalum, I am fine," Jamal responded dryly.

Asalum wasn't too sure of that. His wise old eyes had assessed much. He had arrived at the cottage to deliver some important papers to His Highness to find him sitting outside on the steps, drinking coffee and looking like a lost camel. There were circles under his eyes, which indicated he had not gotten a good night's sleep, and his voice and features were expressionless.

Asalum glanced over to the car that was parked a few feet from where they stood. "I take it the Western woman is still here."

Jamal nodded. "Yes, she is still here."

"Prince, maybe you should—"

"No, Asalum," Jamal interrupted, knowing what his trusted friend and confidante was about to suggest. "She stays."

Asalum nodded slowly. He hoped Jamal knew what he was doing.

Delaney walked into the kitchen to the smell of rich coffee brewing. She was about to pour a cup when her cell phone rang. "Hello?"

"I just thought I would warn you that the Brothers Five are on the warpath."

Delaney smiled, recognizing Reggie's voice. "And just what are they up to now?"

"Well, for starters they threatened me with missing body parts if I didn't tell them where you were."

Delaney laughed. She needed to do that and it felt good. "But you didn't did you?"

"No, only because I knew their threats were all bluster. After all, I'm family, although I must admit I had to remind them of that a few times, especially Thorn. The older he gets, the meaner he gets."

Delaney shook her head. "Didn't Mom and Dad assure them I was all right and just needed to get away and rest for a while?"

"Yeah, I'm sure they did, Laney, but you know your brothers better than anyone. They feel it's their God-given right to keep tabs on you at all times, and not knowing where you are is driving them crazy. So I thought I'd warn you about what to expect when you return home."

Delaney nodded. She could handle them. Besides, when she returned home they would provide the diversion that she needed to help get over Jamal. "Thanks for the warning."

"How are things going otherwise? Is the prince still there?" Reggie asked between bites of whatever he was eating.

"Yes, he's still here and things are going fine." Now was not the time to tell Reggie that she had fallen in love with Jamal. A confession like that would prompt Reggie to tell her brothers her whereabouts for sure. His loyalty to her only went so far. She decided a change of topic was due at this point.

"There is something I need to ask you about," she said, fixing her focus on one object in the kitchen.

"What?"

"The table in the kitchen. Did you and Philip know that it wobbles?"

She could hear Reggie laughing on the other end. "The table doesn't wobble. It's the floor. For some reason it's uneven in that particular spot. If you move the table a foot in either direction it will be perfect."

Delaney nodded, deciding to try it. "Thanks, and thanks again for keeping my brothers under control."

Reggie chuckled. "Laney, no one can keep your brothers under control. I merely refused to let them intimidate me. For now your secret is safe. However, if I figure they will really carry out their vicious threats, then I'll have to rethink my position."

Delaney grinned. "They won't. Just avoid them for the next three weeks and you'll be fine. Take care, Reggie."

"And you do the same."

After hanging up the phone, Delaney poured a cup of coffee, then took a sip. She wondered if Jamal, who was an early riser, was outside practicing his kickboxing as he normally did each morning.

Glancing out the window, she arched her brow when she noted another car parked not far from hers, a shiny black Mercedes. And not far from the vehicle stood Jamal and another man. The two were engaged in what appeared to be intense conversation. She immediately knew the man with Jamal was Asalum. However, with his height and weight, the older man resembled more of a bodyguard than the personal secretary Jamal claimed he was.

Her gaze moved back to Jamal. There was such an inherent sensuality to him that it took her breath away. In her mind everything about him was perfect. His bone structure. His nose. His ebony eyes. His dark skin. And especially his seductive mouth that had kissed her so provocatively last night.

He was dressed in his Eastern attire, which reminded her that he was indeed a sheikh, something she tended to forget at times; especially when he dressed so American, the way he had last night. He'd been casually dressed in a pair of khakis and a designer polo shirt. Today he was wearing a long, straight white tunic beneath a loosely flowing top robe of royal blue. He also wore a white kaffiyeh on his head.

Delaney thought about the decision she had made. Feeling somewhat shaky, she took another sip of her coffee. She knew exactly what would happen once she told him that she had decided to take what he offered. There was no way he would ever know that she loved him, since she had no intention of ever admitting that to him. His knowing wouldn't change a thing, anyway.

She sighed deeply. She had to make him believe she no

longer had any reservations about their future and she had accepted the way things would be.

No longer satisfied with watching him through the kitchen window, she decided to finish her coffee out on the porch the way she normally did each morning. She wanted him to see her. She wanted to feel the warmth of his eyes when they came in contact with hers. And she needed to look into them and know his desire for her was still there.

At the sound of the door opening, Jamal and Asalum turned. Delaney became the object of both men's intense stares but for entirely different reasons. Asalum was studying her as the woman who had his prince so agitated. Having been with His Highness all of his life, he read the signs. Jamal wanted this woman sexually, and in a very bad way. No other woman would do, so there was no need for him to suggest a substitute. He could only pray to Allah that Jamal didn't take drastic measures. He had never seen his prince crave any woman with such intensity.

Jamal's gaze locked with Delaney's the moment she stepped outside of the door. The first thing he thought was that she was simply beautiful. The next thing he thought was that she looked different today. Gone were the shorts and tops she normally wore, instead she was wearing a sundress that had thin straps at the shoulders. Her curly hair was no longer flowing freely around her face but was up and contained by a clip.

"I must be going, Your Highness," Asalum said, reclaiming Jamal's attention, or at least trying to. Jamal kept his gaze on Delaney as he nodded to Asalum's statement.

As far as Asalum was concerned that in itself spoke volumes. Shaking his head, he inwardly prayed for Allah's intervention as he got into the car and drove away.

* * *

Inhaling deeply, Delaney released the doorknob and walked to the center of the porch. Her gaze never left Jamal's and she read in his what she wanted to read. The dark eyes holding hers were intense, forceful and sharp; and the nerve endings in her body began to tighten and the area between her legs filled with warmth with the look he was giving her.

And when he began walking toward her, he again reminded her of a predatory wolf and gave her the distinct impression that he was stalking her, his prey. There was something about him that was deliciously dangerous, excitingly wild and arrogantly brazen. A part of her knew that no matter how far he went today in this game of theirs, she would be there with him all the way. In the end he would succeed in capturing her, but she would not make it easy. She intended to make him work.

When Jamal came to a stop in front of her, dark eyes held hers in sensual challenge. "Good morning, Delaney," he murmured softly.

"Good morning, Jamal," she responded in kind. She then looked him up and down. "You're dressed differently this morning."

A smile twitched his lips, and amusement lit his eyes as he looked her up and down, just as she had done him. "Yes, and so are you."

Delaney smiled to herself. She was beginning to like this game of theirs. "I thought today would be a good day to do something I haven't done since I got here."

"Which is?"

"To try out the hot tub on the back deck. It's roomy enough for two, and I was wondering if you would like to join me?"

Jamal raised a brow, evidently surprised by her invitation

but having no intention of turning it down. "Yes, I think I will."

A tense silence followed. Delaney knew that he wasn't anyone's fool and saw her ploy as seduction in the making and was determined, as he'd done the night before, to turn things to his advantage. He didn't play fair.

She was hoping he wouldn't. In fact, she was counting on it.

"I'll go on out back," she said, her voice only a notch above a whisper. "My swimming suit is under my dress."

"And it won't take long for me to change clothes and join you," he said huskily.

She turned to leave, then suddenly turned back to him. "And one more thing, Jamal."

"Yes?"

"You have to promise to keep your hands to yourself."

A rakish grin tilted the corner of his lips, and a wicked gleam lit his eyes. "All right, I promise."

Delaney blinked, surprised he had made such a promise. She really hadn't expected him to. Without saying another word, she opened the door and went back into the house, wondering if he really intended to keep his promise.

Delaney was already settled in the hot tub when Jamal appeared on the back deck. She found it difficult to breathe or to look away. She finally let out a deep whoosh of air when she broke eye contact with him to take a more detailed look at his outfit.

The swimming trunks he wore were scantier than the boxer trunks he usually wore for kickboxing. Everything about him oozed sex appeal, and she felt inwardly pleased that for the next three weeks he belonged only to her.

"The water looks warm," Jamal said, breaking into Delaney's thoughts.

She smiled up at him. "It is."

Tossing a towel aside, he eased onto the edge of the tub. She watched his every move, mesmerized, as he swung into the water and took the seat in the hot tub that faced her. He sank lower, allowing the bubbly, swirling water to cover him from the shoulders down.

"Mmm, this feels good," he said huskily, closing his eyes and resting his head against the back of the tub.

"Yes, it does, doesn't it," Delaney said, raising a brow. Was he actually not going to try anything? He seemed perfectly content to sit there and go to sleep. He hadn't even tried taking a peek at her swimming outfit beneath the water. If he had, he would have known that she was wearing very little. On a dare from one of her college roommates, she had purchased the skimpy, sheer, two-piece flesh-tone bikini, although she had never worn it out in public.

Feeling frustrated and disappointed, she was about to close her own eyes when she felt him. He had stretched out his foot and it had come to rest right smack between her legs. Before she could take a sharp intake of breath, he had tilted his toes to softly caress her most sensitive area. She closed her eyes and sucked in a deep breath as his foot gently massaged and kneaded her center in tantalizing precision, slowly through the thin material of her swimsuit.

But he didn't plan to stop there. He lifted his foot higher to rest between her breasts. Then with his big toe leading the pack, he caressed the right nipple through the thin material of her bikini top, and when he had her panting for breath, he moved on to the other breast.

When all movement ceased, Delaney opened her eyes to find Jamal had covered the distance separating them and was now facing her in the tub.

"I don't need hands to seduce you, Delaney," he whispered softly yet arrogantly, his lips mere inches from hers. "Let me demonstrate."

And he did.

Leaning toward her he used his teeth to catch hold of the material of her bikini top to lift it up. Growling like the wolf she thought him to be, he sought out her naked breasts with a hunger that nearly made her scream in pleasure. Using his knee he shifted her body so that her breasts were above water. His tongue tasted, sucked, devoured each breast, and she became a writhing mass of heated bliss.

Moments later a moan of protest escaped her lips when he leaned back. She slowly opened her eyes to find him staring at her with raw, primitive need reflected in his eyes.

Her breasts, tender from the attention he had given them, rose and fell with every uneven breath she took. As she continued to look at him, he smiled hotly, boldly, and she knew he was not finished with her yet.

Not by a long shot.

She held her breath when he leaned toward her again and with the tip of his tongue traced the lines of her lips before traveling the complete fullness of her mouth. Automatically her lips parted, just as he'd known they would, and he slipped his tongue inside.

A shudder of desire swept through her, and she wondered what madness had possessed her to forbid him to use his hands. Improvising, Jamal was using his tongue to seduce her as effectively as he would have used his hands. Jamal was an expert kisser and he was using that expertise on her, showing her just how much he enjoyed kissing her. And by her response he knew just how much she enjoyed being kissed.

Moments later he ended the kiss and pulled back. A sexy smile tilted the corners of his lips. "I want to see you naked, Delaney."

His words, murmured softly in the most sensual voice, touched Delaney deeply and sent a surge of emotions through her body. Once again he was able to shake up passion within her that she hadn't known existed—passion she wanted to explore with him.

Moaning, she leaned toward him. She was free to use her hands even if he wasn't. Feeling bold she circled her arms around his neck and kissed him again. Already used to each other, their tongues met, mingled and began stroking intimately.

When she finally lifted her mouth from his, she drew back, looked into his eyes and whispered thickly. "And I want to see you naked, as well."

His eyes darkened even more. "When you are nude will I be able to use my hands?" he asked in a deep, husky tone.

She smiled and instead of answering she asked a question of her own. "When you are nude will I be able to use *my* hands?"

His voice lowered to a growl when he answered. "You can use anything you want."

Her smile widened. "And so can you."

Eight

Jamal was nearly at his wit's end as he watched Delaney towel herself dry. The swimming suit she had on was too indecent, too improper and too obscene for any woman to wear, but he was getting a tremendous thrill seeing her in it. His already ragged pulse had picked up a notch, and his breath was becoming so thick it could barely pass through his lungs.

She would be arrested and jailed if she wore anything so scandalous in his country with the pretense of going swimming in it. The material was so sheer he had to widen his eyes to make sure he wasn't seeing naked skin. And both pieces clung to her curves in the most provocative way, nearly exposing everything. Everything he wanted. Everything he had dreamed about. Everything he craved. And everything he intended to have.

He frowned. She was deliberately driving him mad.

"Like what you see, *Your Highness?*"

And she was deliberately provoking him.

Awareness joined the arousal already flaring in his eyes. He crossed his arms and looked at her assessingly, eager for her to strip. "Yes, I like what I see, but I want to see more." She was inflaming him one minute and frustrating him the next. He knew this was a game to her, a game she intended to play out until the end…and win. She may be amused now but when this was over he would be the one cackling in sensuous delight.

"Anxious, aren't you, Jamal?"

There was no reason for him to lie. "Yes."

She grinned, tossing the towel aside. "I think we should go inside."

He lifted a dark brow. As far as he was concerned here was just as good a place as anywhere. "Why?"

Delaney silently considered his question, sending him a sidelong glance. Did he actually think she would strip naked out in the open? "Because I prefer being inside when I take off my clothes."

Jamal favored her with a long, frustrated sigh. "It doesn't matter where you are as long as you take them off, Delaney. I'm holding you to your word."

"And I'm holding you to yours." She turned to go inside.

Following behind, close on her heels, he crossed the deck and quickly reached out and opened the back door for her.

She looked back over her shoulder and smiled. "Thanks, Jamal. You are such a gentleman," she said in a low, throaty voice.

Jamal smiled. He hoped she thought that same thing a few hours from now. A true gentleman couldn't possibly be thinking of doing some of the things that he planned to do to her. He would try to be a *gentle man* but beyond that he couldn't and wouldn't make any promises. As soon as they were inside with the door closed he said, "Okay, do it."

Delaney shook her head thinking Jamal must have a fetish for a woman's naked body. But she knew the reason he was challenging her and was so anxious to see her naked was because he really didn't believe she would go through with it. He thought she was stringing him along. After all, she had told him she played to win. She glanced around. "Be real, Jamal. I can't strip naked in a kitchen."

He frowned at her. "Why not?"

She shrugged. "It's not decent."

Jamal couldn't help but laugh. "You're worried about decency dressed in an outfit like that?"

"Yes."

Jamal rolled his eyes heavenward. "It's not like you have a whole lot to take off, Delaney. You're stalling."

"I'm not stalling."

"Then prove it."

"All right. I'd feel better taking off my clothes in the bedroom."

Jamal nodded, wondering what excuse she would come up with once he got her into the bedroom. Although he was frustrated as sin, he had to admit he was getting some excitement out of her toying with him, however he much preferred that she toyed with him in quite a different way. This game of hers had gone on long enough.

"Okay, Delaney, let's go to the bedroom."

"I'll need a few minutes to get things ready," she said quickly.

Jamal could only stare at her. Surely she had to be joking. What was there to get ready? She was half-naked already. Before he could open his mouth to voice that very opinion, she said, "Just five minutes, Jamal. That's all I'm asking." She turned and rushed off, not waiting for his response.

"Five minutes, Delaney, is all you will get," he called

after her. "Then I'm going to join you, whether you're ready or not."

Delaney glanced around the room. She was ready.

Because her bedroom was on the side facing the mountains, at this time of the day it was the one with the least amount of sunlight, which was perfect for the darkened effect she needed. The curtains in the room were drawn and lit candles were placed in various spots in the room. Already their honeysuckle scent had filled the midday air.

She had removed the top layer of bedcovering and the two pillows from the bed; arranging them on the floor and adorning each side with the two tall, artificial ficus trees in the room.

She smiled. Everything was set up to make the room resemble a lovers' haven, and as far as she was concerned it was fit for a prince...or a wolf in prince's clothing. It was time the hunter got captured by his game.

She turned when she heard the gentle knock on the door. Taking a deep breath, she crossed the room. Taking another quick glance around, she took another deep breath and slowly opened the door.

Jamal swallowed with difficulty and somehow remembered to breathe when Delaney opened the door, wearing a short, shimmering, baby-doll-style nightie that was sheerer than her bikini had been. Where the swimming suit had left a little to the imagination, this outfit told the full story.

Completely white, the material was a sharp contrast to her dark skin, and he could easily make out certain parts of her body, clearly visible through the transparent chiffon material. The first question that came to his mind was, why would a woman who thought she would be spending a month alone in a cabin out in the middle of nowhere, bring such intensely feminine apparel? He would have to ask her that question later…but not now. The only thing he wanted to do now, other than get his breathing back on track, was to touch her.

But first he needed to think…and then he conceded that his brain had shut down. He was now thinking with another body part. He forced his gaze to move to her face. She was looking at him, just as entranced with him as he was with her. He had changed into a silk robe and from the way it hung open it was obvious he wasn't wearing anything underneath.

The look of desire in her eyes made a deep, heated shudder pass through him, and when she took a step back into the room, he followed, closing the door behind him. He quickly took in his surroundings; the drawn curtains, the candles and the bedcovers and pillows strewn on the floor.

He then gave Delaney his full attention. Reaching out, he placed a finger under her chin. "Take it off, Delaney," he whispered, holding her gaze. "No more excuses, no more games. You have succeeded in pushing me to my limit."

Delaney stared at him, unable to do anything else. Through the haze of passion she saw him, really saw him, and knew that he might not love her, but she had something he desperately wanted. And from the way he was breathing and the size of the arousal he wasn't trying to hide, she had something he urgently needed.

A ray of hope sprang within her. He may be predestined to marry another woman, and he may have a mistress waiting for him in his native land, but now, today, right at this very moment, *she* was the woman he wanted and desired with an intensity that took her breath away.

"Take it off."

His words, Delaney noted, had been spoken…or a better word would be *growled*…through clenched teeth and heated frustration. She would bet no woman had ever given him such a hassle to see her naked. The one thing he would remember about her was that she hadn't been easy.

Reaching up to ease the spaghetti straps off her shoulders, she gave the top part of her body a sensuous wiggle, which prompted the gown to ease down past her small waist, over her curvaceous thighs and land in a pool at her feet.

She met Jamal's gaze when she heard his sharp intake of breath. She watched as his eyes became darker still, and saw how he was focusing entirely on her naked body, seemingly spellbound by what he saw. His eyes roamed over her like a lover's caress, the deep penetration of his gaze blazing a heated path from the tips of each one of her breasts to the area between her legs. Then he reached up and released the clip on her hair, which tumbled around her shoulders.

A thickness settled deep in her throat, and her chest inhaled tightly a faint whisper of air. She thought she would always remember this moment when she had openly displayed herself to him, the man she loved. He was seeing her as no man ever had.

"Now it's your turn," she managed to say in the silence that had settled between them. She watched as he slowly pushed the robe from his shoulders, then stood before her proud, all male, intensely enlarged and naked for her. The glow from the candles reflected off his brown skin.

"I want you, Delaney." His whispered plea penetrated the room. "I want to take you in all the ways a man can take a woman. And I promise to give you pleasure of the richest, purest and most profound kind. Will you let me do that? Will you accept me as I am, accept the things that cannot be and accept that this is all we can have together?"

Delaney stared at him, knowing what her answer would be. This wasn't a cold day in July, and he wasn't coming to her exclusively. Yet she would go to him willingly, without shame and with no regrets. She lifted her head proudly as she fought back the burning in her eyes, inwardly conceding yet again that she loved him. And because she loved him, for whatever time they had left to spend together she would be his, the sheikh's woman, and he would be hers, Delaney's desert sheikh.

She met his gaze, knowing he waited for her response. As much as he wanted her, if she denied him he would accept her decision. But she had no intention of denying him. ''Yes, Jamal, I want to experience the pleasure you offer, knowing that is all I can and will ever get from you.''

For a moment Delaney could have sworn she saw regret, deep and profound, flash in his eyes just before he reached out and gathered her in his arms, sealing his lips with hers.

An insurmountable degree of passion flared quickly between them the moment his tongue touched hers, and the only thing she could do was revel in the fiery sensations bombarding her. His skin felt hot pressed against hers, and when his hand began caressing her backside, instinctively she got closer, feeling him large and hot, intimately pressing against her.

The kiss seemed to go on and on, neither wanting to break it, both wanting to savor every moment they spent together and not rush toward what they knew awaited them. The more they kissed the more fire ignited between them. They began devouring each other's mouths with a hunger that bordered on obsession. His tongue was familiar with every inch of her mouth, every nook and cranny, and it tasted and stroked her to oblivion.

When breathing became a necessity that neither could any longer deny, Jamal broke off the kiss but immediately leaned her back over his arms and went to her breasts. Delaney didn't think her mind or senses could take anything more, with the way his mouth and tongue felt locked on her breasts.

Displaying an expertise that had her weak in the knees, he paid sensual homage to her breasts, lavishing them with gentle bites and passionate licks. The scalding touch of his tongue on her nipples flooded her insides with heat so intense she thought she would burn to a crisp right there in his arms.

"Jamal..."

He didn't answer. Instead he picked her up in his arms and carried her to the area she had prepared for them on the floor. He quickly glanced around the room and saw what she had tried to do. She had attempted to turn a section of her bedroom into an exotic, romantic haven.

Whispering something in Arabic, then Berber, he eased down on the floor with her in his arms, suddenly feeling a deep tightening in his chest when full understanding hit him. She was giving herself to him on a level that was deeply passionate, erotically exotic and painstakingly touching.

Quickly forcing the foreign emotions he felt to the back of his mind, he took her lips once again. While holding her mouth captive to his, his fingers sought out every area of her body, flicking light touches over her dark skin, trailing from the tip of her breasts, down to her waist and naval and along her inner thigh before claiming the area between her legs.

Delaney broke off their kiss, closed her eyes and shuddered a moan when she felt Jamal's fingers touch her intimately, stroking, probing, caressing. She struggled to breathe, to maintain control and to not drown in the sensations he enveloped her in.

She opened her eyes and looked at him. His gaze was locked on hers, and she could tell from the taut expression covering his dark face that he was one step from sexual madness. The erection she felt against her hip was big and hard, and she didn't think it could possibly get much bigger or harder. Nor did she think she could take much more of what he was doing to her.

"I want you in a way I have never wanted another woman, Delaney," he murmured seductively as his fingers continued to stroke the very essence of her. "I want this," he said hot against her ear, pushing his fingers deeper inside of her so she would know just what "this" was.

Delaney could barely breathe. Her only response was a shuddering moan.

He slowly moved his fingers in and out, relishing the tiny purrs and moans she made, knowing he was giving her pleasure.

A sudden tremble passed through his body, and he knew at that moment he couldn't last any longer. He had to get inside of her. Shifting his body to where she lay under him, he sat back on his haunches and looked down at her, glorying in the beautiful darkness of her skin, the magnificent curves of her hip, the flatness of her stomach and the rich sharp scent that was totally her.

Her gaze was holding his, and he saw desire so profound in her eyes he almost lost it. He had to connect with her and sample the very essence of the gift she was offering him. "Are you protected, Delaney?" he asked in a voice so low he wasn't sure she had heard him.

She shook her head. "No, I…"

Whatever it was she was going to say she decided not to finish it. But that was all right, he would protect her. Standing, he quickly crossed the room to gather his robe off the floor. He had placed packs of condoms in the pockets. After putting one on he returned to her and knelt back in place before her, pausing to admire her lying there, waiting for him. Unable to help himself he leaned down and captured her lips again, in a passion that shook him to the core and made everything inside of him feel the need for her.

He tasted her richness as his tongue stroked hers to a hunger that matched his, tantalizing them into a feverish pitch. Breaking off the kiss he whispered something in Arabic as he slid her body beneath him, his gaze locked to hers. A part of him knew that he would always remember this moment as he fitted his body over her, parting her thighs.

His erection was like a radar and guided him unerringly to his destination, the part of her it desperately wanted, probing her entrance before slowly slipping inside, wanting to savor the feel of entering her body. Her heated muscles that encompassed him were tight, almost unbearably so, and held him as he inched his way forward.

He watched as she drew in a deep breath as her body's silkiness sheathed him, and he kept moving forward slowly, until he came to an unexpected resistance. He frowned, then stared at her, not believing what he had come up against, but knowing it was the truth.

"You're a virgin," he whispered softly. Amazed. Dazed. Confused.

She suddenly lifted her legs to wrap around his waist, holding him captive. Meeting his astonished gaze, she whispered sassily, "And your point is, *Your Highness?*"

Jamal couldn't help but smile, although this was not one of those rare times he usually did so. He was always a very serious person when having sex with a woman. He frowned when it suddenly occurred to him that he was doing more with Delaney than merely having sex. With his full concentration on her he responded, "My point is that I don't do virgins."

She reached up and placed her arms around his neck,

lifted her chin and met his stare. "You'll do this one, Prince."

He held her gaze, feeling angry because he knew she was right. There was no way he could retreat. "Why didn't you tell me, Delaney?"

She shrugged and whispered softly, "I didn't think it was such a big deal."

His face became hard as granite. "It *is* a big deal. In my country I would be honor-bound to marry any woman I deflowered."

"Then it's a good thing we're not in your country, isn't it?" She could see the dark storm gathering in his eyes.

"But what about your family? They would expect me to do the right thing."

Delaney's eyes widened when she immediately thought of her brothers. They wouldn't give him a chance to do the right thing. They would take him apart piece by piece instead. "My family has nothing to do with this. I'm a grown woman and make my own decisions. Women in this country can do that, Jamal."

"But—"

Instead of letting him finish whatever he intended to say, she deliberately shifted her body, bringing him a little deeper inside of her. She smiled when she heard his sharp intake of breath. She had him just where she wanted him.

Almost.

"Stop that!" he said, frowning down at her. "I have to think about this."

"Wrong answer, Prince. There's no time to think," she said, as the feel of him throbbing inside of her sent her senses spinning and heat flaring in all parts of her body. She writhed beneath him and felt him place his hands on her hips to hold her still.

"Delaney, I'm warning you."

She stared at him, at the hardness of his face, the darkness of his eyes and the sweat that beaded his brow. He wanted her but was fighting it.

It was time to end his fight. She wanted her memories and she intended to get them.

She lifted her body to capture his mouth and before he could pull back, her tongue skated over his lips. When he let out a deep moan she slipped inside, stroking his tongue into sweet surrender, the way he had done her mouth several times. She knew that once she had his mouth under her control, the rest would be history. There was no way he would not concede.

He groaned deep in his throat and grabbed her wrists, but he didn't release her. Nor did he break their kiss. Instead he became a willing participant, a prisoner of desire of the hottest kind. She knew he was still fighting her, trying to hold on to his last shred of will, his ingrained inclination to do the right thing. But she was beyond that and wanted him beyond it, too.

She felt his hands release her wrists and move to her hips, lifting her to him, and with one hard thrust, he had completely filled her.

Delaney gasped at the first sensation of pain, but it subsided when he slowly began moving inside of her. He broke off their kiss and held her gaze in the fiery darkness of his. "I brand you mine," he growled, nuzzling his nose against her neck as he rode her the way he had dreamed of since that first day, with an urgency that bordered on mania. His hands that were locked at her hips lifted her, held her in place to meet his every thrust.

Delaney closed her eyes, drowning in the pleasure he was giving her. Her fingers dug deeply into his shoulders, and her legs were wrapped tightly around his waist. She opened her eyes to see him looking at her, almost into her soul, and she whispered in a voice filled with quivering need, mind-stealing pleasure. "If you brand me, then I brand you, too, Jamal."

Her words sent Jamal's mind reeling and he knew she *had* branded him. Closing his eyes, he reared his head back, feeling his body connect to her, becoming a part of her, lured to a place he didn't want to go but found himself going anyway. In the back of his mind he heard her whimpering sounds of pleasure as his body continued to pump repeatedly into hers, taking her on a journey he had never traveled before with any woman. And when he felt the tip of her tongue softly lick the side of his face, tracing a path down his neck, he knew then and there he would always remember this but the memories would never be enough.

"Jamal!"

He felt her draw in a shuddering breath. He felt her body quiver tightly around him, clenching him, milking him and elevating him to the same plane she was on. He inhaled deeply, his nostrils flaring when the scent of her engulfed him, surrounded him. Sensations he had never experienced before took control, flooding him to the point where he couldn't think; he could only feel.

He released a huge, guttural groan when the world exploded around him and forged them tighter in each other's arms, as extreme sexual gratification claimed their bodies, their mind and their senses.

And for the first time in his entire life, Jamal felt mind-boggling pleasure and body-satisfying peace. He knew then and there that he would never get enough of this woman.

Nine

Jamal stirred awake as the flickering candles cast shadows in the room. He glanced down at the woman he still held in his arms. She was getting much-deserved rest.

After making love that first time, they had both succumbed to sexual oblivion, quickly falling asleep, only to wake up an hour or so later just as hungry for each other as they had been before. He had been concerned that it was too soon again for her, but Delaney took matters into her own hands, straddling him and seducing him to the point where he had finally flipped her underneath him and given her what they both wanted.

Once again he had experienced something with her he had never experienced before, and knew when they separated he would never find peace. She would always be a clinging memory for the rest of his days.

In the past after having slept with a woman, he would quickly send her away, then shower to remove the smell of lingering sex. But the only place he wanted Delaney was just where she was, in his arms, and he didn't want to shower. In fact, he wanted to smother in the sexual scent their bodies had created.

He looked down at the way they were still intimately locked together, their limbs tangled and their arms around each other as if each was holding the other captive, refusing to let go. He reached out and stroked a lock of hair back from her face thinking how peaceful she looked asleep. She had the same blissful expression on her face that she had the night she had passed out from him kissing her.

He inhaled deeply. He had made love to other Western women, but nothing had prepared him for the likes of Delaney Westmoreland. She was a woman who could hold her own with him. She called him Your Highness with a haughtiness that was outright disrespectful for a man of his stature and distinction. She didn't hesitate to let him know she couldn't care less for those things, and that in his country he might be an Arabian prince but to her he was just a man. No more, no less. Other women gave in to him too easily and were quick to let him have his way. But that wasn't the case with the passionate, provocative and smart-mouthed Delaney.

And then there was the fact that she had been a virgin. Never in a thousand years would he have considered such a possibility, not with the body she had and especially with her nonconservative views. The woman was definitely full of surprises.

He shifted when he began to harden inside of her. As much as he wanted her again, he needed to take care of her. The best thing for her body right now was a soak in a tub of hot water.

"Delaney?" He whispered her name and gently nudged her awake. She lifted sleep-drugged eyes up at him, and her lips, swollen from his kisses, eased into a smile. That smile pulled at something inside of him. It also made him become larger. He saw her startled expression when she felt her body automatically stretch to take him deeper.

He had to find a way to stop this madness. His body was becoming addicted to her. He moved to pull out, but she tightened the leg she had entangled with his. Frowning, he looked down at her. "You need to soak in a tub of hot water," he rasped softly, trying to reason with her and gain her cooperation.

She shook her head. "No. Not now, maybe later." The sound of her voice came out in a sultry purr.

He tried ignoring it. "No, now. Besides, I need to put on another condom before we do this again. If I don't, we run the risk of an accident happening."

He figured that explanation would work on her good sense.

It didn't.

He felt the muscles of her body holding him inside of her tighten. He closed his eyes to pull out of her, but the more he tried the more her muscles held him.

He glared down at her, despising himself for wanting her so much. She was torturing him, and she damn well knew it. "Do you know what you're asking for?"

She met his gaze. "Yes," she murmured softly, while her body continued to milk him into a state of mindless pleasure. "I'm asking for *you,* Jamal."

"Delaney…" Her words were like a torch, sending his body up in flames. He captured her mouth with his at the same time his body thrust deep inside of her, giving her just what she had asked for.

"Mmm, this feels good," Delaney said leaning back in the hot tub.

After they had made love, he had gathered her naked body up in his arms and taken her outside and placed her in the hot tub then got in with her. "It will help relieve the soreness," Jamal said slowly, looking at her. He had decided to sit on the other side of the tub, at what he considered a safe distance away. He couldn't trust himself to keep his hands off her.

"I'll survive a little soreness, Jamal. I am not a weak woman."

He chuckled, thinking that was an understatement. "No, Delaney, you are definitely not a weak woman. You're as strong as they come."

Delaney quirked a brow, not knowing whether he meant it as a compliment or an insult. She knew he was used to docile women; women who were meek and mild. She doubted it was in her makeup to ever be that way.

She glanced around. The sun had gone down, and dusk was settling in around them. "Are you sure it's all right for us to be out here naked? What if someone sees us?"

"I don't have a problem being seen naked."

Delaney lifted eyes heavenward. "Well, I do."

Jamal leaned back and closed his eyes. "This is private property, you said so yourself. And besides, they can look at you all they want, but they'd better not touch."

Delaney stared at him. "Getting a little possessive, aren't we?"

Jamal slowly opened his eyes and met her stare. "Yes." His attitude about that was something he couldn't quite understand. He had never been possessive of any woman, not even Najeen. That thought didn't sit too well with him. Deciding to change the subject, he said, "Tell me about this job of yours as a doctor."

Delaney spent the next half hour telling him about how

she had to go through a period of residency where she would work at the hospital in a pediatric ward.

"Is this hospital a long way from your home in Atlanta?" he asked as he shifted his body below the water line some more.

"Far enough. It's in Bowling Green, Kentucky, so I'm leasing an apartment for the two years I'll be working there." She didn't add that she needed that distance away from her brothers.

When she had first left home for college she made the mistake of going to a school that was less than a two-hour drive from Atlanta. Her brothers nearly drove her crazy with their frequent impromptu visits. The only people who enjoyed seeing them had been the females living in her dorm who thought her brothers were to die for.

For medical school she had decided on Howard University in D.C. Although her brothers' trips to see her weren't as frequent, they still managed to check on her periodically just the same, claiming their parents' concern was the reason for their visits.

"After your residency do you plan to open up your own medical office?" Jamal asked.

"Yes, it's my dream to open up a medical office somewhere in the Atlanta area."

Jamal nodded. "And I hope your dream comes true, Delaney."

She knew he meant that with all sincerity and was deeply touched by it. "Thanks."

Later that evening they ate a light meal that the two of them prepared together. He noticed she had slid the table closer to the window and that it wasn't wobbling. She told him of her conversation with Reggie, who had told her that the problem had not been with the table but with the floor.

"So as you can see, Jamal, things aren't always as they seem to be."

He had lifted a brow at her comment but said nothing.

She smiled. He knew she had been trying to make a point about something, but from his expression it was quite obvious he didn't get it. Delaney felt confident that one day he would.

After dinner she sat in the living room watching television while he sat on the opposite end of the sofa sketching on something. It was the same papers that he had occasionally worked on since she had arrived.

"What are you doing?" she asked curiously when he had finally placed the documents aside.

He reached out his arms to her and she covered the distance and went to him. He placed her in his lap while he showed her what he had been working on. "This is something I plan to build in my country. It will be a place my people can go for their necessities."

She studied the sketch, admiring the structural design. "It's sort of like an open market."

He smiled, glad she had recognized it for what it was. "Yes. It will be similar to the places you refer to in your country as a one-stop shop. Here they will be able to buy their food, clothing and any other miscellaneous items they might need. I also want it as a place for them to socialize while doing so, to come together. Although the majority of my people are like me, both Arab and Berber descent, and are in harmony for the most part, there are those who every once in a while try to cause friction between the two ethnic groups."

Delaney lifted her head. "What sort of friction?"

He smiled at her, feeling her genuine interest. "It's a feud that's dated back hundreds of years. The reason my mother and father married to begin with was to unite the Arabs and the Berbers, producing me, an heir of both heritages. The disagreement is about what should be recognized as the official language of our nation. Right now it's Arabic and has been for hundreds of years, but a group of African-born descendents believes it should be Berber.''

Delaney nodded. ''You mainly speak Arabic, right?''

''Yes, but I am fluent in both. When I become the king, my biggest challenge will be how to get everyone to embrace both languages, since both are a part of my country's heritage.''

Delaney studied his features. ''What are your views on the matter, Jamal?''

He smiled down at her. ''I understand the need for both sides. There is a need to teach the Berber language and preserve and promote the Berber culture. However, since Arabic is the official language, everyone is duty bound to speak it. But I'm not for Arabization being imposed on the Berbers who reside in isolated regions and who want to keep their heritage intact, just as long as they remain loyal to Tahran and its leadership. The needs of all of my people are important to me.''

Delaney nodded. A thought then struck her. ''Speaking of needs, what about medical care? How do your people get the medical care they need?''

He looked at her as if surprised by her question. ''We have hospitals.''

She twisted in his arms, the concern in her features evident. ''But what about those people living in smaller cities who can't make it to a hospital? Don't you think you may want to consider having a clinic just for them?''

Jamal lifted a brow. ''In a market?''

She shook her head smiling. ''Not necessarily in the market but adjacent to it. I believe this entire idea has merit as a way to get people out and about in an open marketplace-type setting. But think of how convenient it would be to them. It might prompt more people who need it to seek medical care.''

Jamal nodded, thinking she had a point. He had often approached his father with concerns of the need for more medical facilities. Keeping his people healthy was another way of keeping them safe. He looked down at the plans he had designed. ''And where do you suggest this facility be placed?''

Delaney's smile widened. She was pleased that he had asked her opinion. For the next hour or so they discussed his designs. She had been surprised when he told her that although his master's degree from Harvard had been in business administration, he had also received a bachelor degree from Oxford in constructual engineering.

That night when they retired to his bedroom, he again told her of his intent to not touch her anymore that day. He just wanted to hold her in his arms.

''Why did you change your mind about us?'' he asked her quietly, holding her close, loving the feel of her softness next to him.

Delaney knew she could not tell him the truth. She did not want him to know that she had fallen in love with him. There was nothing to gain by doing so. ''I took another look at things, Jamal, and decided that I wasn't getting any younger and it was time I did something about being a virgin.''

He was surprised. Women in his country remained virgins until they married. ''You had a problem with being a virgin?''

She heard the censure in his voice. ''No, I didn't have a problem with it, but then I didn't want to die a virgin, either.''

He took her hand in his, letting his fingers curl around

hers and ignoring the sexual rush just touching her invoked. "There were never any plans in your future to marry?"

"Yes, but no time soon. I wanted to establish myself as a doctor before getting serious about anyone."

Jamal nodded. He then thought of another question that he wanted to ask her. "What about your lingerie?"

She lifted a brow. "My lingerie?"

"Yes."

"What about them?"

He cleared his throat. "They are the type a woman normally wears to entice a man. Why would you bring such sleeping attire when you had planned to be at this cabin alone?"

Delaney smiled, understanding his question. She enjoyed going shopping for sexy lingerie and feminine undergarments. Her bras and panties were always purchased in matching sets, and she tended to be attracted to bright colors and for the most part shied away from plain-looking white underthings.

"I like looking and feeling sexy, Jamal, even when there's no one there to notice but me. Whenever I buy lingerie and underthings, I buy what I like for me with no man in mind."

"Oh."

"Now I have a question for you, Jamal," Delaney said softly.

"Yes?"

"Why would you bring all those packs of condoms with you when you had planned to be here alone?"

He grinned sheepishly at her. "I didn't bring them. I purchased them after I got here."

"When?" she asked lifting a curious brow.

"The night you and I went to that all-night supermart," he said, studying her features and wondering how she felt knowing he had planned her seduction even then. He reached out and touched her chin with his finger. "Are you upset?"

"No," she said as a smile curved her lips. "I'm not upset. I'm glad you did have the good sense to buy them."

Long after Delaney had fallen asleep, Jamal was still awake. For some reason the thought of another man sleeping with her, holding her in his arms the way he was doing bothered him. It also disturbed him that one day there would be a man in her life who would see her in all those sexy lingerie and underthings that she liked buying for herself.

When he finally dozed off to sleep, his mind was trying to fight the possessiveness he felt for the beautiful woman asleep in his arms.

"I take it that you enjoyed the movie," Jamal said when he pulled Delaney's car to a stop in front of the cabin.

She smiled, showing perfect white teeth and very sensuous lips. "What woman wouldn't enjoy a movie with Denzel Washington in it."

He searched her face, amazed at the tinge of jealousy he was feeling. "You really like him, don't you?"

"Of course," she responded, getting out of the car and walking up the steps to the door. "What woman could resist Denzel?"

Jamal frowned. "And you would go out on a date with him if he were to ask you?"

Delaney stopped walking and turned around. She studied Jamal's expression, seeing his frown and clenched teeth. As she continued to observe him, she had a sudden flash of insight when something clicked in her brain. He's jealous! Of all the outrageous…

She inwardly smiled. If that was true it meant, just possibly, that he cared something for her. But then a voice within her taunted, *Not necessarily. It could also mean that now that he has slept with you he sees you as a possession he wants to keep and add to the other things he owns.*

"Yes, I would go out with him," she finally answered, and saw the frown on his face deepen. "However, I don't plan on losing sleep waiting for such a miracle to happen. Besides, I doubt he would ask any woman out on a date since he's a married man." She quirked a brow. "Why do you want to know?"

He walked past her and said, "Curious."

She fell silent as she followed him to the porch. When she had awakened that morning he had already left the bed and was outside practicing his kickboxing. By the time she had made coffee and placed a few Danish rolls in the oven he had come inside. They had enjoyed a pleasant conversation, then he had suggested that they take in a midday matinee at the movie theater.

She knew his intention had been to get her out of the cabin for most of the day so he wouldn't be tempted to touch her again. He wanted to give her body time to adjust to their making love before they did it again, although she had tried convincing him that her body had adjusted just fine. She sighed deeply. It was time for her to take matters into her own hands.

Jamal's hands tightened like fists at his side when he stood aside to let Delaney enter the cabin. He didn't understand why an irrational stab of envy had consumed him, making him angry, since he was familiar with Western women's fascination with movie actors and sports figures. But it rubbed him the wrong way to include Delaney in that number.

Closing the door behind them, he watched as she tossed her purse on the sofa. He had admired her outfit the moment she had emerged from the bedroom wearing it. She certainly knew how to dress to show off her attributes to the maximum. The short blue dress stopped way above her knees and showed off her curves and shapely legs. Her high heeled sandals were sexy enough to drive him to distraction.

Then there was that lush behind of hers that always kept his pulse working overtime. He was just dying to touch it, run his hand all over it. He took a deep, fortifying breath as he let his gaze trace her legs from the tip of her polished toes, past her ankles, beyond her knees and up to her thighs that met the hem of her dress. He couldn't help but think about what was under that dress. He shook his head. How had he thought he could go a whole day without making love to her again?

"How does soup and a sandwich sound, Jamal?"

Jamal swallowed. His low reserve of willpower was pitiful. It took every ounce that he had to move his gaze away from her legs and focus on her face. "That sounds good and I'd like to help."

She smiled. "You're getting pretty handy in the kitchen. You seem to enjoy being there."

Jamal's brows furrowed. Not really, he wanted to say. She was the one who enjoyed being in the kitchen. He merely enjoyed being wherever she was. "Things are not always as they seem to be, Delaney."

She studied him for a long moment, then turned toward the kitchen. He followed, trying his best not to notice how the soft material of the dress hugged her hips as she walked ahead of him.

"Do you want to chop the veggies for the soup?"

His mind clicked when he heard a sound. He thought he heard her speak but wasn't sure. "Did you say something?"

She stopped walking and turned around. Her eyes smiled fondly at him as if he was a dim-witted human being. The way he was lusting after her, he was certainly feeling like one. "I asked if you wanted to chop the veggies for the soup I'm making."

"Oh, sure. Whatever you need me to do. I'm at your disposal."

"Are you always this generous to the women you sleep with?"

Jamal tensed, not liking her question and wondering how she could ask such a thing. While he was with her he didn't want to think about other women. "I'm considered a very generous man to a lot of people, Delaney," he said, holding her gaze, refusing to let her bait him.

She nodded and continued her walk to the kitchen.

Jamal sighed. He knew there was an American saying that…if you can't stand the heat stay out of the kitchen. He muttered a low curse. He was following the heat right into the kitchen.

Delaney stopped stirring the ingredients she had already put in the pot and glanced over at Jamal. He was standing at the counter slicing vegetables. "How are you doing over there?"

He lifted his head from his task, and his gaze met hers across the room. "I'm just about finished."

"Good. The vegetables will be ready to go into the pot in a few minutes."

He swallowed hard. "It smells good. I bet it will taste good, too."

She gave a casual shrug. "There's nothing like something smelling good and tasting good," she said before turning back around.

Jamal was doing his best not to remember how good she smelled and how good she tasted. He also tried not to remember other things. Like the feel of her beneath his hands as he held her hips firmly, lifting her as he had entered her; how her eyes would darken each time he thrust into her, pulled out and thrust into her again. And the sounds of pleasure she made, and how her body would tighten around him, holding him deep inside of her, milking him bone dry. At least trying to.

Jamal diced mercilessly into a tomato, furious with his lusty thoughts and knowing his control was slipping. Taking a deep breath he gathered the chopped vegetables in a bowl and on unsteady legs slowly made his way across the room to Delaney.

She turned and smiled at him, taking the bowl he offered. "You did a good job," she said, dumping the chopped vegetables into the steaming pot. "Now all we have to do is wait for another boil and then let things simmer awhile."

Jamal nodded. He knew all about boiling and simmering. He came damn close to telling her that he was already doing both from the feminine heat she generated. For the past thirty minutes he had tried to distract himself from watching her move about in the kitchen. Every move she made had turned him on. When she had reached up into the cabinets looking for garlic salt, her already short dress had risen, showing more leg and thigh and making sweat pop out on his brow. The sight had been pure temptation.

He took a step closer to her. "So what kind of soup are you making?"

She chuckled good-naturedly. "Vegetable soup."

The lower part of his body throbbed from the intensity of his need. He forced a smile. "That was simple enough to figure out, so why couldn't I think of that?"

Delaney placed the lid on the pot, turned the dial to simmer and looked up at him. "Maybe you have your mind on other things." She stepped away from the stove and walked over to the sink.

He followed her. He should have been expecting this, her being one step ahead of him. He wouldn't put it past her to have set him up. "So what do you think I have on my mind?" he asked, looking at her intently.

She shrugged and met his gaze squarely. "I'm not a mind reader, Jamal."

"No," he said, raking his gaze over her body. "Only because you're too busy being a seductress."

"No, I'm not."

"Yes, you are. Do you think I don't know what you've deliberately been doing to me for the past half hour?"

For a long moment neither said anything as their gazes clashed. Then Delaney asked in a deep, sultry voice, "Well, did it work?"

Jamal took a step closer as he muttered under his breath. He reached out and brought her body tightly against him, letting her feel how well her ploy had succeeded. "What do you think?"

She moaned softly and shifted her stance to spread her legs, wanting the feel of the hard length of him between them. Even through the material of their clothing there was simmering heat. Her eyes were half-closed when she said, "I think you should give your body what it wants and stop trying to play hard to get."

He lowered his head and licked her lips, slowly, thoroughly. "I was trying to spare you and give your body a chance to adjust."

Delaney's breath quickened with the feel of his tongue licking her lips as if he was definitely enjoying the taste. "I don't want to be spared, and my body doesn't need to adjust. The only thing it needs is you," she said quietly, shivering inside as his tongue continued to torment her. "I want to be made love to and satisfied. I want you inside of me, Jamal. Now."

The only thing Jamal remembered after that was taking her mouth with an intensity that overwhelmed him as he picked her up in his arms. He wanted her now, too. Quickly crossing the room, he set her on the table and pushed up her dress to her waist and lifted her hips to pull her panties completely off.

Like a desperate man he tore at the zipper of his jeans and set himself free just long enough to push her legs apart. Pulling her to him he then entered her. "Oh, yes," he said, throwing his head back when he felt her heat clutch him, surround him.

"You make me crazy, Delaney," he said, squeezing his eyes shut and placing a tight hold on her thighs, savoring how she felt. He didn't want her to move. He just wanted to stand there, between her legs, locked inside of her.

"Don't move," he ordered when he felt her body shift. "Just let me feel myself inside of you for a minute. Let me feel how wet you are around me and how tight." He wondered how a body so wet could hold him so snugly.

He inhaled her scent. It was like an aphrodisiac, making his sexual hunger all the more intense. "Lie back," he whispered hoarsely, and held on to her hips while she did so. When she was flat on her back on the table he leaned in and pulled her closer to him, going deeper inside of her. He opened his eyes when he felt her thighs quiver and stretch wide to wrap her legs around his waist.

What little control he had left vanished when he leaned down and caught her mouth with his. He closed his eyes and began making love to her with the intensity of a madman, a wolf mating, someone engaging in sex for the last time before facing a firing squad; he was just that greedy, besotted, possessed. He didn't think he could go another single day without getting some of this. All of it. And for a quick crazy moment he thought of taking her back to

Tahran with him—against her will if he had to—just to keep her with him forever.

Forever.

He opened his eyes and muttered an Arabic curse then he mumbled an even worse one in Berber, not believing the path his thoughts had taken. Nothing was forever with him—especially a woman. But as he arched his back to go even deeper inside of Delaney, he knew that with her he had a different mindset. His body had a mind of its own. It wanted to devour her, every chance it got. Sexual intensity flared throughout his body, and he thought nothing could and would ever compare to this.

And moments later when she screamed out her climax, he sucked in a deep whiff of her scent at the same time that he exploded deep in her feminine core. It was then that he realized he wasn't wearing a condom. Too late to do anything about it now, since he had no intention of pulling out, and he continued to pour his seed deep within her as his body responded to the pleasure of their lovemaking.

He clenched his teeth as he drove into her hard, wanting to give her everything that was his, everything he had never given another woman. Finally admitting at that moment that what he was sharing with Delaney Westmoreland went beyond appeasing sexual appetites.

She had somehow found a way to erode his resolve and raw emotions. All his defenses were melting away, the dam around his heart had crumbled. When he realized what was happening to him, shock reverberated through his body, only intensifying his climax.

Then another emotion, one stronger, more powerful, ripped through him. Up to now it had been a foreign element, but at that moment he felt it, from the depths of his loins to the center of his heart.

Love.

He loved her.

Ten

The next week flew by as Jamal and Delaney enjoyed the time they were spending together. Jamal was awakened before dawn one morning by the insistent ringing of his cell phone. He automatically reached for it off the nightstand next to the bed, knowing who his caller would be. "Yes, Asalum?"

He felt Delaney stir beside him, her arms were tight around him, and her naked limbs were tangled with his. Last night they'd had dinner outside on the patio, preferring to enjoy the beauty of the moon-kissed lake while they ate. Then later in his bed they had made love all through the night.

Something Asalum said grabbed Jamal's attention. "Say that again," he said, immediately sitting up. "When?" he asked, standing, and at the same time he grabbed for his robe.

He turned and met Delaney's curious gaze. "I'll contact

my father immediately, Asalum,'' he was saying into the phone. He let out a heavy sigh. When he disconnected the call he sat down on the edge of the bed and pulled Delaney into his arms. Before she could ask him anything he kissed her.

"Good morning, Delaney,'' he whispered huskily, close to her ear when he finally released her mouth. He cradled her gently in his arms.

"Good morning, Prince,'' she said smiling up at him. Then her dark brow puckered in concern. "Is anything wrong?''

Jamal shifted positions to lean back against the headboard, taking Delaney with him. "I won't know until I talk to my father. Before I came to this country I had been involved in important negotiations involving several countries that border mine. The usual issues were under discussion, and after three months everyone left satisfied. But according to Asalum, the sheikh of one of those countries is trying to renege on the agreement that was accepted by everyone.''

Delaney nodded. "So in other words, he's causing problems and being a pain in the butt.''

Jamal chuckled, appreciating the way Delaney put things. "Yes, he is.''

Delaney placed a quick kiss on his lips before slipping out of his arms and getting out of the bed. "Where are you going?'' he asked, when she began gathering up her clothes off the floor. Seeing her naked was making his body stir in desire.

She turned and smiled at him. "I'm going to take a shower. I know you have an important call to make and I want to give you complete privacy to do so.''

He grinned, looking her over from head to toe. "And without any distractions?''

She chuckled. "Yeah, and without any distractions.'' She

gave him a saucy look. "You're welcome to join me in the shower after you finish your call." She then left his bedroom, closing the door behind her.

Jamal didn't finish the call in time to join Delaney in the shower. After talking to his father he discovered the situation was more serious than he had thought and he was needed in Tahran immediately.

He had placed a call to Asalum with instructions to make the necessary arrangements for his return to the Middle East. All his life he had known what was expected of him when duty called, but this was the first time he had something important in his life that meant everything to him.

He hadn't told Delaney how he felt because the emotions were new to him and he wasn't sure it changed anything. She was who she was, and he was who he was. Love or no love, they could never have a future together. But could he give her up?

He knew that somehow he had to let her go. She could never be his queen, and he loved her too much to ask her to be his mistress, especially knowing how she felt about the subject. And then there was that other problem his father had conveniently dumped in his lap. The old sheikh of Kadahan wanted Jamal to marry his daughter as soon as it could be arranged. The thought of marrying, which a few weeks ago he would have merely accepted as his duty, now bothered him to no end. He felt angered at the prospect of having any woman in his life other than Delaney. And he did not appreciate the pressure his father was putting on him to return home and consider marriage to Raschida Muhammad, princess of Kadahan, at once, just to make her father happy.

Jamal shook his head. And why the sudden rush for a wedding? Why did Sheikh Muhammad feel the urgency to marry his daughter off? Jamal had posed the question to his father, and the only answer he got was that the old sheikh's health was failing and he wanted to make sure his daughter, as well as his people, were in good hands should anything happen.

Jamal refused to believe Sheikh Muhammad had serious health problems. He had spent three months with the man while negotiating that contract, and Sheikh Muhammad had still been actively bedding his French mistress when Jamal had left to come to America.

He tightened his fists at his side wondering what the hell was going on. He suddenly felt as if he was headed for the gallows and wished there were some other eligible sheikh the princess could marry. For once he did not want to be the sacrificial lamb.

He inhaled a deep breath. There was nothing left to do but to return to Tahran. It seemed that life had landed him a crushing blow. He felt frustrated and shaken. He was about to leave the only woman he truly loved to return home and marry someone he cared nothing about. A part of him died at the thought, but he knew what he had to do.

He also knew he owed it to Delaney to let her know that he was leaving and the reason why. She deserved his honesty. Chances were that news of his engagement would go out over the wire service, and he didn't want her to find out about it from the newspapers.

It took several moments for him to compose himself, then he left his bedroom to find Delaney.

She was nowhere to be found in the cabin, so he walked toward the lake looking for her. It was a warm, sunny day and birds were flying overhead. A part of him wished he could be that carefree, with no responsibilities and only the commitments that would make him happy. But that wasn't the case. As his father had not hesitated to remind him a few minutes earlier, he was a prince, a sheikh, and he had responsibilities and obligations.

Jamal stopped walking when he saw Delaney. She was sitting on the dock with her legs dangling over the edge, letting her toes play in the water. A light breeze stirred her hair about her face. She tossed it back in place, then leaned back on her hands to stare up the birds; the same flock he had seen earlier.

Leaning against a tree, he continued to stare at her. He smiled. Seeing her sitting there, peaceful and serene, was the most beautiful sight he had ever seen, and he wanted to keep it in his memory forever. And knew that he would.

A battle was raging within him, love versus responsibility. Deep in his heart he knew which would win. He had been groomed and tutored to take on responsibilities all his life. But this thing called love was new to him. It was something he had never experienced, and for the first time in his life he felt lost, like a fish out of water.

A shiver passed through him. He loved her with a passion he hadn't known was possible, yet he had to let her go because duty called.

He forced himself to walk toward her, and when he got to the edge of the dock, he whispered her name and she turned and met his gaze. The look in her eyes and the expression on her face told it all. She didn't know the why of it, but she knew he was leaving.

And from the way her lips were quivering and from the way she was looking at him, she didn't have to say the words, because he immediately knew how she felt. The silent message in her eyes told him everything, just as he knew the silent message in his was exposing his very soul to her. For the first time it was unguarded...just for her.

They had both played the game and won...but at the

same time they had both lost. He hadn't played fair and she had played to win and in the end they had gotten more than they had bargained for—each other's hearts. But now they were losing even more—the chance to be together.

"Come here," he whispered softly, and she stood and came into his arms willingly. He held her like a dying man taking his last drink, pulling her to him and holding her close; so close he could hear the unevenness of her breathing and the feel of her spine trembling. But at the moment all he wanted to do was hold her tight in his arms, close to his aching heart.

They stood that way, for how long he didn't know. He stepped back and looked at her, wondering how he would survive the days, weeks, months and years, without her. Wondering how a woman he had met only three weeks ago could change his life forever. But she had.

He swallowed the thick lump in his throat and said, "Duty calls."

She nodded slowly as she studied his features. Then she asked, "It's more than the business with the sheikh of that other country isn't it?"

He met her gaze. Deep regret was in his eyes. "Yes. I've been summoned home to marry."

He watched as she took a deep breath, saying nothing for a few moments. Hurt and pain appeared in her features although he could tell she was trying not to let them show. Then she asked in a very quiet voice, "How soon will you be leaving?"

He thought he could feel the ground under his feet crumble when he said, "As soon as Asalum can make the necessary arrangements."

She tried to smile through the tears he saw wetting her eyes. "Need help packing, Your Highness?"

A surge of heartache and pain jolted through him. This

was the first time she had called him Your Highness without the usual haughtiness in her voice. He reached out and clasped her fingers and brought them to his lips. In a voice rough with emotion, tinged with all the love he felt, he whispered, "I would be honored to accept your help, My Princess."

He pulled her into his arms and covered her mouth with his, zapping her strength as well as his own. The inside of her mouth was sweet, and he kissed her the way he had kissed her so many other times before, putting everything he had into it.

Without breaking the kiss he gathered her up into his arms and carried her over to the hammock. He wanted and needed her now. And she had the same wants and needs as he did, and began removing her clothes with the same speed he removed his. He then gathered her naked body in his arms and placed her flat on her back in the hammock. Straddling her, he used his legs to keep the hammock steady as he entered her body, almost losing it before he could push all the way inside. His entire body filled with love as he sank deeper and deeper into her. All his thoughts were concentrated on her.

For a moment, like the hammock, he felt his life was hanging by cords, but when she wrapped her legs around his waist and looped her arms around his neck, he knew she was all he would ever need and was the one thing he could never have.

But he would have these lasting memories of the time they had spent together. They were memories that would have to last him a lifetime. He began moving, thrusting in and out of her, his hunger for her at its highest peak, knowing this may very well be the last time he had her this way. Over and over again, he withdrew, then pushed forward again, wanting her and needing her with a passion.

Under the clear blue sky, with the sunshine beaming brightly overhead, he made love to his woman with an urgency that overwhelmed both of them. The muscles inside of her squeezed him, as he pumped into her relentlessly.

In the deep recesses of his mind he heard Delaney cry out as completion ripped through her, once, twice and a third time, before he finally let go, letting wave after wave of sensations swamp his body, and he shuddered deep into her, filling her fully.

He dug his heels into the solid ground to hold the hammock in place as he held her hips in a tight grip, experiencing the ultimate in sexual pleasure with the woman he loved.

Jamal and Delaney heard the sound of Asalum's car when it pulled up in the driveway. The older man had phoned earlier to say a private plane had arrived to take the prince back to his homeland and was waiting for them at the airport.

After making love outside they had come inside and showered together, only to make love again. She had sat on the bed and watched him dress in his native garb, trying not to think about the fact that one day soon another woman would be the one to be by his side.

When he had finished dressing, looking every bit a dashing Arab prince, a handsome desert sheikh, she helped him pack without a word being exchanged between them. There was nothing left to say. He had to do what he had to do.

Delaney inhaled deeply. She had known this day would eventually come, but she had counted on another week with him. But that was no longer possible. It was time for him to return to the life he had without her to marry another. She looked up and saw him watching her. She had been determined to make their parting easier but now...

"Will you walk me to the porch, Delaney?"

"Yes." She felt tears gathering in her throat. Crossing the room to him, she stood on tiptoe and kissed him on his lips. "Take care of yourself, Jamal."

He reached out and stroked her hair back from her face—a face he would remember forever. "You do the same." He inhaled deeply and said, "There were times when I wasn't as careful with you as I should have been, Delaney. If you are carrying my child, I want to know about it. I've left Asalum's number on the nightstand next to your bed. He knows how to reach me at any time, day or night. Promise you will call and let me know if you carry my heir."

Delaney looked up at Jamal, questions evident in her eyes. He knew what she was asking. "It doesn't matter," he said softly. "If you are pregnant, the child is mine and I will recognize it as such. Your child will be *our* child, and I will love it…just as much as I will always love you, its mother."

Tears streamed down her face with his admission of love. It had not been his intent to tell her how he felt, but he couldn't leave without letting her know their time together had meant everything to him, and without letting her know that he had fallen in love with her.

"And I love you, too, Jamal," she whispered, holding him tight to her.

He nodded. "Yes, but this is one of those times when love is not enough," he said hoarsely. "Duty comes before love."

Asalum blew the horn, letting them know it was time for him to leave. Delaney walked him to the door, then stood silently on the porch as she watched his trusted servant help him with his luggage. When that had been done Jamal turned and looked at her after taking a small box Asalum had handed to him.

Walking back to her he presented the box to her. "This is something I had Asalum make sure arrived with the plane. It is something I want you to have, Delaney. Please accept it not as a gift for what has passed between us, because I would never cheapen what we shared that way. But accept it as a token of my undying love and deep affection. And whenever you need to remember just how deeply I love you, just how much I care, take a look at it," he said, opening the box for her to see.

Delaney released a sharp intake of breath. Sitting on a surface of white velvet was the largest diamond ring she had ever seen. It was all of eight or nine carats. But what really caught her eye was the inscription on the inside of the wide band. It read—"My Princess." "But…but I can't take this."

"Yes, you can, Delaney. It belonged to my mother and is mine to give to the woman I choose."

"But what about the woman you must marry, and—"

"No, she is the woman being given to me. In my heart you are the woman I love and the woman I would choose if I could. This is mine and I want to give it to you."

Delaney shook her head as tears began clouding again in her eyes. "This is too much, Jamal. It is so special."

"Because you are too much, Delaney, and you are so special. And no matter who walks by my side, remember that things aren't as they seem to be. You are the one who will always have my heart."

He leaned and tenderly kissed her one last time before turning and walking to the car. He looked over his shoulder before getting inside, and waved goodbye.

She waved back, then stood rooted to the spot, watching the car drive away. She once remembered him saying that he didn't like leaving anything behind broken.

Evidently, it didn't include her heart.

She stood until the vehicle was no longer in sight. It was then that she allowed the floodgates to open, and she gave in to the rest of her tears.

The sun was low on the horizon by the time Delaney finished her walk. The cabin held too many memories, and she hadn't been ready to go there after Jamal left, so she'd taken a stroll around the cabin. But she had found no peace in doing that, either.

Every path she took held some memory of Jamal.

Already every cell in her body missed him, longed for him and wanted him. There was so much she'd wanted to say and wished she had said, but none of it would have mattered.

He had chosen duty over love.

Delaney's heart sank, yet a part of her both understood and accepted. She had known all along that things would end this way. There had been no other way for them to end. Jamal had been totally honest with her from the very beginning. He had not given her false hope or empty promises.

He was who he was. A man of honor. A man whose life was not his own, so it could never be hers.

She sighed when she reached the porch, remembering how they had often eaten breakfast while sitting on the steps enjoying the sun. She also remembered a particular time when he had said something to make her laugh just moments before claiming her mouth and kissing her in a way that had melted her insides.

Inhaling deeply, Delaney knew there was no way she could stay at the cabin any longer. She walked up the steps after making the decision to pack up her things and leave.

Delaney had just closed the last of her luggage when she heard a car door slam outside. Thinking, hoping, wishing, that Jamal had returned for some reason, she raced out of the bedroom to the front door. When she opened it, she swallowed deeply, recognizing her visitors.

Five men were leaning against a sports utility vehicle, and each man had his arms crossed over his chest and a very serious look on his face. Delaney sighed as she studied them.

Dare stood every bit of six-four and was the most conservative of the five. As a sheriff he demanded respect for the law, and those who knew him knew he meant business and not to call his bluff. Thorn stood an inch or so taller than Dare and was considered the prickliest of the five. He was moody and temperamental when it suited him. And he was the daredevil in the family, the one who took risks by racing the motorcycles he built. Chase was basically easygoing when the others weren't around. He stood six-two and relished in the success of his soul-food restaurant that had recently been named one of the best eating places in the Atlanta area. Stone was the most serious of the five, or at least he tried to be. His height fell somewhere between Chase's and Dare's. He enjoyed taking trips to different places, doing research for his books. So far all ten novels had appeared on the *New York Times* bestseller list. Last, but not least, was Storm, Chase's twin. He was as tall as Chase and had dimples to die for. It had always been his dream to become a fireman, and now because of a recent promotion, he was a proud lieutenant in the Atlanta Fire Department.

Even Delaney had to admit they were a handsome group, but at the moment she wasn't in the mood to be intimidated by the likes of the Westmoreland brothers. "You guys are a long way from home, aren't you?" she asked, moving her gaze from one to the other.

Of course it had to be the prickly Thorn who spoke up

by saying, "What the hell are you doing out here by yourself in the middle of nowhere, Laney?"

Before she could answer, Dare chimed in. "I see another
set of tire tracks, you guys. It looks like Laney wasn't here
by herself, or she had a visitor."

Delaney raised her eyes heavenward. "Always the cop
aren't you, Dare?" She sighed. "Why the show of force?
Didn't Mom and Dad tell you I was okay and wanted to be
left in seclusion for a while?"

"Yes, they told us," Stone said easily, but eyed her suspiciously as if she would be the perfect villain for his next
book. "But we had to check things out for ourselves. And
who did that other car belong to?"

Delaney refused to answer. In fact, she had a question of
her own. "How did you find me?"

Storm laughed. "Dare put your picture out over the FBI
wire service as a most wanted fugitive and we got a tip."

At her frown, Storm held up his hand and said, "I was
just kidding, Laney, for goodness sakes, cut the 'I will kill
you dead if that's true' look. Chase took a peek at the folks'
caller ID and got your new cell number. The telephone company was able to trace where the roaming fees were being
charged. Once we had that pinpointed the rest was a piece
of cake."

Delaney shook her head. "Yeah, I bet it was, like none
of you have anything better to do with your time than to
hunt me down. I am twenty-five you know."

Stone rolled his eyes. "Yeah, and the cost of milk was
two-fifty a gallon yesterday, so what's your point?"

Delaney glared at the five of them as she came down off
the porch. "My point is this. I can take care of myself, and
if you start trying to get into my business, I will do the
same for yours."

Four of the men looked uneasy. Of course it was Thorn

who took her threat in stride. "You're welcome to mess things up with me and the woman I'm presently seeing. She's the clingy type, and I've been trying to get rid of her for weeks."

Delaney glared at him. "If your mood hasn't run her off then nothing will." She inhaled deeply knowing her brothers were hopeless. They would never treat her like the adult she was. "Well, since you're all here, you may as well help carry my stuff to the car."

Chase lifted a brow. "You're leaving?"

"Yes."

"You never said whose car those tire tracks belonged to," Dare reminded her.

Delaney turned to go into the house, knowing her brothers would follow. She decided to tell them the truth since she knew they wouldn't believe her, anyway. "The car belonged to a prince, a desert sheikh from the Middle East," she tossed back over her shoulder.

She smiled when she heard Storm say to the others, "And she thinks we're stupid enough to believe that."

Eleven

Jamal gazed out of the window of the private plane as it landed at the Tahran airport. Any other time he would have thought it was good to be home, but tonight was an exception. His heart still ached for Delaney.

What was she doing? Was she thinking of him the way he was thinking of her?

"It is time to disembark, My Prince."

He lifted his gaze and met Asalum's concerned frown. Only someone as close to him as Asalum could know the pain he was feeling. He turned his head to look back out of the window, not saying anything for the longest time, then he said quietly. "I'm no longer filled with obsession, Asalum."

Asalum nodded. "And what is it now, Your Highness?"

"Depression."

Asalum shook his head. That much he had already concluded. The loss of the American woman was having a powerful effect on the prince.

Jamal slowly stood. He had noted the long, black limo parked on the runway. As usual his father had sent an entourage to welcome him home. With a grim set of his jaw he walked off the plane.

Within less than an hour's time he arrived at the palace. Sitting high on a hill it looked like a magnificent fortress, commanding its own respect and admiration, and had served as home for the Yasir family for hundreds of years.

After going through the massive wrought-iron gate, the limo had barely come to stop when a beautiful, young dark-haired woman raced from the front of the house into the courtyard.

''Jamal Ari!''

Jamal smiled for the first time since leaving America and watched his sister come to a stop next to the car, anxious for him to get out. A few moments later he found himself standing next to the car and embracing his sister, Johari.

''It's so good to have you home, Jamal Ari. I have so much to tell you,'' she said excitedly, pulling him through the huge wooden door she had come out of.

Jamal shook his head. If anyone could pull him out of his despairing mood, it would be Johari.

Later that night Jamal heard a soft knock on his door. He had claimed complete exhaustion, and his father had agreed to put off their talks until the next morning. Jamal had escaped to his private apartment in the palace, the entire west wing that was his. Rebakkah, Asalum's wife and the woman who had been his personal servant since birth, had brought him a tray of food a while ago that sat untouched on the table. He had no appetite to eat.

He opened the door to find his stepmother, Fatimah,

standing there. A beautiful woman with golden-brown skin and long, black wavy hair that flowed to her waist, she had retained her petite figure even after giving birth to two children. It seemed she never aged and was just as radiant at forty-four as she had been when she had come into his and his father's lives twenty-two years ago. He was not surprised to see her. Like Asalum, Fatimah knew him well and she knew when something was bothering him.

She stepped into his apartment and turned to face him. Concern was etched in her dark eyes. They were beautiful eyes that were all seeing, all knowing. "What is it, Jamal Ari?" she asked softly, studying him intently. "You are not yourself. Something is bothering you, and I want you to tell me what it is so I can make it better."

Jamal leaned against the door. He couldn't help but smile. When he was younger it seemed Fatimah had always been able to do that—make things better. Even if it pitted her against his father. She had never been outright disobedient, but she had definitely let the king know how she felt about certain things.

"I don't think you can make this one better, Fatimah," he said quietly. "This is something I have to work out for myself."

Fatimah looked at him for a long moment, then nodded, accepting his right to request that she not interfere. *For now.* "Well, whatever has you in such a sour mood will soon be forgotten. I sent word to Najeen that you had returned."

A frown covered Jamal's face. "Najeen?"

Fatimah's feminine chuckle bathed the air. "Yes, Najeen. Have you forgotten who she is?"

Jamal walked away from the door. He didn't want to see Najeen or any woman for that matter. The woman he wanted to see was millions of miles away. "Najeen will no longer be my mistress," he said softly.

Fatimah raised a dark brow. "Why? Do you have another?"

"No." He sighed deeply, not in the mood to explain. But seeing the surprised look on Fatimah's face he knew that he should. "I will be sending Najeen away, back to her homeland where she will be taken care of in the comfort she has become accustomed to until she takes another benefactor," he quietly decreed.

Fatimah nodded as she studied him. Her distress level rose. He was acting in a most peculiar way. "Is there a reason for your decision?"

His lashes lifted and his dark eyes met her even darker ones. Fatimah saw anxiety in their depths. She also saw something else that alarmed her. "Jamal Ari? What is it?"

He crossed the room to the window. The view outside was magnificent, but for the first time he didn't appreciate it. "While in America I met someone, Fatimah. A woman who stirred me in a way no other woman has. A Western woman who initially fought me at every turn, a woman who is just as proud and stubborn as I am, someone who was my complete opposite on some things but then my total equal on others. And…"

Silence. Across the room Fatimah watched his profile. She saw the way his hands balled into fists at his side; the way his jaw hardened and the sharp gaze that was looking out the window without really seeing anything. "And what?" she prompted, hoping he would continue.

Slowly, he turned to face her and she saw the torment in his features. "And someone I fell helplessly and hopelessly in love with."

Fatimah's heart took a lurching leap of surprise in her throat. "A Western woman?"

He met her gaze thinking, *my* Western woman. From the moment Delaney had gotten out of the car that day she had arrived at the cabin, a part of him had known she would be his. He just hadn't known that he, in turn, would become hers. "Yes," he finally responded.

Fatimah studied him. "But you've never liked Western women, Jamal Ari. You always thought they were too modern, headstrong and disobedient."

A smile forced its way to his lips when he thought of Delaney. In her own way she was all those things. "Yes, but I fell in love with her, anyway."

Fatimah nodded. "So what are you going to do? You love one but are planning to wed another?"

Jamal inhaled a deep breath. "I must do what I must do, Fatimah. I am duty bound to do what is needed for my country."

"And what about what is needed for your heart, Jamal Ari?" she asked, crossing the room to him. She had taken him into her heart as her son the moment she had seen him many years ago. "Your heart is breaking. I can sense it."

"Yes," he said, not bothering to deny it. "A good leader's decisions should not be ruled by love, Fatimah. They should be ruled by what is in the best interest of his people. My feelings matter not."

Fatimah looked at him, aware of the coldness settling in him. The bitterness, as well. She smiled sadly. For as long as she had known him, Jamal Ari had always had a mind and a will of his own. Yes, he was as dedicated to the people as his father, but still, he did exactly what pleased him, which usually had been fast cars and beautiful women. But now for what he considered to be the good of his people, he was willing to bend his mind and his will. And in doing so he was slowly destroying himself.

"Your father once thought that way, Jamal Ari, but now he thinks differently," she finally said, hoping to make him see reason before it was too late. "And I hope you will open your mind to do the same. Love is a powerful beast. It can bring the strongest of beings to their knees.''

Without saying anything else, she turned and walked out of the room. The door closed stiffly behind her, bathing the room in dead silence.

That night Jamal dreamed.

Delaney was with him, in his bed while he made love to her. Not caring that he wasn't using protection of any kind, his body repeatedly thrust into hers, glorying in the feel of her beneath him, of him being inside of her. In the darkness he could hear her moans of pleasure that combined with his own. He could actually feel the imprint of her nails on his back and shoulders as she gripped him, her fingers relentlessly pressing deeply into his skin. He felt his body moving closer to the edge and knew what he wanted more than anything. He wanted to impregnate her with his heir, just in case she wasn't pregnant already. He could envision a son with dark, copper-colored skin and a head of jet-black curls and eyes the color of dark chocolate.

His hand reached up and cupped her cheek, bringing her lips to his; lips he now hungered for all the time; lips he would tease into submission. They were also lips whose touch could arouse him to no end, drive him literally insane; lips belonging to a mouth he had branded.

He then gave his attention to her breasts as they thrust firmly and proudly from her body, taunting him to taste, which he did. He loved the feel of them against his tongue, wished he could love her this way forever and never have to stop. Around her he always felt primal, needy, lusty.

So he continued to make love to her, holding her tightly in his arms and whispering his words of love.

* * *

Thousands of miles away Delaney was in bed having that same dream.

Her body felt stretched, filled and hot. Her breasts felt soul-stirringly tender from Jamal's caress, and she could feel him loving her in a way she had become used to: determined, forceful. And very thorough.

His touch felt so right, and she felt a simmering sense that relief was near. She moaned a low, needy sound when a shiver passed through her body, and she gloried in the feel of being made love to this way. Then she exploded into tiny pieces.

Sometime later she opened her eyes, letting them adjust to the darkness. Rejoining reality she found that she was in bed alone. She curled her body into a ball as the waves of passion subsided, sending tremors through her.

She lay there, too shaken to move. Her dream had seemed so real. It had been as if Jamal had actually been with her, inside of her, making love to her. Taking a deep breath she swung her legs down to the floor and eased out of bed.

Going into the bathroom she washed her face in cool water, still feeling the heat of her dream. She inhaled deeply, glad she had returned to her apartment and not done as her brothers had suggested and gone to her parents' home.

She needed time alone—time to deal with everything. Her brothers had relented and had given in to her request for privacy. But she knew their placidness wouldn't last long. For the moment they were humoring her.

Glancing up at the mirror, she studied her red, swollen eyes. After her brothers had left, indicating they would be back to check on her within a few weeks, she had lain across the bed and cried.

She knew she couldn't continue on this way. Jamal was gone and wasn't coming back. She had to get on with her life, and the best way to do that was to go to work. She was not supposed to report to the hospital for another two weeks, but she wanted to go to work now. She would call the chief of staff to see if she could start earlier than planned.

The best thing to do was to keep her mind occupied. She had to stop thinking about Jamal.

Jamal got out of bed drenched in sweat as chills from the night air touched his body, making him tremble. His dream had seemed so real. He inhaled deeply. There wasn't the lingering aroma of sex, that special scent that he and Delaney's mated bodies generated.

He momentarily closed his eyes, memorizing her scent and visualizing in his mind the nights he had been pleasured by her body in reality and not in a dream. He could never forget the sight of her lying on her back…waiting for him. Her legs were shapely, long and sleek, and her breasts, there for him to touch and taste, and he had thoroughly enjoyed doing both. But what took his breath away to just think about it was her rear, perfectly rounded and curvy, making him hard each time he saw it.

The memories were making his body hard, and his breath was ragged. A part of him cursed the fate that had taken him away from Delaney. He acknowledged he would have left eventually, anyway. But knowing that had made every moment with her precious as time had clicked away. The time they had spent together had not been nearly long enough.

He reached for his robe from a nearby chair and put it on, then walked across the room to the door leading to the balcony. Stars dotted the midnight sky and softly lit the courtyard below. With its numerous lush plants, beautiful flowers and exotic shrubs, the courtyard had always been his favorite place to hide out as a child. But no matter how well he thought he could hide, Asalum would always find him. He smiled at the memory, breathing in the scent of gardenias and jasmine.

He then smiled at the thought of what Delaney would think if she ever saw the palace. A part of him could see her feeling right at home here. There was no doubt in his mind that with her Western views she would be a breath of fresh air. Her liberal way of thinking would no doubt scandalize some, but her caring would capture the hearts of others. The same way she had captured his.

Just thinking about her was torment. He straightened slowly and sighed. After he met with his father in the morning he would leave for Kuwait to meet with the other members of the coalition to reach another agreement with the Sheikh of Caron.

Then he would travel to Ranyaa, his estates in northern Africa. And there he would stay until the marriage arrangements had been worked out. He didn't want to be around anyone any more than necessary. He wanted to be left alone…to drown in his misery.

Twelve

Delaney returned the squiggling baby to its mother. "She seems to be doing a whole lot better, Mrs. Ford. Her fever has broken, and her ears no longer look infected."

The woman shook her head smiling. "Thanks, Dr. Westmoreland. You have been so nice to my Victoria. She likes you."

Delaney grinned. "I like her, too. And to be on the safe side, I'd like to see her again in a few weeks to recheck her ears."

"All right."

Delaney watched as the woman placed the baby in the stroller and left, waving goodbye before getting on the elevator. She sighed deeply. During the three weeks she had started working she was getting used to being called Dr. Westmoreland. Her heart caught in her chest each time she heard it. All of her hard work and dedication to her studies had paid off. She was doing something she loved and that was providing medical care to children.

Someone behind her chuckled, and she half turned and saw it was Tara Matthews. Tara was a fellow resident pediatrician whom she had met when she began working at the hospital. They had quickly become good friends.

"Okay, what's so funny?" she asked Tara, smiling.

"You are," Tara said, shaking her head grinning. "You really like babies, don't you?"

Managing a chuckle, Delaney said, "Of course I do. I'm a pediatrician, for heaven's sake. So are you, and I have to assume you like babies, too."

Tara took the stethoscope from around her neck and placed it in the pocket of her doctor's scrubs. "But not as much as you do. I wished I had a camera for the look of awe on your face when you were holding Victoria Ford. You were in hog heaven. And that's with every baby you care for."

Delaney chuckled, knowing that was true. "I already told you that I'm the only girl with five brothers and I was also the youngest. By the time I came along there weren't any babies in my family. And my brothers have declared themselves bachelors for life which means I won't be getting any nieces or nephews anytime soon."

Tara folded her arms under her breasts and nodded. "And for me it was the complete opposite. I'm the oldest of four and I had to take care of my younger sister and brothers, so I can hold off having any children of my own for years to come."

Delaney laughed. She really liked Tara and appreciated their friendship. Like her, Tara had moved to Bowling Green without knowing a soul, and the two of them had hit it off. They lived in the same apartment building and carpooled to work occasionally, and on the weekends they would go shopping and to the video store, then stay up late for hours talking and watching old movies. Being the same age, they shared similar interests, and like her, Tara was unattached at the moment, although Delaney couldn't understand why. With her dark mahogany complexion, light brown eyes and dark brown hair, not to mention her hourglass figure, Tara was simply gorgeous. Delaney knew that a number of doctors had asked her out and she had turned them down without blinking an eye.

But then so had she.

It wasn't uncommon for the single doctors to check out the new unattached female residence physicians. Although Delaney had been asked out several times, like Tara, she had declined the offers. Usually in the afternoons when she left work, unless she and Tara had made plans to do something together that night, she went home, took a shower and went to bed.

And each night she dreamed of Jamal.

"Tara to Delaney. Tara to Delaney. Come in please."

Delaney laughed when she realized Tara had been trying to get her attention. "I'm sorry, what were you saying?"

"I asked if you have any plans for tonight."

Delaney shook her head. "No, what about you?"

"No, none. Do you want to check out Denzel's new movie?"

Wincing, Delaney sucked in a deep breath. Tara's question reminded her that she had already seen the movie...with Jamal. She closed her eyes as she tried to blot out the memory.

"Delaney, are you all right?"

Delaney snapped her eyes back open and met Tara's concerned stare. "Yes, I'm fine." She took in another deep breath of air. "I've already seen the movie, but if you really want to go I can see it again."

Tara looked at her for a moment before saying, "You went with him, didn't you?"

Delaney took a deep breath. "Him who?"

"The guy you won't talk about."

Delaney didn't say anything for the longest time and then she nodded. "Yes, and you're right, I don't want to talk about him."

Tara nodded and reached out a hand to touch Delaney's arm. "I'm sorry. I didn't mean to pry. I have no right."

Delaney shook her head. "No, you don't." A smile softened her features when she added, "Especially since you're harboring secrets of your own."

A gentle smile tilted the corners of Tara's lips. "Touché, my friend. One day, after I've taken one sip of chardonnay too many, I'll spill my guts."

Delaney's expression became serious. "And one day when my pain gets too unbearable and I can use a shoulder to cry on, I'll tell you about him."

Tara nodded, understanding completely. "Good enough."

"I can't marry Princess Raschida," Jamal said, meeting his father's deep stare. He had arrived back at the palace after having been gone three weeks. It had taken all that time for him to make decisions he knew would change his life forever. But there was nothing he could do about that. Delaney was the woman he wanted, and she was the woman he would have…if she still wanted him.

King Yasir held his son's gaze. "Do you know what you're saying?" he asked, pushing himself up from the wing chair he had been sitting in.

Jamal stared into the face of the man who had produced him, a man loved, respected and admired by many—a man

Jamal knew would do anything for his people and a man who, in addition to everything else, believed in honor.

"Yes, Father," he answered quietly. "I know what I'm saying and I also know what this means. I truly thought I could go through with it, but now I know that I can't. I'm in love with someone else, and there is no way I can marry another."

King Yasir looked deep into his son's face. He had known when Jamal arrived home three weeks ago that something had been troubling him. Subsequently, Fatimah had shared with him what that something was. But he had turned a deaf ear to the thought that his son was in love with a Western woman. But now, seeing was believing. Jamal looked tormented and his features were those of a man who was hurting and whose very soul had been stripped away. With all the arrogance and lordliness Jamal was known to have, King Yasir was shocked that a woman had brought his son to this.

"This woman you love is a Western woman, is she not?" he asked gruffly.

Jamal continued to meet his father's gaze. "Yes," he said calmly.

"And you're willing to walk away from a woman of your people and marry someone not like you, of your faith and nationality?"

Chin up, head lifted and body straight, Jamal answered stiffly, "Yes, because, although not like me, she is of me. She is a part of me just as I am a part of her, Father. Love has united us as one."

The king's eyes darkened. "Love? And what do you know of love?" he declared. "Are you sure it's not your libido talking? Lust can be just as strong an emotion as love," he persisted.

Jamal walked closer into the room to face his father.

"Yes, I'm aware of that, and I do admit I was attracted to her from the moment I first saw her. I even thought it to be lust for a while, but it is not. At thirty-four I know the difference. I have had an ongoing affair with Najeen for a number of years, yet I've never thought about falling in love with her."

"You wouldn't have. You knew her position in your life. She was your mistress. If a man of your status were to fall in love it should be with his wife."

"But things don't always happen that way, Father, as you well know. Look at the number of other dignitaries who are besotted with their mistresses. And to answer your question as to what I know about love, I can honestly say that I know more now than I did some weeks ago," he concluded heavily. "I know love is what has me willing to stand before you now and plea for your understanding that I marry the woman who has my heart. Love is what has me in total misery, torment and depression. Love is also what has kept me functioning regardless of those things."

He took a deep breath and continued. "Love is what I see whenever you and Fatimah are together, and love is what has me willing to abdicate my right to succession if I have to."

Shock was reflected in his father's face. "You will give up the right to be my heir—the crown prince, the future king—for this woman?"

Jamal knew his words had caused his father pain, but they had to be said to make him understand just what Delaney meant to him. "Yes, Father, I would. Fatimah was right. Love is powerful enough to bring even the strongest man to his knees. I love Delaney Westmoreland, and I want her for my princess."

"But does this woman want you? What if she refuses to accept our ways? What if she refuses to change, and—"

''I don't want her to change,'' Jamal said vehemently. ''I love her just the way she is. I believe she would be willing to meet me halfway on certain things, and in my heart I also believe she will love our people as much as I do. But Delaney is not a woman who will bend because a man says she has to.''

''This woman is disobedient?'' the king asked, troubled, astounded.

''No more so than Fatimah was when she first came here. If I remember correctly there was some rumbling among the people when you married an Egyptian princess instead of one of your own. But over the years they have come to love and respect her.''

King Yasir didn't say anything for a long moment, because what Jamal had just said was true. Fatimah was loved and admired by all. Finally he released a long, deep sigh. ''Sheikh Muhammad isn't going to be happy with the news that you refused to marry his daughter. He may declare that our sheikhdom lacks honor. Are you willing to abide with that, Jamal?''

Jamal shook his head. That was the hardest thing he had to contend with. ''I will talk to the sheikh and if I have to I will agree to scour the entire countryside and find a replacement that pleases him. But I will not marry his daughter.''

The king nodded solemnly. He then picked up documents off his desk. ''Finding a replacement might not be necessary. Fatimah brought something to my attention a few weeks ago, gossip that was circulating among the servants. It seems that the servants in the Muhammads' household had been whispering, and even with the distance separating our sheikhdoms, the wind carried some of those whispers here. Rebakkah felt it was her duty to make her queen aware of what was being said.''

"And what was being said?" Jamal asked, watching lines of anger form in his father's face.

"Word that Princess Raschida is with child, which is the reason Sheikh Muhammad is in such a hurry to marry her off."

Jamal was taken aback. "I would have married her, not knowing this, and the child would not have been my true heir?"

"Yes," the king answered in a disgruntled voice. "Evidently they were hoping no one would be the wiser since she is in her very early stages."

Jamal became furious. "I can't believe Sheikh Muhammad would do such a thing."

"He was trying to save both himself and his daughter from embarrassment, Jamal. But I agree that what he had planned was dishonorable." He gazed down at the papers he held in his hand. "This report tells everything. When Fatimah brought me word, I had my men look into it, discreetly. It seemed that the princess has been involved in a secret affair—right under her father's nose—with a man who is a high-ranking official in his army."

"Well, the man can have her!" Jamal was appalled at how closely he had come to being taken in. And here Delaney could be—and for some reason he believed that she was—pregnant with his legitimate heir.

"I think you should know, Father," he said, drawing his father's attention, "there is a possibility that Delaney carries my child."

His father's eyes widened. "Do you know that for certain?"

Jamal shook his head. "No. I haven't had any contact with her since I left America. I can only cite my beliefs on male intuition or possibly a revelation from Allah. But I plan to go to her and find out. I also plan to ask her to marry me and return with me as my bride.''

''And if she doesn't want to do that?''

''Then I will convince her otherwise. Whatever it takes.''

King Yasir nodded, knowing just how persuasive Jamal Ari could be when it suited him. ''I much prefer that you marry someone from our country, Jamal, however, you are right, I do understand love doesn't recognize color, national origin or religion.''

''Do I have your blessings, Father?''

The king slowly nodded his head. ''Yes, although I am certain you would still marry her without my blessings. However, before I can fully accept her as the woman who will one day stand by your side to rule our people, I must meet her and get to know her. That is the best I can do,'' he quietly conceded.

Jamal nodded. ''And that is all I ask, Father. You are more than fair.''

King Yasir hugged his son in a strong display of affection, which Jamal returned. After the king released him from his embrace, Jamal turned and walked out of his father's study.

''Delaney, are you sure you're feeling all right?'' Tara asked for the third time that day. ''I hate to be a nuisance but you don't look well.''

Delaney nodded. She didn't feel well, either, but then she wouldn't be feeling well for a number of days to come. She had missed her period and an over-the-counter pregnancy test she had taken that morning confirmed she was carrying Jamal's child. She planned to keep her word and let him know, but decided to wait until after her first appointment with the doctor in a few weeks.

A baby.

The thought that she was carrying Jamal's baby made her extremely happy, and if it wasn't for the bouts of morning sickness she had started having a few days ago, she would be fine. At least as fine as a woman could be who was still pining over the man she loved. Each day she had checked the international news section of the paper for word of his engagement or marriage. So far she hadn't seen anything.

Lovingly she caressed her stomach. Jamal had planted a baby inside of her. His baby, a part of him that she would love as much as she loved him.

"Delaney?"

Delaney looked up and met Tara's concerned stare. She was not ready to share her news with anyone yet. "I'm fine, Tara. I've just been busy lately, preparing for my brothers' visit. I have to get ready, both mentally and physically, for them. They can be rather tiring and taxing to one's peace of mind."

Tara chuckled. "When do you expect them?"

"Sometime later today. They had to wait for Storm to get off work before driving up. And I really appreciate you letting a couple of them stay at your place. There is no way all five of them will fit in my tiny apartment."

"Hey, don't mention it, and I'm looking forward to meeting them."

And there was no doubt in Delaney's mind that her brothers would definitely want to meet Tara. She couldn't wait to see their reaction to her, as well as her reaction to them. Tara was a woman who didn't tolerate arrogance in any man, and the Westmoreland brothers were as arrogant as they came.

On a private plane bound for America, Jamal sat back in the seat, relaxed. Asalum, using his connection with certain international security firms, had been able to obtain a residence address for Delaney in Bowling Green, Kentucky. Jamal planned to go straight to her home from the airport as soon as the plane landed.

He smiled at the thought of seeing her again. Inside of him the yearning to hold her in his arms was so intense it pulled at his inner strength. He laid his head back against the seat. They had been in the air eight hours already, and according to the pilot they had another four hours to go before they arrived in Kentucky.

Asalum appeared with a pillow. "For you, Prince."

Jamal took the pillow and placed it behind his head. "Thank you, Asalum." He looked up into the older man's world-weary and rugged face. "I'm no longer feeling depression."

Asalum couldn't hide his smile. "And what are you feeling now, My Prince?"

Jamal grinned heartily. "Jubilation."

Thirteen

Tara leaned against the closed bathroom door. Concern was etched on her face as she heard the sound of Delaney throwing up on the other side. "Delaney? Are you sure you're going to be okay? That's the second time you've thrown up today."

Delaney held her head over the toilet thinking it was actually the third time. And all this time she thought morning sickness was just for the morning. "Yes, Tara, I'll be fine, just give me a second."

At that moment she could hear the sound of the doorbell. *Oh, my gosh! My brothers are here!* "Tara, please get the door. More than likely it's my brothers, and no matter what, please don't tell them I'm in the bathroom sick."

Tara smiled. "Okay, I'll do my best to stall them, but only if you promise to see Dr. Goldman tomorrow. Sounds like you might be coming down with a virus." She turned and crossed the room when the doorbell sounded a second time.

Opening the door, Tara's breath caught and held at the sight of the four men standing there. Then just as quickly she regained her composure. It took some doing. Delaney's brothers were definitely good-looking and oozing in raw sexuality. Dressed in jeans and T-shirts that advertised the Thorn-Byrd motorcycle, they all had massive shoulders, solid chests and firm thighs.

She cleared her throat. For the longest moment no one spoke. They just stood there staring at her in a way that made her glance down to make sure her T-shirt wasn't transparent or something. She decided it was time to say something. "You're Delaney's brothers?"

A crooked smiled tipped up the side of one of their mouths. He seemed to be a little older than the rest. "Yes, I'm Dare. And who are you?" he prompted curiously, not taking his eyes off her.

"I'm Tara Matthews, Delaney's friend, neighbor and fellow physician," she said, reaching her hand out to him. He took it and held it, a bit longer than she thought necessary, before shaking it. The others did the same when Dare introduced them. She took a step back. "Please come in. Delaney is in the bathroom."

Tara closed the door behind them thinking they appeared bigger than life. All of them were well over six feet tall. "I thought there were five of you," she said when they still gazed at her curiously.

The one whose name was Stone and whose smile was just as sexy as the one called Dare spoke up. "Our brother Thorn had a last-minute appointment and is flying in. He'll get here in the morning."

Tara nodded as she leaned back against the door while the four men continued to look at her. She started to ask them if anyone had ever told them it wasn't polite to stare when Delaney entered the room.

"I see you guys made it okay." Delaney shook her head when they didn't take their eyes off Tara to acknowledge her entrance into the room. They were behaving like any typical male animals that had an irresistible female within their scope.

"Yeah, we made it," Chase said smiling, but not at her, since his gaze was still on Tara.

Delaney bit her lip to keep from laughing. Most women fawned over Chase's killer smile, but Tara didn't appear the least flattered. In fact, it appeared she was beginning to get annoyed at her brothers' attention, if her frown was any indication. "Hey you guys, let up and give Tara a break. She's my friend."

Storm finally released his gaze from Tara and met Delaney's glare. "What are we doing?" he asked innocently.

"The four of you are checking her out like she's a piece of fried chicken just waiting to be eaten." She then glanced around the room. "Where's Thorn?"

"Not in our side," Chase said, finally breaking eye contact with Tara and turning to Delaney and smiling. His response was the usual one the brothers had given over the years whenever someone asked them about Thorn.

"So where is he?" Delaney asked again, hating it when they gave her their smart responses.

"He had a last-minute appointment, some very important customer he had to take care of, so he'll be flying in tomorrow morning," Dare said, finally turning to look at her and leaving his brothers to finish their appraisal of Tara.

"And how long are you guys staying?" Delaney asked. She didn't want to run the risk of being sick around them.

Dare smiled. "Trying to get rid of us already, Laney?"

Delaney frowned. If she'd had her choice they would

never have come. She loved her brothers to death but they could get on her last nerve at times. She didn't want to think about how they were going to handle the news of her pregnancy. "No, I'm not trying to get rid of you, as if it would do me any good even if I were. I just wanted to know for sleeping arrangement purposes. As you can see this place is rather small, and Tara has graciously offered to put two of you up at her place during your visit."

As she had known it would, that statement got her brothers' attention. All eyes returned to Tara, who merely shrugged and said, "It's the least I can do for a friend, but it seems that I need to put some ground rules in place."

Dare gave her a sexy smile. "Such as?"

"I expect you to be good."

Storm smiled and Tara and Delaney didn't miss the by-play gaze that passed between the brothers. "We're always *good*," he said slowly.

Tara lifted a brow and crossed her arms over her chest. "What I mean is *good* as in good behavior. You're to behave like gentlemen and treat me just like a member of the family."

Chase chuckled. "That's going to be a real challenge since you aren't a member of the family."

Tara laughed. "But I get the distinct feeling that the four of you like challenges."

Storm shook his head, grinning. "Thorn is the one who like challenges. We prefer things to be made easy for us."

Tara laughed again as she came to stand before them in the center of the room. "Sorry, I don't do easy. Nor do I do hard, just to set the record straight in case you might be curious. I'm not looking for a serious relationship nor am I looking for a nonserious one. In other words, I'm not into casual affairs. I'm single and although I'm a die-hard heterosexual, I'm not interested in a man at the present time. Do we understand each other, guys?''

Dare nodded and smiled. ''Yeah, you're definitely a challenge, so we'll leave you for Thorn.''

Before Tara could open her mouth and give him the retort Delaney knew was coming, the doorbell sounded. Giving Tara a quick glance, she grinned and said, ''Hold that thought,'' then crossed the room to answer the door.

She opened the door and drew in a breath so sharp her heart missed a beat and a wave of dizziness swept over her. ''Jamal!''

Jamal took a step inside and closed the door behind him. Without saying a word and without noticing the other people in the room he pulled Delaney into his arms and kissed her. Automatically Delaney molded her body to his and placed her arms around his neck and kissed him back.

The intimate scene shocked the other five people in the room; four in particular.

''What the hell is going on!'' Dare's voice bellowed, almost shaking the windows and causing Jamal and Delaney to abruptly end their kiss.

''No!'' Delaney shouted when she saw the murderous expressions of anger on the faces of her brothers when they began walking toward her and Jamal. She leaned back against Jamal, blocking him, and felt him stiffen behind her before he gently eased her to his side.

Her four brothers stopped then, looking Jamal up and down as if he was someone from another planet instead someone dressed in his native Arab garb.

Likewise, Jamal sized them up. He immediately knew who they were. The gaze he gave each one of them was dispassionate, but his features were fierce, sharp, lethal. He was letting them know he would protect Delaney, even from them if he had to.

"I can explain," Delaney said quickly, trying to defuse her brothers' anger before the situation got too far out of hand.

"You can explain things after he's taken care of," Stone said furiously. "Who the hell is this guy? And what is he doing kissing you like that?" And then, noticing Jamal's arms firmly around Delaney's waist, he met the man's dark stare. "And take your damn hands off of her."

"Stone, stop it!" Delaney all but screamed. "The four of you are acting like barbarians, and you're an officer of the law, Dare, for heaven's sake. If you give me a chance I can explain things."

Delaney stopped talking when suddenly a wave of dizziness and queasiness swept over her and she leaned against Jamal. His sharp gaze left her brothers and concentrated on her, turning her quickly into his arms. "Are you all right?" he whispered in concern.

She muttered a barely audible response, saying softly, "Take me to the bathroom, Jamal. Now!"

Reacting with unerring speed, Jamal picked her up in his arms and followed Tara out of the room, leaving the Westmoreland brothers too shocked by the whole scene to speak.

As soon as Jamal placed Delaney on her feet in the bathroom and locked the door behind them, she sank weakly to her knees in front of the commode and threw up for the fourth time that day. When she had emptied her stomach completely for what she hoped would be the last time, she flushed the toilet and tried standing, only to find herself engulfed in powerful arms.

Jamal picked her up and walked over to the counter and sat her on it. He then took a washcloth and wet it and wiped it over her face. Moments later he placed her back on her feet and while he held her around the waist, giving her support, she stood in front of the sink and brushed her teeth and rinsed out her mouth.

After that, he picked her up and sat her back on the counter and stood in front of her. "The prince is already causing problems, I see," he said softly, as he tenderly wiped her face again with the damp cloth.

Delaney gazed up at him still amazed that he was actually there with her. Breath slowly slipped through her teeth as she gazed at him. If it was possible, he was more handsome than before. The dark eyes that were looking at her were gentle yet intent, and his chin was no longer clean shaven but was covered with a neatly trimmed beard that made him look as sexy as sin.

She inhaled deeply. She had so many questions to ask, but what he had just said suddenly came back to her. "What did you say?" She needed him to repeat it to make sure she had heard him correctly.

He looked amused but answered her, anyway. "I said the prince is already causing you problems." And this time he placed a gentle hand over her stomach.

She met his gaze. "How did you know I'm pregnant?"

His smile widened. "I had a feeling that you were. I've been dreaming about you every single night since we've been apart, and the dreams were so real that I would wake up in a sweat and sexually spent. And each time we made love in my dreams, I flooded your womb with my seed, which reminded me of the times I had actually done so at the cabin. I believe the dreams were Allah's way of letting me know of your condition."

Delaney nodded and looked down at his hand on her stomach. "Is that the reason you're here, Jamal? For confirmation that I'm having your baby?"

He lifted her chin. "No. I'm here because I was missing you too much to stay away and couldn't think about marrying another woman. So I told my father I loved you and wanted you as the woman in my life.''

Delaney's eyes widened. ''But what about the princess from that sheikhdom who you were to marry?''

Jamal stiffened. ''It seems the princess needed to marry quickly since she was secretly with child from someone else. It was her dishonorable intent to try and pass the child off as mine.''

''And what about Najeen. Was she well?''

Jamal lifted a brow, knowing what Delaney was trying to ask him in a roundabout way. He decided to rest her concerns in that area. ''I didn't see Najeen. The first night I returned I told my stepmother to make sure she returned to her homeland. She is no longer my mistress.''

Delaney reached out and touched his cheek, remembering how he had once said he would never give his mistress up. ''Do you regret sending her away?''

He met her gaze and smiled. ''The only thing I regret is leaving you, Delaney. I was so miserable without you. The only thing I had to survive on were my dreams,'' he said, his voice soft and husky.

She smiled. ''And I had mine, too. And when I discovered I was pregnant I was so happy.''

''How long have you known?''

''I had an idea when I missed my period last week, and then when I started experiencing bouts of sickness throughout the day I thought I'd better check things out. I took a pregnancy test this morning which pretty much confirmed things. I've made an appointment to see the doctor in two weeks.'' She traced her fingertips softly around his features, especially his lower lip. ''How do you feel about me being pregnant, Jamal?''

He grinned. ''The thought that you carry my child inside of you makes me extremely happy, Delaney. I didn't intentionally get you pregnant, but I was more lax with you than I have been with any other woman, so I think subconsciously I wanted you, and only you, to have my heir.''

Happiness flooded Delaney. "Oh, Jamal."

"And you are the woman that I want for my princess, Delaney. Please say that you will marry me and come live with me in Tahran. There are a number of Americans in your military and private businesses living close by in Kuwait, and if you get homesick we can always come back here to visit at any time. We can even live in your country half the year and in mine the other half if that pleases you. I see my father being king for a long time, which means I won't I have to live permanently in Tahran for a number of years to come.''

He leaned over and kissed her lips. "Say yes you will marry me so I can be yours exclusively.''

Delaney knew there was no way she could refuse him. Her love for him was too great, and she knew she wanted to be with him for the rest of her life.

"Yes, Jamal. I will marry you.''

Filled with joy of the richest kind, Jamal leaned in closer, and captured her lips with his, feeling a jolt of desire shoot down his spine at the contact. His hand moved to the back of her neck, and he ran his fingers through the thick, glossy curls before holding her neck firmly in place to let his mouth make love to hers, wanting to consume her.

He wanted to be reunited with her taste, and he focused his attention on the bone-melting kiss he was giving her. His tongue explored inside her mouth as he licked everywhere before taking her tongue in his and sucking on it in a way he knew would make her scream.

But he didn't want her to scream, or else he would have to hurt her brothers when they broke the door down to see what was going on. So he gentled the kiss, not quite ready to end it. He wanted to taste her some more. He needed to make sure this was the real thing and not a dream.

Jamal continued to let his tongue mate with hers, reacquainting himself with the pleasures he could find only with her.

"What the hell is going on in that bathroom?" Dare asked in a loud, sharp voice as he paced the floor. "I can't believe we're out here and not knocking the damn door down to find out for ourselves what's happening."

Tara glared at him, the same way she had been glaring at the other three since that man had taken Delaney into the bathroom and locked them in. "You're acting just like Delaney wants you to act, calm and civilized, and not like barbarians. She has a right to privacy."

"Privacy hell, she was sick," Stone implored. "And why is he in there taking care of her instead of one of us? We're her brothers."

Yes, but he is the father of her child, Tara wanted to tell them, now that she had figured things out. She sighed deeply. The least she could do for her friend was to keep her brothers under control. "While the four of you are waiting, can I get you to help me with something? I need help with this piece of exercise equipment I'm trying to put together."

They looked at her as if she was crazy. "Nice try, Tara, but we're not moving until we know for sure that Laney is okay," Dare said, smiling at her.

Tara shrugged. "All right. I'm sure it won't be too much longer before they—"

Everyone stopped talking when the bathroom door opened. Everyone who had been sitting down shot up out of their seats. "Laney, are you all right?" Storm asked with a worried look. He glared at Jamal when he saw the man's hand was back around his sister's waist. "I thought you were told about your hands," Storm said, filled with hostility.

Delaney actually chuckled. "Storm, that is no way to talk to your future brother-in-law." Before anyone could recover from what she had just implied, she said, "I never got around to making introductions. Everyone, this is Sheikh Jamal Ari Yasir of Tahran. We met last month at the cabin and fell in love. Before we could make plans for our future he had to leave unexpectedly to return home. Now he's back and has asked me to marry him and I've accepted."

Mixed emotions went around the room. Tara screamed out her excitement, and the Westmoreland brothers stood frozen in shock.

"Marry!" Chase finally found his voice enough to ask, almost in a shout. "Are you nuts! He's not even from this country. Where in the hell will the two of you live?"

Delaney smiled sweetly. "Although we plan to spend a lot of time in America, we will mainly live in Tahran, which is located not far from Kuwait. All of you are welcome to visit anytime."

"You can't marry him!" Stone stormed.

"She can and she will." The room suddenly became quiet when Jamal spoke to everyone for the first time. The tone of his voice reflected authority, certainty and invincibility. "I appreciate all the care and concern you have shown to Delaney for the past twenty-five years and I find your actions nothing but admirable. But as my intended bride, the future princess of Tahran, she now becomes my responsibility. At the exact moment that she consented to marry me, she fell under the protection of my country. My father, King Yasir, has given his blessings and—"

"Your father is King Yasir?" Dare asked in total amazement.

Jamal lifted a brow. "Yes, do you know him?"

Dare shook his head, still semishocked at everything. "No, of course I don't know him, at least not personally, anyway. But a few years ago while I was in the Marines stationed near Saudi Arabia, I got the honor of meeting him when I was in charge of security for a political function he attended. That meeting left me very impressed with the way he carried himself and the care, concern and love he bestowed on his people."

Jamal nodded. "Thank you. I will pass on to him your compliment." He then studied Dare a moment before asking. "So you have resided in the Middle East?"

"Yes. I was stationed there for two years and I must admit the entire area is beautiful and the Persian Gulf is simply magnificent."

Jamal smiled. Pleased at the compliment given to his homeland. "You must visit there again. Delaney and I will have private quarters in the palace and as she has indicated, all of you are welcome to visit."

"Damn," Storm said. "An actual palace?" He grinned. "That day when you told us those tire tracks belonged to a prince, we thought you were fooling." He laughed. "Nobody on the squad is going to believe my sister actually nabbed herself a real-live prince. John Carter walked around with his chest poked out when his sister flew to Tampa and married a professional football player. Just wait until I tell them that Laney is going to be a princess."

Chase frowned at his brother, then turned his full attention to Delaney. Uncertainty and concern were etched in his features. "Are you sure this is what *you* want, Laney? I have to know that this is what *you* want, no matter what *he* wants," Chase said, looking at Jamal. "Is marrying this guy going to make you happy? What about your career in medicine?"

Delaney glanced around the room at her brothers. The deep love and concern she saw in their eyes touched her. Although she had whined and complained about their over-protectiveness through the years, deep down in her heart she knew they had behaved in such a manner because they loved her and had cared for her well-being.

"Yes," she whispered softly, yet loud enough for all to hear. She glanced up at Jamal before turning back to every-one. "I love Jamal, and becoming his wife will be my greatest joy." As well as being the mother of his child, she decided not to add. Her brothers had to adjust to the idea of her getting married. She didn't want to complicate mat-ters with the news that she was pregnant, as well. "And as for my career in medicine, I'm sure it will come in handy in some capacity in Tahran."

"I'm so happy for you, girlfriend," Tara said, smiling brightly and going over to Delaney and giving her a fierce hug.

Storm laughed. "Well, I guess that's that."

Dare shook his head solemnly. "No, that's not that. Thorn doesn't know yet. And, personally, I don't want to be around when he gets in tomorrow and finds out."

Fourteen

That evening Delaney left her brothers in Tara's care while she and Jamal went out to dinner. Although he had invited everyone to join them, she was grateful they had declined, so she could spend an evening alone with him.

However, they had indicated to Jamal, engaged or not engaged, they expected her to sleep in her bed and *alone* tonight. They had made it clear that until there was a wedding they intended to protect their sister's honor. It had been hard for Delaney to keep a straight face at that one. And eye contact across the room with Tara indicated that her friend had figured out her condition and would keep her secret and would do everything she could to help keep the Westmoreland brothers busy until she returned—which Delaney intended to be rather late.

She nervously bit her bottom lip when she thought about Thorn. He could be rather irrational at times and was more overprotective than the others. She would have to talk to him privately just as soon as he arrived in the morning.

"Are you ready to leave, Delaney?"

Jamal's question broke into her thoughts, and she lovingly gazed across the table at him. Earlier that day, after getting nearly everything straightened out with her brothers, he had left to change clothes and had returned two hours later to take her to dinner.

Tonight he was dressed like a Westerner and looked absolutely stunning in a dark gray suit, white shirt and navy-blue tie. She smiled, thinking he was certainly a very handsome man. His dark eyes held her seductively in their gaze and had been doing so all night. "Yes," she said softly. "But it's early yet. You aren't planning to take me straight home, are you?"

He stood and walked around the table to pull her chair back for her. "No. I thought you might be interested in seeing the town house I've purchased to live in while I'm here."

Delaney raised a brow. "You've purchased a town house? But you just arrived today."

He nodded. "Asalum is most efficient when it comes to handling business matters. He took care of all the details and made the necessary arrangements from the jet while we were flying over here."

Delaney shook her head. She doubted she would ever get used to such extravagance. "Must be nice."

He chuckled. "It is nice, as you will soon see." He took her hand in his as they walked out of the restaurant. "And there is another reason I want to take you to my town house."

Delaney had a good idea just what that other reason was but wanted him to tell her, anyway. "And what reason is that, *Your Highness?*"

Jamal leaned down and whispered in her ear. Even with the darkness of her skin, she actually blushed, then smiled up at him. "Um, I think something like that can be arranged, Prince."

Back at Delaney's apartment the Westmoreland brothers and Tara were involved in a game of bid whist. Tara excused herself from the next game and went into the kitchen to check on the cookies that she had baking in the oven.

They had ordered pizza earlier, and with Stone's complaint of not having anything sweet to eat, she had taken a tube of frozen cookie dough from Delaney's freezer and had baked a batch of chocolate chip cookies.

Tara smiled, inwardly admitting that, now that she was getting to know them better, she liked Delaney's brothers. Although she thought their overprotectiveness was a bit much, it was definitely a show of the love they had for their sister.

She was taking the tray of baked cookies from the oven when Delaney's doorbell sounded. She hoped it wasn't one of the neighbors complaining that too much noise was coming from the apartment. Storm had a tendency to groan rather loudly whenever he lost, which was frequently. She smiled, thinking he was definitely a sore loser.

Back in the living room, Chase got up from the table to open the door. He snatched it open, wondering who would have the nerve to interrupt their card game.

He winced when he saw the person standing there. Damn, all hell is about to break loose, he thought frowning. "Thorn! What are you doing here? We weren't expecting you until the morning."

Thorn Westmoreland shook his head and looked questioningly beyond Chase to the table where his other brothers sat playing cards. At least they *had* been playing cards.

Stone had stopped and sat unmoving, like a "stone" right in the middle of dealing out the cards, and both Dare and Storm looked at him as if he was a Martian.

He frowned, wondering what the hell had everyone spooked. Entering the apartment, he walked into the center of the room. "What the hell is everyone staring at? Do I have mud on my face or something?"

Dare, regaining his wits, returned to shuffling the cards. "We're just surprised to see you tonight."

"Yeah," Stone chimed in. "We weren't expecting you until the morning."

Thorn threw his overnight bag on the sofa. "Yes, that's what I heard, twice already. First from Chase and now you guys. So you're all surprised I showed up tonight. What's going on?"

Chase closed the door and walked across the room to reclaim his seat at the table. "What makes you think something is going on?"

"Because the four of you are looking guilty as sin about something."

Dare chuckled. "That's just your imagination, bro." As usual everyone was trying to decipher Thorn's mood and until they did, they weren't making any waves. And they definitely weren't going to say anything about Delaney's engagement. "I take it you got that customer satisfied."

"Yeah, and got a free flight here on his private jet." Thorn glanced around the apartment. "Where's Laney?"

Storm threw out a card. "She went out."

Thorn frowned and checked his watch. It was almost midnight. "She went out where?"

"She didn't say," Stone said, studying his hand.

Thorn's frown deepened. "When is she coming back?"

"We don't know exactly," Chase said, watching his brother, knowing that at any minute they would start seeing smoke come from his ears. It didn't take much to set Thorn off when he was in one of his foul moods. Usually this kind of mood meant he was overdue for getting laid, but it was Thorn's own fault for being so damn nitpicky when it came to women.

Thorn slowly walked over to the table. "And just what do you know, *exactly?*"

Dare chuckled. "Trust us, Thorn, you don't want to hear it. At least not from us. Just have a seat and sit tight until Laney comes home. Or better yet, pull up a chair and join the game. My truck needs a new engine so I need to win some money off you."

Thorn slammed his fist hard on the table, sending cards flying. When he was sure he had everyone's attention he proceeded to say, "I don't know what's going on but I have a feeling it involves Laney. And you guys know how much I hate secrets. So which one of you is going to spill your guts?"

Dare stood. So did Stone, Chase and Storm. Usually it took a combined effort to make Thorn see reason and cut the moody crap. "We aren't telling you anything so sit down and shut up," Dare said through clenched teeth.

At that moment Tara came charging out of the kitchen. She had heard enough. Thorn Westmoreland had some nerve, barging in here at this late hour and causing problems. Just who did he think he was?

Thorn caught her in his peripheral vision the moment she flew out of the kitchen. She stopped walking when he turned and stared at her.

Tara swallowed, wondering why the air had suddenly left the room, making it almost impossible for her to breathe. Her gaze held the muscular, well-built man who stood so tall she had to stretch her neck to look up at him. Dressed in a pair of jeans—and wearing them in a way she'd never known a man to wear them before—he utterly oozed sexuality and sensuality, all rolled into one. He was without a doubt the most gorgeous hunk of man she had ever laid eyes on.

He was staring at her, and his stare was burning intimate spots all over her body, branding her. She blinked, not appreciating the fact that any man, especially this man with his foul mood, could have this effect on her. She didn't have time for such foolishness. Sexual chemistry was too much bother, too time-consuming. Her job and her career came first. Physical attraction, love, sex, babies…and all the other stuff that went with it…was definitely a low priority on her totem pole.

She inhaled deeply, thinking that the best thing to do would be to say her peace and get the hell of out there, on the fastest legs she had. Once she was safe in her apartment, she would try and figure out what was happening to her and why.

With a deep frown she resumed walking until she stood directly in front of Thorn. She placed her hands on her hips and glared at him. "How dare you come here causing problems. Just who do you think you are? The Mighty Thorn? All we need is to give the neighbors a reason to complain. So why don't you do like you've been told and sit down and shut up!"

Taking a deep breath, she then turned her attention to the other four brothers. "I put the cookies on a plate in the kitchen. Help yourselves." After glaring one last time at Thorn, she quickly crossed the room and walked out the door, slamming it behind her.

Thorn forced his gaze away from the whirlwind who had told him off. He slowly turned and looked at his brothers, who for some reason were staring steadfastly at him…with smirks on their faces. "Who the hell is that?"

Dare chuckled as he crossed his arms over his chest. *"That,* Thorn, is *your* challenge."

The same sexual tension that had totally consumed Jamal and Delaney from the moment he had picked her up for dinner increased by umpteen degrees once he had her settled in the warm intimacy of the Mercedes sports car he was driving. Every look they exchanged was hot.

Delaney knew that each time he stopped for a traffic light he took his eyes off the road and turned his gaze to her. Then there was the hand that he simply refused to keep on the steering wheel—the one he preferred to use to caress her legs and thighs instead. And the short dress she had on made her body all that more accessible. It barely covered her thighs.

Her brothers' jaws had almost dropped when she'd walked out of the bedroom wearing it, but thank goodness they hadn't said anything. The look Jamal had given her had been totally different from her brothers' and she had hurriedly ushered him out of her apartment before anyone noticed what seeing her in it had done to a certain part of his body.

"Open."

Jamal's husky command filled the quiet stillness of the car's interior. Delaney couldn't help but notice his hand had worked its way up her inner thigh. Knowing just what he meant for her to do, she slowly opened her legs while studying his profile intently. His eyes were still on the road but she detected his breathing had shifted from steady to unsteady.

Her eyes fluttered shut when she felt the tenderness of his fingers touch the center of her pantyhose between her legs. Boy, she had missed his fingers. Her dream was nothing compared to the real thing. The man was filling her with a purely sexual rush.

Her breathing became heavy when the tip of his finger worked insistently until it poked a hole in her panty hose, to get to just what it wanted. Tonight her panty hose were serving as both panty and hosiery, so once he found his way past the silky nylon all that was left was bare flesh, and his finger found her hot and wet.

"I can't wait to get you home, Delaney," he whispered softly, as his busy fingers continued to touch her, tease her and explore her fully. Her body shivered at the intimate contact, and she felt herself getting hotter and wetter. He felt it, too.

Her mind and thoughts concentrated on what he was doing to her when his fingers began a rhythm that made her arch her back against the seat. She opened her legs wider, which made her dress rise higher on her thighs, thankful that the people riding in the car next to them could not see what was happening inside theirs. Her mouth opened, then closed, along with her eyes, unable to get any words out, just moans…excruciating moans.

"When we get to my place, Delaney, I won't be using my finger. Do you know what I'll be using?"

She slowly opened her eyes and looked at him and saw they had come to a traffic light. He leaned over and whispered hotly in her ear, and the only thing she could think to say was, "My goodness."

Her breath suddenly became shaky and her body began shivering when he began rubbing inside of her harder, increasing the rhythm. The palms of her hands pressed hard against the car's dashboard when everything inside of her exploded, reeling her into a climax. Her body continued to shudder violently.

"Jamal!"

Her head went back and she moaned one final time as pleasure consumed her, slowly leaving her sated, breathless and feeling weak. Once she could get her breathing under control she found the strength to glance over at Jamal. She was too overwhelmed to even feel embarrassed at the fact that he had made her climax in a car while he had been driving with one hand.

"Are you okay, My Princess?"

"Yes," she replied weakly. At some point they had arrived at their destination when she noted he had brought the car to a complete stop in front of a massive group of elegant buildings. As she met his gaze, his lips tilted into an intense sexual smile. He slowly leaned over and placed a light, yet passionate kiss on her lips. "No matter how real my dreams seemed at night, whenever I woke up I could never conjure this."

"What?" she asked softly, barely able to speak.

"The scent of you having a climax. It's a scent that is purely you, private, individual and totally sensual. I wish like hell I could bottle it." He leaned over and kissed her again. "Stay put. I'm coming around the car to get you," he said when he finally released her lips.

She watched as he got out of the car and came around to her side and opened the door. Undoing her seat belt he scooped her up into his arms and, as if she was a precious bundle, he held her gently to him and carried her inside his home.

Jamal took Delaney straight to the bedroom and placed her on his bed. "I'll be right back. I need to lock the door."

Delaney nodded, closing her eyes, feeling blissful yet totally drained. Moments later she slowly reopened her eyes and glanced around. The bedroom was huge, probably big enough to fit two of her bedrooms in. She had noticed the same thing about the other parts of the house when he carried her through to the bedroom. She sat up, and when she noted her dress had risen up past her hips, tried tugging it back down.

"There's no need to pull it down since I'll be taking it completely off you in a second."

Heat filled Delaney's cheeks when she met Jamal's gaze across the room. He was standing in the doorway removing his jacket, which was followed by his tie. Her gaze stayed glued to him, while she watched him undress. She continued to look at him, thinking he was such a fine specimen of a man and that he was hers.

"Jamal?"

"Yes?"

"How soon do you want to get married?"

He smiled as he pulled the belt out of his pants. "Is tonight soon enough?"

She returned his smile. "Yes, but I'd like you to meet my parents first."

He nodded. "Only if you won't let them talk you out of marrying me."

Delaney didn't blink, not once when she said, "No one could do that. I love you too much."

Jamal had taken off all his clothes except for his pants. She remembered the first time she had seen him without a shirt and how her body had responded to the sheer masculinity of him. And her body was responding to him now.

He walked over to where she sat in the middle of the bed. "And I love you, too. I hadn't realized just how much until I had to leave you. Being without you was hard on me. You totally consumed my every thought. There were days when I wondered if I would make it without you."

Delaney looked at Jamal. She knew an admission like

that had probably been hard for him to make. "I will make you a good princess, Jamal."

He sat on the edge of the bed and reached out and pulled her into his lap. "Mmm, will you, Delaney?" he asked, smiling. "Are you willing to salaam me each and every time you see me?"

She lifted a dark brow at him. "No."

"Well then, are you willing to always walk two paces behind me?"

"No. Nor will I hide my face behind some veil," she decided to add.

Jamal couldn't keep the amusement out of his gaze. "You won't?"

"No, I won't."

"Mmm. Then will you be obedient and do *everything* that I say?"

She didn't give that question much thought, either, before quickly shaking her head. "No."

He chuckled as he looked at her. "All right, Delaney, then what *will* you do to make me a good princess?"

She shifted positions in his lap so that she was sitting facing him, straddling his hips. She placed her arms around his neck and met his gaze intently. "On the day I become your desert princess, you will become my desert sheikh. And I will love you more than any woman has ever loved you before. I will honor you and be by your side to do what I can for your people who will become *my* people. I will obey you to a point, but I will retain my right to disagree and make my own decisions about things, always respecting your customs when I do so."

Her gaze became intense when she added, "And I will give you sons and daughters who will honor you and respect you and who will grow up strong in our love and the love of their people. They will share two cultures and two countries, and I believe they will always love and appreciate both.''

She inhaled deeply when she added, ''And last but not least, I will be your wife *and* your mistress. I will take care of *all* your needs and make sure that you stay extremely happy and never regret making me your princess.''

For the longest moment Jamal didn't say anything. Then he kissed her. First softly, then tenderly and finally hotly as his mouth slanted over hers, tasting her fully. He broke off the kiss and slowly stood with her in his arms, her legs still wrapped around his waist.

Placing her on her feet, he pulled her dress over her head, leaving her bare, except for her panty hose and chemise which he quickly removed. When she stood before him completely naked, he removed his pants and boxer shorts, desperately wanting to be inside of her, with his body stroking hers.

Gathering her into his arms, he placed her back in the middle of the bed and joined her there. ''How soon can I meet your parents?'' he asked her, pulling her into his arms.

''I'm scheduled to be off this weekend so we can go to Atlanta then. I plan on calling them in the morning and telling them our good news.''

''Even the news about the baby?''

''No, I want them to get used to the idea of me getting married and moving away before I tell them they will also become grandparents.''

Jamal nodded. ''I told my father there was a possibility you were carrying my heir.''

Delaney raised a brow. ''And what did he say?''

Jamal smiled. ''Not much at the time but I could tell that the thought pleased him. He will enjoy being a grandfather as much as I'm going to enjoy being a father.''

He then placed his body on top of hers, supporting himself on his elbows. "But right now I want to hurry up and become a husband. Your husband, Delaney."

He leaned down and kissed her, wanting to take their kiss to another level like he had that night in the cabin. After tasting her mouth for a few moments, he pulled back. "Stick out your tongue to me."

She blinked, then did what he instructed, knowing what was coming.

"Don't worry," he said huskily. "I won't let you pass out on me again."

When he captured her tongue in his mouth, she gasped for breath with the intensity of his tongue mating so sensually with hers. She moaned with pleasure when he touched those certain places in her mouth that gave her the greatest sexual gratification. The pleasure was so intense, she began to writhe beneath him and he placed his hands on her hips to keep her still.

He finally let go of her mouth and went to her breasts and paid the same homage there, nibbling, sucking and laving her with his tongue.

"Oh, Jamal."

The sound of his name from her lips was like an aphrodisiac, making him want to taste her everywhere. So he did. The scent of her spiraled him on to new heights, new territory and for both of them, a new adventure.

"I can't get enough of you, Delaney," he whispered against her hot flesh before easing his body upward to enter her. The tightness of her surrounded him, stroking the already-blazing fire within him.

"My Princess," he whispered softly as his body began pumping into her as he held her gaze, forcing her to look at him with each and every stroke into her body.

She wrapped her arms around him and targeted his mouth. "My Sheikh," she whispered before thrusting her tongue inside, intent on taking ownership and making love to his mouth the same way and with the same rhythm that he was using on her body.

Delaney released his mouth to look at him. Each time he thrust into her, his neck strained and the tension etched in his face showed the degree of strength he had. Each time he pulled out her thighs trembled as flesh met flesh. Then suddenly he pushed deeper, nearly touching her womb, holding himself still inside of her, refusing to pull out.

He lowered his face to hers and came close to her lips and kissed her in such a way that made both their bodies simultaneously explode in ecstasy, as he filled her completely with the essence of his release making the three weeks they had spent apart well worth the reunion.

He strained forward, lifting her hips to receive him as their bodies exploded yet again, making them groan out when yet another climax struck.

And moments later, completely sated and totally pleasured, they collapsed in each other's arms.

A few hours later Jamal leaned forward over Delaney, breathed in deeply to inhale her scent, before kissing her awake.

He leaned back and watched as she opened her eyes slowly and smiled at him. "You can wake me up anytime, Your Highness."

Jamal chuckled and ran a finger along her cheek. "It's time for me to take you home. I did promise your brothers that I would have you back at a reasonable hour."

Delaney reached down and caressed him, and her smile widened. "And of course you will want to make love again before you take me home, right?"

"That had been my plan," he grinned placing his body over hers. "I will love you forever, Delaney."

"And I will love you forever, too. Who would have thought that what was supposed to be a secluded vacation would bring us together. And to think we didn't even like each other at first."

Jamal leaned down and kissed her lips tenderly. "You know what they say, don't you?" he asked, tracing a path with his tongue down her throat.

"No," Delaney whispered, just barely. "What do they say?"

He smiled down at her. "Things are not always as they seem to be." He kissed her again, then said, "But the love that we share is everything we will ever want it to be and more."

Epilogue

Six Weeks Later

"Another marriage ceremony?" Delaney asked Jamal as they captured some stolen moments in the palace courtyard. All around them, the atmosphere off the desert was hot and humid, yet the fragrance of jasmine and gardenias permeated the air, creating a seductive, erotic overtone. "This makes the fourth."

Their first wedding had been a beautiful garden wedding on her parents' lawn three weeks ago in Atlanta. The second ceremony had taken place last week when they arrived at the palace, with the king, queen and other dignitaries and their wives present. The third had been in the town square, arranged by the people of Tahran as a way to welcome the prince and his chosen princess.

A smile tilted the corners of Jamal's lips. "But think of

how much fun we have with the wedding nights that follow each one.''

Delaney reached out and placed her arms around her husband's neck, leaned up and kissed his lips. ''Mmm, that is true.''

She then turned in his arms so her back pressed against his front while his hand splayed across her stomach where their child rested. She didn't think she could ever be as happy as she was now.

Upon her arrival at the palace last week, she was immediately summoned to hold a private meeting alone with Jamal's father, King Yasir. At first the king had presented himself as the fierce, dictatorial ruler, and had relentlessly interrogated her about her views and beliefs.

She had answered all of his questions, honestly, truthfully and respectfully. In the end he had told her that her sharp tongue and tough stance reminded him of Queen Fatimah, and that he knew she would have no problem being understood, respected and loved. He had hugged her and accepted her into the family.

Jamal's sisters, Johari and Arielle, had also made her feel welcome and said they did not consider her as their brother's wife but as their sister. But it was Queen Fatimah who had endeared herself to Delaney's heart forever by meeting with her and sharing some of the things she had come up against as a foreigner in her husband's land and how she had set about changing things, in a subtle way.

She had even suggested that Delaney give some thought to using her medical knowledge to educate the women of Tahran about childhood diseases and what they could do to prevent them. As well, she suggested Delaney could practice medicine in the hospital the two of them would convince the king he needed to build.

"Ready to go back inside, Princess?" Jamal asked, leaning down and placing a kiss on her forehead.

"Is there another dinner party we must attend tonight?" she asked, twisting around to face him, suddenly captured by his dark gaze. Her body began feeling achy, hot and hungry. She wondered if there would ever be a time she would not be sexually attracted to her husband.

"No. In fact I thought that we could spend a quiet evening in our apartment," he said reaching down and tracing a finger along her cheek.

"That sounds wonderful, Jamal," she said smiling. They hadn't found a lot of time to spend alone except at night when they finally went to bed. She enjoyed the nights he made love to her, reminding her over and over again just how much she meant to him and just how much she was loved. She would fall asleep in his arms at night and be kissed awake by him each morning.

"Everyone should fall in love, shouldn't they, Jamal?" she asked smiling.

He grinned. "Yes, but I bet you would never convince your brothers of that."

She nodded, knowing that was true. "But they were happy for us, even Thorn, once he got used to the idea that I was indeed getting married."

Jamal shook his head, grinning. Thorn Westmoreland had taken great pleasure in being a thorn in his side. "Yes, but look how long it took him to come around. I almost had to call him out a few times. I've never known anyone so stubborn, man or woman, and that even includes you. I don't envy the woman who tries to capture his heart. I doubt such a thing is possible."

I wouldn't be too sure of that, Delaney thought. She couldn't help but recall how Thorn kept looking at Tara at her wedding when he thought no one was watching. Tara had been her maid of honor, and all her brothers had been openly friendly to her, treating her like a member of the family. But for some reason Thorn had kept his distance. She found that rather interesting.

"What are you thinking, sweetheart?"

"Oh, just that it wouldn't surprise me if there is a woman out there who can capture Thorn's heart. In fact, I have an idea who she is."

Jamal raised a curious brow. "Really? Who?"

Her mouth curved into that smile that he adored. "Um, you'll find out soon enough."

Later that night, after making love to his wife, Jamal slipped from the bed, leaving Delaney sleeping. Putting on his robe, he left the confines of their apartment and walked down the stairs to the courtyard to find a private place to give thanks.

A half hour later on his way back to his apartment he met Asalum lurking in the shadows, always on guard to protect his prince.

Asalum studied Jamal's features. "Is all well with you, Your Highness?"

Jamal nodded. "Yes, my trusted friend and companion, all is well."

Silence filled the space between them, then a few moments later Jamal asked, "Do you know what I'm feeling now, Asalum?"

A smile curved the older man's lips. He had a good idea but asked anyway. "And what are you feeling, My Prince?"

Suddenly Jamal began to laugh. It was laughter of happiness, joy and contentment, and the rapturous sound punctured the silence of the night and echoed deep into the courtyard.

Moments later Jamal spoke when his laughter subsided. ''Exultation.''

* * * * * *

DESERT WARRIOR

BY
NALINI SINGH

Nalini Singh has always wanted to be a writer. Along the way to her dream, she obtained degrees in both the arts and law (because being a starving writer didn't appeal). After a short stint as a lawyer, she sold her first book and from that point, there was no going back. Now an escapee from the corporate world, she is looking forward to a lifetime of writing, interspersed with as much travel as possible.

To Mum, Dad and the Amazing FMP, for Everything

One

"Do not put even one foot on Zulheil soil unless you are ready to stay forever. You will not get past the airport gates before I kidnap you!"

Hands trembling, Jasmine skirted around the small groups of people in the waiting area and headed for the glass doors that would lead her out of the airport, and into Tariq's land.

"Madam." A dark hand fell next to hers on the handle of the luggage trolley.

Startled, she looked up into the smiling face of a man who appeared to be an airport official. "Yes?" Her heart started to pound in a mixture of hope and fear.

"You are going the wrong way. The taxis and hire cars are on the other side." He gestured toward a long corridor leading to another set of glass doors. Desert sands glittered in the distance.

"Oh." She felt foolish. Of course Tariq wouldn't complete his threat so literally. He'd been angry enough to scare her when he'd warned her against coming to his land. Now, Tariq was a cool, controlled man, whom she'd seen a number of times on television, leading peace talks between warring Arab states. Her Tariq was now Tariq al-Huzzein Donovan Zamanat, the Sheik of Zulheil, the leader of his people.

"Thank you," she managed to say. When she began to move again, the pale blue fabric of her ankle-length dress swished around her legs in time with her steps.

"It is my pleasure. I will escort you to the vehicles."

"That's very kind. What about the other travelers?"

The corners of the stranger's eyes crinkled. "But madam, you were the only foreigner on this flight."

Jasmine blinked, thinking back over the trip. All she could remember were lilting vowels and flowing hands, beautiful sloe-eyed women and protective Arabian men.

"I didn't realize," she admitted.

"Zulheil has been closed to visitors."

"But *I'm* a visitor." She stopped, wondering if it was too much to hope that Tariq would actually kidnap her. No sane woman would want to be captured by a desert sheik who held her in contempt, but she was long past logic and sanity.

Her guide paused, and she could have sworn that he blushed under his golden skin. "It...Zulheil began letting in people again this last week."

At his graceful wave, she started to push the cart down the marbled floor once more. "Was it closed because of mourning?" Her voice was quiet, respectful.

"Yes. The loss of our sheik and his beloved wife was a tragic blow to our people." His eyes momentarily darkened with pain. "But we have a good sheik in their only son. Sheik Tariq will lead us out of the darkness."

Jasmine's heart skipped a beat at Tariq's name. From somewhere she found the strength to ask, "He's ruling alone, your new sheik?"

If the man told her that Tariq had taken a wife during the period of media blackout since his parents' deaths, she'd get on the next plane out of Zulheil. Even now, her lungs protested every breath she took, and she hung on the edge of control.

The look her guide threw her was assessing. He nodded sharply, but waited until they were outside before speaking. The harsh heat of the desert hit Jasmine like a physical slap, but she stood firm. Wilting was not an option, not when this was her last chance.

There was a black limousine parked at the curb. She'd started to move away from it when her guide halted her.

"That is your taxi."

"That's definitely not a taxi." Hope, she understood, came in many forms. Hers had arrived in the shape of a long, sleek piece of gleaming machinery.

"Zulheil is rich, madam. These are our taxis."

She wondered if he expected her to believe that. Biting her lip to muffle the slightly hysterical urge to giggle, she nodded and let him put her cases into the trunk. She waited, heart pounding and mouth dry with anticipation, until he came around to the back passenger door.

"Madam?"

"Yes?"

"You asked if our sheik rules alone. The answer is yes. Some say it is because his heart has been broken." His voice was a low whisper.

Jasmine gasped. Before she could continue the conversation, he swung open the limo door. Her mind in a whirl, she stepped inside the luxurious air-conditioned interior.

The door shut.

"You really did it," she whispered to the man sitting across from her, his long legs encroaching on her space.

Tariq leaned forward, his hands on his knees. The darkness inside the limo threw the sharp lines of his face into vivid relief. None of the softness she'd seen in her Tariq was present in this hardened stranger.

"Did you doubt me, my Jasmine?"

Her body went into delayed shock at the sound of his voice. It was deep and compelling. Beautiful and dangerous. Familiar yet...different. "No."

Tariq frowned. "And yet you are here."

She bit her lower lip again and drew in a ragged breath. His eyes, deceptively dark in the confines of the vehicle, were fixed on her like those of a predator waiting to pounce. The opaque partition between passengers and driver was raised, further collapsing the space, leaving her nowhere to turn.

"Yes. I'm here." The car moved off at that moment, unsettling her precarious balance. She fell forward and barely caught herself on the edge of the seat. Tariq's arms came around her anyway and he lifted her into his lap.

Jasmine clutched at his wide shoulders, the fine material of his white tunic crumpling under her fingers, but she didn't fight, not even when he gripped her chin with his fingers and forced her to meet his gaze. He was so angry. She could see the turbulence in his vivid green eyes.

"Why are you here?" He tightened his hold around her when the car bounced over something on the road. His muscled body was so much bigger than hers that Jasmine felt surrounded, overwhelmed. But still she didn't fight.

"Because you needed me."

His laugh was a harsh, ragged echo of pain that hurt her inside. "Or have you come to have a liaison with an exotic man, before you marry the one your family has chosen?" With an oath, he dumped her unceremoniously back into her seat.

Jasmine pushed her fiery plait over her shoulder and lifted her chin. "I don't have liaisons." His distrust of her was clear, but she refused to let that silence her.

"No," he agreed, his voice cold. "You would have to have a heart to experience passion."

Her already fragile confidence was shaken by the direct hit. All her life she'd struggled to be special enough to deserve love and acceptance. Now it appeared that even Tariq, the one person who'd ever treated her as if she were worth cherishing, found her wanting.

"You can't hold a man like Tariq. He'll forget you the minute some glamourpuss princess comes along."

Uninvited, Sarah's spiteful words from four years ago burst into Jasmine's mind. Back then, they'd delivered the last emotional blow to her belief in herself, coming from an older sister who knew so much more about men. What if it hadn't just been spite? What if Sarah had been right?

When Jasmine had made the fateful decision to find Tariq again, she'd been uncertain of her ability to reach the man she'd known. How could she hope to reach the man he'd become? Buffeted by doubt, she turned and stared out the tinted windows. There was nothing to see but endless desert.

Strong fingers on her jaw forced her attention back to the panther lounging opposite her. His green-eyed gaze caught her own and held her in thrall. "I will keep you, my Jasmine." It was a statement, not a question.

"And if I don't wish to be…" She paused, unable to think of the right word.

"Owned?" Tariq suggested in a silky whisper.

Jasmine swallowed. A part of her was terrified of the dark fury she saw swirling in his eyes, but she'd come too far to fall victim to her fears now. "Like a slave?" Her voice was husky, her lips parched. However, she didn't dare moisten them with her tongue, afraid of how Tariq would react.

He narrowed his eyes. "You think I am such a barbarian?"

"I think you're going out of your way to give me that impression," she retorted, before she could caution herself not to bait the panther.

The corners of his lips tilted upward in a slight curve. "Ah, I had forgotten."

"What?" She lifted a hand to his wrist and tried to break his hold on her jaw. It proved impossible. Under her touch, his pulse beat in a slow, seductive rhythm that promised her both exotic pleasures and darkest fury.

"That the fire of your hair does not lie." He moved his thumb over her lower lip and frowned. "Your lips are dry. Moisten them."

Jasmine scowled at the command. "And if I don't?"

He lifted one brow in response to the defiance in her tone. "Then I shall do it for you."

Betraying color stained her cheeks at the erotic image of

Tariq moistening her lips. His intense gaze made her feel like a tasty morsel he'd be only too happy to devour. Breathing in shallow gasps, she flicked out her tongue and wet her lips.

"Better." His approval was apparent in the deepening timbre of his voice and the way his thumb slowly swept over her lower lip, now soft and wet. When he abruptly set her free, surprise kept her perched on the edge of her seat for a moment, leaning toward him. Sanity returned with a shock. Face flushed, she scrambled back and across the seat until she was in the opposite corner of the car.

"Where are you taking me?"

"Zulheina."

"The capital?"

"Yes."

"Where in Zulheina?" She refused to back down despite his repressive monosyllabic replies.

"To my palace." He lifted one foot and placed it next to her right hip, effectively caging her against the door. "Tell me, my Jasmine, what have you been doing these four years?"

It was clear that he wasn't going to answer any more questions. Jasmine bit back her frustration, wanting to push but aware that she was on very shaky ground. "I was studying."

"Ah, the business management degree." His words were a soft taunt, a reminder of the times she'd cried on his shoulder, sobbing out her dislike of the subject.

"No." *There,* she thought, *let him suffer for a minute.*

He moved and suddenly he was sitting next to her, his shoulders blocking her vision, his legs caging her in the corner. He wasn't the one suffering.

"No?" His deep voice evoked memories of huskier tones and sensual laughter. "Your family let you change?"

"They had no choice." She'd followed their dictates and cut herself off from Tariq, but it had almost destroyed her. Her weak state had alarmed even her family, and no one had commented when she'd switched studies. By the time they'd tried to change her mind, she'd grown up. Disillusionment with the selfishness of those she'd trusted had followed fast on the heels of her sorrow.

"What did you study? Hmm?" He curved one big hand round her neck in a blatantly possessive gesture. The heat from his body swirled around her.

"Do you have to sit so close?" she blurted out.

For the first time, he smiled. It was a smile full of teeth, the smile of a predator tempting his prey to venture out into the darkness. "Do I bother you, Mina?"

He'd called her Mina. She remembered the way he'd always shortened her name to Mina when he'd been coaxing her to do something, usually involving kissing him until she felt like liquid honey inside. He hadn't needed to coax much. One look of sexy invitation, the husky whisper of her name against her lips, and she'd softened like a sigh in the wind.

When she didn't answer, he leaned down and nuzzled her neck, his warm breath seeming to burrow through her skin and into her bones. He'd always loved to touch. She'd relished his affection, but right now it was making her more off balance than she already was.

"Tariq, please."

"What do you want, Mina?"

Jasmine swallowed. He traced the movement down her throat with his thumb. "Space."

He raised his head. "No. You have had four years of space. Now you are mine."

His intensity was almost frightening. As an eighteen-year-old, she'd been unable to cope with his sheer, charismatic power. Though he was only five years older than her, his strength and determination even then had been enough to command unswerving loyalty from his people. Now, four years later, she could see that he'd grown impossibly stronger, impossibly more charismatic. However, she was no longer a sheltered young girl, and she had to learn to cope with Tariq if she wanted a future with him.

Holding his gaze, she lifted her hand and placed it over the one curled around her neck. When she tugged, he released her, his curiosity apparent in the quizzical look in his green eyes. Raising his hand to her cheek, she turned her face to drop a single kiss on his palm. His breath grew harsh, loud in the confines of the car.

"I studied fashion design." His skin was warm against her lips, his masculine scent an irresistible aphrodisiac.

"You have changed."

"For the better."

"That remains to be seen." His eyes narrowed. The hand against her cheek tightened. "Who taught you this?"

"What?" Shivers threatened to whisper down her spine at the sound of that dark, rough tone.

"This play with my hand and your lips." His jaw could have been carved out of granite.

"You did." It was the truth. "Remember the time you took me to the Waitomo caves? As the canoe floated in the glow-worm grotto, you picked up my hand and you kissed it just so." She moved her head, and he loosened his hold enough to allow her to repeat the soft caress.

When she looked up, she knew that he'd remembered, but his features remained stony and his eyes boiled with emotions she didn't have the experience to identify.

"There have been others?"

"What?"

"Other men have touched you?"

"No. Only you."

He curved his hand around to tug at her plait, arching her neck and making her vulnerable to him. "Do not lie to me. I will know," he growled.

He was threatening to overwhelm her. In response, she relaxed into the exposed position that he'd engineered and slid her arms around his neck. "I will know, too," she said quietly. Under her fingers, his hair was soft, tempting her to stroke. Below that was the living heat of his skin.

His jaw firmed. "What will you know?"

"If you've let other women touch you."

Tariq's eyes widened. "When did you become fierce, Mina?

You were always so biddable.'' She knew he was taunting her with the way she'd let her family control her life, even to the extent of ignoring her heart.

"I had to grow claws to survive."

"And am I supposed to be frightened of your puny claws?" He raised one dark brow, daring her.

Deliberately, Jasmine sank her fingernails into the back of his neck. She forgot that she was goading a panther. To her surprise, her panther didn't seem to mind her claws. He smiled down at her, a dangerous, tempting smile.

"I would like to feel those claws on my back, Mina," he whispered. "When you are in your place—flat on your back, under me—then I will."

"In my place?" Jasmine jerked out of his hold. When he continued to loom over her, his body crowding her against the door, she pushed at his chest. Masculine heat seared her through the fine fabric. "Move, you...you male!"

"No, Mina." He put one hand against her cheek and turned her toward him. "I will no longer follow your commands like a dog on a leash. From this day forth, you will follow mine."

He held her in place as his lips descended over hers. He needn't have bothered. Jasmine was transfixed by the raw pain she'd glimpsed on his face, before his shields had risen. She'd done this to her panther. It was, she acknowledged, his right to demand restitution.

Two

Tariq couldn't fight the driving, primitive urge to taste Mina, to claim her in this small way. Not even the knowledge that she was feeling overwhelmed and trapped could halt him. He tried to be gentle in his possession, but he hungered too much to stop. Then small, feminine hands clutched at his nape, holding him to her, inciting him. The painful craving he'd leashed for years battered at his control, pleading for freedom. He wanted to gorge on Mina. To feast on Mina.

Not now, he decided.

When he took her, he wanted hours, days, weeks in which to linger over her. But that long-suppressed craving had to be fed something, or it would shatter the bonds he'd imposed in order to keep from being eaten alive. Anger threatened to flame at the edge of his consciousness as he crushed her soft lips under his. He'd kill any man who'd dared to touch her. He would never forgive her if she'd allowed a single caress.

Mina was his.

And this time, he wouldn't let her forget.

In his arms, she shivered, and the simmering need inside him threatened to take complete command. He stroked his tongue across the seam of her lips. She opened at once. The taste of her was an elixir, a drug he'd starved for for years. His feelings for her were as wild and chaotic as a desert storm. How dare she leave him? How dare she take four years to return? When she gasped for breath, he breathed into her mouth, feeding her even as he took from her.

"No one else has touched you." He found some peace in that. Not much, but enough to rein in the beast.

"And," Jasmine responded in shocked surprise, "no one else has touched *you*."

He smiled that predator's smile. "I'm very hungry, Mina."

Jasmine felt her body begin to react as it always had to Tariq's dark sensuality. "Hungry?"

"Very." He was stroking her neck with his thumb in an absent fashion, feeling the vibration as she spoke.

"I need time." She was unprepared for the reality of the man he'd become. Dark. Beautiful. Magnificent. Angry.

He raised his eyes from his perusal of her throat. "No. I am no longer willing to indulge you."

She had no response to that flat statement. Four years ago, Tariq had delighted in letting her have her way. She'd never had to fight this warrior. Back then, he'd been careful with her innocence, but when he'd touched her, Jasmine hadn't felt like an outcast. She'd felt cherished. Today, she didn't feel that beautiful but fragile emotion. Tariq wasn't acting like a lover, but rather a conqueror with his prize. The true depth of what she'd lost was only now becoming clear.

He moved and set her free, but remained on her side of the car, one arm slung negligently over the back of her seat. "So, you have been studying fashion design."

"Yes."

"You wish to be a famous designer?" He threw her a look full of male amusement.

Jasmine bristled. Though used to her family mocking her

dreams, she'd never expected it from Tariq. "Why is that funny?" She aimed a scowl at his savagely masculine features.

He chuckled. "Sheathe your claws, Mina. I simply cannot see you designing those ridiculous things on the catwalks. Your dresses wouldn't be see-through, hmm, displaying to the world treasures that should only be viewed by one man?"

She blushed at his heated gaze, ridiculously pleased that he wasn't laughing at her.

"Tell me," he commanded.

"I want to design feminine things." Her dream was real to her, no matter what anyone said, but until this moment, no one's opinion had truly mattered. "These days, the male designers seem to have an incredibly macabre idea of the female form. Their models are flat boards with not a curve in sight."

"Ah." It was a wholly male sound.

She looked up, suspicious. "Ah, what?"

Tariq spread one possessive hand over her abdomen. She gasped. "You're full of curves, Mina."

"I never pretended to be a sylph."

His warm breath close to her ear startled her. "You misunderstand. I'm delighted by your curves. They'll cushion me perfectly."

Biting hurt turned to red-hot embarrassment and shocking desire. Blinded by longing, she barely finished her explanation. "I want to design pretty things for real women."

Tariq regarded her with a contemplative expression. "You'll be permitted to continue this."

"I'll be *permitted* to continue my work?"

"You will need something to do when I'm not with you."

She gave a frustrated little scream and shifted until her back was plastered against the door, making it possible for her to glower up at him. "You have no right to *permit* me to do anything!" She poked him in the chest with her index finger.

He captured her hand. "On the contrary, I have every right." The sudden chill in his voice stopped her.

"You are now my possession. I own you. That means I have the right to do with you as I please." This time there was no hint of humor in his expression, not even the shadow of the man she'd once known. "You would do well not to provoke me. I have no intention of being cruel, but neither will you find me a fool for your charms a second time."

When, after a frozen moment, he released her and moved back to the opposite side of the car, she gathered the shreds of her composure around her and turned to the window. Had she done this? she asked herself. Had she with her cowardice so totally destroyed the beauty of what had once been between them? She wanted to cry at the loss, but something in her, the same something that had urged her to come to him when she'd heard of his parents' deaths, refused to surrender.

Unbidden, she remembered the way he'd held her so protectively in his arms when she'd run to him, frightened by the suffocation of her home.

"Come home with me, my Jasmine. Come to Zulheil."

"I can't! My parents…"

"They seek to capture you, Mina. I would set you free."

It was a bitter irony that the very man who'd once promised her freedom was now intent on caging her.

"I was only eighteen," she exclaimed abruptly.

"You are no longer eighteen." He sounded dangerous.

"Can't you understand what it was like for me?" she pleaded, despite herself. "They were my parents and I'd only known you for six months."

"Then why did you—what is your phrase?" He paused. "Yes…why did you lead me on? Did it amuse you to have an Arab royal at your beck and call?"

He'd never been at her beck and call. At eighteen, she'd had even less self-confidence than she did now, but he'd always made her feel…important. "No! No! I didn't…."

"Enough." His voice cut through her protests like a knife. "The truth is that when your family asked you to choose, you did not choose me. You did not even tell me so *I* could fight for us. There is nothing further to say."

Jasmine was silenced. Yes, it was the truth. How could she even begin to make a man like him understand what it had been like for her? Born with a mantle of power, Tariq had never known how it felt to be crushed and belittled until he didn't know his own mind. Shrinking into her corner, she thought back to the day that had changed her forever. Her father had forbidden her to see Tariq, threatening to disown her. She'd begged on her knees but he'd made her choose.

"The Arab or your family."

He'd always called Tariq "the Arab." It wasn't racism, but something much deeper. At first she'd thought it was because they expected her to marry into another high-country farming family. Only later had she understood the ugly reality of why they'd crushed her small rebellion under their feet.

Tariq had been meant for Sarah.

Beautiful Sarah had wished to be a princess, and everyone had assumed it would happen. Except, from the moment he'd arrived, Tariq's eyes had lingered on Jasmine, the daughter who wasn't a daughter, the daughter who was a cause for shame, not celebration.

The huge spread in the hills, which had been Jasmine's home, had been in the Coleridge family for generations. As the beneficiaries of that heritage, Jasmine's parents had been used to controlling everything in their high-country kingdom and they had feared Tariq's strength of will. Added to that, his choice of Jasmine over Sarah had made him anathema. To let Jasmine have him when their darling Sarah couldn't, would have meant being continuously faced with both their failure to manipulate Tariq *and* the wrong daughter's happiness. It was ugly and it was vicious, but it was the truth. Jasmine was no longer a needy child, and couldn't pretend that they'd had her best interests at heart.

"Did you implement that irrigation system?" Her voice was softened by pain. They'd met when he'd visited New Zealand to learn about a revolutionary new watering system discovered by a neighboring family.

"It has been operating successfully for three years."

She nodded and laid her head against the seat. At eighteen, she'd made the wrong choice because she'd been terrified of losing the only people who might ever accept her, flawed as she was. A week ago, she'd turned her back on those very people and ventured out to try and recapture the glorious love she'd had with Tariq.

What would he say if she told him that she was now alone in the world?

Her father had carried out his threat and disowned her. But this time she hadn't compromised her soul in a bid for acceptance. She'd walked away, aware that she'd made an irrevocable decision. There would be no welcome back.

The only things Jasmine had in the world were her determination and a soul-deep love that had never died, but she couldn't tell Tariq that. His pity would be far worse than his anger. She'd chosen him and completely forsaken everything else. But was it too late?

"We are approaching Zulheina, if you wish to look."

Grateful for a chance to escape the distressing memories, she pressed a button by her elbow and the window rolled down. Warm air floated in, caressing her cold cheeks. "Oh, my," she whispered, distracted from her emotional agony.

Zulheina was a city of legend. Very few foreigners were ever allowed into the inner sanctum of Zulheil. Business was usually carried out in the larger town of Abraz, in the north. She could see why the people of Zulheil guarded this place with such zeal. It was utterly magnificent.

Fragile-seeming minarets reached for the heavens, illusions that touched the indigo-blue sky. The single river that ran through Zulheil, and eventually fed out into the sea, passed by in a foaming rush. The white marble of the nearest buildings reflected its tumbling, crystalline beauty.

"It's like something out of a fairy tale." She was fascinated by the way the water flowed under them as they drove over the bridge and entered the city proper.

"It is now your home." Tariq's words were a command.

Strange and wondrous smells drifted to her on the warm breeze. Sounds followed, then the vibrant living colors of the people as the limousine passed through a busy marketplace.

Hard male fingers encircled the soft flesh of her upper arm. Startled, she faced Tariq. His green eyes were hooded, hiding his emotions from her. "I said that it is now your home. You have nothing to say to that?"

Home, Jasmine thought, a sense of wonder infusing her. She'd never had a real home. Her smile was luminous. "I think that it will be no hardship to call this place home." She thought the panther opposite her relaxed a little. In the next moment, she saw something out of the corner of her eye that made her gasp. "I don't believe it. It can't be true." Ignoring the firm but strangely gentle grip on her arm, she stretched her neck to peer out the window.

Rising in front of her was the most fragile-looking building she'd ever seen. It seemed to be formed out of mist and raindrops, the artistry in the carving magnificent beyond imagining. The crystal-white stone of the building seemed to glow with a pale rose luminescence that had her transfixed.

She turned to Tariq, wide-eyed, forgetting his anger in her amazement. "I could swear that building is made of Zulheil Rose."

Though Zulheil was a tiny desert sheikdom, enclosed on three sides by bigger powers, and on the fourth by the sea, it was a rich land, producing not just oil, but a beautiful, precious stone called Zulheil Rose. The striking, clear crystal with the hidden fire inside was the rarest gem on the planet, found only in Tariq's land.

"If your eyes get any bigger, my Jasmine, they'll rival the sky," Tariq teased.

Jasmine forgot the stunning building the moment she heard the quiet humor in his tone. Tariq had apparently decided to put aside his anger for the moment.

"That is your new home."

"What?" She lost any composure she might've attained.

He eyed her flushed features with amused interest. "The royal palace is indeed made of Zulheil Rose. Now you see why we do not let many foreigners into our city."

"Good grief." Earnestly, she leaned forward, unconsciously

putting her palms on his thighs for balance. "I know the crystal is harder than diamonds and impenetrable, but don't your people, um, get tempted to chip off pieces?"

His voice was rough when he answered, "The people of Zulheil are happy and well cared for. They are not tempted to lose their place in this society for money.

"And the palace is considered sacred. It was carved where it stands by the one who founded Zulheil. Never in the history of our land has anyone discovered another such concentration of the crystal. It's believed that as long as the palace stands, Zulheil will prosper."

Hard male muscles flexed under her fingers. Jasmine jerked up her head. Blood rushed through her veins to stain her cheeks bright red. Flustered, she removed her hands and scrambled back into her seat.

"That, Mina," Tariq said, as they came to a stop in the inner courtyard of the palace, "is something you're permitted to do at will."

Hot with a combination of embarrassment and desire, she muttered, "What?"

"Touch me."

She sucked in her breath. It was clear that while Tariq had been prepared to wait for intimacy when she'd been eighteen, he was no longer so patient.

They stepped out into the heart of the palace complex—a lush garden protected from the outside by curving walls of Zulheil Rose. From where she stood, Jasmine could see a pomegranate tree heavy with fruit in one corner of the garden. A fig tree dominated the other. Bright, luxuriant and glossy flowers spread like a carpet in either direction.

"It's like a page of the *Arabian Nights* come to life." Any second now she expected a peacock to come strutting out.

"These gardens are opened every Friday to my people. At that time I meet with those who would talk with me."

Jasmine frowned. "Just like that?"

Beside her, Tariq tightened his clasp on her hand, his big body shifting to dominate her field of vision. "You do not approve of my meeting with my people?'' The bright sunlight made his hair glitter like black diamonds.

"Not that. From what I've read, your people adore you.'' Pausing, she turned her head to avoid his penetrating gaze. "I was thinking about your safety.''

"Would you miss me, my Jasmine, if I was gone?'' The question escaped Tariq's iron control, betraying emotions he refused to acknowledge.

"What a thing to ask! Of course I'd miss you.''

Yet she'd walked away from him without a backward look, while he'd bled from the heart. "It has always been done this way in my land. Zulheil is small but prosperous. It will only stay that way if the people are content. None would hurt me because they know I will listen to their concerns.''

"What about outsiders?'' Her hand clenched around his.

He was unable to restrain his smile, seeing in her intent expression echoes of the bright young girl who'd claimed his soul. "The minute a foreigner enters our borders, we know.''

"Your driver tried to convince me this was a taxi.'' Her gentle laughter was as light as the desert dawn.

At the happy sound, something deep inside Tariq was tempted to awaken. He had ached for her for so long. Ruthlessly, he crushed the urge. This time, he would not give Jasmine either his trust or his heart. Not when the scars from the hurt she'd inflicted in the past had yet to heal.

"Mazeel is a good driver, but not the best of actors.'' He looked up at the sound of approaching footsteps.

"Your Highness.'' A familiar pair of brown eyes regarded him with barely veiled disapproval. Tariq wasn't worried. Hiraz might let him see his anger, but his loyalty would keep him silent on what mattered.

"You remember Hiraz.'' He nodded at his chief advisor and closest friend, allowing the woman in his arms to turn.

"Of course. It's nice to see you again, Hiraz.''

Hiraz bowed, his manner stiff and formal. "Madam.''

"Please, call me Jasmine.''

Under Tariq's hand, her back felt incredibly fragile. He

didn't fight the surge of fierce protectiveness that thundered through him. However angry he was with her, Mina was his to protect. *His.*

"Hiraz does not approve of my plans concerning you, Mina." His words were a subtle warning.

"Your Highness, I would speak with you." Hiraz blinked in understanding, but his stance remained stiff. "Your uncle and his entourage have arrived, as have all the others."

"And he only calls me Your Highness when he wants to annoy me," Tariq murmured. "It is not the address of our people." It took an effort to keep his tone even after the blithely delivered message. The arrival of those who would stand witness to the events of this night, brought his plans one step closer to fruition.

Hiraz sighed and relaxed, unable to continue on in such an unfamiliar way. "So you actually did it." His gaze settled on Jasmine. "Do you understand what he has planned?"

"Enough." Tariq made the words an autocratic warning.

Hiraz merely lifted a brow and moved aside. He fell into step beside them as they entered the palace.

"What have you planned?" Jasmine asked.

"I will tell you later."

"When?"

"Jasmine." His quiet, implacable tone usually commanded instant obedience.

"Tariq." At the unexpected echo, he paused and turned, to find Mina scowling up at him.

Hiraz's chuckle provided welcome respite from the sudden shock of recognizing that Jasmine was no longer the fragile girl of his memories. "I see that she has grown up. Good. She will not be easy to control. You would crush a weak woman."

"She will do as I say."

Jasmine wanted to protest at the way they were ignoring her presence, but Tariq's dark expression stole her faltering courage. He'd humored her in the final minutes of the journey, but the man in front of her was the Sheik of Zulheil. And she didn't know this powerful stranger.

Inside, the palace was surprisingly comfortable, with nothing ornate or overdone. Light came in through lots of tiny carved windows, bathing the rooms in sunlight lace. Though beautiful, it was very much a home. Jasmine was still admiring her surroundings when a woman dressed in a long flowing dress in a shade of pale green materialized at her elbow.

"You will go with Mumtaz," Tariq decreed. He lifted their clasped hands and kissed Jasmine's wrist, his gaze locked with hers. Her blood raced through her body, frenetic with the effect of the simple caress. "I will see you in two hours." Then he was gone, striding down the corridor with Hiraz.

Three

Mumtaz showed her to her rooms—a suite in the southern end of the palace. While one room she was shown into had a very feminine feel, the others in the suite were full of masculine accoutrements. She commented on the fact.

"I...do not think there was enough warning of your arrival." There was an odd catch in Mumtaz's voice.

Jasmine attributed her faltering explanation to embarrassment over discussing Tariq's business. "Of course," she agreed, wishing to put the friendly woman at ease.

"Where do these doors go?" she asked, after they'd put her clothes away in the huge walk-in closet.

"Come. You will like this." Mumtaz's ebullient smile was infectious. With a flourish, she flung open the doors.

"A garden!" Under Jasmine's bare feet, the grass in the enclosed garden was soft and lush. A small fountain in the middle of the circular enclosure sent arcs of water tumbling over the Zulheil Rose carvings at its base. Benches surrounded the fountain, and were in turn encircled by millions of tiny blue flowers. A haunting fragrance drifted to her from the huge tree in the corner, which was covered with bell-shaped, blue-white blossoms.

"This is the private garden of…" Mumtaz stumbled over her words. "I am sorry, sometimes my English…"

"That's okay." Jasmine waved her hand. "I'm trying to learn the language of Zulheil, but I'm not very good yet."

Mumtaz's eyes sparkled. "I will teach you, yes?"

"Thank you! You were saying about the garden?"

Mumtaz frowned in thought. "This is the private garden of the people who live behind these…entrances." She pointed to Jasmine's door and to two other similar ones to the left. Together, they encircled three quarters of the garden. A high wall overrun with creeping vines completed the enclosure.

Jasmine nodded. "Oh, you mean it's the guests' garden."

Mumtaz shuffled her feet and gave her a smile. "You like your rooms and this garden?"

"How could I not? They're stunning."

"Good, that is good. You will stay in Zulheil?"

Jasmine looked up, surprised at her tone. "You know?"

Mumtaz sighed and took a seat on a bench near the fountain. Jasmine followed. "Hiraz is Tariq's closest friend, and as Hiraz's wife—"

"You're Hiraz's wife?" Jasmine choked. "I thought you were…never mind."

"A maid, yes?" Mumtaz smiled without rancor. "Tariq wished for you to be with someone you felt comfortable with when you arrived. I work in the palace and will be here every day. I hope you feel you can ask me for anything you need."

"Oh, yes." A little spark of warmth ignited inside Jasmine. Tariq had cared enough to arrange for this lovely woman to welcome her. "But why didn't he say anything?"

"Both he and Hiraz are terrible when they are in a temper. Tariq is angry with you, and my husband with me."

"Why is Hiraz angry with you?" Jasmine's curiosity got the better of her.

"He expects me to agree with something he and Tariq are

doing, even though he himself does not agree with Tariq.'' Before Jasmine could question her further, Mumtaz continued, ''Hiraz told me the story of what happened in your country. But it is common knowledge in Zulheil that Tariq had his heart broken by a red-haired foreigner with blue eyes.''

Jasmine blinked. ''How?''

''Hiraz would go to his grave with Tariq's secrets, but others in that party were not so…loyal,'' Mumtaz explained. ''You are a mystery, but it is good you have come now. After his parents' deaths, Tariq is much in need.''

''He's furious with me,'' she confessed.

''But you are in Zulheina. It is better to be near him even if he is angry, yes? You must learn to manage your h—''

The sudden look of distress on Mumtaz's exotic face alarmed Jasmine. ''What is it?'' she asked.

''I…I have forgotten something. Please, you must come inside.''

She followed, bemused by Mumtaz's sudden change in mood.

''A bath has been drawn for your comfort. Afterward, please wear these.'' Mumtaz pointed to clothing that had appeared on the bed.

Jasmine touched the soft and incredibly fine fabric with her fingers. It was as weightless as mist and the color of Zulheil Rose—pure white with a hidden heart of fire. There was a long flowing skirt sprinkled with tiny shards of crystal that would catch the light each time she moved. The top was a fitted bodice bordered with the same sparkling crystals. Though the long sleeves would end at her wrists, the garment itself was short and would leave her midriff bare. Multiple strands of fine gold chain lay beside the top. Clearly, they were supposed to go around her waist.

''These aren't mine,'' Jasmine whispered.

''There is a special…meal, and your clothing is not correct. This is for you as, uh…''

''A guest?'' she suggested. ''Well, I suppose if this is normal practice, then it should be okay. I just wouldn't feel comfortable wearing something so expensive otherwise.''

She had to repeatedly ensure Mumtaz that she'd be fine before the other woman would leave. "It's something formal, this dinner?" she asked, just before Mumtaz walked out.

"Oh yes. Very formal. I will return to do your hair and make sure you look beautiful.''

As Mumtaz left, Jasmine was certain that she heard her muttering under her breath, but the delicious promise of the scented bath distracted her.

"I feel like a princess," Jasmine whispered, almost two hours after she'd entered the palace. She touched her hand to the gold circlet that Mumtaz had insisted on placing about her head. Her deep-red hair had been brushed until it shone. Now it flowed in riotous waves to the middle of her back, the fine gold strands within it complementing the simple circlet.

"Then I have done my job." Mumtaz laughed.

"I thought flesh wasn't meant to be shown?" Jasmine put her hand on her abdomen. The fine gold chains about her hips were lavish and utterly seductive.

Mumtaz shook her head. "We are reserved in public only. Zulheil has no strict laws, but most women prefer modesty. In our homes with our men, it is acceptable to be more…'' She waved her hands at her own clothing. She was wearing wide-legged harem pants in a pale shade of yellow, cinched at the ankle, and a blouse fitted much like Jasmine's. However, her clothing didn't glitter with sparkling crystal shards.

"I won't be overdressed?" Jasmine didn't want to change. She'd been imagining the look in Tariq's eyes at her appearance. Maybe he'd think her beautiful, because for the first time in her life, she felt that way.

"You are perfect. Now we must go.''

A few minutes later they entered a room full of women, all dressed in stunning costumes bursting with color. Jasmine's eyes widened. At their entry, conversation stopped. A second later, it started again in a chaotic rush. Several older women came over and invited her to sit on the cushions with them. With Mumtaz acting as a translator when necessary, Jasmine was soon laughing and talking with them as if with old friends. Something about them seemed familiar, but she couldn't put her finger on what.

The innate tensing of her body was the only warning she needed half an hour later. She looked up and found Tariq standing in the doorway. Unbidden, her legs uncurled and she stood. Silence reigned again, but this time it was full of expectancy, as if everyone was holding their breath.

He looked magnificent, dressed in a black tunic and pants, the only ornamentation being gold embroidery on the mandarin collar of the tunic. The starkness of his clothing set off the dark beauty of his features. He walked across the room and took her hand. She was vaguely aware of other men following him inside, and the rustle of cloth as the women around her stood up.

His eyes blazed with heat when he gazed at her. "You look like the heart of the Zulheil Rose," he whispered, for her ears only, his eyes on her hair. He drew back, but she felt as if she was in the center of an inferno.

"I have a question for you, my Jasmine." This time the words were crystal clear in the otherwise silent room.

She stared up at him. "Yes?"

Green fire met her. "You came to Zulheil of your own free will. Will you stay of your own free will?"

Jasmine was confused. Tariq had made it clear that he wasn't going to let her leave. Why ask her this now? However, she instinctively knew that she couldn't question him in front of witnesses, not without doing damage to his pride and standing among his people. "Yes."

Tariq's smile was quick and satisfied. He reminded her of a panther again and she suddenly felt stalked. "And will you stay *with me* of your own free will?"

The question was the trigger her mind needed. She understood what was happening, but the knowledge didn't change her answer. "I will stay," she said, and sealed her destiny.

The savage satisfaction in his eyes burned unfettered for one bright second. Then his lids lowered and hid the fire. He lifted her hand to his lips and turned it over, to lay a single kiss on the pulse beating rapidly under her skin. "I take my leave of you, my Jasmine…for now."

Then he was gone, leaving her standing, her mind in shock at what she'd just done. Giggling women came to her side and directed her back to her cushion. Jasmine caught Mumtaz's worried expression as the other woman took a seat next to her.

"You know?" The whisper reached only her ears, muffled by the buzz of conversation in the room.

Jasmine nodded. Aware that she was the center of attention, she tried to appear calm, even though her heart beat so hard she was afraid that it was going to rip out of her chest. The secret that she'd successfully buried under her love for Tariq raised its head, like a cobra readying itself to strike, taunting her with its inevitability. Unable to face his rejection, she'd planned to tell him once she was certain of her welcome in his life. Now it was too late. Much too late. How could she tell him the truth now?

"Jasmine?" Mumtaz interrupted her thoughts, reminding her of the act that had just taken place.

"When he asked me those questions…"

"I wished to tell you the truth, but they forbade it."

"And your loyalty is to Tariq." Jasmine couldn't hold the omission against Mumtaz. The other woman had done everything she could. "I thought the country was in mourning?"

"One month we have mourned, but it is part of Zulheil's culture that life conquers death. Our people would rather live joyously as an offering to those who are gone, than shroud ourselves in darkness."

Someone put a plate of sweetmeats into Jasmine's hands. She nodded an absentminded thanks at the woman, but didn't attempt to eat. Her stomach was in knots. Suddenly, she knew why the guests around her seemed so familiar. All of them had an unmistakable regal bearing that reminded her of

Tariq—of course his family would be in attendance on this night.

"Do you know what happens next?" At the negative shake of her head, Mumtaz explained. "The questions are the first step in the marriage ceremony. Second is the binding, which will be performed by an elder. The final part is the blessing, which will be sung outside. You will not see Tariq again until it is over."

Jasmine nodded. Her eyes went to the lacy window set in the middle of the dividing wall. Her future awaited on the other side. "I've never heard of such a ceremony."

"Zulheil's ways are not those of our Islamic neighbors. We follow the ancient paths," Mumtaz explained. "You truly answered him knowing the consequences?"

Jasmine drew in a deep breath. "I stepped off that plane with only one goal. I didn't expect this, but he's the only man I've ever wanted. I could never say no to him."

Mumtaz's smile was understanding. "He is angry, but he needs you. Love him, Jasmine, and teach him to love again."

Jasmine nodded. She had to teach him to love her, or she was going to spend her life as the possession of a man who didn't care about her love. A man who, unless he loved her, would reject her once she revealed her shameful secret.

By the time she stepped out of this room, she would be married to the Sheik of Zulheil.

"It is time for the binding." Mumtaz nodded toward an aged woman, clad head to toe in vibrant red, who had just entered the room.

Coming to kneel next to Jasmine, the elder smiled and picked up her right hand. "With this I bind you." She tied a beautiful red ribbon with intricate embroidery around Jasmine's wrist.

Leaning close, Jasmine saw that the embroidery was writing—flowing Arabic script. When the elder raised her wrinkled face, there was power in those dark eyes. "You will repeat my words."

Jasmine nodded jerkily.

''This binding, it be true. This binding, it be unbroken.''

''This binding, it be true. This binding, it be unbroken.'' Her voice was a whisper, her throat clogged with the knowledge of the finality of her actions.

''With this bond, I take my life and put it in the keeping of Tariq al-Huzzein Donovan Zamanat. For ever and eternity.''

Jasmine repeated the words carefully and exactly. She'd made her choice, and she would see it through, but a deep shaft of pain ran through her at the thought that her parents weren't present on this day. They'd cut her adrift with a callousness she still couldn't comprehend.

Once she'd finished, the elder picked up the other end of the ribbon and fed it through the lacy window halfway up the wall. A minute later, Jasmine felt a tug on her wrist.

Tariq had just been bound to her.

For ever and eternity.

The haunting chant that began outside seemed to echo in her soul.

Tariq stared at the small aperture that was his only window into the room where his Jasmine sat. As the blessing chant grew in volume around him, he kept his eyes trained on the opening. Images raced through his mind, competing to hold his attention.

Mina, wearing the dress of his land. He felt fierce pride in the way she'd carried herself. A princess could not have been more regal.

Mina, her red hair a fall of sunsets that beckoned him with promises of warmth. Soon he'd collect on that promise.

Mina, looking at him with eyes that betrayed her awakening sensuality. Yes, Jasmine had grown up. It would be his pleasure to teach her the secrets of the bedroom.

His need to possess her clawed at him, but underlying it was a deeper need and an even deeper hurt, things he refused to acknowledge. He allowed only a sliver of hunger to escape his control. Mina had always belonged to him, but in a few more minutes, the ties between them would become unbreakable.

Then he would claim his woman.

He was very hungry.

Tariq's words in the car refused to leave Jasmine's mind. How was she supposed to relax, knowing that a hungry panther was coming to lay claim to her? With a groan, she sat up in the huge bed in the room next to hers. Tariq's masculine presence was everywhere.

The flimsy nightgown that she'd found on the bed was scandalous as far as she was concerned. The superfine white linen fell to her ankles like a sheet of mist. It was laced with blue ribbon down to her navel, and had long sleeves tied with the same ribbon at the wrist. Thigh-high slits on either side bared her legs with every movement she made. The sleeves were also slit from wrist to shoulder, exposing her skin. All that wasn't as bad as the fact that the material was almost sheer, her nipples and the darker triangle between her legs far too visible.

"They might be reserved in public but they could give lessons in eroticism," she muttered, standing beside the bed.

Uncomfortable in the sensual clothing, she crossed to the closet, with the intention of finding a robe to throw on over it. She found a large blue silk one that was clearly Tariq's. It would have to do, she thought, and pulled it out.

"Stop."

Startled, she swiveled around. She hadn't heard him enter. Hadn't heard him move across the room. Tariq was almost upon her, his eyes hot as they skated over her body. Her gaze fixated on his naked chest. He was magnificent. His shoulders were wider than she'd imagined, the muscles thick and liquid when he moved. The ridges on his abdomen appeared hard and inflexible, pure steel under skin. The only thing saving him from nakedness was a small white towel.

"I did not give you permission to cover yourself."

Jasmine bristled at his autocratic tone. "I don't need your permission."

With a single flick of his wrist, he pushed the robe from her nerveless fingers and captured both her hands in one of his own. "You forget that I now own you. You do what I wish."

"Rubbish."

"If it comforts you, feel free to disagree," he said, magnanimous in victory. "But know that I am going to win."

Jasmine stared up at him. Not for the first time, she wondered if she'd taken on more than she could handle. Maybe Tariq really was the despot he was acting. Perhaps he did consider her a possession.

"I wish to see you, Mina." He turned her with such speed that she would've lost her balance had he not clamped an arm around her waist. His other arm came to lie under her breasts.

When she looked up, she found, to her shock, that they were standing in front of the full-length mirror in the corner. Her hair was exotically red against the white of her nightgown, her pale skin a stark contrast to the darkness of his arms. His big body was curved over hers, his shoulders blocking out the night.

"Tariq, let go," she begged, unable to take the erotic intimacy implied by the reflection. She turned her face to one side, so her cheek pressed against his chest. Her worries about him were buried under the river of need that flooded her body.

"No, Mina. I wish to see you." He nuzzled her neck, brushing aside the strands of her hair in his path. "I have fantasized about this for years."

His rough confession made her tingle from head to toe. It no longer felt wrong to know that his eyes were on the mirror, seeing everything she attempted to hide. It felt completely right, as if she had been born for this moment. Born to be the woman of the Sheik of Zulheil.

"Watch me as I love you." He nipped at the side of her neck, then suckled the spot.

She shook her head in mute refusal. Despite the feeling of

rightness, she was too innocent, too untouched, to easily accept this level of sensual discovery. Tariq kissed his way up her jaw and over her cheek. Her earlobe was a delicate morsel to be sucked into his mouth and savored. He ran his teeth over her skin in a gentle caress. Jasmine shivered and stood on tiptoe in an unconscious attempt to get closer.

"Look in the mirror," he whispered, spreading his fingers across her stomach and under her breasts. "Please, Mina."

His husky "please" broke through her defenses. She turned her head and looked. And met his burning green-eyed gaze. Holding her eyes, he moved the hand under her breasts until he was cupping one full globe. She gasped and gripped the arm at her waist. In response, he squeezed her aching, swollen flesh. It wasn't enough. She needed more.

"Tariq," she moaned, shifting restlessly against him.

"Watch," he ordered.

She watched.

He moved his hand up until his thumb lay near her nipple. Under her wide-eyed gaze, he rubbed his thumb over the throbbing peak once, twice, and again. She was panting for breath. Behind her, she heard his own breathing alter, felt his body harden, muscles and tendons settling into unyielding lines. She cried out when he stopped caressing her, only to sigh and whimper when he repeated the teasing stroking on her other breast. His hands were big, sprinkled with dark hair, and Jasmine ached to feel them everywhere. When he moved, she dropped her hands to her sides.

He left her breasts aroused and hot. His hands moved over her stomach, smoothing their way to her hips. There, he very carefully spread his hands so that his thumbs met in the middle across her navel. She dug her fingers into the rigid muscles of his thighs behind her when she saw the way the action framed the shadowy curls between her legs. He murmured in approval against her ear and rewarded her with another teasing nibble of her sensitive earlobe.

Then he smiled at her in the mirror, a very male, very satisfied smile. Still holding her gaze, he moved his thumbs. The curving arc rubbed the top of her curls. Jasmine tried to shift but his upper arms held her shoulders pinned to his chest. She watched in helpless fascination, her heart thudding in her throat, her knees losing their strength, as he slowly, deliberately pushed his thumbs down and inward.

The sudden pressure on the tiny bundle of nerve endings hidden under the fiery curls made Jasmine scream and bury her face against his chest. He let her recover before repeating the intimate caress again and again, until she was arching into every touch, urging him on. Dazed, she met his gaze. His eyes were hooded and dark, but the flush high on his cheekbones assured her that he was as affected as she was.

"No!" she cried, when he removed his hands.

"Patience, Mina." His breathing was irregular, but his control intact.

Jasmine squirmed in an effort to make him return. Instead, he gripped her gown at her hips and started to gather the soft material into his big hands. She was bare to her thighs before she registered his intent.

"No!" She tried to lift her arms but he squeezed with his biceps, trapping her. Unable to watch as he claimed her so blatantly, she pressed her eyes shut. And felt his lips on her neck, on her temple, on her cheek. He stopped raising the nightgown.

"Mina." It was an invitation into sin. Jasmine couldn't resist. She opened her eyes and watched him bare her to the waist, mesmerized by the rich sensuality of his voice.

"Oh, God." She felt like a complete and utter wanton, standing there unveiled, her legs parted for balance, Tariq a dark masculine shadow behind her.

His thigh muscles moved fluidly under her hands as he changed position. To her shock, she felt one thickly muscled thigh slide between her legs. He began to rub it across her aroused flesh, a gentle abrasion that set her senses reeling. There were no barriers between his heat and her moist warmth. Her hands were free but she no longer wanted to stop him.

"Ride me, Mina." He shored up the gown with one arm

and slid his other one between her legs. Jasmine thought she would lose her mind when she saw his fingers part her curls. He shifted his leg again, inciting her to do what he wanted. Jasmine moaned and, almost without volition, began moving her hips. His fingers stroked her pulsing flesh even as his leg pushed harder and lifted her toes off the floor.

Lost in his touch, she closed her eyes and rode. Desperate for an anchor, she curled her hands around his biceps, but it was too late. She felt the explosion building, and then suddenly, she crashed. It was as if every part of her had broken apart and then reintegrated. Sobbing with her release, she lay against Tariq, trusting him to hold her up.

"Mina, you're beautiful." His voice was reverent.

Jasmine lifted her head and found herself looking at her image in the mirror, her legs spread apart, Tariq's thigh holding her up. Too full of pleasure to blush, she raised her head and met his eyes. "Thank you."

Tariq shuddered, almost undone by her surrender. "I haven't finished yet."

The gown whispered down her lovely legs as he released it. Her fever-bright eyes watched him untie the laces. He took his time, enjoying the culmination of years of erotic dreams. When she moved, he felt the faint shivers that rocked her. Pleased, he flexed his thigh against her sweet heat, knowing it would send shards of pleasure rocketing through her.

"Tariq, don't tease." She tilted her head toward him.

He dropped a kiss on her lips, enchanted by the feminine complaint. "But you are so teasable." He finished with the ribbons and the gown gaped open, baring her breasts. His arousal became almost painful in its intensity, at the sight of a reality that outstripped his every fantasy. Closing one hand around the taut flesh, he squeezed gently.

Mina's eyes drifted shut and she arched into his touch. He nudged her hips, needing her to feel him, to understand this claiming. This branding. He wanted to mark her so deeply that she'd never think of walking away from him again. The urge was primitive and uncivilized, but when it came to this woman, his emotions had never been polite or bland.

Opening her eyes, she smiled at him in the mirror, a smile full of newly realized feminine power, and then began to move her body up and down. The slow dance was an unmerciful tease, but the feel of her was indescribable.

He growled in warning. ''Witch.''

''Tease,'' she accused.

He started to fondle her breast again, rubbing her nipple between his fingertips. She was so exquisitely sensitive, it was a temptation he couldn't resist. ''Perhaps,'' he agreed, ''but I'm also bigger than you.''

Before Jasmine could take another breath, Tariq lifted the gown and tugged it over her head. Her arms came up of their own volition, her mind unable to defy the compulsion. She heard him throw the garment aside at the same time he withdrew his thigh from between hers. Only his arm around her waist kept her upright.

Jasmine pushed aside the hair in her face and gasped at the sight of her naked body displayed so openly for him.

''You are mine, Jasmine.''

This time, the blatant possessiveness of his words didn't scare her. No man could touch a woman as tenderly as Tariq was touching her if he only saw her as a possession. Somehow, she had to reach the man she knew existed behind the mask.

She'd hurt Tariq more than she could've imagined when she'd ended their relationship. Now she had to love him so much that he would never doubt her again. Her panther had to trust in her loyalty before he'd allow himself to trust in her heart. And he would, because she had no intention of giving up. She couldn't allow herself to think that there was no hope of winning him back. That was a nightmare she couldn't face.

His eyes met hers in the mirror, daring her to deny him. Instead of answering the silent challenge, she took a deep breath and said, ''I want another ride.''

Four

Tariq's arm tightened convulsively around her waist and the
fire in his eyes blazed out of control. "No, this time *I* will
ride." He turned her in his arms and picked her up without
effort. "A long, slow ride. You can have another turn later."
A hard kiss on her lips sealed the rough promise.

He laid her on the sheets after pushing aside the blanket.
For the first time, Jasmine saw him completely naked. He was
big. She hadn't thought about just how much bigger than her
he was, until that moment.

His eyes met hers and she knew he understood her apprehension. "I won't hurt you, Mina." He moved onto the bed
and covered her body with his own. The heavy weight of him
was like a full-body caress, a feast for her senses.

"You always call me Mina when you want to get your own
way." She spread her thighs for him and wrapped her arms
around his neck.

Tariq rewarded her trust by slipping his hands under her
waist and cupping her buttocks. "I'll always get my way from

now on." His statement was uncompromising, as was the blunt tip of his erection against her.

Then he kissed her, his tongue mimicking the ultimate sensual act. Jasmine knew she was ready; she'd felt herself slick and moist against his thigh. She knew it, but it took his kiss on her breast, his huskily uttered, "I'll take care of you, Mina," to make her believe.

"Now," she whispered.

He gripped her hips and pushed. At the same time, he captured one strawberry-pink nipple into his mouth and suckled. Hard. Jasmine screamed and bucked under the onslaught of feeling, inadvertently easing his way. He surged inside her, tearing through the thin membrane that had protected her innocence. She gasped, her body taut.

"Mina?" He was frozen above her.

She dug her fingernails into his shoulders. "A long, slow ride," she reminded him in a breathless murmur, still adjusting to the feel of his heat inside her.

Three torturously slow strokes later, she was begging him to go faster.

"You are too impatient," he reprimanded her, but his body glistened with sweat and she could feel him trembling with the effort to hold back.

She tightened her legs around him and drew her nails down his back. His eyes flashed as his control fractured and then he slammed into her. Jasmine bit his shoulder when her desire reached a crescendo, and then she felt herself explode for the second time that night. Above her, Tariq went rigid as his own climax roared through him.

His body was heavy when he collapsed on top of her, but she was so exhausted she couldn't move. Instead, she nestled her face in the crook of his neck and fell asleep.

Jasmine awoke sometime in the twilight hours when her stomach growled. Only then did she realize that, as a consequence of her nervousness, she hadn't eaten since she'd left New Zealand. She attempted to shift, and found she couldn't.

One heavy male leg pinned her lower body to the bed and the arm curved possessively under her breasts immobilized her torso. Her stomach growled again.

"Tariq." She turned her head and kissed his neck. Under her lips, his skin was warm and tasted faintly of the desert and the salt and spice of their loving. "Wake up."

He groaned in his sleep and tightened his embrace. Sighing, Jasmine put her hands on his shoulders and shook him.

"You wish for your ride already, Mina?" His sleepy question made her turn bright red. Now that she wasn't in the grip of passion, she couldn't believe her boldness.

She frowned. "I wish for food. I'm starving."

He chuckled and rolled over, taking her with him. She ended up sprawled on his chest. His eyes glinted at her from behind half-closed lids. "What will you give me if I feed you?"

Her stomach growled again. Loudly. "Peace."

This time he laughed, his chest rumbling under her hands. "Ah Mina, you are never what is expected." He gave a long-suffering sigh. "I'll see if I can find you food."

He put her aside with careful hands and slipped out of bed. Jasmine couldn't help watching him. The well-defined muscles of his back bunched as he stood up and bent over to pick up the robe he'd pushed out of her hands.

"Like what you see?" he asked, without turning around.

Jasmine felt herself blush again. "Yes."

He was pleased by her answer. She saw his smile when he turned to walk out, shrugging into the robe.

"Where are you going?"

"There is food in the dining area. I'll bring it to you."

After he left, Jasmine quickly found her rumpled gown and slithered into it. She was sitting cross-legged on top of the blankets, hoping the shadows hid the sheer quality of the gown, when he came back. Not saying anything, Tariq put the tray of food in the center of the bed and lounged on the other side like a lazy panther, watching her eat.

"So, what's my name now?" she asked, once the sharp edge of her appetite had been dulled to something bearable.

"Jasmine al-Huzzein Coleridge-Donovan Zamanat."

Jasmine's eyes widened and her hand stopped midway to her lips. She stopped chewing. "Good grief. What a mouthful! I didn't know that I got to keep my maiden name."

"Zulheil's women have always been cherished." He stretched lazily. "It's why we do not ask them to convert their religion upon marriage. The choice is yours."

The words sent a warm glow through her. Yes, she thought again, there was hope. "So Donovan was your mother's name?"

A flicker of darkness seemed to shadow his eyes, but his response was easy. "You know she was Irish." He plucked a fig off Jasmine's plate and put it into his mouth. For a minute, she just stared at the sensuous shape of his lips, reminded of the things he'd done to her with that clever, clever mouth.

"When we have a child, he or she will have al-Huzzein Coleridge Zamanat as their name. Al-Huzzein Zamanat is the name of the ruling family, but their mother's name is also always carried by the children."

He glanced curiously at her when she didn't reply. She blushed and transferred her attention back to her food. The thought of carrying Tariq's child caused bittersweet pain. She knew she had to tell him her secret…but not now.

"You have her eyes."

"Yes. And…" He paused. When Jasmine looked up, he smiled his dangerous smile. "Some would say I have her temper."

"They're obviously bright people." She picked up a dried apricot and fed it to him. He caught her wrist in a lightning-fast move and licked her fingers clean, like a great big cat lapping at his meal. His eyes never left hers.

"You must miss them." Swallowing, she fought the sensual promise in the air to address something far more important.

He looked away from her, into the shadows. "They are gone. I must lead my people now. I have no time to mourn."

Jasmine hurt for him. Everyone should be given the chance to grieve. Even a sheik. She'd opened her mouth to offer her support when he took the tray of food and put it on the floor. "Enough talking." He tumbled her to the bed.

Tariq did not wish to talk of his parents. The pain of their deaths had been intense. What he'd discovered afterward had almost driven him mad with grief. His beautiful, loving mother had been dying of cancer. His parents had been on the way back from a clinic when the car crashed.

The woman he'd trusted most in the world had kept a secret that had stolen her from him before her death. He'd had so many things to tell her, but because she hadn't had enough faith in him to share her secret, he would never get the chance. And he'd never know if there was something he could've done that would have averted tragedy.

Shaking off the memories, he pressed Jasmine into the mattress, pleased by her instant acceptance. Here, there would be no lies between them. There would be no secrets in the pleasure their bodies found in one another. He shoved aside the errant thought that there couldn't be such passion without emotional consequences, unwilling to concede that this tiny woman, with her gentle smiles and lush sensuality, might have already found a foothold in the lost places of his soul.

"You are sore?"

He could tell that she blushed by the hotness of her skin under his palm. Her heart's ragged beat became even faster.

"No." She hid her face against his neck.

"I won't force you, Mina. Never will I take what is not freely given." He stroked her back and pressed a line of kisses down her throat, luxuriating in her softness. Mina's delicious curves made him want to conquer her feminine secrets with slow, languorous enjoyment.

"Can I force you?"

He was startled for an instant by the suggestive whisper, and then he smiled. "Do you want me so much then, my wife?"

"You know I want you." Those eyes of hers flashed fire

at him, unexpected and delightful. Again he had to acknowledge that this Mina wasn't the same girl who'd almost destroyed him four years ago.

He leaned down and tasted her lower lip. Her teeth scraped gently over his in return. Yes, he thought, this Mina was no tame kitten to be ordered to heel. This Mina had claws. Would she use them to fight him or fight for him?

New excitement flickered through his bones.

Two days later, he walked into a turret room at one end of their suite, just in time to see Mina raise her arms above her head and say, "Perfect!"

Surrounded on three sides by clear glass, the room was bathed in sunshine. As Mina danced across the floor, dust motes whirled with her, as if excited by her laughter. His whole body clenched. Buried feelings shook off their bindings. So easily, she could once again hold his heart in her hands.

Shocked by the knowledge of his susceptibility to a woman whose loyalty had never belonged to him, he fought off the tenderness she'd aroused.

"What's perfect?" he asked at last.

Startled, Jasmine froze and met Tariq's dark gaze. His power and charisma seemed to have increased in the hours that they'd been apart. "This room," she managed to answer. "I thought I'd use it for a workroom. Is that okay?"

Tariq moved farther inside. "This is your home, Mina. Do as you wish."

His generosity gave lie to his harsh words in the car. Jasmine smiled and hugged him. He didn't react, and she drew away before he could think to push her away. Affection was something completely different from touching in bed, and Tariq had given no sign that he wanted anything from her outside of that sensual arena. The knowledge hurt, but she was determined to break through the barriers between them.

"Thank you." Walking over to one of the windows, she found that it looked out into their private garden. "This room would be perfect for your painting. Where's your studio?"

The vibration of the floor beneath her bare feet warned her of his approach. Seconds later, he put his hands on her shoulders and turned her around. "I am a sheik, Mina. I don't have time for such things."

Jasmine frowned. "But you loved painting." She treasured the painting he'd done for her in New Zealand. It had become a talisman of sorts, keeping her focused on her dream.

"We do not always get to do what we love."

"No," she agreed, shaken by the implacability of his statement. Her Tariq, who'd been gentle enough in his heart to truly love, was now buried under the stoney facade of this sheik. Doubts about her ability to reach him surfaced once again, though she tried to fight them. For a woman who'd never been loved by those who were supposed to treasure her despite her faults, it was a task that required a mix of defiant courage and desperate hope.

Tariq closed his hands around her neck and caressed the sensitive skin with his thumbs, his eyes hooded and mysterious. "We do not have the time for a wedding journey, but I am scheduled to visit one of the desert tribes tomorrow. You will come."

He was giving her no choice, but Jasmine didn't want one. She'd spent four years apart from him. It was enough. "Where are we going?" Her skin felt as if it was on fire.

Tariq rubbed his thumb over one particular spot. "I marked you this morning."

Her hand flew to her throat and touched his hand. "I didn't realize when I chose this blouse."

He looked at her, the green of his eyes altered by emotion to something close to black. "You are mine in every way, Mina."

She didn't know what to say to the possessiveness in his tone. It was a little frightening to be the wife of this dangerous man. Sometimes her Tariq appeared, but mostly, all she saw was this cold, glittering mask.

"Such soft, white skin, my Jasmine." His throaty words made her relax. Tariq's desire she could cope with, but when he retreated behind his shields, she wanted to scream with frustration. "You mark so easily."

"Tariq, what—" she began, surprised when he started to undo the buttons on her scoop-necked blouse.

He ignored her fluttering hands. Eyes wide, Jasmine watched his dark head dip and then felt his mouth on her breast. *Sizzling.* It was the only word to describe the sensation of his lips against her skin. She clutched at his silken hair as he began to suck at the soft flesh. Her body felt like one big flame, his touch the fuel. A minute later, he moved away.

Picking up her hand, he touched one finger to the small red mark on her breast. "See this and know that you are mine."

She stared at him, stunned by the possessive act. Yet she was also aroused beyond comprehension, her body reacting to the primitive maleness of his actions.

"Keep thinking those thoughts." He kissed her once, a kiss calculated to keep her aching. "I will satisfy us both tonight." Then he turned on his heel and strode out.

Jasmine felt her knees begin to buckle. She grabbed the window ledge behind her for support. Unbidden, one hand rose to her breast. He'd deliberately marked her as a gesture of possession, of ownership. She remembered the glittering satisfaction on his face, the harsh lines of his cheekbones, the lush sensuality of his lips, and shivered. Part of it was desire, but the other part was a painful uncertainty. She didn't want to believe that Tariq felt only lust for her, not when he treated her so tenderly at times, but this act of branding had been driven by something darker than love or affection. Something that she instinctively knew could destroy their relationship if she didn't find and confront it.

The next day dawned with skies of crystal clarity and beauty so pure and pristine it made Jasmine's heart ache. Such glory humbled her and yet gave her courage.

They left Zulheina in a limousine for the five-hour journey into the hinterlands of Zulheil. From there, they would have to go by camel to the important, though small, desert holding of Zeina.

"Who are the others following us?" she asked Tariq, after they had pulled out of the palace.

"Three of my inner council are coming." He crooked a finger. Jasmine smiled and moved to sit beside him. He cradled her against his body. Unlike the steely intensity of his passion the night before, today he was relaxed, content to just hold her. "At the end of the road, we'll be met by two guides sent from Zeina to lead us to the outpost."

"It sounds isolated."

"It is the way of our people. We are not like the roaming Bedouin tribes, because we settle and set up cities. But for the most part, our cities are small and isolated."

"Even Zulheina isn't that big, is it?"

Tugging off the tie at the end of her plait, he unraveled her hair. Jasmine laid her head against his chest and basked in his unexpected affection. Just yesterday, she hadn't believed it possible that he'd enjoy this gentle touching.

"No. Abraz is the biggest city, the city we show to the outside world, but Zulheina is the heart of the sheikdom."

"Why is Zeina important?"

He moved his hand to her nape and began to rub his fingers over the sensitive skin in a slow caress. She arched into his touch like a cat. "Ah, Mina, you're a contradiction." His amused words made her tilt her head back to meet his gaze.

"In what way?"

He touched her parted lips with his fingers and said, "So free and uninhibited in my arms and yet such a lady in public. It's a delightful combination."

"Why do I know you're going to add something else?"

"I find I relish stripping away that ladylike facade in my imagination. It's very enjoyable to spend time planning exactly how I will make you cry out."

"Now every time I look at you, I'll think you're thinking that." She blushed.

"You would probably be correct." His laughing eyes

warned her of his intention before he covered her lips with his own.

Jasmine wrapped her arms around his neck and relaxed into the slow and lazy loving. Tariq was in no hurry. Pulling her into his lap, he caressed her breasts with hands that knew every inch of her, and gave her a lesson in the pleasures of kissing. He tasted the inner sweetness of her mouth and nibbled at her lips when she needed to breathe, then returned to tempt her with his tongue, seemingly willing to do this forever. She was the one who got so heated she began to wriggle.

"No more," she gasped, and broke the kiss, aware of the hard ridge of his arousal under her bottom.

His eyes were slumberous, his desire clear, but he pulled down her tunic and settled her beside him on the seat again. "You're right, Mina. I would need hours to finish this."

Flustered and aroused, she scooted to the other side of the car. "Tell me about Zeina before you start your work."

His smile was very male as he gazed at her heaving breasts. "Zeina is one of the major suppliers of Zulheil Rose. For some as yet unknown reason, the gem only exists alongside deposits of oil. It is a strange crystal."

Jasmine whistled. "Talk about double dipping."

"It could be like that, but over centuries, the tribes of Zulheil have set up an interconnecting system that means that not just those people living near such bounty will benefit. For example, the Zulheil Rose leaves Zeina in a condition close to its raw state. It then goes out to two tribes in the north, who train the best artisans in the world."

Jasmine knew Tariq's pride was justified. The artisans of Zulheil were considered magicians. "Wait a second." She frowned in thought. "If the crystal is only found next to deposits of oil, why isn't Zulheina an oil center?"

"Zulheina is odd in more than one sense. Contradictory as it seems, our engineers and geologists insist there is not an ounce of oil in the area," he informed her. "So we think of the palace crystal as a gift from the Gods."

"I can't argue with that. It's so beautiful." She sighed in remembrance. "What's the purpose of this trip?"

"We're a scattered people. I make it a point to visit each tribe at least once a year." He stretched out his long legs, taking up even more of her space. "I'm afraid I must read these reports now, Mina." He gestured to some papers that he'd slipped into one of the pockets lining the limousine doors.

She nodded in acquiescence, thinking over everything he'd said. It was clear that while Tariq didn't yet trust her with his love, he had no qualms about sharing the business of his sheikdom with her. For the first time in her life, she felt a part of something greater, not just an outside observer. With hope renewed in her heart, she plucked a small sketchbook out of her purse and began to design a dress of moonlight and silver.

Tariq looked up from his papers to find Mina's hand flying in graceful strokes across the page. Her face was intense in concentration, her mouth set in a way that suggested something had caught her attention. He was fascinated.

When they'd first met, she'd been a student, but her studies hadn't captured her interest. Today, she was fully absorbed in her thoughts. This was, he realized with a sense of wonder he couldn't fight, the first time he'd truly come face-to-face with the woman his Mina had grown into.

"May I see?" he asked, wanting to learn about this new Jasmine, this woman who threatened to catch him in a net far stronger than the one that had ensnared him four years ago.

Startled blue eyes looked into his, but then a slow smile bloomed. "If you like." At the shy welcome, he moved to sit beside her, his arm along the back of the seat.

He looked over her shoulder. "An evening gown."

"I thought that I'd use material shot with silver."

Her hair was soft against his fingertips as he leaned down to study the clean lines of the drawing. "You're talented. This is lovely."

Her cheeks flushed with color. "Really?"

There was hunger in the need she tried to hide. He recalled

her defensiveness about her designing when he'd first questioned her—the reaction of someone whose dream had never received support. Distanced from the rapier-sharp pain of the past, he began to see a glimmer of the forces that had shaped this woman and her decisions. A kind of furious tenderness for her rose inside him. The urge to punish those who had hurt her while she'd been lost to him was so strong, he had to exercise conscious effort to control it.

"Yes, really. You might find some material to your liking in the shipment that comes from Razarah in the next month." In fact, he'd make sure that bolts were delivered for her perusal. "Tell me about your designs."

Eyes bright, she did. The journey passed in easy companionship that surprised him. Since he'd ascended to the throne, he'd never been free to simply "be" with anyone. Now Mina, with her laughter and her dreams, was tempting him to relax. To play. Did he trust her enough to unbend that much?

Five

"**I**'m scared," Jasmine blurted out.

Tariq turned to face her. "Scared?"

She nodded. "They're so big and…"

To her surprise, he walked over and pulled her into a gentle embrace. "Don't worry, Mina, I'll take care of you."

"Promise?" Her voice was shaky. She hadn't thought through the idea of what a trip on the back of a camel would entail. It had been something vague and slightly exotic.

"What is this?" Tariq moved back, his hands on her shoulders, eyes dark with concern. "You're terrified."

She nodded, miserable. "I can't stand heights and their backs are so high."

"There is no other way to reach the tribe or we'd take it." He cupped her cheeks in his palms.

"It's okay. I can handle it," she lied.

"So brave, Mina." He rubbed his thumb over her quivering lower lip. "The car is still here. You may return home."

Jasmine's head jerked up. He'd been so domineering in his

demand that she accompany him that this concession was a real surprise. "You don't want me to come anymore?"

"I would not have you suffer."

She bit her lower lip. "How long will this trip take?"

Tariq dropped his hands to her waist. "It'll take three days to reach Zeina. With the time I must spend there and the return trip, a week and a half is an optimistic guess."

A week and a half! She couldn't bear to be parted from him for that long. "I'll come. Can I ride with you?"

He nodded. There was approval in the soft kiss he dropped on her lips. "You can snuggle your face against my chest and close your eyes, just like you do in bed."

She blushed. It was true that she liked to sleep with her head on his chest, her arms and legs spread over him, but she hadn't realized that he'd noticed her preference. She raised her hand and stroked his jaw, which was shadowed by his white head covering. "Thank you, Tariq."

"You are welcome, my wife. Come, it is time to go."

Sometimes, Jasmine thought, as Tariq helped her mount the sway-backed creature, her husband could be the most thoughtful of men. He mounted behind her before she could begin to panic. For the ride, both of them were in wide-legged pants and tunics, their heads and necks also covered from the harsh sun.

Her stomach lurched at the camel's first step, but she kept her eyes resolutely forward, determined to conquer this fear if it killed her. The endless desert vista was an unexpected ally, tranquil and beautiful. By the time they stopped for the day, she was watching everything with wide eyes. The camel's rolling gait was a little disconcerting, but as long as she didn't look directly at the ground, no nausea arose. And in truth, her husband's strong grip around her waist almost gave her the confidence to do that as well.

However, she understood that even he couldn't help her with a sore rear. They had stopped at a hidden desert oasis for the night when she discovered just how bad it hurt. After they arrived, she excused herself and walked until she was out of sight of the men. She quickly took care of her needs and then stood in the shadow of a small tree, rubbing her sore behind.

Tariq's low chuckle made her spin around, face flaming. He was standing less than a foot away, his arms crossed over his chest, a wide smile on his aristocratic face.

"What are you doing here?" She dropped her hands and started to walk past him, embarrassed.

He caught her around the waist with one arm and swung her against his hard body. She turned her face away. Tariq nuzzled her neck affectionately. "Don't be angry, Mina. I was worried when you didn't return to camp."

Mollified, and melting from his warm touch, she decided to be honest. "It hurts." For the first time since she'd arrived in this land, she felt ill at ease, a foreigner unused to the ways of these exotic people. She needed Tariq's comfort. What she got was something totally unexpected.

His hands dropped to her bottom and began to massage her aching flesh with soothing strokes. "It will get worse before it gets better. I believe that's a Western saying."

She groaned, too relieved to be embarrassed. His hands felt like magic, but she knew that if he kept going, she'd do something silly like ask him to make love to her. Shoving at his chest, she backed away, her legs shaky.

"We, um…better return or we'll miss dinner." She didn't look him in the eye, afraid of her own hungry desire.

His disappointed sigh was loud in the silence. "You are correct, Mina. Come." He held out his hand. Jasmine slipped her palm into his and they made their way to camp.

Her wicked husband leaned over and said, "I promise to soothe your sore muscles tonight, my Jasmine. I wouldn't have you so aching from riding that I couldn't ride you," just as they reached camp. A blazing blush stole over her.

The other men took one look at her and smiled knowingly. Ignoring them, Jasmine sat down next to Tariq. He sat to her left and a little in front of her, protecting her from the curious looks. Jasmine almost smiled at his possessiveness, but didn't challenge him. Aside from the fact that she was relieved she didn't have to face everyone in her current state, she would never dishonor Tariq in front of his people. In private, she felt free to question him, but deep instinct told her it would be a betrayal to do so publicly.

It wasn't just that Tariq was sheik in a desert land, where men possessively protected their women even as they cherished them. It was him. He was a very private man, a man who met the world wearing a mask. His pride was tied to his inherently private nature.

To his people, Tariq was approachable and kind, but he maintained an aristocratic reserve that was appropriate to his role. However, in New Zealand, he'd utterly frozen out her family, his contempt for their manipulative games completely undetectable. Yet with Jasmine he'd been warm, playful, teasing and, most of all, loving.

Four years later, she understood that only she had seen the man behind the mask. He'd trusted her. Even now he was really himself with her only occasionally—times when he seemed to forget the past. The rest of the time, he wore a mask for her, that of a man who would "own" his woman. It *was* a mask, she told herself. Her Tariq was hidden behind it.

After the evening meal, there was a short discussion in the native language of Zulheil. It was a beautiful language, but one she hadn't yet mastered.

"You were discussing sleeping arrangements?" she asked Tariq, when he turned to her. His eyes were hooded by the edge of his headgear, but she could see the campfire reflected in their depths. Her body began to burn with an inner blaze that was hotter than anything the desert could create.

"Yes. We carry tents with us if you wish to use one."

Jasmine shook her head. "No, I want to see the stars."

He smiled, as if she'd made him proud. "We will sleep away from the rest of the men."

Remembering his promise, she blushed. "Won't that be a problem?"

He raised an aristocratic eyebrow. "No man would let his

woman bed down where other men may look upon her sleeping face.''

''That sounds very…''

''Primitive? Possessive? I am all those things where you are concerned, Mina.''

With the wild desert surrounding them and the night sky sparkling overhead, his words sounded exactly right. He was a warrior into whose keeping she had given her life, and she knew that he would always protect her.

''What, no arguments?'' he asked, when she remained silent.

''How can I argue with a man who has promised me a massage?''

For once, her controlled husband looked disconcerted. It only lasted a moment, but it was enough. The desire between them was mutual, a living, breathing thing. Unlike the loneliness of her love, when he took her in his arms, they were very much partners.

''I think it is time to retire.'' As he spoke, Tariq's eyes glowed with inner fire, not reflected flames.

They left the others soon afterward, carrying their own bedding. Tariq waved off offers of help, saying that if he couldn't make a bed in the desert, he wasn't worthy of being sheik. His men nodded solemnly, pleased with their leader.

He made Jasmine wait while he lay the bedding on top of a thick patch of some springy vegetation that would cushion their bodies from the hard ground. Then he held out his hand. ''There is one thing, Mina.''

''What?''

''Tonight, you cannot make a sound. We are too close to the others.'' He'd already removed his headgear. Now he took hers off and put it aside, before tangling his hands in the heavy fall of her hair. A rough sigh betrayed his pleasure. ''Not a single sound, my Jasmine.''

''Not a single one.'' Her promise was softly whispered.

She didn't make a sound when he stripped her and then himself. She managed to remain silent when he kept his promise to loosen her muscles, his powerful hands tender on her abused flesh. She even bit back her cries when his mouth enclosed her engorged nipples. Then his hand moved between her legs.

Jasmine bit his shoulder. He continued to play with the soft, moist folds between her thighs until she couldn't breathe. She sank her teeth farther into firm muscle in an effort to control her scream. Finally, after tormenting her for what seemed like hours, he lifted her hips and thrust into her in one smooth stroke. This time, she muffled her cries against his neck. He gritted his teeth against his own cry of satisfaction, his face a study in restraint.

They lay with arms and legs tangled until their skin began to chill from the cool night breeze. Tariq rolled off her and sat up to zip the attached sleeping bags closed. When he propped himself beside her, Jasmine saw what she'd done.

"Oh no." She was horrified at the deep, red marks.

"What is it, Mina?" His concern was clear.

"I bit you." She touched the evidence of her crime with her fingertips.

He grinned. "Thank you."

"I'm really sorry."

"I do not mind. There are two more nights we must spend in the desert. Perhaps you will give me another two souvenirs?"

She remained concerned. "Are you sure it doesn't hurt?"

"Why don't you kiss it and see?" he invited.

Jasmine immediately reached over and laved the spot with her tongue and then pressed a tender kiss over it.

"*Now* I hurt," he growled against her ear. The hardness pressing impatiently against her thigh explained why. "But we'll travel far tomorrow. You must have your rest. Turn around and stop tempting me."

Jasmine laughed at how disgruntled he sounded, but she fell asleep in seconds, despite the embers of desire glowing between them. When she wakened, Tariq was already dressed, which was probably just as well. The look in his eyes said that if she'd wakened a few minutes earlier, he'd certainly have delayed the entire party.

"Good morning, Mina."

"Morning." She sat up and rubbed at her eyes.

"I let you rest as long as possible, but we must be away soon if we are to make the next oasis by the time daylight fades." Tariq's deep voice was a caress in itself, full of sensuous memories.

Fighting off her blush, she replied, "I'll be quick. Give me ten minutes."

"Ten minutes." A hard kiss sealed those words.

Jasmine watched him stride away into the lush foliage, her body craving his touch. Hurried along by the cool wind, she shook off the desire that lay heavy upon her senses, and rose. The morning air was crisp, almost chilly, with no hint of the fire and heat that would descend as the sun rose higher. As she completed her toilette, Jasmine was struck by the way her husband reflected the hidden glory of his land.

Tariq could be ice, and he could be fire. Since arriving in Zulheil, she'd experienced both. Four years ago, she'd never seen the ice. Had she known only half the man? Four years ago…four years lost. Suddenly, she was starving for knowledge of Tariq's life in those lost years. The longing was a physical ache inside of her. Tariq had rebuffed her attempts to discuss the past, but she knew that until they did, they'd never truly be at peace.

"Mina! Are you ready?" Tariq's call cut through her unwelcome thoughts. The warmth in it was an arrow to her heart. Despite her hunger to know, she couldn't bear to disrupt their new harmony by bringing up the past.

She parted the branches protecting her from his view. "Are we leaving?" Other than a few bent shoots of grass, nothing revealed that they had camped in this desert haven.

"I would not starve you. Not when I am the cause of the hunger you must be feeling." The rumble of his voice washed over her. She smoothed her pants, inexplicably shy.

Straightening from his leaning position against the trunk of

a tree heavy with dark green, glossy foliage, Tariq skated his
eyes over her modestly garbed form with a possessiveness she
couldn't mistake. Her breath hitched. When he looked up, she
thought she might just beg him to take her.

He crooked a finger.

Some feminine instinct protested that arrogant action, even
as the needy part of her wanted to run over and say yes, please.
Instead, she stuck one hand on her hip and copied the gesture,
with a boldness that, around her husband, felt right.

Tariq's smile was a slash of white in the duskiness of his
face. To her surprise, he obeyed her command and walked
over to stand in front of her, so close that her breasts brushed
his chest with every breath she took.

"What would you do with me, my wife?"

Now that she had him where she'd wanted him, she couldn't
think of what to say.

Mina's sudden shyness surprised Tariq. He traced a finger
down the cool smoothness of her cheek. She ducked her head,
but brought her hand up to cover his. He smiled and bent his
knees to bring himself to her level. He surprised her with his
sudden descent, and that was the only reason he saw the shadows in her eyes.

He rose to his full height, thunder pouring through his veins.
She was hiding something. "What is worrying you?"

She jerked her head up. Hair the color of shattered rubies
tumbled over his hands. Blue eyes displayed her distress at
being found out. "What do you mean? I'm fine."

Her small lie only made him more determined. What was
she thinking that she had to hide it from him? Where she was
concerned, he'd learned to trust his instincts. Mina called to
the part of him that was wild, primitive, untamed, a part that
could be dangerous if he didn't keep it leashed. Complete
possession of Mina was the payment demanded by the wildness for four years of imprisonment.

"I am your husband. You will not lie. Answer me." He
thrust his hands through the fiery silk. The last time she'd
hidden her thoughts from him, she'd been convincing herself

to walk away. It had almost destroyed him. He didn't think he would survive if she ran from him a second time.

"We'll be late," she protested.

Time was no longer important. "They will wait." His voice was made rough by his knowledge of his vulnerability to her.

"This isn't the place." She put her hands on his chest, as if to push him away.

"You *will* answer me."

The small hands on his chest curled into fists. "You are so arrogant, sometimes I want to scream!"

The explosion almost made him want to smile. Mina's temper delighted him. Only the knowledge that she was hiding something from him curbed the urge. His mother had hidden her illness and it had cost him his chance to say goodbye...and maybe more. Mina's secret could cost him his wife. "I am simply willing to go after what I want."

"So am I." Her voice was fierce. "I came to you."

"And you will stay." He would not give her a choice. "Is this primitive land starting to lose its charms?"

She rolled her eyes, impertinent in her anger. "No, but you're driving me crazy with your questions."

"Answer me and I will ask no more." His logical response made her grit her teeth. Those magnificent eyes flashed lightning at him.

"I'll tell you later."

"*Now.*" He kept her in place with his hands in her hair, clenching thick handfuls of the luminous strands.

She looked away from him. Her body was poised for flight but there was nowhere for her to go. In its blinding starkness, his land was his greatest ally. As he watched, the realization of her weakness dawned on her.

"You're taking advantage of your strength." Her hunted expression accused him.

"I will use every advantage I have." He would not, could not, lose her. She was as vital to him as breathing.

For a second, their eyes met. Silence hung between them, his implacable words almost visible in the air.

"What does it matter what I was thinking?" He knew she was clutching at anything that might offer a reprieve. The hint of victory sharpened his hunter's instincts.

"You belong to me, Mina." This time she'd have no secrets from him. Perhaps, he acknowledged, her youth had made her vulnerable to the pressures she'd been put under four years ago. But if he'd known of those pressures, he would have been ready to fight for her and might not have had his heart ripped to pieces.

Her sigh signaled defeat. "I was thinking of the past."

Some of the chill that had retreated under the fire of their heated conversation returned with a vengeance. "Why do you think of such things?" The past held only pain and betrayal.

"I can't help it. Not when it stands between us." Her expression was earnest, her words passionate.

As Jasmine had feared, the mention of the past blighted the incipient joy of the day. Tariq's smile was only a memory now, this hard-visaged desert warrior the reality. He didn't deny her statement and the silence grew until it pressed heavily upon her. Wary of the stranger he'd become, she lay her hand on his left bicep. The muscle was inflexible.

"Four years, Tariq." Her emotions were naked in her voice. "Four years we were apart, and you refuse to share even a crumb of your life during that time."

His expression grew even darker. "What would you know?"

The question stunned her. She'd been expecting a harsh reprimand or perhaps cold dismissal. For a moment, shock kept her silent, but then words tumbled out of her. "Anything! Everything! Not knowing about those years is like a hole inside me, a part where you're missing."

"You made that choice."

"But now I've made another choice!"

The infinitesimal turning away of his face was his only response.

"Please," she begged.

He released her. Startled, she swayed before regaining her

balance. Stepping back, he regarded her with eyes darkened to the color of ancient greenstone. "I was the subject of an assassination attempt by a terrorist organization on my way back from New Zealand."

"No! Did they…?"

He shook his head in a sharp negative as an answer to the question she couldn't bring herself to ask. "They had no chance." When he returned to his position by the tree, her sense of isolation almost overwhelmed Jasmine.

"Are they still active?"

"No, they were supported by their government, which was overthrown two years ago. The new government is friendly and will sponsor no more such attempts."

She thought that he was trying to soothe her obvious pain. That gave her the courage to continue, even though the ice in his voice was an obvious command to withdraw. She almost expected to see the air fog with her breath.

"But even one!"

That was when he delivered a blow so staggering that he might as well have backhanded her. "They thought me weak and an easy target, because a woman had brought me to my knees."

Jasmine wanted to scream in agony. To have almost lost him…and to finally comprehend that her mission would be a thousand times more difficult than she'd believed. Maybe even impossible. The night before, she'd begun to understand the depths to which her husband's honor and pride were intertwined with his private nature. Today, it was painfully clear that Tariq's pride had been savaged by the reason behind the attempt. His strength as a leader, as a warrior, had been questioned because he'd allowed himself to feel. He would not forgive the woman who had been the cause of the insult.

A call from one of the guides interrupted the heavy silence. Tariq replied without shifting his gaze from her, his eyes dark, impenetrable. The syllables sounded brusque and guttural, as if he, too, were keeping strong emotions in check.

"We must go."

She nodded, numb from shock. Unable to trust herself not to break down, she followed him to the main area. He put food in her hands, and when she didn't move to feed herself, he leaned down and whispered in her ear. "Eat, Mina, or I will put you in my lap and feed you."

She believed him. As quickly as possible, she forced the food down. She had her pride, too.

Tariq carefully picked up Jasmine and placed her on the camel, once she'd bolted down the meal. He could see her fighting the urge to bring up the food, but he was ruthless in his protectiveness. She would need her strength to survive the desert journey. He would not let her mistreat herself.

When he mounted behind her, he made sure not to jostle her. She'd been silent since his revelation about the assassination attempt. He didn't like her stillness. His Mina was fire, life, joy. Yet he knew his harshness had caused her withdrawal. He had spoken to his wife in anger, and now that it had passed, he did not know how to bring her back to him.

"Hold on," he said, as the camel stood up, even though there was no need. His arm was a band around her waist. He would never let her fall, never let her be hurt.

She clutched at his arm, but let go the minute the camel was up. Her white headgear gave her a hiding place and frustrated him. He needed her to talk to him. The discovery made him scowl. A sheik didn't need anyone. A man would be a fool to need a woman who'd proved incapable of loyalty. He'd merely become used to her presence and voice over the past day. It was nothing more than that.

"Will you sulk all day?" He knew he was being unfair, but was unable to stop himself. He wanted her to fight back, wanted her to feel as much as he did, even if it was only anger.

"I'm not sulking." Her response held a hint of her customary fire.

Something he didn't want to acknowledge inside him eased

at her response. She hadn't been beaten or broken. "It's better that you know the truth."

"That you'll never again allow me close to your heart?"

Her blunt question threatened to unsettle him. "Yes. I will not be such an easy target a second time."

"Target?" It was a husky whisper. "This isn't war."

His mouth twisted. "It's worse." After her rejection, he'd barely been able to function. He had loved her more than he loved the endless deserts of his homeland, but it had been the desert wilderness that had helped him heal the wounds she'd inflicted.

"I don't want to fight with you."

Her words calmed him and made him gentle in his response. "You belong to me now, my Jasmine. There's no reason for us to fight. This is forever." He would not trust her with his heart again, but neither would he let her go.

Forever. Jasmine lay her head against Tariq's chest and swallowed her tears. At one time she would've crawled on her hands and knees across broken glass for the promise of forever with Tariq. Now that wasn't enough. Forever with a Tariq who didn't love her and would never love her wasn't enough.

The obstacles in her path had grown to almost insurmountable proportions. Convincing Tariq of her loyalty would not be enough. He might eventually forgive her for not fighting for their love against her family, but she doubted it would be easy. But would he ever forgive the second staggering blow to his warrior's pride?

And what if she caused a third, with the secret that had broken a child's heart?

Panic threatened to choke her. No! No one would know about her illegitimacy! No one would shame her husband. Only her family knew, and they valued their position in society too much to let the truth slip out.

You think your prince would marry a girl who can't even name her father? Keep dreaming, little sister.

Four years ago, Sarah had picked at her most vulnerable spot and then kicked hard. Jasmine still hadn't recovered from

the blow, because she knew her sister was right. How could
Tariq accept her, much less love her, if even her adoptive
parents hadn't been able to?

He wouldn't believe that she'd been so overwhelmed by the
marriage ceremony, she'd forgotten the one vital fact that
made her the wrong choice to be his wife. As a girl of eighteen, she'd planned to tell him...until Sarah had bluntly
thrown the consequences in her face. Believing her sister, Jasmine had kept her hurtful secret, and her family had used it
to batter her down when they'd asked her to choose.

"You will speak to me." The rough order jerked her out
of her maudlin thoughts. He liked her speaking to him, did
he? Yesterday, he'd teased her that she chattered like a mag-
pie.

Allowing a smile to escape, she let hope fill her heart about
her ability to inspire love in this complex man. So the fight
would be harder. So what? She'd almost died living apart from
him. As long as there was the slightest hope, as long as her
panther liked to talk to her, as long as he touched her body
like he was starving for her, she'd persevere.

Maybe one day he'd trust her enough, love her enough, to
accept all of her. Until then, she'd keep the secret she desperately needed to share, the anguish she needed to fight with
his love, deep within her. And she'd make up for that one lie
by fighting for other truths, however much it hurt.

"Tell me." Her tone was quiet but determined.

"What?"

"Tell me exactly what they tried to do."

"Mina." Tariq's annoyance was clear. "I have said that the
past is the past. If you do not wish to fight, we will not speak
of this." His hard body moved behind her as he made an
adjustment to the reins held negligently in his left hand.

"And I'm supposed to obey your decree without question?"
She was unable to let such an arrogant presumption pass.

He was silent for a long moment. "No one challenges the
sheik when he has spoken."

"You're my husband."

"Yet you don't act as a submissive wife should."

His tone was so neutral that she almost missed the wry undertone. He was teasing her, no longer cold, as he'd been after the revelation in the oasis. Jasmine decided to continue her quest for the truth, despite his implied forgiveness for the pain she'd reawakened that morning. If she let it go now, Tariq would always refuse to discuss the past. An incredibly strong man, he needed a woman who would challenge him when required, not buckle under to his demands.

"If you wanted submission, you should've gotten a pet." She didn't add that a submissive wife would bore him out of his aristocratic skull within a week.

His arms tightened around her. "No, Mina, I need no pet. Not when I have you to pet."

The wordplay made her blush. "You speak English just fine when you put your mind to it," she noted. "But I'm not going to be distracted."

"No?" Under her breast, his arm suddenly came to life. Muscle flowed and shifted, caressing her without any visible movement.

"No." Her voice was firm, though desire crackled through her like white lightning.

He slid his hand down to press against her stomach. Then, without warning, he said, "We stopped in Bahrain on our return, for diplomatic reasons. On the way from the airport, my car was separated from the cavalcade by two large trucks."

"Hiraz?"

"I was not good company at that time." Tariq's quiet response drove another nail into the bruised flesh of her heart. "Hiraz was riding in the foremost car with two guards. Another two were in the following car."

"You were alone." Instinctively, her hands left the pommel and pressed over his.

"I am never alone, Mina." His words were as close to a complaint as she'd ever heard. Even a sheik, she understood, needed privacy. A man like Tariq would need it more than most. "My driver is always a trained guard."

"What happened next?" She was caught in the destructive grip of a past that could have physically stolen Tariq from her. As it was, the emotional damage caused by the attack was profound.

He leaned down and moved her headgear aside so he could whisper into her ear. The intimate gesture made her glad that they were riding at the back of the group.

"We took care of them." His masculine scent surrounded her, his warmth an experience she didn't want to escape.

"That's all you're going to say?" she protested, disturbed by the way he seemed to be withdrawing once again.

"There isn't much else. They were religious zealots from a troubled nation who sought to kill me with their bare hands. I disabled three, my driver two." He nuzzled her neck, a gesture so achingly familiar that tears threatened. The tone of his voice belonged to an exasperated man tired of a topic, rather than one bent on rebuilding an impenetrable wall.

"And the other guards took care of the rest after breaching the barrier of trucks?" she guessed.

Tariq drew back from her and pulled the covering close around her face. "You are too fair," he grumbled.

"Maybe I'll tan." There was always hope.

His response was a disbelieving snort. "Enough of this. We will talk of other things."

She might've argued with him, but he'd already relented a great deal after his initial refusal to speak about his life. Pushing her luck could backfire. "All right."

"I don't believe you." He sounded so male, so put upon.

"Drat." She fell back into the relationship as it had been before she'd learned the awful truth about how Tariq had been targeted for assassination because of his perceived weakness in loving her. She needed to feel his happiness, to find hope in his laughter.

"How are you feeling?" he asked.

She thought he was referring to their fight. "This is a beautiful day. It's a day to be happy."

His chuckle startled her. "I was asking how your sweet bottom was feeling."

She blushed and elbowed him. "Behave." The last traces of frost were long gone. Fire surrounded her. She swallowed tears of bittersweet happiness. There would be no more pain this gorgeous day. She'd pretend that the world was perfect and that the man holding her so carefully, loved her, too.

However, that night, Jasmine couldn't keep pretending that everything was okay. Not when her heart was threatening to break under the strain. "Would it be okay if I retired early?" she asked Tariq. The firelight, which had seemed so romantic the night before, now made her eyes feel dry and achy.

From his protective position slightly in front of her, Tariq glanced over his shoulder. "You do not wish to remain?" His voice had a dark edge that she couldn't decipher.

"I'm tired. This is new for me," she confessed, hiding one truth behind another.

Her husband moved until he was sitting next to her. Then, to her surprise, he pulled her against his seated form. Tariq rarely touched her in public. She hadn't yet found the courage to ask him whether it was because he didn't want to, or because of the circumspection demanded of his position.

"I apologize, Mina. You don't complain, so I forget that this journey must be hard for you." Deep, sensuous, caressing, his words washed over her like soft, welcoming rain.

She nestled her head against his shoulder, finding that some of her inner ache had disappeared. He held her as if she mattered. "Am I expected to stay because I'm your wife?"

His muscled arm firmed around her as he shifted her a tiny bit nearer, eliminating any hint of space between their bodies. "Your intelligence is one of the reasons you are my wife," he murmured. "My people judge those not of our land. It's a flaw in us and yet it's so much a part of Zulheil that it may be our saving grace. We do not trust easily." Jasmine had known that the first moment she'd met him.

"Even though they've accepted you because you are my

chosen wife,'' he continued, gazing down at her upturned face, ''and you'll receive obedience, the amount of respect you receive will be determined by a thousand things, among them your ability to endure this harsh land.''

She understood what he would never articulate. His honor was now bound inextricably to hers. It was a fragile link that could shatter as it had once before, and rip even this shaky relationship from her grasp. ''I'll stay. Just hold me?'' She winced at the neediness of her voice.

He answered by touching her cheek with his free hand, his dark eyes fierce with what she wanted to believe was pride. Another knot melted inside her. When he looked away, she watched the play of the firelight on his face. He was at once beautiful and dangerous. A panther momentarily at rest. A warrior at home among his people.

Jasmine smiled. Her earlier frustration and pain had faded to a dull ache. Strangely content now, she stared up at the jewel-studded night sky, wondering if within those pinpricks there was a candle to light her way into her husband's heart.

Six

By the time Tariq returned from a last-minute consultation with one of the guides, Mina was curled up and half-asleep. No light from the campfire reached their bed and neither did the voices of the men. He stripped down to the loose pants designed by his ancestors to offer respite from the unrelenting heat of the desert, glad for the small lagoon that had allowed the entire party a chance to bathe.

Memories of watching over his wife while she swam sent familiar need racing through him, but it was clear that Mina was exhausted. Tenderness overwhelmed him. She looked so small and fragile, and yet she made him feel so much. Too much. Heart clenching with emotions he didn't want to accept, he lay down beside her, wrapped her in his arms and let her rest. For a while.

Unfortunately, he didn't get to wake her with slow, sensuous caresses as he'd wanted, because deep in the night she jerked upright beside him, and he could almost smell her fear. He reached up to pull her back into his arms.

"Tariq!" She turned blindly toward him.

"I'm here, Mina." He succeeded in trapping her fluttering hands and held her tight against his body, disturbed by the too-fast thudding of her heart.

"Tariq." This time her voice was a husky whisper, but no less desperate than her first fearful cry. She clutched at his shoulders with small hands.

"Hush. You are safe, my Jasmine." He stroked the curved line of her spine, trying to calm her. When she continued to shiver, he flipped her over onto her back and pressed his body along the length of hers. Some of her tension seemed to seep out of her at the full-body contact. "Mina?"

"They hurt you."

"Who?"

"The men in the trucks. I thought they took you from me."

He hadn't thought that his revelation would have this effect. "I am safe. They did not succeed. You did not lose me." When she looked as if she disagreed, he held her tightly. "You will not worry about these things."

Wrapped in Tariq's strong arms, Jasmine felt her fears start to dissipate. "I'll try. It was probably because I was tired."

"We will not talk of it anymore."

"Wait—" she protested.

He squeezed the breath out of her. "I have decided. You may sulk if you wish, but we will not talk more of it."

"You can't just decide that on your own," she snapped.

"Yes. I can." His voice was neutral, but she heard the steely determination. When he closed his eyes, she knew that any further words would only strengthen his resolve. Sighing, she conceded defeat…for tonight.

Wide-awake, she thought back over her nightmare. Unlike the dream, the real assassins hadn't succeeded in killing him, but they'd broken the connection between her and Tariq, torn the emotional threads. Their taunts had destroyed whatever had been left after she'd walked away.

A man's pride was a fragile thing.

A warrior's pride was his greatest weapon.

A sheik's pride upheld the honor of his people.

She had to learn to deal with the power of all three.

"We're going to finish what we started last night."

"No. I will not have you disturbed." Though Tariq wasn't surprised by Mina's stubbornness, his first duty was to protect her. The memory of how she'd trembled in fear made him hug her against his body as the camel picked its way across the golden sand.

"I'm a big girl. I can handle it."

"No." He would *not* allow her to be hurt.

"Tariq! Don't do that. Don't protect me by keeping me in ignorance." In his arms, her small body was stiff with anger and frustration. "I'm not eighteen anymore."

Her perception about his motives startled him, proving the truth of her words. "Perhaps not," he allowed.

"Then the assassins—"

"You know all there is to know, Mina." This time he acknowledged the quiet pain of the memories. "You *know*."

After a small silence, she leaned back in his embrace. "I'm sorry."

Unable to bear her sorrow, he held her close and told her stories of the desert and his people, and after a long time, she smiled again. And as they rode, he considered her persistence. Four years ago, she would never have challenged him. Since she'd returned to him, she'd never stopped fighting him. Some men would have been dismayed by the change. Tariq was intrigued.

On the morning of the fourth day, they rode into the small industrial city of Zeina. Despite their functional nature, the steel and concrete buildings of the city had been designed with curved edges and flowing lines. Overlaid with the omnipresent sand, the low-rise structures almost blended into the desert. The two-lane highway snaking out of Zeina in the opposite direction from their route showed how oil was moved out of such an isolated spot. To Jasmine's surprise, they continued through the city and a good distance beyond, to where a number of huge, colorful tents sprawled across the desert sand.

"Welcome to Zeina," Tariq whispered against her ear.

"I thought that was Zeina back there." She jerked her head to indicate the city they'd passed.

"It's part of Zeina. This is the heart."

"No houses, just tents," she mused out loud.

"Arin and his people prefer it this way. As they are happy, I have no right to question."

She pondered that for a moment before asking, "I assume many of them work in the industrial section—how do they get there?"

Tariq chuckled. "There are camels for those who prefer the old ways but also several well-hidden all-terrain vehicles."

"Why didn't we travel in those?" She scowled at the thought of the abuse her rear had suffered.

"Some of the areas we passed through are too treacherous to trust even those vehicles. They also cause much damage to the delicate ecosystems of the desert. But, for commuting the distance to the metal city, they are useful," he explained. "Arin's people may be old-fashioned but they are also eminently practical. See the pale blue tents?" He pointed.

"There's quite a few."

"They appear the same as the others, but look closely."

Squinting, she did. "They don't move with the wind! What are they, plastic?"

"A durable type created by our engineers," Tariq confirmed. "Each houses sanitation facilities for use by four closely related families."

Given the dimensions of the tents and the typically small size of Zulheil's families, the allocation appeared generous.

"How ingenious." Jasmine was impressed by the way old and new had been merged so creatively.

"Arin is certainly that."

She met the intriguing Arin minutes later. He was a huge

bear of a man with a short, neatly trimmed beard, but his warm smile took the edge off his menacing appearance.

"Welcome." He waved them both inside his large tent after exchanging greetings. "Please, sit."

"Thank you." Jasmine smiled and sat down on one of the luxuriant cushions arranged around a small table.

"I forbid you to smile at this man, Jasmine."

Jasmine stared at her husband in shock. "Did you just forbid me to smile at the man in whose home we are guests?"

Her subtle reprimand made her husband's lips curve in an inexplicable smile and Arin howl with laughter. She looked from one to the other, belatedly aware that she'd missed something. When Tariq continued to smile with that hint of mischief in his eyes and Arin to howl, she threw up her hands. "You're both mad."

"No, no," Arin answered, his shoulders shaking with mirth. "This one is just afraid of my power over women."

Intrigued, Jasmine turned to Tariq for an explanation, but he just grinned. Shaking her head, she busied herself trying to follow their conversation, which could not be undertaken in English, as their host wasn't fluent enough for the subtleties required.

"My apologies." Arin seemed discomfited by that fact.

"Oh, please don't say that," she said earnestly. "This is your land. I should be the one to learn your language. While I'm learning, it would be better for me to be surrounded by it."

The big man looked relieved. Tariq squeezed her fingers once in silent thanks. Warm, strong, male, his hand represented so much of who he was.

If she concentrated, she could follow the bare bones of their talk. They appeared to be catching up with each other's news but there was an undercurrent of seriousness. The sheik was asking after the health of his people.

As she listened, the changes in Tariq struck her again. When they'd first met, he'd been every inch a royal, but more relaxed, having the support of his parents, a much-loved royal couple. Now the mantle of authority sat on his shoulders alone, and he wore it as if it had been made for him.

He'd always been touched with the promise of greatness. Before her eyes, that promise was being fulfilled.

"Enough," Arin announced at last in English. "I am a poor host to keep you so long even before the dust is gone from your clothes." He uncurled his legs, incredibly graceful for such a big man, and began to stand.

"Terrible," Tariq agreed, but his eyes were full of laughter as he followed their host's example. Jasmine's guess that the two were good friends was confirmed by the back-slapping embrace they exchanged, before Arin led them toward the much smaller tent that had been prepared for them. Members of Arin's council had greeted Tariq's advisors upon arrival, and it was likely that they'd all settled in by now.

"Your tent should be larger. I would give you mine but your husband, he is not wanting to be treated like royalty." Arin scowled at Tariq over Jasmine's head. The two men had bracketed her between them as soon as they'd exited. She felt like a shrimp between two very large carnivorous beasts, but one of the beasts was hers and the other appeared friendly.

"If I am in that cavern you call a tent, people will not come to me as willingly as they do if I am in something approximating their own homes." Without breaking his stride, Tariq reached over and tugged Jasmine's headgear around her face, protecting her from the sun. "With you it is different. They have known you their whole lives."

With a sigh, Arin abandoned trying to get Tariq to change his mind. "This—" he waved to a small dun-colored tent "—is to be your home for the next three or four days."

Despite the dull exterior, the interior was beautifully appointed. Colors created bright splendor through the room, in cushions scattered about and gauzy silk hangings decorating the walls. Delighted, Jasmine peeked around the partition dividing the space and discovered a sumptuous sleeping area.

"Thank you. It's beautiful," she exclaimed, bestowing a dazzling smile upon Arin. He looked taken aback.

Tariq scowled. "You will go now," he ordered. "I wish to talk to my wife about the smiles she gives away so easily."

Arin laughed good-naturedly and left, but not before he threw Jasmine a wink. She ran to her husband and tugged his head down for a kiss. He picked her up off her feet to facilitate the soft, urgent caress.

"That is permissible, Mina." He set her down on her feet. "You are welcome to kiss me at any time."

"Gee, thanks." She stepped back to escape him but he was too quick. Tariq held her against him, his hands splayed over her bottom. When she wiggled, he took mercy on her and slid his hands to her waist. "Why did you forbid me to smile at your friend?"

"Because women like him too much. It is very provoking." His complaint was without heat.

"I think he's nice." Her husband's playful mood was a rare treat, one she fully intended to enjoy.

He lifted her up until they were eye to eye. "Really?"

"Mmm." She wrapped her arms and legs around him. "But I think you're the nicest of all."

Tariq's grin was pure male. Her reward for her honesty was a kiss that was so hot, she felt singed.

They ate dinner with Arin and other members of the camp in Arin's huge tent. Jasmine liked being able to watch her sheik among his people. He was magnificent. Charisma flowed from him like a physical substance, bright and clear and utterly seductive. People listened when he spoke, and answered his questions without hesitation, basking in his attention.

"Your accommodations are suitable?" Arin asked.

She had to force herself to look away from her husband, aware that the moment she did so, Tariq glanced at her. His obvious awareness of her, even in the midst of a busy dinner, warmed her to her toes.

"They're lovely. Thank you." She smiled. "I've been forbidden to smile at you because women like you too much."

Arin stroked his neat beard. "It is a curse I must bear. It makes finding a wife difficult."

Jasmine thought she'd misunderstood. "Difficult?"

"Yes." He looked mournful. "How can a man pick one lovely fruit when every day he is confronted with an orchard?"

She clapped a hand over her mouth to muffle her laugh at his outrageousness. No wonder he and Tariq were friends. Right then, her husband tugged at her hand. Though he was talking to someone else, it was an unmistakable sign that he wanted her attention on him. She knew that he wasn't really worried about Arin's affect on women, so his possessiveness puzzled her.

"He is like a child, unwilling to share you," Arin whispered, leaning over. "He is correct in this."

She ignored the last part of that statement and concentrated on the first. It was true. Tariq was unwilling to share her— sometimes. He liked having her interact with his people and make friends such as Mumtaz, so he was no controlling oppressor. However, he seemed to want to keep her close.

What she didn't know was whether he wanted her near because he needed her, or because he didn't trust her out of his sight. She swallowed her hurt at the possibility that it was the latter, and smiled brightly at the woman sitting across from him. Taking that as a sign of encouragement, the woman drew Jasmine into conversation.

"Today, I intend to view several Zulheil Rose mines." Tariq finished his breakfast the next morning and stretched. The power and beauty of his impressive musculature made Jasmine catch her breath. "It will require hard riding, so unfortunately you cannot accompany me."

She scowled in disappointment. "Maybe next time. After we get back home, you have to teach me to ride those beasts."

He smiled at her mock shudder. "I'll do that, Mina. While you are here, you may wish to…I do not know the word, but it would be good if you would walk among the people."

"Oh, you want me to mingle?"

"Yes. Especially with the women. Out here in the desert, a lot of them tend to be shyer than their city counterparts."

"So you want me to talk to them and make sure they're doing okay?"

He nodded. "You are a woman and you are friendly, especially as you continue to smile at everyone." His tone was disgruntled but his expression approving. "Most of the Zeina citizens will try to come to meet us. It is the way we strengthen the bonds that tie our land together. The men tend to wait for me, but the women will feel easier with you."

Jasmine bit her lip in sudden indecision. She felt more than saw Tariq's relaxed body tense.

"You do not wish to do this?"

"Oh, I do. It's just that…do you think I can? I'm just an ordinary woman. Will your people talk to me?" All her life, she'd never been good enough. Sometimes the past threatened to overcome her hard-won self-esteem.

"Ah, Mina." Tariq tugged her into his lap and held her close. "You are my wife and they have already accepted you."

"How do you know?"

"I know. You will trust your husband and do as he bids."

His autocratic command made her want to grin. If he trusted her with this, then he had to have some faith in her. Perhaps it was even the beginning of a deeper kind of trust. The flame of hope inside her, which had been threatening to go out ever since he'd revealed the assassination attempt, started to flicker with fiery life.

"Aye, aye, Captain." She adopted a meek expression that made him laugh and kiss her.

He rode out ten minutes later into the crisp desert morning. After waving him off, Jasmine took a deep breath and began to walk toward the heart of the camp. Within moments, she was surrounded by Zeina's women, surrounded and welcomed.

It was only as dusk began to descend in purple strokes

across the desert that she returned to their quarters. After washing the grit and dust of the day from her body, she dressed in an ankle-length skirt and fitted top in a beautiful shade of gold and lay down on one of the low couches to wait for her husband. Lulled by the soft chatter outside, she closed her eyes, intending only a moment's rest.

Once again, Tariq found Mina asleep. This time he needed to wake her, to satisfy not carnal hunger, but something far more dangerous. "Wake up, my Jasmine." His voice was rough.

"Tariq." With a wide smile she opened her eyes and her arms and tempted him into her embrace. "When did you return?"

"Perhaps forty minutes ago. Now you must awaken so we can eat." Nevertheless, he leaned toward her and let her put her arms around him. Spending the entire day apart from her for the first time since their marriage had brought old pain to the surface—raw, jagged pain that mocked him for pretending he didn't need her. The truth was that he needed her far more than she would ever need him.

"With Arin?"

"No." He smoothed the tangled strands of her hair off her face. "Just me. Tomorrow we'll dine with our people again."

Not wishing to face the emotions she aroused, he started to leave. She held him tight. "Don't go. I missed you."

"Did you, Mina?" He couldn't keep the edge out of his voice. He needed her, but would never again chance entrusting her with that knowledge.

"Yes. I kept looking for you all day." Her eyes were soft, her body warm from sleep.

"Show me how much you missed me, Mina. Show me." He clasped her to him possessively, the wounded beast inside him unsatisfied with less than complete surrender.

He stripped her so quickly that she gasped, but made no protest. He laid her down on the thick rug on the floor, inflamed by the sight of her creamy skin and fiery hair against the scarlet-and-gold material. She was like some pagan fantasy, a dream designed to drive men wild.

Wrapping his hand around her neck, he kissed her, claimed her. He tasted every corner of her mouth while his free hand roamed her body, then covered the soft mound of one breast, making her whimper. Finally breaking the kiss, he bent down to take a tightly beaded nipple into his mouth. He sucked. Hard.

She bucked under him and her hands clenched in his hair. "Please...please..."

The broken sounds urged him on. Nudging apart her legs with his knee, he settled in between them, opening her to him. One hand flat on the rug beside her, he raised his head and looked down at her as he moved his other hand to her stomach and inexorably lower. Sky-blue eyes bled into indigo and lush lips parted in a fractured breath as he found the small nub hidden in her curls.

Though he was careful not to hurt her, this woman of cream and fire, his strokes were firm. Mina clutched at his arms and he could feel pleasure exploding inside her. He stroked harder, leaving her only for the instant it took to lift her right leg and place it over his hip, giving him full access to her secret places.

Her moan when he touched her again wasn't enough. He needed more. He needed Mina's utter and total submission. He needed her to hold nothing back from him. Needed her to need him like he needed her. Needed her to love him so much she would never leave him again.

Reaching lower, he slipped a finger inside her. Her body jerked. Her skin dampened. Then he lowered his head and lightly, carefully, bit the underside of one plump breast. Around his finger, her muscles clenched in an intimate fist so tight he was drenched, surrounded. It was at that moment, as she shoved a fist in her mouth to muffle her cries, that he removed his hand, released himself from his pants and surged into her. Unable to control the spasms overtaking her, she held on to him, biting his shoulder to silence her gasps and moans.

He welcomed the sweet pain. Mina had fallen over the edge

and he could feel it beckoning, but he wouldn't surrender. Not yet. Gripping her hips, he thrust hard. Fast. Deep.

Branding her.

"You're mine, Mina. Only mine." The words were wrenched out of the part of him that raged to claim her for all time.

Only when she lost the battle to muffle her pleasure and her cry rode the night air did he allow himself to fall into the beckoning void.

It was at the final dinner with Arin that Jasmine learned about the relationship between the two men. While Tariq was deep in conversation, Arin answered her questions.

"Tariq spent time in each of the twelve tribes after he turned twelve. This was to teach him about his people."

Jasmine thought that the experience must have been unutterably lonely. He would have been one of them but also, as their future leader, set apart. Her heart ached for the boy he'd been, but she could see the results of his training. Tariq mixed as effortlessly with these desert dwellers as he did with his people in the city.

"He came to Zeina at fifteen and we became friends."

Arin's words were simple, but she understood the depth of that friendship. Her husband didn't bestow his trust lightly. And once that trust had been breached...

"And you've remained friends." She swallowed her sudden apprehension and turned a bright smile on Arin.

The big man nodded. "He is my friend, but he is also my sheik. Make him just your husband, Jasmine, not your sheik."

His advice echoed her thoughts of not so very long ago. She knew that Tariq needed freedom to lay aside the heavy burden of leadership, even if only for a few hours each day. It was easy to say but hard to put into practice, especially where her stubborn husband was concerned. Without warning, he could change, seeing in her the shadows of the past.

A memory of the bittersweet glory of their lovemaking yesterday flickered through her mind. The complex man she'd married, a man even more fascinating than the prince who'd been her first love, would give neither his trust nor his love into her keeping, unless she proved herself worthy. But she refused to quit trying to breach the walls around his heart. She could be just as stubborn as him.

That night, Jasmine sat cross-legged on their silken bedding and watched Tariq undress in the warm glow of the lanterns. He turned and motioned her over with a tilt of his aristocratic head. She rose and walked toward him. Without words being exchanged, she knew what he wanted. She began to help him remove his clothing. His back was golden heat under her light touch, his body beautiful to her.

"You'd make a perfect harem slave," he commented, tongue in cheek.

She bit him on his back for that remark. "I don't think this primitive desert atmosphere is good for you."

He chuckled at her response. She drew back when he was dressed only in loose white pants. To her shock, he held her gaze and pulled them off in one smooth motion. She couldn't move as he threw the last piece of his clothing aside and stalked to her. It wasn't as if she'd never seen him naked, simply that he had never acted with such sexual aggressiveness. Even his furious loving last night hadn't been this… blatant.

He was a sleek, muscled warrior, rippling with strength kept in check for his woman. She knew that Tariq would never physically hurt her, which only made his maleness more compelling. Lips parted with sensual longing, she raised her head to meet his green eyes, shadowed in the dim light from the lanterns.

"You're overdressed for a harem slave," he murmured, and tugged her nightshirt over her head, leaving her naked.

"What about women?" she managed to ask, though her throat felt dry with need and her thoughts were scattered like tangled skeins of thread.

"Hmm?" He nuzzled her neck. It was, she was beginning

to realize, one of his favorite preludes to lovemaking, as well as a gesture of affection.

"Did they have harems?"

He raised his head to meet her laughing eyes. "You wish for a harem, Mina?"

She frowned as if considering it. He squeezed her tightly. "Okay! Okay! I think I can handle only one of you at a time," she stated.

"You will only ever handle me," he said with a masculine growl.

Jasmine smiled and, without stopping to consider her words, said, "Of course. You're the only one I love."

Tariq turned to stone. She wanted to take back her hasty declaration. He wasn't ready; she knew he wasn't ready. But the words had welled up in her heart and escaped before she could control them.

"You do not need to say such things." Under her hands, liquid silk turned to steel and his warm flesh was suddenly searingly cold.

"I mean it. I love you." There was no going back. Throwing away her pride, she gazed at him, silently begging him to believe her.

Tariq's eyes were midnight dark in the lantern light. "You cannot love me."

"How can I make you believe I do?" She ached for the loss of their joy, their laughter, their blindingly beautiful love.

Too late. She was four years too late.

He shook his head, answering her with silence. In the past, his control over his emotions had fooled her into thinking that his feelings didn't run as deep as hers. Only now, when it was too late, did she understand that she'd hurt him more than she could have believed possible. He'd given her his warrior's heart and she'd thrown it away in her ignorance of its value.

How could he possibly believe the truth after such a betrayal? And yet the truth existed. Her love for him was deeper, richer, more intense now. The child-woman who'd first loved him had matured into a woman who loved him so much she sometimes thought she'd die from the sheer intensity.

When he kissed her, she gave herself up to his embrace, swallowing her tears. Tariq played her like a well-tuned musical instrument, drawing every note of pleasure out of her. But he didn't give her his heart. Her warrior didn't trust her not to hurt him again.

Long after he'd fallen asleep, Jasmine lay awake, thinking of the past and how it had indelibly marked her future. Her husband's distrust was like a razor in her chest, making each breath incredibly painful. Even worse was the knowledge that he believed love weakened him.

"...You'll never again allow me close to your heart?"

"Yes. I will not be such an easy target a second time."

The memory of his implacable expression and his determination to never again fall prey to love haunted her. How could she fight her warrior's pride and his distrust in her loyalty at the same time?

Jasmine woke to find Tariq gone. She missed him. Missed his smile, his morning caresses, his body sliding into hers, completing her in a way that she'd never known was possible between a man and a woman. When their bodies were one, it was as if she could see into his soul for one blinding instant. But only sometimes. Last night he'd shut her out, loving her body with exquisite care but giving her nothing more than his physical passion.

She stood up and quickly ran through her toilette when her musings threatened to make her teary. Then she pulled on a long skirt in a soft peach fabric over her naked skin. She felt exposed even in the confines of the tent and wanted to get covered before she worried about underwear. In her rush to dress, she forgot that they were traveling today and she would need to be in pants.

Her fear was justified. She was reaching for a bra when the tent flap opened behind her and a warm breeze touched her back. Apprehensive, she glanced over her bare shoulder.

"Oh." Relief flowed through her.

Tariq raised a dark eyebrow. "You were expecting someone else?" The flap closed behind him, hiding the incipient brightness of the day.

She blushed. No one would dare enter without his express permission. "I just can't get used to the openness of these tents." With a shake of her head, she turned and picked up the bra.

"Leave it." Husky and rough, Tariq's unexpected command startled her into dropping the piece of lace and satin.

The feel of his naked chest against her back startled her even more. He'd been fully dressed when he'd entered, and she'd turned her back on him only a few seconds before. Unlike last night, this morning his hands were impatient, cupping her breasts and teasing her nipples with more heat than expertise, while he kept her trapped in front of him. He was a little rough and most possessive.

She felt a hot rush of liquid heat between her thighs. It was as if Tariq knew. He slipped one hand under her skirt. Continuing to caress her breast with the other hand, he slid a single finger through her curls.

"You are ready." His husky voice held a note of satisfaction, as if he was pleased at her responsiveness.

Before she knew what was happening, he pushed her skirt up her back and bared her buttocks to him. Too needy to be embarrassed, she gripped his thighs when he put both hands around her hips and pulled her onto him, sliding her down so slowly she thought she would go mad.

"Tariq, please, please," she moaned. "Oh, please."

From the way he growled in approval and gave her what she wanted, she knew that he liked her obvious need, liked the way she wriggled on him and urged him to go faster. Out of nowhere, an image of what Tariq had to be seeing as their bodies joined in wild surrender burst into her mind. It was the final erotic stroke. Her climax was thunder and lightning. She knew that she took him with her, his throaty cry mixing with her scream of release.

Afterward, he held her in his lap, their bodies still joined. She tilted her head back against his firm shoulder and tried to get her racing heart to calm down. A long time later, she swallowed and wet her dry lips. "Wow."

Tariq chuckled against her ear and nibbled on the soft flesh of her earlobe. "Not too fast? I hear women like it slow." His tone was pure provocation, daring her to deny the way she'd burned like wildfire in his arms.

She nudged him with an elbow. "You're a horrible tease, but I'm too sated to argue with you."

She heard his smile in his reply. "So this is what I must do to get your complete cooperation. It could become exhausting."

Jasmine laughed. Tariq closed his hands over her breasts in a final sweet caress before he reluctantly pulled away. "We must prepare to leave, my Jasmine. It is time to go home."

Just before they left the tent, she took a deep breath and put her hand on his muscular forearm. Under the white material of his shirt, skin and muscle moved over bone, seducing her with their effortless flow.

He gave her an indulgent smile, still enjoying the aftereffects of their wild mating. "What is it? I promise you we can play when we get home."

His sensually teasing response made her blush. It was as if last night had never happened. She had her husband back. The shields had dropped, but only as far as they had been before her declaration. It wasn't enough. If she let him deny her love, then this half-life would be all she ever had. And she was tired of never being good enough. Tired of never being loved. Perhaps her flaws made her unworthy of love, but until there was no hope, she would try. This time, she wouldn't let anyone, even Tariq, keep her from fighting for their love.

"Your eyes are getting bigger and bigger." He raised one finger and ran it across her lips.

"I meant it. I love you."

His face underwent a sudden change, from open and teasing

to totally reserved. "We must go." He turned away without another word and preceded her outside.

She sucked in a breath of air that felt like a knife blade slicing across her heart. Oh, it hurt so much to have her love not even acknowledged. But her struggle would be worth it if she succeeded in getting back what she'd lost so carelessly in her naiveté.

Tariq waited for Jasmine outside their tent, careful to keep his emotions from showing on his face. It would not do for his people to see their leader in turmoil.

Why did she do this?

Did she truly believe that she could control him with a declaration of love? Words so easily said…promises so easily broken. He'd offered her his very soul four years ago, and she'd thrown it back at him as if it was a worthless token, after promising him forever. Though he would never let her know it, he still hurt from that emotional blow.

Part of him wanted to believe her, whispering that she was no longer the scared girl who'd crumbled under the slightest pressure, but a woman strong enough to fight him at his angriest. However, Tariq refused to listen to that voice. His heart was still raw from her rejection, not yet convinced of the depth of her commitment.

More than once, when she'd thought him occupied, he'd glimpsed shadows in his wife's blue eyes. His pride had stopped him from hounding her, as he had in the desert, but the knowledge ate away at him. Even now, even after he'd told her so much, she kept her secrets, and that he could not forgive. Women's secrets had always caused him pain.

By force of will, he buried that part of him that had become entranced by her. It shocked him just how close he'd come to laying his heart at her feet once again, even when it was clear that she didn't trust him. He wouldn't make that mistake twice. He couldn't. Not when his vulnerability to her ran so deep it had become his greatest weakness.

Seven

The next few days felt as if they'd sprung fully fledged from Jasmine's worst nightmares. Tariq had withdrawn so completely from her that it scared her. No matter what she tried—humor, anger, pleas, protestations of love—none of it reached him. The strength of will implied by such total emotional excision was a huge blow to her fragile confidence. Tariq could apparently cut her out without a thought.

"Tariq, please," she said, in the car on the way back to Zulheina, "talk to me." She was frantic to make him respond.

"What do you wish to talk about?" He looked up from his papers, his eyes holding the mild interest of a stranger.

"Anything! Stop shutting me out!" She was close to tears, which horrified her.

"I do not know what you mean." He bent his head again, dismissing her.

With a cry torn from deep inside, she pulled away the papers and threw them aside. "I won't let you do this to me!"

His eyes flashed green fire as his hand snaked out and

gripped her chin. "You have forgotten the rules. I no longer follow your demands." No anger, no fury, only calm control. Even his touch gentled and then he let her go.

"I love you. Doesn't that mean anything?" she asked in a broken whisper.

"Thank you for your love." He picked up the papers she'd hurled aside, and sorted them. "I am sure its worth is the same as it was four years ago."

The subtle, sardonic barb delivered in that smooth, aristocratic voice hit home. "We're not the same people as we were then. Give us a chance!" she begged.

He met her gaze with eyes so neutral they were unrecognizable as her panther's. "I need to read these."

He'd beaten her. Tariq's anger she could deal with, but she had no defense against this cold, inaccessible stranger. It was clear that he regretted the indulgences he'd allowed her in Zeina, the small things that had caused her guard to slip. She could imagine his thought processes. He probably thought that she believed she could control him now, because he'd allowed her so much, been so open.

Despite that knowledge, she didn't buckle. Tariq was stubborn, but she'd realized that when it came to loving him, she was obstinate beyond belief.

Their first night back, she was tempted to sleep in her own room, hurting and unsure of her welcome. Instead, she brushed her hair in front of Tariq's mirror and lay down in his bed. And when he reached for her, she went to him. In this place, they connected. Their loving was always wild, always passionate. It gave her hope, because how could he touch her like that, how could he whisper, "You're mine, Mina. Mine!" as he moved inside her, if only lust was involved?

A week later, Jasmine pinned some silver cloth in place and picked up her scissors.

"I wish to talk to you, my wife."

Startled by the deep rumble of Tariq's voice, she dropped the pins she'd been holding in her mouth. "Don't sneak up on me like that!'' She put one hand on her T-shirt, above her heart. ''And stop looming.''

He frowned, and she knew he was about to remind her that he gave the orders around here. Since their return from Zeina, he'd been more autocratic than usual, and colder. It was hard to battle this warrior every day, but his anger strengthened her resolve. Anger this powerful had to spring from deep emotion.

And, she realized, she was willing to fight the warrior because he was a part of the man she loved. The ice that tempered the fire.

Mentally rolling her eyes, she raised her arms and smiled in invitation. Loving him was the only way she knew to prove that she'd changed. For a moment, she thought that he would refuse, and her heart clenched in anticipation of another bruise. But then he came down on his haunches beside her.

She wrapped her arms around his neck and kissed him. He let her be the aggressor, remaining quiescent in her arms, but Jasmine couldn't forget the power humming just under the surface. He could have taken over at any second, but he let her control the kiss, seemingly content to taste her.

When she drew back, he removed her hands and clasped them between his own. ''I am going to Paris for the week.'' Any fire that her kiss might have aroused was carefully hidden, if it existed at all.

''What?'' She couldn't conceal her surprise. Her hands curled into fists in his grasp. ''When?''

''Within the hour.''

She blinked. ''Why didn't you tell me sooner?''

His jaw firmed. ''I have no need to tell you such things.''

''I'm your wife!''

''Yes. And you will stay in your place.''

The unexpected verbal reprimand hit her like a slap. She bent her head and took a deep breath. ''You know some of the French designers are putting on shows this week. If you'd told me earlier, I could've gone with you.'' She'd come to expect his need for control, could even understand it, but he'd never treated her so harshly, as if he cared nothing for her feelings. She hadn't known that he regretted what had happened in Zeina that much.

He released her hands and gripped her chin between his thumb and forefinger, forcing her to face him. "No, Jasmine. You cannot leave Zulheil."

She frowned. "You don't trust me, do you? What do you expect me to do—run away at the first available opportunity?"

"I may have been a fool once, but you will not make me one twice," he nearly growled.

"I came and stayed of my own free will. I won't run."

"You did not know what you faced when you came." His features were expressionless as he brushed aside her words. "I am not wrapped around your little finger, as you no doubt expected, and I do not intend to be. Because you know this, you will wish to escape. I do not intend to lose you."

She shook her head in denial, but he didn't release her. "I love you," she repeated firmly. "Don't you know what that means?"

"It means that you can turn your back and walk away at any time." Rapier sharp, his jabs made her bleed. But she still wasn't beaten.

"How long are you going to act this way?" she asked him in desperation. "How long are you going to punish me? When is your revenge going to be complete?"

His green eyes had darkened to the color of the deepest sea. "I do not do this to punish you. To want to take revenge, I would have to feel something for you beyond lust, which I do not. You are a possession, prized but not irreplaceable."

She felt the color leave her face. She couldn't speak. Her heart felt as if it was bleeding. In a desperate attempt to hide her grief, she bit the insides of her cheeks hard enough to taste blood, and waited for him to finish.

"I will be involved in matters of state. Hiraz knows how to get in touch with me."

She remained silent, barely able to hear him through the painful buzzing in her ears. When he bent his head and placed a possessive kiss on her lips, she accepted it dully, too stunned to respond. Tariq seemed to take her reaction as subtle defiance because he moved his hand to her hair and tangled his fingers in the long ponytail, gripping her head.

"You will not deny me," he growled against her lips. Because he knew her every sensual weakness, he was right. She couldn't deny him. Not when she'd been starving for him for so long.

When he drew back, cold satisfaction gleamed in his eyes. "I can make you pant for me anytime I wish, Jasmine, so do not try and manipulate me with your body."

The sensual fires he'd aroused were doused instantly by his taunt. Thankfully, he didn't continue the lesson.

"I will be leaving in forty minutes." With that, he rose and strode out the door of her workroom.

Jasmine didn't know how long she sat there, unable to function. She felt as if he'd ripped out her heart and then laughed at her agony. She hurt too much to feel the pain. When she finally rose and made her way to the wide glass doors that led out to a balcony overlooking the main gardens, it was to see Tariq walking to a royal limousine.

He was dressed in a black suit, his tie the vivid green of his eyes, his beautiful hair brushed back. She saw him stop and look up at the balcony. Quickly, she stumbled back into the room. From this far, she couldn't make out the expression on his face, but she knew he hadn't seen her. Then he stepped inside and the car drove off.

It was as if his departure released the paralysis that had protected her from her own anguished emotions. Suddenly close to an emotional breakdown, she scurried through the corridors, praying she wouldn't meet anyone along the way. Once safely behind the locked doors of the exquisite room that was her own, she walked out into the private garden and hid under the spreading tree with the blue-white flowers. The branches were so heavy with blooms that they almost touched the ground, providing her with a scented cave of darkness in which to let go of her torment.

Her sobs came from somewhere deep inside, wrenched out

of her body with such force that she didn't have breath enough to make a sound. She was destroyed by the sudden insight that she'd been fooling herself. She'd believed that she could love Tariq enough to make him love her, a girl who'd never been loved. She had allowed him every liberty, going so far as to tie herself to him for life. She'd given him her body and her soul, keeping nothing back.

And now he'd rejected her gift in the cruelest of ways. She was nothing but a possession to him, prized but not irreplaceable. He felt nothing but lust for her. Lust! Her illusions of time healing the wounds of the past shattered under the realization that his actions weren't born out of pain. He just didn't care if he hurt her.

Had he married her only to humble her? Crush her?

She curled into a ball at the base of the tree and wrapped her arms around her shaking body, trying to breathe through the pain that lay like a rock in her throat. Dusk fell outside but she didn't notice. She'd cried all the tears she had inside, but her pain was so great she couldn't move.

Freed, the demons that she'd drowned in tears descended upon her, wanting their pound of flesh. In Tariq's land, in Tariq's arms, she'd almost managed to forget the lack in her. The missing part that made her incapable of being loved. Suddenly, the memories of that terrible day in her childhood when she'd understood the truth flooded over her.

"Does it bother you that you demanded half of Mary's inheritance before you'd adopt Jasmine?" Aunt Ella had asked the woman Jasmine had thought was her mother. "After all, Mary is our baby sister."

"No. She should've known better than to get pregnant by some stranger in a bar. I don't know what possessed her to have the child." The sound of ice cubes hitting crystal had penetrated the library door. "We aren't some charity. How else were Jasmine's expenses going to be covered?"

"You got a lot more than that," Ella had persisted.

"Mary's inheritance from Grandpa was twice the size of ours."

"I think of it as adequate compensation for having to accept bad blood into my family. Lord only knows what kind of a loser Jasmine's father was. Mary was so drunk, she couldn't even remember his name."

Later, when Jasmine had forced herself to ask, Aunt Ella had taken pity on her and told her about Mary. Apparently, in order to avoid any hint of scandal, Mary had moved to America after Jasmine's birth. She'd never returned. The people who'd raised Jasmine, Mary's older sister, Lucille, and her husband, James, had already had two children, Michael and Sarah, and had been unwilling to take on another, until they'd been given a financial incentive. Yet they'd gone on to have another child of their own—a beloved younger son named Mathew.

That day, Jasmine had been slapped in the face with the fact that any care she'd ever known had been bought and paid for. Searching for someone to love her, she'd written to Mary, saying hello. The response had arrived on her thirteenth birthday, a cool request to make no further contact because Mary had no wish to be associated with a past "indiscretion."

An indiscretion. That's all Jasmine was to her birth mother. And to her adoptive mother she was bad blood. Neither Mary nor Lucille had been able to love her. Today, she was forced to accept that the lack hadn't magically disappeared. She was still unloved. Still unwanted.

The next day, Jasmine decided there was nothing to be gained by crying over something she couldn't change. Despite the hurt that existed inside her like a living, breathing creature, she forced herself into her workroom and picked up the scissors she'd dropped the day before.

She had to do something until she figured out how to handle the situation with Tariq, the man whom she'd married in a blind haze of love. Perhaps she'd made the biggest mistake of her life, but she didn't want to think about that now. Neither did she want to think about the way her old fears and insecurities had tormented her last night.

An hour into her work, she heard a telephone ring, but ignored it. There was a knock on her door a minute later.

"Madam?"

She looked up to find one of the palace staff at the door. "Yes, Shazana?"

"Sheik Zamanat wishes to speak with you."

Jasmine's throat locked. About to ask Shazana to tell Tariq that she was busy, she recognized the possible consequences of asking a loyal staff member to lie, and nodded.

"Please transfer the call to this phone." She indicated the one near the door of the turret.

Shazana nodded and left. The phone rang seconds later. Jasmine stood up and walked over. She picked up the receiver...then hung up. Heart thudding, she hurried down the hallway, into her bedroom and out into the garden. The phone rang again just as she escaped. She hid under her tree.

It was cowardly to hide from Tariq but she couldn't bear to talk to him, couldn't bear to hear the voice that she'd dreamed about for years rip her to pieces with the painful truth about her inadequacy. Last night, she'd believed that all her illusions had been destroyed, but today she realized she couldn't face the total loss of hope. Not yet. Not yet.

Perhaps an hour later, she emerged and made her way back to her workroom. There was a message on the table by the phone. She picked it up with shaking hands. It instructed her to call Tariq at a given number.

"Go to hell!" She crunched the note into a ball and threw it into the wastebasket, then began to work on the top she was making. Her movements were jerky and uncoordinated, as for the first time, anger began to simmer under the hurt and sorrow. So Sheik Zamanat expected her to come to heel when he hollered? She almost stabbed the material with her scissors.

He was about to learn that his wife was not some toy he could throw aside and pick up whenever he felt like it.

Tariq hung up the phone for the fourth time. He was annoyed by his wife's subtle rebellion, but another, more dangerous emotion threatened. That emotion would not let him forget the naked pain in Mina's eyes when he'd last spoken to her.

After so long, the anger and hurt he'd ruthlessly controlled for years had shattered its bonds and lashed out. When Mina had voiced her love, he'd felt as if she'd torn open wounds that had barely begun to heal. The almost unbearable pain had sprung from a need that he didn't want to accept. It had caused him to say things he shouldn't have.

Guilt was not something he was familiar with, but pangs of it had been stabbing him since the moment Mina hadn't appeared on the balcony to bid him goodbye. His sense of loss had shaken him. He felt as if he'd damaged something fragile between them. Only angry pride had kept him from returning to her.

But Mina didn't hold grudges. Once he spoke to her, she would return to normal. And the next time he picked up that phone, he *would* talk to her.

Jasmine felt as if she was getting ready for a knock-down, drag-out fight. She'd ignored Tariq for two days. At first, it had been blind instinct, an attempt to save herself from rejection. She'd had enough of that in her lifetime. Later, when she'd calmed down, she'd realized that she needed some time and distance to sort out her feelings. Tariq had given her a rude shock, waking her up forever to the fact that the man she loved was not the man she'd married.

Did she love this Tariq?

Her mind wasn't completely made up, but her anger refused to be ignored any longer. This time, Tariq would get an answer to his call. A call that came as soon as dawn was breaking over Zulheil. She picked up the phone on the second ring.

"Prized possession speaking." It slipped out without thought. She was horrified, but just a little proud of herself.

There was complete and utter silence on the other end of the phone. "I am not amused, Jasmine," he said finally.

"Well, since I'm not a comedienne, my ego isn't too badly wounded." Sitting in bed, her legs hanging off the edge, she felt the simmering anger start to bubble. "Did you have anything to say or did you just ring to remind me of my place?" Where had that come from?

"You are being obstinate."

"Yup."

"What did you expect when you returned?" A thread of anger crept into his so far calm tone. "That nothing would have changed? That I would lay my trust in your lap?"

"No. I expected you to have forgotten me." It was a cruel truth. "But you didn't. You took me and you married me, giving me a place in your life. How dare you now treat me like…like an object? Like something to scrape off the bottom of your royal shoe? How dare you?" Tears threatened, riding the crest of her anger.

"Never have I treated you as such!" His response was a harsh reproof.

"Yes, you have. And you know what? I don't want to talk to a man who treats me like that. I could almost hate you. Don't call me anymore. Maybe by the time you get home I'll have calmed down. Right now, I have nothing for you. Nothing!" It was the raw pain of her emotions speaking.

"We will talk when I return." His voice held a note she'd never before heard, a note she couldn't understand.

Jasmine hung up the phone with shaking hands, surprised by her own outburst. She'd planned belligerence, but had ended up ripping apart the shields protecting her heart. She hurt. And yet it felt cleansing. She *was* worth more than this treatment. She might not be loved but she was worthy of respect.

Something her husband might never give her.

I could almost hate you.

Tariq stared out at the cobbled streets of Paris, Jasmine's words ringing in his head. He was used to being adored by her, being the center of her attention, as he'd been since their first meeting. He'd never considered being with a Jasmine who didn't treat him that way.

He didn't like the sensation. Not when his need for her ran so deep that he missed her every moment she wasn't by his side. He'd only survived the four years without her by working night and day, striving for mindless exhaustion. Her laughter and affection since her return had been a balm to the hunger inside him. Now she was furious with him.

He'd underestimated the woman she'd become. A woman who apparently felt things more deeply and wildly than he'd given her credit for. She'd always had quiet feminine courage, but this was the first time she'd dared to rebuke him for his actions with such blunt honesty. He finally listened to the inner voices he'd been ignoring, accepting that she'd changed dramatically from the Jasmine he'd known.

That Jasmine would never have hated him.

That Jasmine had also walked away from him.

If he opened his heart just a little, what would this Jasmine do? Would she treat him with the same disregard she'd shown four years ago or…? The possibilities were as intriguing and as tempting as the evocative scents borne on the Paris winds.

But first, he'd have to win Mina back. She was his. She wasn't allowed to hate him.

Eight

"**W**hat do you mean, he's in the courtyard?" Jasmine cried, shoving her hands through her tumbled hair.

Mumtaz shrugged her delicate shoulders. "I persuaded Hiraz to delay him so I could warn you."

"But it's Friday night. He wasn't supposed to be back until Monday!"

Heavy footsteps sounded in the hallway. Mumtaz's eyes widened. "I must go. I wish you luck." She slipped out the door. Jasmine heard her say something to Tariq.

With a muted cry of frustration, Jasmine secured the azure silk robe around her waist. It was too late to change. She didn't want to greet Tariq wearing a robe that hit her midthigh, with her hair loose around her shoulders, but the doorknob was turning. Quickly, she settled onto the stool in front of her dressing table and picked up her brush. At least this way, if her legs collapsed, he wouldn't know.

She heard Tariq enter the room and close the door. Her fingers tightened convulsively around the carved wooden handle of the brush, but she continued the smooth, full-length strokes, ignoring his presence. She felt him move until he was standing behind her. He leaned forward and put both hands on her dressing table, one on either side of her, effectively caging her with his body. She kept brushing her hair, though she couldn't feel her fingers anymore because they were shaking so hard. She didn't look in the mirror, avoiding the trap of green fire that awaited her.

"How's your throat infection?" He reminded her of one of her earlier excuses, not referring to the last painful call.

"Much better."

"I can hear that. And you're feeling well?"

"Yes." She tried to avoid touching her head to his chest. Every time she moved an inch away, he leaned closer, until she was on the edge of her stool with nowhere to go.

"Good. I was worried, as you seemed to be sleeping so much when I called." Though his tone was calm, she knew he had to be furious. He wasn't a man used to being reprimanded.

And she wasn't ready to face his anger. Despite her bravado, she didn't hate Tariq. Her feelings for him were raw and undefined, but they didn't come close to hate, and their depth and promise scared her. What if she began to love him even more deeply than she had all these years?

The heat of his body seemed to surround her. She wondered if he'd subtly moved. It was becoming difficult to continue to brush her hair, because with every stroke, she touched him. She chanced a peek at his arms and saw that he'd lessened the gap between them. He was wearing a blue shirt, his jacket discarded.

He reached out, took the brush from her nerveless fingers and put it on the dresser. Then he tucked her hair behind her ears, baring her face. She froze as he stroked the knuckles of one hand down her cheek in a simple but powerful caress, reminding her of the times he'd done that after they'd made love. She curled her fingers into fists and gritted her teeth against the response he could call forth so easily. The memory of his parting gibe helped, but it wouldn't hold up forever against this gentle persuasion.

"Will you also refuse to talk to me now that I am home?" He continued the lazy caress.

"I'm talking to you right now." She was overjoyed when her voice didn't break.

"No. You are answering my questions and hiding yourself from me."

She didn't say anything.

"You are very angry with me, my Jasmine?" The husky timbre of his voice was close to her ear, his body almost totally enclosing her. "You have not calmed down?"

"I'm not angry." Her heart thudded hard against her ribs. The anger had long since burned out, leaving behind a residue of hurt so deep she felt ravaged.

He kissed the lobe of her ear. A shiver raced through her. She couldn't disguise the instinctive reaction, but neither did she do anything else.

"Ah, Mina, you cannot lie. Come, look at me. Welcome your husband home."

His words were an unwanted echo of his commands before he'd left. "Do you wish to have sex? If you'll move, I'll get on the bed." Dark and violent emotions rose in her throat, daring her to release them. She stifled the urge, refusing to let Tariq see just how badly he'd hurt her when he'd brought her deepest fear to the surface and given it form.

His body turned to stone around her. She could feel his muscles tensing as if to strike. He drew back so fast that she nearly fell off the stool, unbalanced. She'd barely got herself grounded when he lifted her and stood her in front of him. In bare feet, she only came halfway up his chest. Startled, she almost met his eyes but managed to fix her gaze on his shoulders.

"Mina, do not do this. You know you will turn into liquid fire in my arms." He curved one hand over her hip and used the other to cup her cheek, but didn't force her to look up.

"Yes, I know you can make me *pant* at any time." She

swallowed the lump in her throat as she repeated his taunt. A taunt so true it made her cry inside. If he touched her much longer with those sensitive fingers, she'd shatter like fine crystal. Something wild and needy in her recognized his touch and wouldn't let her pull away. "I'm not going to fight you."

He growled at her response and pulled her into a bruising embrace, holding her head against his chest. Jasmine had to fight every instinct she possessed not to respond. Her hunger for him was a clawing being inside her. She reminded herself that she was prized but not irreplaceable. *Not irreplaceable.* He felt only momentary lust when he touched her. When she remained stiff, arms at her sides, he released her.

"Go to bed, Jasmine." He sounded tired and defeated. Leaving her standing in the center of the bedroom, he pushed through the connecting door and into his room.

The door shut with a quiet click.

Out of nowhere, exhaustion slammed into Jasmine. Dreading this confrontation, she'd barely slept the past five nights. Still wearing the silk robe, she crawled under the blankets. However, a sense of loss kept nudging her awake. She knew it was a lie. She'd never had anything to lose. Still, she wanted to go to her husband and hold him…soothe him.

"No." No, she wouldn't give in to the need, when he clearly saw nothing wrong with his treatment of her. Respect, she repeated to herself. She was worthy of respect.

Tariq threw his balled-up shirt across the room. She'd denied him! He'd never expected that from Jasmine. He had relied on her generous nature to forgive him. Time and distance, and Jasmine's passionate anger, had made him regret his cruel words. That day in her solar, he'd allowed the wounded beast inside him to speak, full of years of pent-up anger and pain. It would have been better to keep that uncontrollable part of himself locked up.

He'd been feeling instead of thinking, and the words that had slipped out had been weapons aimed at his wife. More than that, they'd been untrue. He had four years of midnight awakenings to attest to the fact that she was irreplaceable.

What if the damage was irreversible? What if Mina did hate him? Her body had been so stiff in his embrace, her lips so silent. She'd been like a small creature frozen in front of a predator. The painful image forced him to accept that what he'd felt from Jasmine hadn't been anger or a need for revenge, but...hurt. His temper vanished in the face of that truth. He had hurt his wife, his Mina. There was no satisfaction in that knowledge, only disgust at himself. She was his to protect. Even from himself.

For the first time in an eternity, Tariq was uncertain about his next act. A sheik could rarely indulge in indecision, but it appeared that a husband had plenty of opportunity to do so. He knew he'd acted badly, but he wasn't a man accustomed to asking for forgiveness. With a sound akin to a growl, he stalked into the shower, his mind on the small woman with big blue eyes next door.

Familiar hands, rough but gentle, stroked the naked line of her spine. Jasmine frowned, sure that she'd been clothed before sleep, but in this dream, skin touched skin. A kiss on her nape, on each vertebra, possessive hands grasping her hips... She moaned and turned onto her back, welcoming her lover. When he pressed his lips to her breasts, she arched into him. Waking thoughts merged with hazy dreams as her fingers tangled in thick silky hair. A beard-roughened jaw angled across her breast. She shivered and the spot was immediately kissed.

"Tariq," she whispered, awake and aware. It was too late to stop her response. Her whole body was open in invitation. Jasmine sighed and gave in to the inevitable. Whatever he said, whatever he did, he was hers. How could she possibly deny him when he touched her as if she was precious?

When he kissed her, she returned his kiss joyously, unable to hide how much she'd missed him. He shuddered against her and broke away to drop kisses across her breasts. Under her fingers, his shoulder muscles bunched as he moved down her body, dropping a line of kisses across her stomach and flicking his tongue over the indentation of her navel.

Shivers racked her body as he found an unexpectedly sensitive spot. Her reaction made him repeat the quick caress. Her stomach muscles clenched and her hips jerked upward without conscious control. Pressed so close, she could feel his heartbeat in the pulse of his body.

She parted her thighs for him without prompting, but he didn't rise to possess her. He lifted her left leg and placed it over his shoulder. Her sensitive skin burned from the heat of his body. Then he rubbed his rough jaw across the tender skin on the insides of her thighs.

She gasped. "Tariq, please."

He soothed the roughness with his tongue, sending her nerves into further disarray. Then he repeated the whole process with her right leg. Just when she thought that she could feel no more pleasure, he dipped his head and bestowed the most intimate kiss of all upon her.

She screamed and would've squirmed away, but his hold on her hips kept her in place as he slowly, and with great care, introduced her to this shatteringly intimate form of loving. His only aim was her pleasure.

With the tiny slice of her brain that was functioning, she knew this was Tariq's apology. Her warrior was adoring her body, cherishing her response. He couldn't say the words, but he was showing her that she was more than an object to satisfy his lust. How much more, she didn't know, but even the depth of her hurt couldn't survive against this kind of tenderness.

She clutched handfuls of the sheets and gave herself up to his caresses. Once more, she gave her heart and soul to Tariq, her vows to keep him at bay disintegrating into dust. She felt the change in him immediately. His intense, concentrated caressing continued, but his shoulders were no longer so tense under her thighs, and his hands were anchors rather than vices forcing her to stay in place. And then she couldn't think. She found the kind of freedom that she could only find in his arms and splintered on the wings of pleasure. He held her until the tremors subsided and then gently entered her, as if unsure of his welcome.

Tears pricked her eyes at his hesitation. He wasn't acting the autocratic despot now. The silent question delivered the final blow to any lingering hurt. She deliberately clenched her inner muscles and held him prisoner, telling him without words that he was wanted, needed, loved. At the same time, she curled her arms around him and dropped kisses across his shoulders. With a groan, he began to move.

"Welcome home," she whispered, just before she crested the highest pinnacle of desire for a second time that night.

A long while later, she gathered enough confidence to ask, "Why did you return early?"

Tariq spooned her deeper against him and dropped a kiss on the curve of her shoulder where it met her neck. "The trade agreement was completed earlier than expected."

"Did you…" She began to ask him about the agreement, then stopped, unwilling to be rebuffed. He'd loved her with fire, but she was afraid that she'd be waking up beside the cool, reserved stranger he'd become after Zeina.

"What, Mina?"

"Nothing."

He was silent for a while and then said, "Zulheil now has a contract with several Western states that will allow our artistic products to cross their borders without duty."

She took the olive branch, prepared to meet him halfway. "Why artistic products?"

"Zulheil's jewelry and other artistic products are highly prized. They are our third biggest export. The agreement goes both ways." He chuckled, warming her heart. "They think their goods will flood our markets, but they're wrong."

"How do you know that?"

"Because, Mina—" he squeezed her with unexpected playfulness "—we have had such an agreement with the United States for years."

"Really? But there's no mass-market stuff in your streets." She snuggled into him, her head pillowed on his arm.

"My people are used to the best handcrafted goods. The riches of the land are shared by all. The cheap things they send are never bought."

"You're snobs."

Her husband shrugged. "But we are rich enough to be so."

His unrepentant reply made her laugh. She couldn't temper her responses to him when he let his shields fall. "So you're getting the best of this bargain? Why don't they know about the experience of the Americans?"

"Nobody likes to admit their mistakes. What would it look like if the world's biggest power had been...I have lost the word," he paused, waiting for her.

"Conned?" she suggested cheekily.

"Yes. It would not look good for them if they were seen to have been *conned* by a tiny sheikdom from the desert. A poor, primitive people."

She laughed so hard that she cried. "Primitive!"

When she'd stopped giggling, Tariq bit her lightly on her shoulder to catch her attention. She turned into his arms, aware that she'd capitulated too easily, without waiting for words of apology to banish her heartache. But she'd always known that Tariq would never humble himself in such a blatant fashion. He was too much the desert warrior for that. For now, his incredibly tender loving was enough.

It was a start.

Early the next morning, Jasmine sat on the edge of her Zulheil Rose fountain, listening to the cool splash of the water and the quiet sounds of the birds. Kept awake by her newly reinvigorated demons, she'd made the decision to leave Tariq sprawled in bed, and face them. Face them and defeat them.

First, she accepted that she'd never truly been loved. Not the way she needed to be loved.

Perhaps if she'd chosen Tariq four years ago, he might have learned to love her like that. Perhaps. However, back then, she'd been young and needy compared to Tariq's strength and confidence. While he'd cherished her, he'd also been her caretaker. Her love for him had been deep and achingly true, but it had been the love of a girl growing into womanhood. Tender. Easily bruised.

Though her hurt had made her doubt her feelings, since she'd come to Zulheil her love had matured and grown, fed by her awakening emotions for the man Tariq had become. All vestiges of the youth were gone, but in his place was a man of integrity, power and charisma. A man who touched her with tenderness that turned her heart inside out. A man who was, quite simply, magnificent.

She loved this Tariq with an intensity that even his anger couldn't destroy. This love was tougher and gave her the courage to look behind his remarks, to the pain she'd caused. This love gave her the strength to fight for her lover.

From the first day she'd arrived, Tariq had been demanding. Now, she saw that as a gift. He no longer thought of her as a girl to be protected, but as a woman who had to confront her mistakes.

That was the first truth. The second was that she still wasn't loved. And that terrified her. Her naive belief in her ability to reach Tariq with her love had been smashed beyond repair that day before Paris, and she couldn't face that kind of torment again. She'd been rejected so many times in her life that once more might break her. So, while she would continue to fight for her sheik's trust, she wouldn't do it by offering him her heart…or betraying her hunger to be loved in return.

"I think we're getting somewhere," Jasmine said to Mumtaz two weeks later. They were browsing in an art supply store in Zulheina. "He's talking to me."

"Talking about what?"

"Business, mostly." She was drawn to the easel in the corner.

"Hmm, that is good, but what about your relationship?"

Jasmine ran her fingers down the polished wood of the easel. Perfect. Leaning down, she picked up several prepared canvasses and stacked them on the easel. Tariq had always liked to prepare his own, but these would do for a start.

"I don't want to ruin it by pushing." She wandered over to the oil paints and began selecting tubes. Pthalo blue, burnt umber, viridian hue…

"You are waiting for something?" Mumtaz absently added titanium white to Jasmine's collection.

"I want some sign that… I can't explain it." Ever since his return from Paris, Tariq had treated her with kid gloves, keeping an emotional barrier between them. He didn't hurt her with his anger any longer, but conversely, she couldn't breach his shields to teach him to trust in her again.

This lukewarm companionship was simply wrong.

Nothing had ever been lukewarm between them. Their love had been a blaze and their separation pure pain. Even the anger and hurt between them was jagged and sharp enough to draw blood. The sudden change in his behavior mystified her.

"Do not worry about explaining. Simply do what you must." Mumtaz squeezed her hand.

"Good advice, I think." But, Jasmine thought, what *could* she do to breach the wall her enigmatic husband had erected?

"Are you busy?" She peered into Tariq's office. At the sound of her voice, he looked up from his desk.

"You are always welcome, Jasmine."

She ignored the desire to rile him just to get him to respond with more heat. What sane woman would prefer an angry, simmering lover to a friendly, warm one? She had to be insane, because she definitely favored honest fury over a gentle illusion. At least then she knew his emotions ran deep.

Pushing aside those disturbing thoughts for the time being, Jasmine ducked out and picked up the pile of purchases and put them on his desk. The easel she left outside, unwilling to spoil his surprise.

"What is this?" He tugged at the string around the brown paper wrapping.

"A present. Open it!" She moved around to his side and perched on the arm of his chair.

He frowned and immediately curved one arm around her waist. "You will fall in such a position."

"Here." She wiggled and fell into his lap. "Now open it."

He seemed nonplussed by her unexpected cuddling. When she pushed at his hands, he picked up his letter opener and cut the string. His body stilled around hers when he saw the canvasses, paints and brushes.

"I know you're busy," Jasmine began, before he could talk himself out of it. "But surely you can find an hour each day? Think of it as doing something for your sheikdom."

He raised an expressive eyebrow at that.

She smiled. "A workaholic sheik will become stuffy and stressed out, and of no use to his people." She ignored his snort of disbelief. "You used to paint as a way to relieve the stresses of the day. Why not try that again?"

"My responsibilities—"

She stopped him with a hand on his lips. "An hour. That's not too much to ask. And I'll help you."

"How?"

"I'm sure I can do something to lighten the load for you. Filing? Summarizing reports? I'm smart, you know."

He chuckled at her earnest words and his shoulders subtly relaxed. "I know you are smart, Mina. I've always known that. All right. You may assist me and you must also sit for me."

"You're going to paint me?" She sat up on his lap, excited. "Will it be a nude?"

He frowned at her impudence. "Such a painting would never be seen by the world and would be burned upon my death."

Jasmine kissed his cheek, delighted by his acceptance, and scrambled off his lap before he could stop her. "There's an easel, too." She collected the materials. "I'll put this in a corner of my workroom and come back to help you."

She ended up spending the rest of the day with him, reviewing reports. He told her she could leave at any time, but when she saw the amount of work that required his attention, she was more than happy to sit down and dig in.

One of the reports gave her an unwelcome shock. "Tariq?" He raised his head at her sharp tone.

"It says here that the sheik can have more than one wife." Her brow furrowed.

Tariq's lips twitched a little. "That is an ancient law."

"How ancient?" She didn't intend to share her husband. *Ever.*

"Very. It is a historical oddity. Both my grandfather and my father had only one wife."

"Your great-grandfather?"

"Four." It seemed to her that his eyes were bright with withheld amusement. "Do not worry, I believe I have only enough stamina for one wife."

"I'm going to get this law repealed," she declared.

"The women of Zulheil would salute you. It only applies to the sheik, but the law seems to threaten Zulheil's modern image, some say."

Jasmine nodded, her fears soothed by his practical words. At least another wife was one problem she wouldn't have to contend with. She settled back to work. There was, she discovered, a kind of quiet satisfaction in helping her husband bear some of the burdens he carried on his shoulders.

"Enough, Mina." He stood up and stretched, his powerful body drawing her attention.

She'd been sitting on the sofa in one corner of his study, curled up. Putting aside a report, she stood and stretched as well, loosening tight muscles.

"You may regret your offer." He came to stand by her. "I find your summaries excellent. I will conscript you often."

Pleased by his compliment, she smiled and put her hand in his. "Good. Now let's go before someone else catches you."

Today, for the first time, she'd realized just how many people thought that Tariq was the only one who could possibly provide an answer to their problems. Often they turned up in person. Hiraz and Mumtaz deflected a lot of them, but some were insistent. The relaxed system of government in Zulheil astounded her. However, it appeared to work fantastically well for the small and sparsely populated land.

"Would you protect me, Jasmine?" His smile said he found that a ludicrous idea, given that he was twice her size.

"I think you need someone to run interference. Mumtaz and Hiraz have trouble because they're not seen as royal." She was serious about her observations. "But I am. I could deal with most of what they came to you for, leaving you free to take care of bigger matters."

Tariq was ominously silent. She looked up to find him staring at her, his expression thoughtful.

"I mean, if you want me to." She was suddenly uncertain. A lifetime of never being good enough tended to overcome her efforts at self-confidence. "I know I'm a foreigner..." With a corner of her mind, she shoved aside the secret that threatened to float to the surface. She didn't want to think about that now, not when her husband was looking at her with eyes that held something close to tenderness.

Tariq stopped her with a finger on her lips. "You are my wife. I have told you that my people have accepted you as such. What about your designing?"

"I wanted to speak to you about that," she said. "Would my having business interests damage the royal image?"

He shook his head. "I have many such interests. You wish to develop your designs?"

"I was thinking of a small fashion house. One that markets to the retail sector, but has no shops of its own."

"You will do well." His answer was just a simple statement of confidence in her abilities, yet it filled her with immense joy. No one had ever believed in her.

"But, much as I'll miss not giving the majority of my time to design," she ventured, "I think it'll have to slip into second place."

"Second place?"

"As your wife, my place is here, with you." She didn't

betray the love driving her decision. Until she was sure of Tariq's feelings for her, she'd keep that beautiful emotion to herself. Another rebuff, even a gentle one, would tear her to pieces. "My designing will have to be like your painting. Something I do for myself, after serving our people." It was a sacrifice, but one she made willingly. By marrying Tariq, she'd accepted that the country's needs would sometimes come before her own. And Tariq needed a partner who could bear some of the many duties of a leader.

Approval glimmered in his eyes. She was encouraged. It was time for her to grow up and accept the responsibilities that came with being the sheik's wife. He hadn't pushed her, allowing her to do as she wished, but her place was with him.

"If you wish to do this, then I accept."

Jasmine smiled and leaned closer. The slight tensing of his body was his only response. By the time they got to her workroom, he was relaxed again. She frowned in thought.

"I'll work here," Tariq announced.

She looked up, her introspection momentarily interrupted. Tariq was gesturing to the semicircle of windows in the southern end of the room. The light was brilliant in that corner. She nodded and helped him set up.

"Now, you'll recline on this."

Jasmine dutifully stretched out on the plush red chaise longue that he'd dragged opposite his easel. Before beginning to paint, he put a cushion under her elbow to prop her up. She knew that he never bothered with sketches, preferring a light watercolor outline on the canvas itself.

He was, she thought with pride, very, very talented. She cherished the tiny painting that he'd given her a month before they'd separated. It was a Zulheil seascape that he'd painted from memory to show her his homeland.

"You're frowning."

She smiled. "Better?"

"Hmm."

For some reason, his masculine murmur reminded her of her earlier thoughts. Tariq appeared to find physical affection from her somewhat disconcerting. No, perhaps that wasn't the right word, she thought, stopping herself from frowning again. It was more that he seemed to be taken by surprise. He didn't reject her touches, he just didn't seem to expect them. She carefully thought back over the past weeks, and then over the six months they'd spent together four years ago.

Tariq had always loved touching her. Though a highly sensual man, he liked to touch as a gesture of tenderness as well. He'd been autocratic and reserved with everyone else, but with her, he'd been very affectionate. Conversely, she'd been used to the repressive formality of her own home. It had taken him months to make her comfortable enough in his presence to risk even the simple touches that he'd taken for granted.

"Mina." Tariq's disapproving look made her aware of her frown. She shot him another cheerful smile and waited for him to return to his paints. Once he did, she relaxed.

Since she'd come to Zulheil, he'd touched her often. For the first turbulent weeks, it had mostly been sexual and erotic. She'd understood that he wasn't ready to trust her with his affection. But in Zeina, it had been like being in heaven. After spending so much time pressed together on the back of a camel, their casual touching had merged seamlessly into their lives.

However, since his trip to Paris, their tiny instinctive gestures of togetherness had disappeared. Now it seemed that Tariq was controlling the intensity of their lovemaking. Though he made love to her without fail, and took care to make sure that she always reached her peak, something was missing. The heady eroticism of their earlier encounters had been dampened.

Why? Jasmine asked herself. Why would he seek to limit their sensuality, the one place where they'd always been in perfect accord? Surely he wasn't holding against her the fact that she hadn't welcomed him with open arms the minute he'd returned? She almost shook her head to dismiss that idea.

Tariq had apologized to her in his own way, she was sure of that. They'd made their peace.

Then why? The answer flitted just out of her reach.

"That is enough for now, Jasmine."

Nine

Startled, Jasmine blinked. Only when she attempted to get up did she comprehend how long she'd been in the reclining position. Reaching over her head with her hands, she stretched in a luxurious curve, feeling muscle after muscle relax.

"I'm going to head off to the shower. See you at dinner," she murmured.

Tariq looked up. Desire burst into life in the green fire of his eyes. He stifled it almost as soon as it arose, but answering heat rushed over her in reaction to that single searing glance. So, his passion ran as deep as ever. He'd just decided to hide it from her. Relief that he wasn't truly indifferent to her made her almost dizzy.

"But why would the thought of a shower set it off?" Jasmine muttered to herself. She was in the shower before she figured it out. "Idiot." She laughed at herself. Tariq was the man who'd made love to her in front of a mirror. The sultry possibilities presented by soap and water would be tantalizing to him. They were already affecting her.

It stunned her that she wanted to be in a shower with her husband. She could imagine the darkness of his hand against her sudsy skin, and almost feel his big body pressing her against the wall. As a result of her imaginings, she stepped out of the shower hotter than when she'd entered. Her predinner preparations were undertaken in a state of sexual anticipation.

"I have to entice him into a shower with me," she decided. "Otherwise this fantasy is going to drive me crazy." She would much rather be driven crazy by Tariq himself.

Midway through brushing blush onto her cheekbones, she paused, hit by a thought that she'd earlier rejected as implausible. Her hair was already secured on top of her head in an elegant knot, with a few loose tendrils around her face. Those tendrils now framed her startled eyes.

"What if he thinks our passion doesn't affect me with the same power it does him?" One simple fact that she'd always known was that her husband desired her deeply. His hunger was palpable, or it had been until he'd begun to withdraw. Even at his angriest, Tariq had made love to her until she screamed. She tapped her nails on the wood of her dresser in a staccato beat. "I did manage to resist him after Paris, but that was because I was hurting so much, and even then…he could've seduced me if he'd stayed another minute."

However, Tariq didn't know that. To him, it would appear as if her need was nowhere near the strength of his. To a warrior like him, that would be a blow. It wouldn't just affect his masculine pride, but would be hurtful. He stubbornly refused to believe in her love, but he'd accepted her passion as real and unfeigned. Jasmine wondered what it would be like if someday she began to believe that Tariq didn't want her with the same fervor that she needed him. It would rock the one solid foundation in their relationship.

"Goodness." Her eyes widened in the mirror, bright with realization. "I have to convince him that I want him, or he'll just continue to withdraw and I won't even have our passion to build on." However, the idea of seducing her husband was daunting. He tended to take charge in bed, and his control was amazing. It was annoying, too. If she was going to lose control, then he could damn well do so, too.

"Hmph. Any ideas?" she asked her reflection.

"Do you always talk to yourself?" The amused question had her spinning around in her seat. Tariq lounged in the doorway between their rooms. For a second, she thought he might have heard too much, but his expression was the by-now-familiar warm and extremely irritating one.

"It's good for the soul," she quipped. Out of habit, she went to secure the tie on her robe. Then she noticed the way he was looking at her under his eyelids. If she hadn't been concentrating, she would have missed it. She changed direction, picked up the blush again and turned to the mirror.

When she leaned forward, she was well aware that her robe parted in the middle, offering an enticing view of the rounded curves of her breasts. Or at least she hoped it was enticing. It would kill her if the reason for him keeping his distance was that he no longer found her sexually compelling.

"Ridiculous," she muttered. Tariq's fires were the kind that would burn forever. That was what made him so precious.

"What is?" He moved to stand behind her, hands in the pockets of his slacks. While he normally wore traditional garb, sometimes he preferred Western dress. Today he was wearing a blue silk shirt and black pants, the solid colors setting off his rugged masculine beauty in vivid relief.

Her nape prickled with awareness of his nearness, supremely sensitive to his presence. The urge to lean back and rest her head against his firm stomach was so enticing that she had to issue a firm reprimand to herself to behave. If she gave in now, her beautiful, arrogant, sexy husband would once again have her screaming in ecstasy while he remained in control.

With that thought to spur her along, she leaned forward a bit more. It seemed that a lot of seduction in her life went on in front of mirrors, she thought, in an effort to fight her anxiety over her sudden decision to seduce a man who'd proved so capable of controlling his physical passion. Ignoring the voice of fear, she crossed her legs in a movement that looked unconscious. As she'd expected, the robe parted over her thighs and slid off the leg on top, leaving her practically naked.

"Oh, I was just thinking about some of the recent designs on the catwalks." She waved airily and put down the brush, then picked up the lipstick. Curving her lips into a softer-than-normal pout, she began to smooth on the pale bronze with deliberate slowness. It was more of a gloss, which left her lips looking wet and full, rather than a rich hue. She knew her husband preferred to kiss her lips devoid of lipstick, and tonight was about her husband. By the time they got through dinner, the gloss would be gone, but she hoped that by then she wouldn't need its seductive qualities. Right now, the glistening sheen looked like a brazen invitation.

Tariq coughed and shifted behind her, but didn't move away. Jasmine took that as a good sign, but wondered how far she could go. She didn't want him to guess her plan before she had him safely in bed and at her mercy. She grinned.

"What is so funny?" His voice was rough. She recognized that timbre. Anticipatory heat blossomed in the pit of her stomach. Her heart's beat turned ragged and needy.

"Homosexual male designers and their ideas about the female body," she stated with a decisive nod, proud of herself for being able to keep her head while her hormones were in full riot mode. "I mean, look." She swept her hand over the curves of her breast and hip, lingering just a millisecond too long. "As we discussed before, women are rounded, right?"

"Yes." He sounded as if he was strangling.

"Then why—" she spread her hand on her bared thigh, drawing his attention to the way the fiery curls at the apex of her thighs were barely covered by the blue satin "—are the latest trends going toward boxes and flat, jagged edges?"

When he didn't reply, she looked up into the mirror. Before he met her eyes, she gleefully noted the flush along his cheekbones and the heavy-lidded gaze on her thigh. She thought he'd forgotten what they'd been talking about. Wonderful.

"I am sure you are correct in your view," he said at last.

Nodding in vigorous agreement, she returned to her makeup, aware that he was watching her in the mirror. Keeping a straight face was difficult, but her need to make him feel the same sensual hunger as her gave her the strength. She took her time finishing her makeup and then stood up and crossed to the wardrobe. To her pleased surprise, Tariq lay down on the bed to wait, his arms crossed behind his head. He reminded her of a lazy panther, all liquid muscle and barely contained strength.

Her scowl only surfaced once she was inside the closet. How was she supposed to seduce him with artless ease if he couldn't see her? The bed was placed parallel to the dresser and faced away from the closet behind it. That meant Tariq's eyes were on the bedroom door and she was behind the headboard. Frowning, she pulled an almost-sheer blue skirt off its hanger. The two thin layers of chiffon were just opaque enough for decency, and she'd never before worn the skirt, but today, it was war.

The matching top had tiny cap sleeves trimmed with fine silver braid, and was cut to fit snugly under her breasts, leaving her abdomen bare. She didn't bother to grab a bra because the top was tight enough, and every time she bent forward, the scoop neck would hint at that revealing fact. Walking out of the closet, she put her clothes down on a nearby chair. She almost shimmied into them in haste, before she suddenly understood exactly how sneaky Tariq was.

Far from not being able to see her, her husband had a perfect view of her in the mirror. Her hands went to the knot of her robe. She heard Tariq shift on her bed, and out of nowhere, a belated wave of nervousness hit her. Playing with him was one thing, but could she actually do a striptease?

Before she lost her courage, she undid the robe and shrugged it off. When she leaned forward to throw it across the top of the chair, she thought she heard Tariq's breath hitch. Her own wasn't too steady, but she kept going. She picked up her panties and forced herself to speak.

"Where are we having dinner?" Jasmine slid on the fragile creation of lace and satin, smoothing it over her bottom with fingers that trembled. She snatched them away before he could notice in the mirror, and grabbed the skirt.

Instead of dropping it over her head, she bent over to step into it. She could imagine the picture she presented, and it was making her blush. She hoped the dimness of the light near the closet concealed that betraying fact.

"I had thought the main dining room with Hiraz and Mumtaz, but I've changed my mind. We'll eat in our private dining area." Jasmine didn't miss the possessive edge in his voice. She hadn't heard it for two weeks. At one time, she'd believed it meant he thought of her as an object. She was beginning to understand that Tariq would always be possessive about his woman, even if he loved her. He was simply that kind of man. His possessiveness and protectiveness were traits that she could get used to, she decided. In fact, they made her feel almost cherished.

"Hmm." She buttoned her skirt at the side, picked up the top and turned a little so that her breasts were displayed to him, though her face remained in shadow. She decided that she deserved a medal for bravery. Who would have believed that shy, quiet Jasmine would be trying to entice her virile, sexy husband with such an audacious exhibition? Certainly not her.

The top buttoned down the front, so she slipped it on and then did up the row of five tiny buttons made of white crystal. It was unexpectedly tight across her breasts, which surprised her. However, when she looked down, the line of buttons wasn't distorted, so it appeared that the design required that final snug fit.

Finally, she stepped into a pair of Arabian sandals that she could easily shuck off. Their private dining area was in essence a room full of huge cushions.

"Almost finished." She was thankful that the breathy quality in her voice wasn't too evident.

"There's no hurry." He sounded at ease.

Jasmine wondered if she was mistaken and he hadn't been watching. Walking over to stand beside the bed, she put her hands on her hips and twirled around.

"What do you think?"

He unobtrusively bent his leg at the knee, but wasn't quick enough to hide the arousal straining against the material of his pants. She swallowed a sigh of relief.

"Perfect." His mild tone didn't fool her.

"Hmm, but I think I need some jewelry."

The stroll to her dresser took every ounce of nonchalance she possessed. She didn't even glance in the mirror to check her appearance, not wishing to meet Tariq's eyes and give herself away by accident. From inside the built-in jewelry drawer, she pulled out the fine gold chains that she'd looped over her hips on her wedding day, and put them on. Then she clasped a necklace around her neck. It was pretty but unremarkable, except for the fact that the long spherical Zulheil Rose pendant fell between the globes of her breasts.

"Come on, lazybones, I'm starving." She beckoned to him and pushed through the connecting door to his room. She could have reached the dining room through the corridor, but she couldn't resist the temptation of leading him past the huge double bed. The one in her room had never been used, except for the week that he'd been in Paris.

She heard him mutter, "Me, too," as he rose from the bed. His tone was distinctly bad tempered. She smiled. A starving panther was more to her liking than one attempting to play at being a pussycat.

Her hand was on the knob of the door that led into the dining area when Tariq gripped her waist. Burning heat sizzled through her nerve endings where his hands touched bare skin. His big body pressed her against the door.

"You will wait here while the servants finish."

"It's okay, I don't mind helping them."

His fingers tightened on her skin. "You *will* wait here." Spinning her around, he sealed her next protest with a hard kiss. Giving her a warning glance, he opened the door. It shut with a click behind him.

Jasmine lifted her hands to her tingling lips. He hadn't kissed her like that for weeks. She leaned against the wall because her knees felt as if they'd crumple at any moment. The imprint of his hands on her waist was a living touch that continued to burn her skin.

"I guess I can put up with the arrogance this once," she said out loud, a smile wreathing her face. But she couldn't figure out why he hadn't let her enter the room. Then she happened to glance at the mirror. Her jaw dropped.

She almost ran into the other room to cover herself. The skirt wasn't *almost* sheer. It was absolutely, utterly, scandalously sheer. The outline of her legs was visible with stark clarity, and when she moved, the cloth revealed more than it hid. To make matters worse, the lace front panel of her flimsy panties didn't exactly hide anything, either. The gauzy blue of her skirt granted any watcher blatant hints of the dark red curls at the juncture of her thighs.

The top, which she'd thought sexy but not too revealing, was outrageous in its eroticism. The fabric hugged her breasts with loving care, outlining them with clear precision; her nipples were visible, shameless points of desire against the thin silk. The tightness of the top controlled her breasts, but it also lovingly plumped them up. Soft, white flesh overflowed the neckline.

"Oh my God." She clutched at the wall behind her. No wonder Tariq had forbidden her from entering the other room. She looked like a houri. She felt like a woman dressed to please her master in any way he chose. A wave of apprehension hit her. In desperation, she took a deep breath. In and out. In and out. The added oxygen must have revived her brain cells, because a bright ray of hope stood out from the chaos in her mind.

"He didn't tell me to change," she whispered. "In fact, he said I looked perfect." If Tariq had been put off by her sexy outfit, he wouldn't have been so insistent on leaving her in his bedroom to wait, wouldn't have agreed on her choice, and surely wouldn't have kissed her.

Grinning, she skipped over to the huge bed and perched on the end, away from the mirror. She pasted a bored expression on her face just as Tariq opened the door. He stopped. She saw him swallow, and for once she knew exactly what her husband was thinking. He wanted to throw her on the bed and teach her not to tease him. Except he wasn't sure that she was teasing. And, Jasmine decided, he was too much in control if he could resist that primitive urge.

She jumped off the bed and walked over. "Ready?"

He nodded but didn't seem to remember that he was blocking the door. Successfully fighting the urge to tease him, she pushed at his chest. He obediently moved aside to let her pass, then followed.

Once inside, he didn't take a cushion on the other side of the low table set with food. Instead, he sat down beside her, propping himself up with one hand flat on the cushion behind her. His shoulder and chest pressed against her and when she leaned back a little, his arm provided a hard masculine backrest.

Jasmine tried to steady her breathing, and picked up a plateful of small tarts of some kind. She offered the plate to Tariq. He lifted one dark eyebrow in invitation. With a blush she couldn't control, she picked up a tart and fed it to him. He almost caught her fingers on his second bite. Laughing, she pulled away just in time.

Her husband had a definite glint in his eye, but she was determined that she wouldn't be the only one losing control tonight. He was coming with her. However, attempting to ignore the way the panther by her side was throwing her body into chaos was proving to be difficult.

With a forced smile, she picked up a tart and took a bite. "I've never eaten anything like this." The savory pastry was spicy, with a hint of unfamiliar herbs, but delicious. To her surprise, Tariq reached out and filched the rest of it.

"Hey!" Surprise overcame her inner trembling.

"I told you I was hungry. Feed me quickly."

Jasmine told herself she was imagining the double entendre in his words—surely he hadn't meant that he was *hungry?* She was getting ahead of herself. She mock-scowled at him, but picked up a kebab and fed it to her sheik. He sprawled beside her, seemingly content to eat whatever she chose, as long as she offered it to him. Tariq had never done this before and Jasmine found that she enjoyed cosseting him. Today, for the first time, she'd begun to understand precisely how enormous his duties were. It made her want to fill his life with pleasure, so that those duties wouldn't burn out the bright light inside him, though that same light threatened to make her love for him impossibly stronger.

"I don't think I can eat dessert." Some time later, she put a hand on her stomach. It wasn't terribly full, but she was aware that she might be engaging in some strenuous exercise soon.

Tariq's eyes traveled in a slow journey from her lips to her breasts, to the curve of her stomach. This time she couldn't fight the glow that tinged her skin the color at the heart of Zulheil Rose. The instant he became aware of her response, he ran a finger across the top of her breasts. The fleeting caress made her feel weak and tingly inside.

"We'll leave it here." Tariq rose to his feet and held out a hand to help her up. "In case you get hungry later."

Jasmine almost stumbled when she caught the meaning of his husky words. However, when she looked up, she saw that he continued to exercise rigid control over his expression. If she surrendered now, she wouldn't be any closer to breaking through the sensual barriers between them than she'd been at the start of the evening.

What now? she thought, frantic at the prospect of failure. He wasn't aroused enough if he wasn't ripping off her clothes. She was sick of being gently undressed each night. She wanted her passionate, insatiable and teasing lover back. He led her into their bedroom, stopped by the bed and lifted his fingers to the buttons on her blouse.

Jasmine took a deep breath and pushed Tariq's hands away. They dropped at once, but he'd already half unbuttoned her blouse, leaving her breasts in imminent danger of falling out.

"You do not wish to proceed?" He was painfully correct in his speech.

"Tariq, would you grant me a boon?" The old-fashioned words seemed appropriate. She was dressed like a princess from a fairy tale, or perhaps a sensual goddess from myth, and in front of her stood a dark warrior she had to woo to her side or all would be lost.

"You do not have to ask a boon, Jasmine. I accept your desire not to…" He began to back away. Only the way he clenched his fists at his sides revealed his true feelings.

She gripped his shirt in desperate appeal. "I want you."

His hands went to her buttons again. She shook her head.

"What is it, Mina?" He sounded impatient, more like the lover she'd known before he'd started to withdraw. And he'd called her Mina.

"I just…" She bit her lip. "Would it be okay if I touched you tonight?" This time, she went for *his* buttons.

He groaned. "I've told you, touching me is permitted at any time."

"But I want you not to touch me."

"I do not understand." He was wary again.

"I lose my mind when you touch me, and for once I want to be able to explore you. Please?" She knew asking him to give her control was a risk. But if he said no, she'd just keep trying, she decided. He was already acting with more heat than he'd shown for the past two weeks. She undid the button she'd been toying with and moved on to the next one.

His hand touched her hair in a light caress before he pulled out the pins. The soft curls tumbled to her shoulders in a fiery waterfall. "And what am I to do while you…explore me?" She didn't miss either the slight hesitation or the abrasive roughness of his voice.

Ten

Jasmine undid another button. "Just lie back and enjoy it. I'll do all the work."

Silence filled the room, broken only with the sounds of their breathing. Jasmine bit her lip again and stopped herself from pleading.

"I'll allow you to do this." His hands settled on her exposed hips, his skin warm against hers.

Jasmine smiled and reached up on tiptoe to press a soft kiss to his lips. "Thank you."

He appeared startled by her open enjoyment of the situation, but was willing to do as she wished. She drew back and finished unbuttoning his shirt, then pulled the tails out of his pants to complete the task. His beautiful chest felt as hard as steel under her questing fingers. Delighted by the freedom to explore, she ran her fingernails down the center line of his chest. He sucked in a breath.

"I love your chest." She threw caution to the winds. "Every time I see you come out of the shower, I want to pull you into bed and kiss you everywhere.'' She moved her fingers to his flat male nipples and then ran her nails over both. His groan was music to her ears.

Emboldened by his response, she wrapped her arms around his rigid body and put her hands flat on his back. His skin was so hot it almost burned. Then she flicked her tongue over one of his nipples. His hand moved up her back to clench in her hair. Delighted, she continued to kiss his chest, alternating soft warm kisses with wet openmouthed ones. She kissed her way down to his abdomen until she was kneeling in front of him. When she reached the waistband of his pants, he tugged on her hair with innate gentleness and pulled her back up.

''Mina,'' he whispered, against her mouth. ''Have you had enough exploring?'' His voice was heavy, sensual, encouraging.

She gasped when he sucked her lower lip into his own mouth. He took his time kissing her, bestowing nibbling love bites on her lips before urging her to open. When she did, his tongue swept in and proceeded to taste her with arrogant thoroughness. It was a long, lazy kiss that left her feeling as if she belonged to him. When he released her, she shook her head, breathless and aroused. ''I've just begun.''

She trailed her fingers down the bare part of his arms. His golden skin strained to contain the pure strength of the muscles beneath. Lifting his hand to her mouth, she sucked one finger into the moist recesses. He released his breath in a forceful hiss. One by one, she sucked each of his fingers and then repeated the hot, sweet caress on his other hand, before moving to undo the buttons on the cuffs.

By the time she finished, Tariq's vivid green eyes echoed the perfect clarity of shattered emerald shards. ''Would you like this off?'' He motioned to his shirt.

''Yes.'' Walking behind him, she helped tug it off. The skin of his shoulders was hot and smooth. Jasmine molded her hands over them, captivated by the way they tensed.

The shirt fell to the floor. After pushing it aside with one foot, she shucked her slippers. When he would've turned, she wrapped her arms around his waist and plastered herself against him. "Stay. I want to touch your back." The shudder that went through him vibrated against her sensitive nipples and reached deep within. It was as if a part of Tariq was inside her, touching her in the most intimate way.

Pressing her palms against his chest, she drew back just far enough to appreciate the sculpted planes of his back. Muscles moved like liquid steel under his skin when he raised his hands and put them over her own.

"You're so strong." She blew a warm breath onto his skin, entranced by the way he groaned and leaned backward. His reaction was the strongest of aphrodisiacs. "So beautiful."

His chuckle was hoarse. "It is you who are beautiful. I am a man."

She bit him just under his shoulder blade. "Absolutely, utterly beautiful."

He squeezed her fingers. "I am pleased you find me beautiful, Mina. However, you are not to tell this to anyone."

Jasmine laughed at the mock warning and tugged her fingers from his grasp. Once free, she began to trace the defined muscles of his back with slow deliberation. His breathing hitched, then restarted in a shallower rhythm.

"Would it damage your reputation as a tough, macho sheik?" She began to kiss her way down his spine. Her half-exposed breasts pressed against him, exciting her as much as she hoped the contact was stimulating him.

He took a deep breath. "I do not know this word *macho*."

She started to undo the remaining buttons of her blouse, while continuing to caress his back, pressing urgent kisses against his slightly salty skin. "Macho means you." She grazed his ribs with sharp little teeth. "Strong, manly, very masculine." The blouse came undone. She pulled it off her shoulders and then licked her way back up his spine with her tongue. There was a swish as the blouse fell behind her. Her mind spinning with the extravagant sensuality of the moment, she plastered herself against him once more.

Electricity sizzled between them as skin touched skin.

Tariq's groan was a rumble deep in his throat. Sensing that her panther was reaching the end of his tether, she moved to stand in front of him. Her lover's expression was devoid of disguise, his eyes so dark they were almost black, his desire etched in stark lines.

Aroused beyond bearing, Tariq had to touch Mina. He raised one hand and cupped the warm weight of one breast. She gasped and her fingers pressed into his chest.

"No, please." It was a husky whisper, a sensual plea.

"You will kill me with this exploring, Mina." He picked her up and put her on the bed, aching to claim her. The disappointment that flickered in her eyes at having her exploration cut short fanned the flames of his passion as nothing else could have done. Keeping his eyes on her body, he kicked off his shoes and unzipped his pants.

"Yes?" He paused, waiting for her instruction.

Eyes wide, she nodded.

He peeled off his underwear with his pants. Jasmine stunned him by reaching out and trailing her finger down the length of his erection. His body was racked with tremors. "Move aside, Mina, or I will be on top of you and this will end."

She shifted with an alacrity that made him feel like the most desired of men.

He lay down on the bed on his back, his arms folded under his head. "I think you have about five more minutes," he warned, his gaze skating possessively over her body. He'd thought he could manage the beast inside him, dictate what he felt for this woman, but all he'd done was starve himself. The weeks of enforced calm disintegrated, and the primitive urge to take Mina ate away at his control.

As he watched, Jasmine straddled his thighs. Her gauzy skirts settled around them like curtains of mist.

"In that case, I'll get right to the crux of the matter." Without warning, she wrapped her fingers around his erection.

Swamped with ecstasy, Tariq growled low in his throat and pushed into her hands. Her fingers were delicate and feminine around him, her expression utterly fascinated. Seduced by her delight in his body, he surrendered and let his wife have her way with him.

Encouraged by Tariq's unhidden enjoyment, Jasmine increased the pressure and began to move her hand up and down. Velvet over steel. Burning fire and searing heat. A soft moan escaped her lips. She could feel herself being seduced by his reactions. Tariq's face was a study in raw passion. His cheekbones stood out against his flushed skin and his teeth were gritted against the pleasure. Aching with the need to give him more, to give him everything, she dipped her head and replaced her hands with her mouth.

Tariq's thighs went as hard as rock under her. He jerked up into a sitting position and clenched his hands in her hair. When he shuddered under her inexpert caresses, Jasmine's fear of not pleasing him evaporated. Exhilarated by his hoarse cries, she settled into the task she'd set herself.

Mina's attentive exploration snapped the threads of Tariq's control. "Enough." He pulled her up, his hands rough.

Her heavy-lidded, passion-hot face inflamed him further. With another throaty groan, he hauled her up his body, until she was almost astride him. Then he reached under her skirt and found the lace of her panties. The sound of lace and satin ripping was drowned out by the loud panting of their breaths. Tariq threw aside the torn pieces and touched her with his fingers. Creamy heat welcomed him.

"You're so wet, Mina." His voice shook with the discovery.

Sensitized beyond bearing by their erotic play, Jasmine moved demandingly against his fingers. "Now. Now!"

Tariq didn't argue, sliding her onto his hard length. He was too slow for her. She gripped his sweat-slick shoulders and pushed down, surprising him. He lodged to the hilt inside her and groaned in satisfaction. She saw the look on his face and knew that this time, her lover would be coming with her on the incandescent final ride. He had, after all, ripped off her clothing. With a smile, she gave in and rode him to surrender.

* * *

Tariq drew a line down Jasmine's breastbone with his finger. She squirmed under the light caress. Tariq let her capture his hand in her own and place it over her heart. She was almost asleep, apparently exhausted by their wild mating.

"You were aroused just by touching me," he commented.

"Tariq," she murmured, her cheeks red.

"So shy now?"

Opening her eyes, she made a face at him. "Tease." But she wriggled closer and wrapped her arms around him.

He stroked her back, as if petting a cat. "Always?" Under his hand, she was warm and smooth.

"What?" she asked sleepily, burrowing into his chest.

"Are you always aroused by touching me?" he persisted, even as he cuddled her close to him. The need he'd hidden deep within rebelled against being ignored any longer.

Eyes closed and body relaxed almost totally, Jasmine muttered, "I get aroused just by looking at you. It's because I love you. Now go to sleep."

"Mina, when you touch me like that, I could almost believe you." He knew she didn't hear him, because she'd already fallen asleep. Stroking her hair off her face, he wondered if she would remember her declaration tomorrow. It didn't matter, because he would. The fist that had been clenched around his heart loosened. Maybe being unable to control his feelings wasn't the disaster he'd thought. Not if this was the outcome.

While she slept, Tariq couldn't help but compare the woman he'd seen over the past week to the girl to whom he'd given his heart, only to have it rejected. In his arms, she was fire, unafraid of her sensuality. Yet in the desert, though her persistence had angered him, she hadn't given up probing for the truth of the past. The autocratic part of him that expected instant obedience bristled at her audacity. But there was a bigger part of him that was awed by her feminine strength. This was a woman with whom he could rule.

Since Paris, he'd wanted to take a chance on his wife. Tempted by the promise of the last few days, he found that the urge to let his barriers fall was almost irresistible. He wanted to give her his trust. Except the last time he'd done that, she'd almost destroyed him. Did he dare to try again, even knowing that she still hid something from him?

She had her panther back.

"You will follow my orders. You will not venture into Zulheina today." Tariq slammed the flat of his palm on his desk, the sound as loud as a pistol shot in the quiet study.

Jasmine put her hands on her hips and scowled. "Why not? I've always been able to do so before."

"I have given an order. I expect it to be obeyed."

She blew out a breath through pursed lips. And she'd wanted this fiery, hot-tempered creature to come back? "I'm not a servant to be given a command!" She lost her temper for the first time. After the powerful intimacy of the last few days, he could act with a tad more consideration. "Give me an explanation that makes sense and I'll stay."

Tariq stalked around his desk and put his hands on her waist. Then he picked her up until they were eye to eye. Her feet dangled off the floor. Jasmine placed her hands on his shoulders and refused to be intimidated.

"Has a terrorist organization infiltrated Zulheina?" she guessed wildly. "No, I've got it. Today is the annual Kill-the-redhead Festival. No, no wait, is it Tariq-is-going-to-act-like-a-dictator Day? Am I right? Come on, am I even close?" She pushed at his shoulders, furious at the way he was demonstrating his greater strength.

His shoulders started to shake. She squinted at his face. "Arrgh! Let me go, you... No, I can't call you an animal because that would insult the animal." Tariq laughed harder, his eyes sparkling. "Stop it you...you husband!"

"Mina." His smile was blinding. "Mina, you're magnificent."

That made her pause. It had sounded like a compliment. She looked at him suspiciously. "Are you going to tell me?"

"It seems I have been insulted into submission."

"Hah! Your hide is as thick as a rhinoceros's. Anything I

say just rolls off,'' she muttered under her breath. ''Put me down.'' He wrapped his arms even tighter around her and walked through the door, into the corridor.

''Tariq, what are you doing?'' She glanced around, hoping against hope that no one else was around. His official study was in the main wing of the palace. ''My feet are bare. My slippers fell off when you picked me up.''

''Then it is just as well I am carrying you.'' His reply was insufferably male.

She gave up. Wrapping her arms more firmly around his neck, she hung on, realizing that he was taking them back to their rooms. ''Are you planning to lock me in our suite?''

He paused and then resumed his ground-eating stride. ''I had not thought of that. It is an excellent idea.''

Jasmine shook her head and tipped her head back, but she couldn't catch his eye. ''Bad idea. Very bad idea.'' When he didn't reply, she narrowed her eyes and tried to shake his shoulders. ''You wouldn't…would you?''

''I must have a way to deal with the bad-tempered hellcat I've married.'' He pushed through the doorway to their suite and headed for their bedroom.

''Bad tempered!'' She scowled. ''Me? I think you've got your wires crossed.''

''At least it's not my eyes.''

''Eyes? What…I can't believe it. You made a joke?'' She gave a theatrical gasp that turned into a cry of surprise when he dropped her onto the bed. ''Be still my heart.''

Tactile pleasure shimmered over her when he lowered his body full-length over hers. He started to stroke her with his talented hands. ''Is this supposed to be a distraction?'' she demanded.

''Would it be successful as one?''

''Oh, yes,'' she sighed. ''But tell me the truth, please?''

''Persistent little creature,'' he complained, but his tone was affectionate. His eyes were heavy with sensual promise when he looked at her. ''Today is the festival…''

Jasmine's giggles caught her completely by surprise. Tariq

tried to frown her into submission. When that didn't work, he kissed her until she was boneless.

"As I was saying, it is the festival of the virgins." He kissed the side of her neck. "If you'd arrived a few weeks later, you could have joined it. No, that's a lie. You would not have remained a virgin long enough. I almost took you in the car as it was."

"Stop that," she ordered.

"What?"

"Making me crazy."

"I like making you crazy." Satisfaction simmered in those green depths when she shivered under his stroking. His lips curved into a grin.

Jasmine didn't know what to do with him in this mood. In the end, she decided that the safest option was to ignore the gleam in his eye and bask in his attention.

"So tell me." She traced a design over his chest with her fingertip, enjoying touching him through the fine linen. Tariq had never once curtailed her sensual explorations after she'd shown him just how much she adored his body.

"It's a day when female virgins of a certain age make a pilgrimage to a sacred place."

"Where?"

He looked chagrined at her question. "No man knows."

Her interest was piqued. "Really?" At his nod she asked, "How old is this festival?"

"As old as Zulheil."

"And why couldn't I go outside?"

Tariq pressed his forehead to hers and spoke against her mouth. "If you would let me finish, Mina, I will tell you."

Jasmine pursed her lips and slanted him an encouraging look. He continued to speak against her mouth, lips on lips, sorely tempting her to open up.

"I do not know what they do and that is probably just as well. No man is allowed on the streets at the time."

Jasmine frowned, the question stuck at the back of her throat. Tariq read her mind.

"Patience, little hellcat. There is no danger because the married women go with them, including the policewomen."

She couldn't keep her mouth shut. "Policewomen? Zulheil allows its women such occupations?" Once more, the way the people of Zulheil guarded their privacy so zealously left her feeling at a loss. She had so much to learn. And a lifetime in which to learn it, she reminded herself, ignoring the dart of fear that threatened to ruin the moment. Tariq would trust her again and wouldn't denounce her when he discovered her illegitimacy. Maybe, her heart whispered, if she wanted his trust, she should begin by giving him hers?

"I have told you our women are cherished. We protect but do not cage." He ran his tongue over the line of her lips in a teasing stroke. The urge to surrender almost overcame her.

"Why couldn't I go then?"

"Because—" Tariq took advantage of her open mouth to sip from her lips "—aside from the virgins, only married women who have borne children or been married for five years can do so." He spread his fingers over her stomach in an unmistakable message. "When you have borne my child, then you may go."

Jasmine swallowed. The thought of bearing Tariq's child was a dream she hadn't dared consider. And still couldn't, so long as she hid the truth of her own birth. She had to tell him. But not now, not when he sounded as if he cared for her. "How do you stop foreigners from disturbing the pilgrimage?"

"Zulheil annually closes its borders the week prior to this journey. Those already inside have visas that expire that same week. Recalcitrant visitors are escorted out."

"You closed your borders after your parents passed away, didn't you?" She'd spoken without thinking, but as soon as the words were out, she braced herself. Tariq had remained staunch in his refusal to talk about his loss.

He kissed her. It was a gentle kiss full of warmth, but without overt sexual overtones. Jasmine returned the caress, though she didn't understand what was happening.

"Yes," he whispered into her mouth. "For two months, Zulheil was closed to foreigners. Our people needed to come to terms with the grief and I needed time to heal the fractures."

"Two months? Don't you mean one?" Jasmine stroked his cheek. She wanted to cry with joy. He was trusting her with something important, something that had hurt him to the core. "I came one month afterward, remember?"

Eleven

Tariq's lips curved in a smile. "You were granted a very
special visa."

She stopped breathing. "You knew. You knew all along
that I was coming."

He shrugged. "I am the Sheik of Zulheil. I knew. Why did
you come then?"

It was the one question that he hadn't asked before, and the
one that she couldn't answer without giving away almost everything. Jasmine stroked her fingers into his hair and knew
she'd tell him the truth. Four years ago she'd been a coward
and it had cost her his love. Perhaps she could win it back
with bravery. There would be no more hiding the strongest
emotion in her heart because she was afraid of being rejected.

"I came because I heard about your loss and I thought that
maybe you might need me." Tariq's body tensed against hers.
She understood his silent rejection of the thought of needing
her. He wasn't ready to make himself that vulnerable. Perhaps
he never would be, his pride having been savaged too badly

the first time. She swallowed the feelings of hopelessness and continued. "But more than that, I needed *you*. I'd already decided to come long before. I'd laid the groundwork."

"Why, Mina?" His eyes were dark and impenetrable. His fingers dug into the soft skin of her upper arms hard enough to leave bruises, but she was heartened. If he cared enough to lose control over his strength, then she had to have a chance.

She felt tears rise in her eyes. "Because I couldn't live without you anymore. I just couldn't bear it. I woke up each day thinking of you and fell asleep with your name on my lips. I love you so much, Tariq, you can't even imagine."

He didn't answer in words. His kiss was tender and almost forgiving. She didn't force the issue. It would take time to heal the wounds of the past, but she hoped her bravery would buy her that time.

Tariq rolled onto his back and fitted her to his side. "I miss them."

Jasmine took a deep breath and just let him speak.

"I was brought up with knowledge of the responsibilities that awaited me, but my parents made sure I had a childhood and a relatively free young adulthood." He cuddled her closer, as if needing her warmth. "I traveled and I learned. I was given a chance to grow into a man without being shaped by my role. For that, I'll always be in debt to my parents. Any child of ours will have the same chance."

"They sound like they were wonderful people," she dared to murmur, though not wanting to break this fragile rapport.

"They were." He paused, as if debating whether to continue. His next words shocked her to the core. "My mother was dying and she did not tell me."

Jasmine sucked in a breath. "Dying?"

"Cancer." His voice was harsh. "They were on their way back from a treatment when the crash occurred."

Unable to imagine the depth of his suffering, she blinked back tears and asked, "Do you blame her for their deaths?"

He shook his head. "I blame her for not trusting me, for stealing my chance to try to help her. And to say goodbye."

"She was protecting her son." Jasmine understood his mother's actions instinctively, but she could also understand her warrior's pain. His mother's secrecy had rendered him helpless and he would hate that feeling. "It wasn't about trust. It was about a mother's love."

"I have almost come to accept that, but part of me remains angry with her for making the choice for me. Perhaps there was something I could have done. Now I will never know." His voice was haunted. "When they died, I was ready to assume my duties, but not to lose my parents. I felt adrift, lost emotionally. You have to understand, I was an only child, and despite close friendships, no one except my parents understood the demands of our position in this land.

"We are the rulers and guardians of our people. It's an honor and the gravest of responsibilities. For my people I had to be strong, but I felt as if I was enclosed in a cave of ice, unable to feel, until…"

"Until?" She held her breath, waiting for words that she knew might never come, but couldn't help hoping for.

"Nothing." Quick as lightning, he changed their positions, so that she was pressed under him.

She didn't protest. He'd given her far more than she'd expected. His mother's secret explained so much. It hurt Jasmine to think what damage it would have done to the proud and loyal man she'd married, to know that his mother had not trusted him with the truth of her health. Her reasons had been born out of love, but they'd wounded her son. Jasmine bit her lip, unable to escape the inevitable conclusion. What would her cowardice in keeping her secret cost him?

It was her last thought before Tariq pulled her into the heat of his passion.

Tariq held Mina in his arms after their loving, deeply affected by her confession of need. The raw honesty of it was undeniable, but it was hard to trust her completely. While he'd begun to let down his shields, his wife kept secrets that turned her blue eyes dark without warning. Though he'd vowed to have nothing but honesty between them, he wouldn't beg her for this secret. He wouldn't humble his pride for her. Not again. Never again.

He'd thought that she'd fallen asleep, but suddenly, she spoke, "I...have to tell you something."

Keeping his sudden tension from showing in his body was a struggle. He merely moved aside the hair covering her face from him. "Yes?"

She kept her eyes on the bedspread, her fingers playing with the embroidered swirls. "When we first met...I was so frightened of losing you. That's why I never told you."

"What?" He felt a mixture of hope and despair. Was she going to try and give him more excuses? He'd begun to believe that she'd matured, become someone he could trust, but that woman wouldn't try to ease her way with excuses.

"Promise me something first?" she asked.

It was the naked vulnerability of her voice that made his response gentle. "What would you have of me, Mina?"

"Don't hate me for this." Her tone was ragged, as if she no longer had any protective walls, and suddenly, he knew that there were going to be no excuses from this woman.

Hate her? Though he'd walked close to the line, he'd never hated Mina and couldn't imagine doing so. "On my word of honor as your husband." He gathered her closer, tenderness for her overwhelming him. He did not like to see her hurting.

On the sheets, her graceful hand clenched into a fist so tight that cream turned to white and tendons stood out across her wrist. "I'm illegitimate."

She'd given him no warning, no sign of the strength of her secret. "Illegitimate?" In his arms, she shivered. He reached over and covered them with a blanket, tucking her close to him, almost able to see her need to be touched.

"My...parents are really my aunt and uncle. My birth mother, Mary, had me when she was a teenager." Jasmine swallowed. "I found out when I was a child that my parents only adopted me because they received part of Mary's inheritance. They n-never loved me. To them I was...bad blood."

The words came out on top of each other, like a flood bursting its banks. Her fist loosened and then curled again.

Reaching out, he covered her hand and uncurled her fingers, smoothing them out. Her hurt was almost palpable. He'd never liked her parents, but at this instant he could have done physical violence to them. How dare they not treasure his wife, his precious Jasmine? "And you think this matters to me?" He was a little hurt by her distrust.

"You're a sheik. You should've married a princess or at least someone who can claim royal blood. I don't even know the name of the man who fathered me." Her breath was ragged.

That was shameful, he acknowledged, but the shame was not hers, *never* hers. The shame was of the man who'd given his seed to create this lovely woman and then walked away, of the woman who'd borne a child and abandoned her, and of the people who'd asked payment for the priceless gift of this woman.

"Look at me." He turned her in his arms. Jasmine raised her head and met his gaze, vulnerable but willing to face whatever he had to say. Pride in her courage burned in him. "Our people have barbarian roots. Chieftains still occasionally give in to the urge to carry off the women of their choice." He ran his finger over her lips, reminding her of his actions. "A desert male's choice is what is important. And I chose you to be my wife."

"You aren't angry that I didn't tell you?" Her blue eyes shimmered with moisture.

"Of course I'm not angry with you, my wife. I would that you had told me earlier, but I am not such a barbarian that I can't understand your reluctance." He kissed her again, knowing she needed to be physically reassured. Her body felt incredibly fragile under his hands, needing exquisite care.

When she started to relax, he asked, "Why didn't you tell me this when we first met?" Back then, he'd been open in his adoration of his flame-haired girl.

She bit her lip and took a deep breath. "I…just wanted…

I didn't expect Mary to keep me…but I thought after I was older she might want to get in touch. I wrote to her.'' She swallowed. ''She told me never to contact her again. I was…an indiscretion.'' Her breath had become ragged again, her tears barely held in check.

''Then you… I wanted to…to not be an outcast.'' Those eyes of hers brightened with tears, but his brave little Mina didn't let them fall. ''I just wanted to be accepted.''

He heard the important words in that emotional confession. ''Then have no fears. You are accepted. As my *wife,* Jasmine. What you were before only matters if you wish it to.'' Any hurt and anger he might have felt died a quick death under the overwhelming need to shelter her from further pain.

His Mina, his gentle, sensitive wife, had grown up in a place where she had not been nurtured, where her softness had been mocked. It made him furious that this lovely woman in his arms had suffered so much pain and rejection. Knowing what she'd been through, he could forgive her for trying to protect herself. And yet she'd told him her secret. She'd laid her heart at his feet, and then given him the weapons to destroy it. It was an offering of immense trust and courage, and he intended to treat it with the care it deserved.

Slowly, almost shyly, she wrapped her slender arms around his waist. ''Truly?'' At that soft sound, his heart clenched in a wave of tenderness as fierce as the desert sun.

''Are you saying that the Sheik of Zulheil would lie to you?'' He saw a tremulous smile edging her lips and was proud he could make her smile. Mina was his to care for.

''Maybe. If he thought it would get him his own way.'' Her voice was less teary, her smile wider.

He grinned at that. ''I think you are right, but in this thing, never doubt me. You are now equivalent to a queen. No one has the right to make you feel an outcast.'' He would destroy any man or woman who tried to make his Mina feel a lesser being. ''No one. Do you understand, my wife?''

Finally, she nodded, and her smile was glorious. Tariq kissed her, knowing that she'd just shattered the strongest barrier keeping him from loving her, heart and soul. How could he continue to fight his feelings for her, now that he knew what had driven her? How could he hurt his Mina as her family had hurt her, by not loving her as she needed to be loved?

Jasmine closed the door on the last guest of the day and headed to Tariq's study. Since she'd started to spend her days helping her husband, her pride in herself had grown. All her life she'd been told that she didn't measure up, but the people of Zulheil thought she was doing a fine job. And, she thought with a smile, the look in her husband's eyes as he helped her pick up the reins of royalty was magic itself.

"You are looking pleased with yourself."

"Tariq." Jasmine flowed into his arms. Her need to touch him grew daily. "I thought you'd be in your office."

"I have completed my work for today. You make my duties much easier to bear." He cupped her cheek and tipped up her face. His expression was unexpectedly serious. "You are not taking on too much, Jasmine? I would not have you become ill."

She smiled and turned her face into his palm. "Do I look ill or tired?"

He shook his head. "You glow like the crystal of this palace."

"That's because I've found a place where I can belong at last." She was struck by the truth of that statement.

Tariq didn't stop her when she began to walk toward their apartments. He slipped his fingers into hers and shortened his stride to accommodate her steady pace. The ageless beauty of the tapestries and carvings lining the hallway didn't hold her attention while her mind was on things past, but she was constantly aware of Tariq's protective presence. She led them out into the private garden behind their rooms.

"It's like the sun is smiling at the world." When she held out her hands, the thick yellow-orange sunlight shot through her fingers like warm, liquid satin. In the sky, red, orange and yellow vied for prime position in the soft pink glow of sunset, and all seemed at peace.

Tariq tucked a wayward strand of hair behind her ear. "You belong in the sun, Mina."

She turned and smiled at him. "I belong *here*."

"Yes." He curved his arm around her and cradled her against him. One arm around his back, she rested her head on his muscled chest. They didn't speak until there was more red than yellow in the sky and pink was segueing to violet.

"I know you did not feel you belonged in your parents' home. Was there any reason aside from your birth?"

The question was unexpected, but she welcomed the chance to make Tariq understand the girl she'd been. "I've never talked to you about this. I think I was afraid you'd begin to feel like everyone else."

"No one can control me, my Jasmine. Tell me."

She knew his words were supposed to comfort her, and to a certain extent, they did. However, they also reminded her of the divide that existed between them. Tariq was treating her like a partner as far as running Zulheil went, but in their personal relationship…would he ever trust her again?

"You know my sister Sarah is a stunning beauty." Sarah had the kind of beauty that made people stand in the streets and stare, something Sarah certainly knew. She'd been using her beauty her entire life to bewitch and control those around her. Even her parents could deny her nothing.

"She is cold. She does not have your fire," Tariq stated, as if it were a simple truth.

Jasmine's eyes widened. "Do you really think so?"

"A man would be a fool to be captured by the glitter of false gold, overlooking the quiet, ageless beauty of purity." He wasn't looking at her and Jasmine didn't know if his words were a compliment or merely a statement.

"Sarah never liked me. I don't know why, but it hurt so much when I was younger. She's my big sister and I wanted her to be my friend."

Tariq was compelled to ease the bewildered pain in Jasmine's voice. "She was jealous of you. I could see it when I first met her. As you grew older, you became competition, and Sarah is not one who would countenance such a thing."

Jasmine snorted. "Thanks for the flattery, but I'm nowhere near her in the beauty stakes."

He hugged her tightly. "Your fire burns not only in your hair but in your spirit. Your sister was aware that she would grow colder and colder until she felt nothing. She knew you would burn hotter with each passing year, your beauty growing apace with the unfurling of your wings." He hadn't meant to admit that much, wasn't sure enough of Jasmine to show her that she was gaining a foothold in his heart.

"That's the most wonderful thing anyone's ever said to me." The shimmering joy in her eyes soothed him. If letting Mina see that she mattered to him healed her hurts, then he would risk giving her this insight into his heart.

"Your sister…what is the word?…propositioned me, after I had made my interest in you clear." He frowned at the memory. "She placed her fingers on my chest."

Jasmine's eyes widened. "No."

"I found it distasteful. I simply removed her hand." Implicit was the fact that he'd chosen her over Sarah.

Jasmine remained silent for a moment, mulling over that information. It put a new slant on Sarah's utter viciousness while Tariq had been in New Zealand. She'd known that Sarah wanted Tariq, but not that he'd rejected her advances.

"Tell me the rest, Mina."

Still unsettled, she continued, needing him to know. Needing him to love her despite her flaws. "Because of Sarah and how my parents always took her side, I never felt like I fit there. Then there were Michael and Matthew."

"Your brothers hurt you?" Tariq's dangerously calm voice startled her.

"Oh, no. Michael's a certified genius. He's older than me, and spent most of his life in his lab or with his head in his books. He was kind to me when he remembered my existence. Matthew's just turned twenty-one. We were born…" she paused "...over a year apart. Matthew is the baby of the family. He's also a natural athlete. He's been studying in the United States on a football scholarship for the past three years."

"I don't see what you're trying to say." Tariq turned her around. She saw the frown on his face and knew that he was telling the truth.

"I was so ordinary." Even now, her childish fear that he'd begin to treat her as her family had lay like a malevolent shadow over her heart. "I sort of got lost among those three and their brilliance. I was just...me."

"Even in a crowd of a million people, Mina, you would stand out. I saw you with your family that first time and I saw only you." His voice was quiet but the words roared through her. "Your family did not appreciate your worth. It is good you came to me." With that, he folded her in his arms and dropped a kiss on her hair.

Seduced by his unexpected gentleness, she almost told him again that she loved him, but the part of her that needed so badly to be loved in return stopped her. She couldn't bear it if he ignored her, or worse, looked at her with puzzlement, because that was clearly not the nature of their relationship. As they stood there watching the sun set, a vague sense of impending wrongness worried her. She couldn't shake the feeling that she was going to lose Tariq.

However, as busy days drifted into sultry nights, her fears seemed to grow groundless and without substance, as airy as the desert wind. She convinced herself that she'd been imagining things, and stopped looking over her shoulder.

Days later, dressed in an ankle-length dress of pale green, her arms covered by full sleeves cuffed at the wrist, Jasmine circulated among Zulheil's people in the palace gardens, bathed in the fading evening light.

"Jasmine al eha Sheik." A touch on her elbow halted her.

She turned to smile at the elderly woman who'd stopped her. Absently, she made a note to ask Mumtaz exactly what

the address meant. More than one person had greeted her that
way this day. "Hello." She attempted Zulheil's native language.

The old woman's wrinkled face lit up. "You speak the language of Zulheil?" she asked in the same tongue.

Haltingly, Jasmine answered. "I try but...I am slow."

The woman patted her on the arm with the warm familiarity
that the people of Zulheil seemed to feel toward their rulers.
It was as if they were considered part of every single family
in the land. She found the easy acceptance wonderful.

"You are of Zulheil. Soon you will speak the language well.
My name is Haleah and I come from the farthest corner of
Zulheil."

"A long journey."

Haleah nodded and fixed her with a shrewd eye. "I was
sent to look at the new sheik's wife by the chieftain of our
tribe."

Jasmine knew from her visit to Zeina that Zulheil's system
of government was made up of a number of chieftains who
exercised local power. In turn, they'd sworn allegiance to their
sheik and followed his dictates with unswerving loyalty and
even fiercer dedication.

"And what will...you tell...them?" She continued to speak
in the beautiful lilting language of her sheik's land, not discomfited by learning the reason for Haleah's presence. For the
past month, she'd been on the receiving end of such scrutiny
from a number of messengers.

Haleah gave her a slow smile. "I will say that you have
hair like fire and eyes like the blue of the sea on our coast. I
will say your heart is open and that you will love our people
as you love our sheik."

Jasmine's composure fractured. "I...thank you."

Haleah squeezed her arm. "No. I bring you the gratitude of
my tribe for making our sheik feel happiness again. The sadness in his heart was felt keenly by all."

Jasmine bent and accepted the kiss on her cheek. Haleah

moved away with a wave, heading for the car that would take her back to her lodgings and then to her home.

A tug on her arm brought Jasmine around to face Mumtaz.

"As your advisor, I have some information." Mumtaz's eyes held an amused look.

"Spit it out," Jasmine said, easy in the presence of this woman who'd become her closest friend.

"Keep your eye on that one." Mumtaz nodded discreetly toward an exotically beautiful woman.

"Why?" Jasmine hadn't talked to the woman, but had admired the way she managed to dress demurely yet still look sexy.

"Hira's family is the most powerful one in Abraz and they wished for her to become Tariq's wife. She was also happy with the idea. Then you came. It does not hurt to know those who might bear you grudges." Mumtaz raised her brows and blended back into the gathering.

Though her confidence had grown since her marriage, Jasmine found it a shock to come face-to-face with her competition.

He'll forget you the minute some glamourpuss princess comes along.

Like a bad dream, her sister's contemptuous laughter whispered out of nowhere, perfectly describing Hira's lush sensuality. That same voice taunted that with women as stunning as Hira around, it was a wonder Tariq had married her at all. Love was a fool's dream. Jasmine gritted her teeth and fought off the ghosts. Tariq had married *her* and he wasn't a man who felt lightly.

Tariq watched Jasmine move about the garden. Her smile was bright and her grace unique. She was at home among his people, a confident woman, sure of herself. No hint remained of the needy child-woman who'd hurt him so badly that he'd had to return to his homeland to heal.

After her emotional confession, he'd made sure that she understood that she was accepted without question or hesitation. It had taken time, but his reward for patience had been seeing her faltering smile grow in brilliance. He was fascinated by her gentle blooming. Four years ago, she'd been a barely open bud who'd been badly mishandled, even by him. It was a hard thing to acknowledge, but he did it with the same ruthless honesty that made him a good leader.

He'd been older and emotionally far stronger. His wife's family had not nurtured the fragile confidence of his Jasmine, and as a result, she'd been easily bruised. He'd put pressure on a vulnerable eighteen-year-old to choose him against her family—an unfair choice. He could understand that childwoman's fears when faced with his arrogant demands, and even forgive her for the choice she'd made. And yet he couldn't deny that he still needed her to choose to fight for him, needed her to love him so much that fighting for him was the only choice she'd ever make.

The last time the choice had had to be made, her family had used her powerful need for acceptance to emotionally beat her into submission. Seeing this new Mina, he couldn't help but wonder whether, if the choice had to be made again, she'd stand firm and refuse to give him up.

Could it be so simple? The difference between the weakness of a child and the gentle strength of a woman? Perhaps he could chance trusting this lovely woman. This woman who quite simply took his breath away.

He planned to go to Sydney in a week, and this time, he decided, he wouldn't leave Mina behind. The woman his Jasmine had grown into deserved to be free. And she deserved his trust.

Seeing that she was having a quiet moment by the small reflection pool in the corner, he strode toward her.

"Why so quiet, my Jasmine?" Tariq's question was whispered against her ear.

"I'm amazed each time I realize that your people have accepted me." It was neither a lie nor the whole truth. Haleah's words had made her wonder just how obvious her love for

Tariq was. If his people could see it, why couldn't her husband?

The pensive look in his green eyes gentled. "You are my wife. There was never any question." He touched her lower back. "Now, tell me what is truly on your mind."

His perception startled her. "Hira."

His brows rose. "One of my advisors needs to learn discretion."

"She's my advisor now, thank you very much," Jasmine retorted. "I appreciate being in the know."

Tariq's eyes glinted with male amusement. "Gossip, you mean."

"Essential information." She smiled in return. "So?"

"How can women say so much in one word?" He squeezed her when she opened her mouth. "Hira's family wished a political match. I didn't."

The practicality of his words calmed Jasmine. "She's very beautiful."

"Beautiful women cause men only trouble." His eyes lingered on her, but it was the tenderness of his tone that made her heart stop beating.

Touched by the subtle compliment, she did something she rarely indulged in, unsure how Tariq would react. Reaching up on tiptoe, she dropped a quick kiss on the corner of his lips. "Ditto for outrageously handsome men."

His surprised laugh drew all eyes their way, bringing smiles to the faces of their audience. However, the royal couple weren't disturbed.

"What does Jasmine al eha Sheik mean?" she asked, since she had him to herself for a few minutes, and the hand curved over her hip told her he was quite happy to be there.

Tariq's smile held an unusual hint of mischief. "You will not like it, my independent little wife."

She tilted her head to the side, struck by his tone. Unless she prompted him, her husband was rarely so playful. "What?"

"The literal translation is 'Jasmine who belongs to the sheik.' The sheik's Jasmine. They know you're mine."

She smiled and shook her head. "They are as bad as you."

He shrugged, unrepentant. "It is an address of honor. If they had not liked you, they would have called you this." He rattled off an unfamiliar phrase.

"What does that mean?"

"It means, 'One who is married to the sheik.'"

She frowned. "What's wrong with that?"

"Strictly speaking, it is respectful, but if a sheik's wife is addressed as such, the people do not believe that she is the one who should stand by their ruler's side."

"How strange. Does that mean you're Sheik al eha Jasmine?"

Tariq grinned but didn't get a chance to answer, because at that moment, a couple interrupted them to say their farewells. Kanayal and Mezhael were ambassadors from another corner of Zulheil.

"I wish you good journey." Tariq's demeanor underwent a subtle change. He remained warm and approachable, but the mantle of authority settled around him like an invisible cloak. It made Jasmine aware of just how different he was with her when they were alone.

Kanayal bowed at the waist, approval on his face. Mezhael clasped her hands together and bent her head in respect.

"We will go back to Razarah with joyful news for our tribe." Kanayal's eyes rested briefly on Jasmine. "I will tell them of sunsets and blue skies."

"All is well in Razarah?"

Jasmine knew that Tariq's question was more an issue of protocol than real inquiry. This afternoon, when the ambassadors had arrived, they'd both been invited to a private meal with Tariq. Her husband had insisted that Jasmine attend, telling her that he valued her intuitive insights.

Kanayal's hazel eyes were warm. "All is well in Razarah."

"As always, you will be in our prayers." Mezhael's eyes met hers. "Jasmine al eha Sheik, I will sing for you."

Not understanding the undercurrent in Mezhael's statement, Jasmine nevertheless knew that it was offered as a compliment. She inclined her head, imitating Tariq's regal action without conscious thought. "Thank you. I wish you good journey."

When they left, Jasmine saw that they'd been the last guests. The others had drifted out, happy to communicate their goodbyes through Hiraz, Mumtaz or the other advisors scattered around.

"Come, I will answer your question in our suite."

"How did you know I was going to ask you a question?" She let Tariq lead her inside the palace.

"You always get a certain determined look in your eye. It is most disfiguring. You should stop asking questions."

"You're a horrible tease, you know that, don't you?" She was laughing, safe in the knowledge that he liked her curiosity and her desire to learn.

"I have you to tell me." Tariq tugged her inside their bedroom and closed the door. He pressed her against the door before running his hands over the smooth material of her dress. "Where are the buttons?"

Tariq's passion was so hot, Jasmine felt scorched. As a result of the inferno, they didn't get around to dinner until very late. Jasmine only remembered to ask her question when they were in bed. She turned in Tariq's embrace and propped herself up on his chest.

"Why would Mezhael sing for me?"

Tariq's eyes were hooded, his expression that of a sated panther. He ran his finger across the fullness of her lower lip. "The Song of Gifting is unique to Zulheil." His tone was indulgent as he explained. "As you know, our country follows the old ways. It is what sets us apart from our neighbors."

"The Song of Gifting." She mulled that information over, enjoying Tariq's lazy but affectionate exploration of her face. "So she's singing it as a gift?"

"No. She will sing it to ask for a gift for you."

Jasmine kissed his fingers when he stopped at her lips again. He smiled and carried on, trailing his fingertips across her cheek to trace the rim of one ear.

"What gift?"

The glint in his eye was the only warning she had. "A child. There will be many such songs sung across Zulheil in the coming weeks." Tariq chuckled at her gasp. "My people have decided that you are the woman to bear the next sheik."

"They don't waste time, do they?" She wriggled up his body until her lips were over his.

"You are young, Jasmine, and not yet with child. If you wish, we will wait."

They'd already lost so much time, Jasmine thought with a pang of old pain. "I may be young but I've always known that I would bear your child."

His expression was suddenly bleak. "Come, Mina. Love me and convince me of that truth."

She gave him everything she had, but somehow knew that it wasn't enough. Tariq needed something else from her, something that he'd never ask for and that she couldn't divine. She fell asleep with a lump in her heart. The fear that had been eating away at her returned in full force, haunting her dreams with premonitions of loss and suffering.

Twelve

"**Y**ou are not excited about this journey, my Jasmine?"

Jasmine turned her face from the airplane window. "Of course I am. Attending Australian Fashion Week will be a wonderful learning experience for me."

Tariq frowned. "Yet you seem preoccupied."

She bit her lip, thrown by his perceptiveness. "I guess I am a little. It's the first time you've let me leave Zulheil."

The hand he'd placed on her own tightened a fraction. "And you will return to Zulheil." His voice was hard, eliminating her misty dreams of trust.

"Yes." She would go wherever Tariq resided. "Will you be very busy with the energy conference?"

His face underwent a subtle change at her calm acceptance of his decree. However, the fact that he'd entertained even for a second the belief that she might defect, told her that deeper issues of trust and forgiveness lay buried within his heart. Even her agreeing to have his child had not rebuilt their broken bond.

"I'm sorry you cannot participate." His mouth twisted in a wry smile. "Zulheil may allow its women full participation, but most of the Arab states at this conference hold different views. Those who agree with Zulheil's approach are helping me to try and change the others' thinking, but progress is slow."

"And to challenge them openly with my presence at this juncture could well destroy everything that you've achieved?"

He threw her a quick grin. "Correct. Even though this conference involves the leaders of the Western world as well, including their women, our neighbors are the ones we must be careful of. I cannot afford to take a too-radical stance and alienate the massive powers that surround our borders."

She nodded, understanding the delicate balance he sought to maintain. "One step at a time. Perhaps by the time I'm fifty, I'll be able to chair such a conference," she joked.

Tariq didn't answer. When she turned her head, she found him staring at her. "What?"

"We will have been married for twenty-eight years by then."

"Goodness. I didn't even think of that."

"Then perhaps you should."

His enigmatic statement kept her company throughout the journey. They landed at Sydney Airport around 2:00 a.m. Going through customs, Jasmine confused her two passports.

"Sorry. This is the one you need." She handed over her newly issued Zulheil passport and put the other one away.

Tariq didn't say anything until they were in the limo on the way to the hotel. "Why did you bring both passports?"

Looking out at Sydney's lights, Jasmine replied absentmindedly, "The New Zealand one was in the pocket of my carry-on bag from when I entered Zulheil. I forgot all about it."

He didn't say anything further on the topic and came to sit beside her, teasing her for her open delight in the night scenery. She teased right back, but once in their hotel room, exhausted by the long flight, she fell into immediate slumber.

* * *

Tariq woke just before dawn. Mina was asleep, her head resting on his chest. He tangled his fingers in her glorious hair, feeling an urgent need to touch her, to appease the slowly healing creature inside him. He'd made the decision to trust Jasmine's loyalty on this trip, aware that she was no longer a teenage girl. What he hadn't counted on was his possessiveness and the frailty of this new accord between them. He'd needed his Mina to himself for a while longer.

He hadn't meant to snap at her on the plane, and had been immediately sorry that he had done it, seeing the hurt in her expressive eyes. But his generous wife had forgiven him. He would, he vowed, try to control his edgy possessiveness. It was not her fault that they were in this country, which had to remind her of her homeland. And it was not her fault that he was…afraid. Afraid that once again she'd make a choice that would shatter his soul. He hated that feeling.

Yet he couldn't have left her in Zulheil. It would have broken her tender heart if he'd forced her to remain behind—one more rejection on top of so many others. He touched her cheek and felt something deep inside him sigh in defeat.

Unbeknownst to her, his wife once more held his heart in her hands.

"I have tickets to most of the shows." Jasmine waved the pieces of paper in Tariq's direction. He stopped in the process of buttoning up his white shirt and stalked over.

"You will be accompanied by Jamar."

She stood up to finish buttoning his shirt. "He'll be bored stiff."

Tariq gripped her wrists, forcing her to meet his vivid green eyes. "I do not do this to clip your wings, Mina. You are the wife of the Sheik of Zulheil. There are those who would hurt you to reach me." His words were gentle.

She gasped in surprise. "I hadn't considered that. I guess I'm still not used to being your wife." She knew she'd said the wrong words the moment they left her mouth.

Tariq's jaw firmed into a determined line that she knew well, and his grip on her wrists suddenly felt like steel hand-cuffs. "That will never change, so get used to it." He dipped his head and took her lips in a profoundly possessive kiss, his body rigid against hers. "You belong to me."

She thought he was going to leave her with that image of distrust, wounding her. Instead, he turned at the door and walked back to her, his shoulders taut. "Mina." His eyes were dark and turbulent. The gentle touch of his finger on her cheek was an apology.

Carefully, she reached up and kissed him softly on the lips. "I know I am your wife, Tariq. I *know*."

He nodded, an expression in his eyes that she couldn't read. "Take care, wife. I would not lose you." Then he was gone, leaving her shaken by the power of that statement.

Whether it took place in Sydney or Melbourne, Australian Fashion Week was one of the biggest shows on the planet, full of every type of style, color and decadence. Jasmine was entranced, though she never forgot Tariq's words. Did love drive her husband's possessiveness, or something less beauti-ful? Her mind continuously went over the words.

However, she didn't have to worry about Jamar. Her mus-cled bodyguard enjoyed watching the women on the catwalks, if not the fashions. He was commenting on a curvy brunette when a hand on her shoulder made Jasmine cry out in surprise. Jamar moved so fast she didn't see him shift. Suddenly, his big bulk blocked her field of vision.

A throaty feminine laugh breached the barrier.

"Jamar, it's okay." Shocked, Jasmine pushed around his side when he refused to budge from his protective stance. "She's my sister."

"Hello, Jasmine," Sarah drawled.

"Sarah." Her sister's beauty seemed even brighter.

Sarah's mouth curved into a smile that was without warmth. "So, what's it like being part of a harem?"

After all these years, Tariq's revelation had given Jasmine an insight into her sister's cruelty. "I'm Tariq's wife."

Sarah didn't hide her surprise fast enough. A bitter look tinted her beautiful eyes for a second. "Well, well. Caught the big fish, after all." She looked over her shoulder. "It's been lovely but I must rush. Harry's probably looking for me."

Sarah turned and disappeared into the dimness beyond the lights of the catwalk before Jasmine could reply. The minute-long meeting left her feeling a confusing mix of emotions.

"She is not like you." Jamar moved to her side once more, his blunt features set in disapproving lines.

"No. She's beautiful."

"And icy. That one is cold."

Jamar's words reminded Jasmine of Tariq's statements. Suddenly, her heart felt lighter, more carefree. Her husband had chosen her. He thought she was good enough just as she was, and that was what mattered.

"How did the initial negotiations go?" Jasmine asked Tariq over dinner. She'd decided to eat in their suite, aware that he'd be craving some peace and quiet.

He ran his hand through his damp hair, having just showered. Under the terry-cloth robe that he'd thrown on to placate her sense of modesty, his tanned skin glowed with health. "It is as I expected. Those with oil wish to keep their position of power and are unwilling to look at alternatives."

"Isn't that short-sighted? Oil will eventually run out."

His eyes gleamed with intelligence. "Exactly. And it is not only money but our world that we must consider."

Jasmine reached across the table and touched his hand. "As an ex–New Zealander, I'd have to agree with you. Kiwis are very big on clean and green."

"Are you?" He trapped her hand beneath his.

"Am I what?"

"Are you an ex–New Zealander?"

She paused. "Aren't I? I thought after marrying you, I gained Zulheil citizenship?"

He nodded once. "Zulheil allows dual citizenship."

"I didn't know that." She smiled. "My heart belongs to you and your land, Tariq. It's home."

He began to rub his thumb in tiny circles across her wrist. "You have no wish to return to your family?"

She knew her smile was a little sad. Even though they'd hurt her so much, they were her family. A lifetime couldn't be easily dismissed. "I saw Sarah today."

"Your sister is well?" His question was innocuous, but his eyes were alert.

She shrugged. "You know Sarah."

He didn't say anything, simply watched her face with eyes that seemed to see through to her soul. When he stood and came around the table, she was ready for him. That night, his lovemaking was tender and careful, as if he was trying to soothe her hurt. She forgot Sarah's barbs with his first touch, her heart overflowing with love for her desert warrior.

Her grip on her husband's strong body was fierce, her loving equally tender, his comments at dinner having given her an insight into his mind. Her husband had been afraid that she'd be tempted by the proximity of her country of birth. He didn't know that Zulheil was the only place that she truly thought of as home, and only because it was his land.

Jasmine spent most of the next day shopping for gifts. Jamar tagged along like a good-natured, if extremely large, puppy, even offering suggestions on prospective purchases.

"Your sister is approaching us," he stated suddenly.

Jasmine looked up in surprise. Sure enough, Sarah was making her way through the small boutique in Darling Harbour.

"How about lunch, little sister?" For once, there was no sarcasm or bitterness in her words, and Jasmine couldn't resist the invitation. Old habits were hard to break and this hint of an olive branch from an always-unapproachable sister was too good to pass up.

Before they reached the car, Sarah asked her if they could

stop in at a travel agency. "Have to pick up some tickets."
She smiled and wiggled her fingers at Jamar.

The bodyguard, who'd been hanging back, moved closer.

Jasmine smiled at him. "We're just going to stop by a travel
agent's office. Can you tell the driver?"

Jamar frowned but did as she asked, taking the front passenger seat, while Jasmine sat in the back with Sarah. As the
vehicle was a courtesy provided by the Australian government,
there was no glass partition between the two compartments.
Mindful of that, Jasmine kept her voice down as she chatted
with Sarah, catching up. When she admitted to missing her
family, Sarah said, rather loudly, "So, when do you want to
leave for New Zealand? I'll book your ticket right now."

Jasmine responded in a quieter tone. "I'll see if Tariq has
some free time after the conference." She wondered if she
could convince her husband to return to the place where they'd
hurt each other so much.

To her surprise, lunch was pleasant. Starved for news about
her family, she drank in every one of Sarah's words. "Thank
you," she said, after paying the bill for both their meals. "I
needed to know about everyone."

Sarah smiled slowly. "Perhaps we'll see each other again.
We're both adults now."

Jasmine nodded. She was no longer the naive girl she'd
once been, and it seemed her sister respected that. And maybe
after marrying Boston blue-blood Harrison Bentley, Sarah had
matured and forgotten her spiteful anger toward Tariq.

Jasmine had no premonition of the sheer wrongness of her
belief until late that night.

She was in the shower when Tariq returned sometime after
eight. When she walked out into the bedroom, wrapped in a
towel, she found him waiting for her, eyes glittering with what
she immediately recognized as unadulterated rage.

"Tariq? What is it?" She froze, suddenly afraid.

He remained on the other side of the room, his big body

held tightly in check. "Did you have fun laughing at me, Jasmine?" His quiet voice vibrated with anger.

"W-what are you talking about?"

"Such innocence! And to think I'd believed you'd changed."

He raked her body with eyes that were so angry, she didn't want him anywhere near her. At the same time, it hurt that he stayed as far as physically possible from her.

"Unfortunately, your sister gave away your plans."

Her head jerked up. "What plans?"

"Your sister commiserated with me over your desertion. She said I had to understand that you could not bring yourself to marry a man like me."

Shocked, Jasmine just stared. When he ripped something out of his pocket and threw it against her chest, she didn't move to get it.

"You did not tell her I was your husband! What were you planning to do after you left? File for divorce, or just ignore your Zulheil marriage?" The sharp pain in his voice cut her.

Sarah had done this, Jasmine thought dully. But she wouldn't win. Her lie was too enormous, too unbelievable. Surely Tariq would see the truth. He *knew* Sarah. "I'm not planning on leaving you. She lied."

He looked even more furious. "Do not make this worse with further lies. The plane ticket in your name that Sarah wished me to give you does not lie."

With shaking hands, Jasmine picked up the ticket, barely able to keep the towel around her. The ticket was in her name, and even worse, her passport details were listed. That was odd, but only seemed to damn her further in her husband's eyes.

"No," she cried. "I would never do this. My family had all these details on file."

His mouth twisted in disbelief. "Enough! I was foolish to believe in you despite it all, but Jamar heard you discussing your defection!"

Jamar had obviously not heard her response to Sarah's

words. She reached for Tariq, forgetting the towel. "Listen—"

"The truth is clear. I have always known your choices. Your body is not enough to make me a fool again. Though if you wish, I can avail myself of the invitation." His dismissive glance broke her heart. He was so cold, so uninterested.

Unbearably ashamed of her nakedness, she pulled the towel around her with fingers that trembled, and tried to reason with him. "Please, Tariq, listen to me. I love you…" She gave him her heart in a frantic attempt to make him listen.

He laughed. "You must think me a great fool, Jasmine. Your love is worthless."

Brokenhearted at the bald-faced rejection, and no longer able to figure out a way to make him understand that her love and loyalty belonged to him without reservation, Jasmine threw the balled-up ticket in his face. "Yes, that's the truth!" she lied. "I'm going to New Zealand and I'm going to divorce you!"

Tariq didn't speak. His face resembled a mask carved out of stone. The rage driving him had been tempered to cold fury.

"I'll go back and marry someone more suitable. I don't know what I was thinking of, marrying you!" She wanted to break down and cry, but some final piece of pride held her in check. If she gave in to the urge, she might never stop.

"You will not leave Zulheil."

"I'm already out of Zulheil! I won't go back!"

The anger on his face should have scared her, but she was past fear, mercifully numb. "You will return," he declared.

"No!" Her anger crested. "You have no right to make me!"

"Get dressed. We are leaving today." His voice was without emotion, as if he'd suddenly tripped a switch. "If you try to make it difficult, I will personally make sure that you get to Zulheil."

"You wouldn't make a scene." The room separated them, but it was the distance in his eyes that broke her heart.

His eyes narrowed. "I will do what it takes."

Confronted with the Sheik of Zulheil, she knew that she'd lost this battle. He had the political power to do whatever he wished. "I have nowhere else to go." The wistful words fell from her lips like long-held tears. "I gave up everything for you. Everything. *Everything.*"

Her only response was the slamming of the door behind him as he left the room.

Slumped outside the hotel door, his control shattered, Tariq could barely think. He knew what Sarah was like, and so, when she'd told him, he hadn't believed her. Even with the evidence of the ticket, he hadn't believed her. Making sure that she knew of his disgust with her for her troublemaking, he'd gone to find Jasmine. He'd wanted to protect her from her sister's maliciousness. Then Jamar had seen him heading to their suite, and had asked if Jasmine had talked to him about leaving for New Zealand. His expression had been dark.

"On their way to the travel agent's, her sister asked Jasmine al eha Sheik when she would like her ticket booked." The bodyguard had started to say something else, but was interrupted when the head of security beeped him. He'd excused himself.

Tariq had felt his heart break with Jamar's words. It was fortunate that the guard had left, because otherwise he would have seen his sheik's composure crack, like fine porcelain under a heavy boot.

Jamar was a loyal guard, one with no reason to lie, especially since he clearly adored Jasmine. Tariq called himself a fool for accepting Jasmine's explanation for carrying her New Zealand passport. He'd broken his longest held vow and had trusted her when she'd said it was an oversight. Even after what she'd done to him the first time, he'd *trusted* her. He'd wanted to protect and keep her safe in his arms.

An image thrust into his mind, turning a knife inside him. Of a tiny woman with hair of flame pleading with him to believe her, her shoulders and legs bare. A woman with shame in her eyes when he'd mocked the inherent sensuality that was her nature. Sensuality that he had always treasured, that he'd taken time and care to nurture.

Another knife joined the first.

He forced himself to remember the reason for his anger. There was no reason for him to feel as if he'd broken something beyond value. Except he couldn't think for the anger and pain blinding him. The wounded thing inside him was in agony, but he refused to acknowledge that, refused to examine exactly why this betrayal hurt with the pain of a thousand suns on his naked skin. He'd survived Jasmine once before and he'd do it again.

Even if what he felt for her was a hundred times stronger than before…and the pain threatened to drive him to madness.

Thirteen

They landed in Zulheil midmorning. Jasmine couldn't help but remember her first trip through the gleaming white corridors. Then, she'd believed that if she loved him enough, the man beside her would grow to love her, too.

Now, she knew that if he could convict her on such flimsy evidence, he had to have no trust in her loyalty. And no love in his heart. She'd failed to make him see that she was worth loving, and if Tariq couldn't see that, then the flaws in her had to be fatal. Battered by emotional storms, her defenses crushed, Jasmine couldn't fight those old demons any longer.

Once they reached the palace, she let Tariq haul her through the corridors, humiliating as it was, knowing that if she fought, he was angry enough to do something truly unforgivable. But when, after pulling her into his bedroom, he turned to leave, she stopped him. She wasn't someone he could lock away and forget.

"Where are you going?"

Tariq didn't even look at her. "Abraz."

Speak to me, she wanted to cry. *Give me something to hold on to.* Even after his accusations and distrust, her heart refused to give up. She loved him. Needed him. And this time, she would fight for him until there was no hope. "Why?"

He did look at her then, his eyes dark green with pure fury. "I am going to marry my second wife. You no longer amuse me. Perhaps she will have more loyalty than you have shown."

Jasmine's heart turned to ice. "You're taking another wife?"

"I will marry her in Abraz. You would do well to get used to a submissive role."

"How can you do this to me?" She prayed that he was only striking back at her because he was angry at her supposed betrayal. Then she remembered gorgeous Hira. Hira, who'd wanted to marry Tariq…and who lived in Abraz. Hira, the glamourpuss princess that Sarah had taunted her with so long ago. Jasmine's worst nightmare had just come to life.

Tariq's beautiful face was cruel with distaste as his merciless eyes raked her trembling body. "The same way you plotted to betray me."

"No! I didn't. Why don't you believe me?" She reached out to grab the edge of his jacket, but he shrugged her off.

"I do not wish to be late." Throwing her another dismissive glance over her shoulder, he walked out the door.

Jasmine didn't go out to the balcony this time. At that moment, something priceless deep inside her broke with an almost audible snap. But she couldn't allow herself to feel the pain, because if she did, she'd die from the wound. Instead, as a self-defense mechanism, she started to plan her escape. She'd been prepared to put up with Tariq's anger, his distrust, even his rejection of her, but this…

"I will never share him. Never."

Sarah's derisive voice seemed to haunt her, telling her she hadn't been woman enough to hold her husband.

"No!" Sarah had probably only meant to cause a fight, but Tariq's deep-rooted distrust of his wife had given her the greatest of victories. Jasmine refused to give her vindictive sister any more power.

Spinning on her heel, she walked to her room and locked the door. She needed to think. There was no way she was going to get a flight out of Zulheil. Tariq would have alerted his men to watch for any attempt on her part. He wanted her to suffer. He wanted to punish her. Previously, she'd let him, certain that her love would win through.

"Not anymore." He'd gone too far this time.

She couldn't take to the roads. The border guards were well-trained and scrupulous. Aside from that, her red hair was a beacon of recognition among the desert people.

"Water." She stopped, her heart pounding. Zulheil had a narrow seacoast and a thriving port. It would be relatively easy to slip on board one of the foreign ships when it stopped to refuel. Sailors were an independent lot, and the harbor authorities couldn't monitor each and every individual movement. Aside from that, they were more worried with keeping people out of Zulheil than policing those wanting to depart.

She knew she had to leave everything behind, so that no one would guess her plan. That seemed to sum up her fate. She was leaving everything. Her heart. Her dreams. Her hope.

Taking a calming breath, she went to the small safe in the bedroom. After their marriage, Tariq had shown her the safe and told her that it would always hold cash for her use. At the time, she'd been touched by his thoughtfulness, but today, she just felt humiliated. Though she didn't want to take his money, accessing her New Zealand savings accounts would immediately give away her plans. Shouldering aside her pride, she keyed in the combination. There was enough cash to buy her passage and support her for a few weeks.

As she turned away from the safe, a flash of silver on a corner chair caught her eye. She had finished the beautifully beaded blouse with such hope, just before their departure to Australia. Now she could barely bear the sight of it. She folded it up and left it on the bed, with a note for Mumtaz. Her friend might hate her for fleeing, but she was the one for whom Jasmine had chosen the material.

Once she was ready, she walked to her writing desk and picked up a pen. Her fingers threatened to shake under the force of her emotions, but she disciplined them with strength that came from somewhere so deep inside, she'd never known it existed before that instant.

Tariq,
Ever since I came to Zulheil, you've been waiting for me to betray you and leave. Today, I'll live up to your lack of belief in me, but I won't leave in silence like a thief.

I love you so much that every time I breathe, I think of you. From the moment we reunited, I had no thought of ever leaving you. You were my first love, my only love. I thought I'd do anything for you, even bear your punishment over my choice four years ago, but today I've discovered my limits. You're mine and mine alone. How can you ask me to share you?

Your pride will urge you to search for me, but I beg you, if you ever had any feelings for me, please don't. I could never live with a man who I loved but who hated me. It would kill me. I don't know what I'll do, I only know that my heart is broken and I must leave this place. Even if I never see you again, know that you'll always be my beloved.
Jasmine al eha Sheik

Dry-eyed, her pain too great even for tears, she folded the letter and sealed it in an envelope. When she'd begun, she'd thought to pen something hateful, hurting him as much as he'd hurt her, but she couldn't. Picking up her purse and the letter, she walked out to his study, the one place no one would venture until his return. She placed the letter in the center of his desk, where he would immediately see it. Her hands stroked the smooth mahogany in a final aching goodbye. In this room, they had come to learn about each other and she'd begun to help him shoulder his burdens.

"But it wasn't enough." Teeth gritted, she almost ran from the room, unable to bear the deluge of memories. Outside, she slipped on her sunglasses while the driver brought the car around. Within two minutes, she was on her way.

The beautiful minarets and colorful marketplace outside the windows of the car brought tears to her eyes. Her sense of loss was overwhelming. This place had become home. The exotic scents, the heavy heat, the bright-eyed and laughing people—they were all a part of her and would be forever.

Just like Tariq.

The docks were bustling. The driver parked in front of the popular waterside café she'd indicated. "I'm meeting a friend for lunch, so you can go elsewhere if you wish."

"I will wait here." His dark eyes didn't reflect his automatic smile.

She hadn't expected anything else. Tariq had been in a rage, but he'd given orders designed to keep her prisoner.

The minute she stepped outside, people waved and called out. They had accepted her without question, these generous desert people. Yet not even for them could she bear to share Tariq. After greeting her people with forced smiles, she made her way into the restaurant and sought out the hostess.

"Jasmine al eha Sheik, you will take a table?" The woman was beaming.

"Thank you, but I was wondering if you could help me?" Her voice was soft, but didn't waver as she'd half expected.

"Of course." The hostess's smile became impossibly wider.

"Somehow, a foreign news crew has managed to enter Zulheil and they've been tracking me. If you could show me your back entrance, my driver has instructed another driver to pick me up. It's annoying to be hounded like this."

The hostess's eyes lit up. Jasmine knew she should feel guilty about lying to her, but she was too numb to care. The back door opened onto a narrow alley. Though the lane was clean, there was a deserted, quiet air about it. The hostess looked around, a frown wrinkling her face.

"There is no driver here."

"Oh, he's waiting down there. Thank you." Before the woman could protest, Jasmine stepped out and began to stride confidently down the narrow cobbled path. Once out of sight, she changed direction and headed toward the water.

Lady Luck decided to give her a chance. A cruise ship was tethered at the docks, there only for a three-hour stop to refuel. In the crowd of European tourists allowed out to wander the docks, Jasmine no longer stood out. The authorities were vigilant about anyone attempting to get out, but nobody noticed a small female merging *into* the colorful mass of humanity.

Jasmine found that the cruise liner was happy to pick up an extra paying passenger, having lost some due to illness at the last stop. As an almost instinctive precaution, she used the New Zealand passport that had planted suspicions in Tariq's mind. Globe-trotting Kiwis were more likely to be present on the ships in port than the reclusive people of Zulheil. Or perhaps she used it because she couldn't bear to see her married name written there.

An hour later, she watched Zulheil's sparkling sand retreat to the horizon. She stood on the deck, her cheeks whipped by the wind, unable to look away. A part of her believed that if she didn't lose sight of the land, the final threads tying her to Tariq wouldn't be cut. Then night fell, spelling an end to even that impossible dream.

The moon shimmered over the minarets of Zulheina, but Tariq could find no surcease from the gnawing sense of loss that seemed to reach inside his soul and steadily eat away at any hope of happiness.

He'd been halfway to Abraz by the time his sense of betrayal and anger had dissipated, gentled by his homeland. Pulsing hurt had taken its place. He'd given Mina his heart and she'd cut it to pieces for a second time. He hadn't quite known what he would do to survive. No one but Mina would ever be wife to him, but how could he remain with a woman who could betray him so easily?

His mind had kept replaying the most painful image—the naked agony in Mina's eyes when he'd told her that he was taking another wife. That he was rejecting her, just as her family had. He'd felt as if he'd struck her, as if *he* was the one who needed forgiveness.

Something desperate and primitive in him had kept saying that he'd made a mistake and had to return home. Searching for any hint of hope, he'd finally stopped reacting and had started to listen.

When looked at logically, without the blindness caused by heartbreak, none of it made sense. If Jasmine had wished to leave him, she could have done so without Sarah's help. Dread had crept into Tariq's body when he'd realized that, but it was the memory of Jamar's revelation that had almost stopped his breath. Why would the bodyguard tell him about betrayal in such a casual way—in the hallway of a hotel, where anyone could have overheard?

Unwilling to believe that the mixture of distrust and anguish in him had caused him to make such a terrible mistake, but knowing deep inside that he had, Tariq had ordered the car to return to Zulheina in all haste. The wild part of him that had always belonged to Mina had *known*. He'd picked up the phone in the back of the car for something to do, a shield against his fear that he'd lost his wife for good.

The guard had answered after one ring. "Sir?"

"Jamar, I was thinking of a gift for my wife and recalled what you said in Australia. Was Jasmine enthusiastic when her sister asked about booking tickets to New Zealand?" His hand had been clenched tight around the phone.

"I heard Jasmine al eha Sheik say that she was going to speak to you about whether you might have some free time. I believe she would enjoy the gift of a trip." There had been a smile in his tone at being asked his opinion. "I was called away before I could ask if I could be her guard on any such trip. I know I ask much but...I did not like the feel of her sister.'' The guard's tone had been of someone expecting to be rebuked for the criticism, but he'd put his duty to protect above his own status. His judgment of Sarah also explained his scowling expression that day in Sydney.

"I agree, Jamar. And thank you.'' Tariq had been barely able to speak. His blood cold with the realization of his incalculable error, he'd returned to Zulheina.

Too late.

Far too late.

The crackle of paper made him glance down in surprise. He felt as if he was looking at a stranger's hand. A stranger who'd crushed the fragile material in his palm beyond recovery, with brutal efficiency. Uncurling those fingers that he was forced to acknowledge were his own, he pulled out the page and tried to flatten it against the dark wood of his desk. The whole time, he knew that no matter how hard he tried to smooth the wrinkles, it would never be enough.

As he would never again be able to enjoy the perfect joy of his Jasmine's love. He'd beaten and battered her heart so many times, in so many different ways, and yet she'd continued to love him, her feminine courage quiet and strong. But even her generous nature wouldn't forgive this most recent blow.

Tariq was prepared to accept that. He wasn't prepared to accept that he'd lost her for good. The woman his Mina had grown into had changed him forever. Her strength, her ability to lead beside him, her glorious sensuality...she was irreplaceable. He couldn't bear to live without the other half of his soul, even if she hated him.

"You belong to me, Mina.'' Only the desert heard his voice. Only the desert sent sighs of agreement on the wings of the cool, evening wind. Only the desert understood his desolation...and his determination.

Jasmine spent the entire voyage secluded in her cabin, eschewing attempts by the social activities' staff to draw her out.

She didn't cry. Her tears were frozen in her heart along with the rest of her emotions. She just wanted to forget.

Except Tariq wouldn't leave her alone. Each night, he came to her in her dreams, strong, virile, unwilling to accept her decision. She tossed and turned, her body covered with sweat, trying to fight him, but in the end he always won.

"You belong to me, Mina." His hands stroked her.

"No."

"Yes!" That male arrogance was apparent even in her dreams. His shoulders gleamed in the moonlight, as they'd done those nights they'd spent in the desert. The desert, where she'd learned that a warrior's pride could be a harder thing to fight than any physical enemy.

"Tariq," she whispered, reaching out a hand to touch that warm, tempting skin. Nothing met her searching hands but cold emptiness. "Tariq, no!" Invariably, she woke up with his name on her lips, a cry for him to believe her…to love her.

The liner docked at a number of Middle Eastern destinations, but she didn't depart, not wanting to take the chance that someone might recognize her. Two weeks passed in self-imposed isolation. Then the ship made an unscheduled stop on a small Greek island, due to a passenger's need to disembark because of an emergency. Exhausted by her sense of loss and lack of sleep, Jasmine slipped off the ship and never returned. It was as good a place as any, she thought without enthusiasm. And because it wasn't a scheduled stop, even if Tariq searched for her, he'd be unlikely to locate her.

She managed to find a small garret apartment after she left the ship. On the night she arrived, she curled up on the bed and couldn't make herself move again. Thoughts of Tariq haunted her night and day, building shadows under her eyes and adding to the weight loss she'd suffered on board ship. Her mind replayed that final terrible fight over and over again, trying to find another way, another avenue. There were none.

"It's over. Accept it," she told herself each day, and each day she woke with her heart heavy with need and her body aching.

A week after her arrival, she dragged herself out the door, fighting the depression. She was strong, she told herself. She'd survive. So what if half her soul was missing? She'd given that away by choice. And she couldn't bring herself to regret it. By chance, she saw a sign in a shop window seeking a seamstress. Taking a deep breath, she pushed open the door and walked inside.

That night, as she picked up a pair of scissors to begin an alteration, her numbness suddenly broke. It was as if her body realized that by doing something beyond bare survival, she'd decided to live again. With the sudden shift came thoughts and memories and heartache.

Her first emotion was fear—fear that she'd never forget Tariq. And then suddenly, she was terrified of forgetting. He lived inside her, part of her. Paradoxically, there was peace in knowing she would never stop loving him. Despite that knowledge, she avoided newspapers and magazines, aware that if she saw Tariq with his new bride, she would surely lose the tentative control she'd regained over her emotions.

Tariq picked up the brush and squeezed out paint the color of rich cream. Add a tinge of palest rose and he would have the living hue of his Jasmine's skin. A single stroke and one graceful arm came to life. She was almost complete, this creation of paint and emotion. Painstakingly, he began to fill in the details that made Mina unique. Pure sky-blue for those big, always innocent eyes. Even after he'd taught her the ways of pleasure, a part of Mina had remained forever the innocent.

A memory of those eyes bruised with hurt when he'd done something she couldn't forgive taunted him as he painted her portrait. It didn't matter if she never forgave him. He couldn't let her go. He needed her more than she would ever need him. She made his life a gift rather than a burden. She was a piece of his soul, and if he had to, he'd search forever for her.

He told himself that she was no weak woman who would suffer in silence when he dragged her back. His Mina had spirit. She would fight him, and as long as there were words, he would fight for her.

There was a movement near the doorway. "Yes?" His concentration was immediately and utterly focused on Hiraz.

"We tracked down some passengers who saw her on board after the ship left the Middle East. They do not recall seeing her after Greece." Hiraz paused and suddenly said, "I cannot believe she has done this to you again. Let her go."

"Hold your words!" Tariq snapped. "Because you are my friend, I will forgive you that indiscretion, but you will never again speak against Mina. I am the one to blame." It would have been easy to blame Sarah, but Tariq knew it was his own fierce protection of his heart against further pain that had caused this. Sarah had merely been the catalyst.

His advisor's skepticism was obvious. "You? You treated her like a princess."

"I told her I was going to take another wife."

Hiraz froze. Sadness settled over his features, so deep it turned his brown eyes black. "I do not think even my Mumtaz would forgive me such a hurt."

"It does not matter. Jasmine is mine and I will never let her go." Tariq touched his hand to the letter that he constantly kept with him. "Prepare the aircraft. We will fly to Greece. You have a list of the stops the cruise ship made?"

Hiraz nodded. "There were only two." A brief flicker of hope glittered in his brown eyes.

Tariq didn't feel hope. He felt certainty.

Jasmine ignored the impatient knocking for as long as she could. When it didn't stop, she put down some mending and made her way across the small garret, prepared to face off with her landlord. She'd paid up. He had no cause to hound her.

"You!" Her knees buckled when she saw the man filling the doorway. His arms reached out to catch her as she fell. Behind him, the door slammed shut. The garret seemed suddenly minuscule, the light slanting in under the eaves not bright enough to soften the intense darkness of emotion. "Let me go."

"You'll fall."

"I'm fine now." She pushed at Tariq's shoulders. To her surprise, he released her without complaint, holding her only long enough to gauge that she could stand on her own.

Stumbling backward, she wrapped her hands around her waist and stared. "You've lost weight." His face was shadowed with the beginnings of a beard, and his eyes looked dark and haunted, but it was the way his clothes hung on him that worried her. "What's happened?"

"You left me."

Jasmine hadn't expected that response. She shook her head and backed up until she hit the wall. "How did you find me?"

He didn't release her from his bleak gaze. "I went to New Zealand first."

Her heart thudded at that.

"You didn't tell me that you'd completely turned your back on your family to come to me."

Jasmine didn't answer, torn up at the thought that he'd cared enough to search for her. Perhaps, a traitorous part of her wondered, half of him was better than nothing? Immediately, she discarded that dangerous idea. No. No. No!

"You chose *me*, Mina." His voice was rough with the understanding of what she'd done. "You chose me above all others, above everyone else in the world. Did you think I would let you walk away once you'd become mine?"

"I won't come back." Seeing him with another woman would rip her to shreds.

"Mina." He reached out his hand.

"No!"

He didn't heed her, moving to trap her against the wall. The white silk of his shirt was soft under her fingertips when she tried to push him away. At the same time, she hunched her body against the exposed beams of the wall, afraid that her craving for his touch would override her vows to resist him.

"I won't share you." It took an effort to sound strong.

"Because you love me and you chose me."

She nodded, and lost the battle to stop the flow of tears. This close, she just wanted to hold him and forget her anguish in his arms. And the force of his words almost made her think that he believed in her love.

"Mina, you must come back with me. I cannot live without you, my Jasmine. I need you like the desert needs rain." Framing her face with his hands, Tariq used his thumbs to gently rub away her tears.

The pain in his green eyes echoed her own. She tried to shake her head but he held her in place. "I chose you, Jasmine. You are my wife. It is not a bond that can be broken." The fervor of his words made her body thrum in recognition. "I love you. I *adore* you."

"But you've taken…" She couldn't complete her sentence.

"I would never do such a thing," he murmured. "I was very angry with you that day, but I was also hurting. I believed that you had trampled on my heart again. It was the only weapon I possessed and I used it. Then, I did not believe that you cared enough to be heartbroken. I am so sorry, Mina."

"You weren't planning to take another wife?" She managed to get the question past the obstruction in her throat.

"Never. You are the only one. *Always* you'll be the only one. In my heart and in my soul, I have known from the moment we met that you would be the only one. That is why I felt so betrayed. I would never marry another."

"Never?" she whispered, beginning to understand, to believe. Her husband had turned on her like a wounded animal that day, shattered by her apparent betrayal after they'd seemed to be reaching peace. The broken pieces inside her began to heal under the heat of the truth in his eyes. Unconsciously, her hands drifted to rest at his waist.

"I waited four years for you to grow up. I stayed faithful to the love between us. Do you think I could ever take another woman to my bed, much less into my heart?" His eyes glittered with the power of what he was confessing.

Stunned, she didn't know what to say. She hadn't known

of the depths of her panther's devotion. Her heart seemed to be crying and laughing at the same time, but all she could do was drown in the promise she saw in his eyes.

"Forgive your foolish husband, Mina. Around you, he does not always think with calm." His expression was penitent, but the way he had her trapped against the wall told her that he intended to persuade her, no matter how long it took.

Her husband might be apologizing, but he didn't know the meaning of being humble. Jasmine smiled slowly. She wouldn't have him any other way. "Only if he'll forgive me for making the wrong choice four years ago."

"I forgave you the instant you stepped foot on my land, Mina." He smiled his predator's smile. "I just needed time to salvage my pride."

"And is it salvaged? Will you doubt me again?"

"All I needed to know was that you'd choose to fight for me if you ever had to make the decision again."

So simple, and yet she hadn't been able to figure it out. She touched his hair with tentative fingers. "There is no question of choice. You come first."

"I know that now, Mina." He leaned into her gentle caress.

There was something more she had to know. "Do you think...loving me is a weakness?"

There was no pause. "Loving you is my greatest strength. The assassins sought to blind me to that truth. With heart, I can reach those who would otherwise be lost. I have never stopped loving you." His hands moved down her body to clasp her buttocks and press her close. "Will you return with me?"

Jasmine laughed at the way he was trying to act as if he was giving her a choice, when they both knew he wasn't leaving the room unless she was with him. "Do you promise to be a good, amenable husband from now on and follow my every command?"

He scowled. "You're taking advantage of me."

"It's not working, is it?"

"I don't know." He glanced speculatively at the tiny bed

in the corner. "If that cot holds up under our weight, I'll permit you to take advantage of me." The sparkle in his eyes belied his solemn tone, but before Jasmine could accept the offer, she had to know.

"I love you. Do you believe that?"

Tariq's face was fierce with joy. "Mina!" He crushed her to him. "Your love for me is in your eyes, in your touch, in your every word. Even your farewell letter, which you wrote when you were feeling abandoned and so hurt, rings with the richness and truth of your love. I do not feel worthy of it, but I will not give you up. You are mine."

Jasmine swallowed and laid one fear to rest. There was no room for doubt in the passion of her husband's voice. "Do you believe I betrayed you?" She leaned back so she could look into his eyes.

He laid his forehead against hers as his big body curved over hers in a familiar protective stance. Vibrant male heat seeped into her bones, a deep caress that made her want to melt, but there were questions yet to be answered.

"Once I was no longer blinded by pain and anger, I realized the truth. I did not need Jamar's explanation. My heart knew you would never do such a thing to me." Tenderly, he cupped her cheek in one hand. "I am afraid I am possessive beyond reason where you are concerned, and the closeness of your homeland had me on edge. My fear of losing you turned me a little mad. I was returning to beg your forgiveness when I was told that you had disappeared."

"I didn't want to go," she confessed.

"You will promise to never leave me again. Promise," he growled, no longer gentle and compassionate, the panther tying his mate to him. "Fight, get angry, but do not leave!"

"I promise, but you must talk to me. Promise me that."

He smiled. "I promise you, my Jasmine, that I will talk to you. I cannot change who I am. I am possessive and you will have to become adept at dealing with such a husband."

"As long as you let me deal with you. Don't push me away.

Don't go cold and silent on me. When you do that, it's like a part of me is missing.''

He pulled her to him again, the hand on her nape holding her against his chest. "Forgive me, Mina, because I cannot forgive myself for the hurt I have caused you."

"I think I could forgive you anything." Her vulnerability to him no longer terrified her, not when he loved her with all of the passion in his warrior's heart. "My only regret through everything is that we wasted four years."

He chuckled. "Not wasted, Mina. I thought I would give you five years to grow up. I was being very patient, was I not?"

She smiled and touched his cheek in a familiar caress. He turned his face into her hand, his stubble rough but enticing against her skin. "You were. And after five years?"

"You would have decided to take a trip to the desert."

"I would have?"

"Umm." He leaned down and kissed her, as if he couldn't resist. She softened, she melted, she became his. When he drew away, the masculine scent of him swirled around her, enclosing her in an embrace more intimate than the physical one. "And once there, you would have married a man who has always known that you were meant to be his."

"So I could've waited another year and saved myself the trouble?" she dared to tease.

"Perhaps I would not have lasted five years. My patience was wearing thin." His next words were uncompromising. "You were born to be mine, Mina."

The strength of his vow made her want to weep. Tariq loved her, flaws and all. The hole inside her heart closed forever. She leaned up and kissed him, a soft, loving kiss that held everything she felt.

"Does this mean I am truly forgiven?" he asked.

"Just give me your promise to talk to me if you ever feel angry or hurt, and we'll wipe the slate clean."

"I do not intend to let you out of my sight, so that is a

moot point.'' He laughed when she pushed at his chest and raised her scowling face to his.

''You still don't trust me?''

''I trust you with my heart and soul,'' he told her, his green eyes bright. ''I also need you so fiercely that it would please me should you wish to spend your hours by my side.'' He touched his fingers to her throat in a light caress. ''You asked me a question once. The answer is yes, as you are Jasmine al eha Sheik, I am Tariq al eha Jasmine. I belong to you.''

The raw honesty of his words humbled her and yet made her heart burst. Tariq was proud and strong, as enduring in his vows as Zulheil Rose was in its beauty. For him to surrender to her in this way meant more than could ever be put into words. Her panther had placed his happiness into her keeping, and she intended to protect that trust with every breath in her body.

''Do your people hate me?'' She bit her lip.

''*Our* people are used to the tempestuous women of sheiks.'' He grinned. ''In the first years of my parents' marriage, my mother once camped in Paris for two months.''

''Oh.'' Though the news about their people made her happy, Jasmine was even more pleased to hear the affection in Tariq's voice. It appeared that his frustrated anger toward his mother was passing with time.

''It is I who would be considered a poor sheik if I could not persuade you to return.'' He leaned close. ''My honor is in your hands.'' There was a teasing light in his eyes.

''Come, husband who belongs to me.'' She tugged his hand. ''Your wife wishes to take advantage of you.''

''I would never deny my wife, Mina,'' he breathed into her mouth.

The cot did indeed hold their weight.

Epilogue

There was a roar from the crowd below when Jasmine stepped out onto the balcony, her six-month-old baby son cradled in her arms. Behind her, Tariq put a protective arm around her waist and leaned down until his lips touched her temple. "You are loved, my Jasmine." His smile was tender.

Jasmine stretched up and touched her lips to his. "I know," she whispered. The roar of the crowd was drowned out by the passionate thunder racing through her veins. "As are you, Tariq al eha Jasmine. From the heart and soul."

This incredible man was hers, she thought, without limits or restrictions. Or worry. His birthday present to her had been the repeal of the old law that had made her believe his angry threat to take another wife.

"Our son will be a warrior." Tariq touched one waving fist. "He was conceived in passion."

"Tariq, hush." Her cheeks bloomed at the memory of their reunion on that tiny Greek island. Out of their love and hunger, they'd created a tiny, beautiful human being.

"Our people cannot hear us." He smiled.

That smile made her heart beat faster and her mouth go dry. Every day that they spent together, she fell more in love with her husband. In front of her eyes, he was growing into a powerful, compassionate leader, adored by his people and respected by both his allies and his foes. But what turned her heart over was the way he loved her. The way he saw greatness in her, too.

"I could not have chosen a better woman to lead by my side. You are magnificent." His hand stroked the fiery fall of her hair, unconsciously echoing her thoughts.

Jasmine thought back over the past year and a half. "I feel like I've grown more since I married you than I did in all the years before." Tariq's faith in her had made her dig deep to find the skills he needed in a wife. She'd become adept at behind-the-scenes negotiations, and even better at listening to what people didn't say.

He touched her cheek and the caress turned the crowd wild. "You have also taught me much. Your gentle ways are turning foes into allies. That's why I married you, of course."

His teasing of her hadn't changed. "I told you, by the time I'm fifty, women will be at those conferences."

"I have faith that you will accomplish the impossible." Tariq's confidence in his wife ran deep and true. Mina could do whatever she put her mind to. Look how well her designing was going. His lovely little wife was becoming famous, not only for her diplomacy but for her artistry.

"You are not working too much?" He looked down at her luminous beauty and could understand why their people openly thanked the stars for her. Just as her husband did.

"How could I?" She turned an exasperated face up at him. "If it's not you, it's Mumtaz or Hiraz telling me to rest. Honestly, I could shoot that man at times."

"My advisors know how important you are to their sheik's happiness." Tariq's tone was light, but his need for her very real. Without her, he would not be the man he was today. She had taught him about love so strong it humbled him. He could never articulate all that she meant to him, but he could say, "Thank you." It was a rough whisper.

He looked down at that tiny being cradled in his wife's arms and thanked him, too—for teaching him about a parent's love. The minute Jasmine had laid Zaqir in his arms, he'd forgiven his mother for her choice.

"You're welcome." Jasmine's throat closed with withheld tears. She understood what her desert warrior couldn't say. Tariq no longer hid either his very real love or his need for her. He'd filled the emptiness in her with so much love that sometimes she hurt with the beauty of it.

Moving closer to him until he was supporting their son with an arm under hers, she raised her free hand to the gathered masses. These desert people were her family, her home. Zaqir was a beloved son, the embodiment of the love between her and Tariq. Her husband was her hope and joy.

"We are going in. You are cold." After one final wave, Tariq rubbed her arms and nudged her inside.

Once there, she raised her face to his. "I think we should dine alone tonight. In our private dining area."

He raised a brow, his eyes darkening at her husky tone. "Will the little sheik be asleep?"

"Your son is beginning to be very well behaved." She kissed their baby's soft cheek. "Unlike his father."

Tariq laughed. "If I began to behave, Mina, you'd be most disappointed. Bored." He pulled her into the circle of his arms, warm and strong.

She let him cuddle her to him, their baby between them. "I don't think forever with you would bore me."

"Come then, Jasmine al eha Sheik, let us put this one to bed." He nuzzled her and then kissed Zaqir, his love for their child open and unashamed. "I wish to adore my wife, little one. You will have to be good tonight."

Jasmine smiled in sheer joy. Around them, the rare beauty of the Zulheil Rose glowed with an inner warmth, but between her and Tariq, there burned an even more precious incandescence. As she went to lay Zaqir in his crib, Tariq by her side, Jasmine knew that this glory would only grow stronger with time. Like the crystal, it would endure.

* * * * *